PRINCIPLES
TO LIVE BY

PRINCIPLES
TO LIVE BY

DAVID
ADAMS
RICHARDS

DOUBLEDAY CANADA

Doubleday Canada and colophon are registered trademarks of Penguin Random House Canada Limited

Library and Archives Canada Cataloguing in Publication
Richards, David Adams, 1950-, author
Principles to live by / David Adams Richards.

Issued in print and electronic formats.

ISBN 978-0-385-68245-9 (bound).—ISBN 978-0-385-68246-6 (epub)
I. Title.

PS8585.I17P75 2016   C813'.54   C2015-906347-7
                                              C2015-906348-5

This book is a work of fiction. Names, characters, places and incidents are products of the author's imagination or are used fictitiously.

Cover design: Andrew Roberts
Cover image: Tim Robinson/Arcangel
Printed and bound in the USA

Published in Canada by Doubleday Canada,
a division of Penguin Random House Canada Limited

www.penguinrandomhouse.ca

10 9 8 7 6 5 4 3 2 1

Penguin
Random House
DOUBLEDAY CANADA

FOR MY FRIEND CRAIG CARLETON, QC

"You accused him of everything but his genius. That, my dear, you tried to claim for yourself."

Sue Van Loon

Then out spake brave Horatius
The Captain of the Gate:
'To every man upon this earth
Death cometh soon or late.
And how can a man die better
Than facing fearful odds,
For the ashes of his fathers,
And the temples of his Gods.'

Thomas Babington Macaulay, *Lays of Ancient Rome*

PART ONE

1.

In March of 1999, sometime after work, after the lights came on in the houses and the fog came in on the snow, Bunny McCrease was chasing a boy across a field in Saint John, New Brunswick. It was in fact the first boy he had ever chased. He was a big man with a heart generally kind, and a kindness generally, but this was a special circumstance. He was puffing and panting as he ran, stopping every twenty-two yards to bend over and cough.

The boy was from Bunny's own foster house, and had left without warning. He had been locked in his room earlier, but had managed to slip out the window and shimmy down the old drain. He was thirteen years of age. Bunny and his wife had taken the boy in as a favour, and now this had happened.

Moms McCrease, a woman of proportion and common sense, had told Bunny to bring the boy back.

"The goddamn Limey bolter," she said. "I knew we'd have a problem with him." And she was upset that she hadn't refused to take him two weeks before. "The little bastard," she said.

Bunny sighed, got up from his paper and went out wearing just a scarf and his old suit jacket and forlorn torn rubber boots. He saw the boy in the field and called out, "Hey, Jackie!" And the boy stopped for just a second.

He was a strange boy, a noticeable boy without anyone else in the world. He had been brought to the McCrease family with four words whispered: "He is a lunatic." The police constable, Melonson, had taken him in and put him in lock-up, and now he was in a foster home. No one knew much about him or what to do with him.

He was a liar. And, Melonson said, probably a thief.

He had been found on the street looking for his parents, with no ID on him at all. He said he only remembered his first name—Jack. He said people were supposed to meet him in this city and straighten everything out. But Melonson thought this was a ruse.

"My name is Jack," the boy told people over and over again, more and more hopefully every time he said it.

"Jack and the beanstalk," Melonson said.

So Melonson started asking around for any information about the boy. But he found little.

So where was this Jack from, and who was he—and who did he belong to? For a few days before the boy was placed in foster care, this took up the constable's time. But then Melonson got the idea that the boy was simply a runaway making up stories because he didn't want to go back home. And he felt he knew exactly who he was.

"He's just a little runaway kid from Upper Gagetown," he and another constable decided, "and the only notable fact about him is he is great at making up stories."

Now, did they know a person had run away? Well, they believed one had—and he was here, so this one fit.

The police looked into it, finally wrote down the boy's name as Jack Toggle from Sackett Corner—and sent him into foster care. This was done without any fuss, and was forgotten.

But Jack Toggle wanted to tell someone about something. Whether he was lying or not, he pressed ahead with his story, and made his foster family agitated every night at supper.

"Here he goes again," they said.

"Yes, Sebby kept me alive as long as he could—" Jack would begin where he left off "—but then when they came, he hid me—but I was sent here. For my dad. I remember Mom said we were Canadian. But I must be in the wrong city, for no one was here to meet me. I thought my uncle was supposed to meet me—everything was supposed to have been taken care of by last November. I think it was called external affairs."

"External affairs last November. Is that right? External affairs. Of course you would be too good to live here. I should have known that with a boy like you, we'd have to contact external affairs." Moms laughed gaily at this, scratched her face a bit and then told the boy if he wanted to see his uncle, his uncle was a Toggle man who was in jail for poaching deer.

Now, catching up to him, Bunny asked this boy why he had his bag with him.

"You can't just leave—you have to come back. Look, if you are really who you say, I promise we will find out!"

But the boy turned and Bunny began to chase him again, grabbing at his bag and his coat, and the boy gyrated, moved to right and left over some burdocks, and managed to slip out of both bag and coat. As he did, he grabbed at a ticket he had hidden in his pocket—holding it, he ran again.

Then, close to Saint's Cliff, Bunny made a final lunge for him.

"Stop or you'll go over," Bunny yelled.

The boy turned and tried to say something, but tumbled backward— and fell, without a sound.

Ninety-two feet.

Bunny McCrease went to the side of the cliff and looked down. He waited for the sound of a body hitting. There was nothing. He saw snow swirl in the grey dark beneath him; it was like looking into an abyss. For a long time he couldn't speak.

"Hey," he whispered, "hey—hey, Jackie? Are you there? Say something. Sometimes people don't know what to do when you begin making up stories—about Africa and elephants and shit like that there."

He said this haltingly and wiped his face with a large hand as the snow fell on his head.

Bunny was not so fortunate and not so bright. He owned a little second-hand bookstore and took in foster children on the side.

This boy made it five they were keeping—and he came in at 560 bucks a month. Everything had been run-of-the-mill. There'd been no great crises—over the years, boys came and went.

Moms got them up and fed them. She didn't much love them. But she and Bunny did what they could. Now suddenly—and suddenly it was—this had happened. Of all the boys they'd had, Moms had a particular lack of empathy for this boy—thought he was "too big for his britches," walking around despising everyone and saying things about external affairs. Moms tried her best to get the other boys to dislike him. That was her way—and she was clever at it, giving extra desserts to those who would mock him, and sending Melon Thibodeau from the table because he would not partake.

Bunny now looked into the boy's bag and saw some socks, a pair of shoes and a shirt. They were strange to the touch, almost in a frightening way—as if they had come from some extraordinary world, perhaps an extraordinary journey. This frightened Bunny and he immediately began to believe the boy had been telling the truth. That would make things even worse for them now.

He called the boy's name again, and then again.

And he now thought that when the boy said, "I was sent by plane to Canada to find my dad," he seemed to be telling the truth.

"Lunatics always sound sane," Moms had said just two nights ago.

She told the boy he had an uncle in jail, so the boy had begged to see his uncle five days ago, and they'd decided to take him to the jail in Harcourt.

Uncle Marvin—who was sitting in a jail cell—said, "Goddamn me all to hell is he ever a Toggle, he's got them Toggle eyes, though, don't he?"

So they drove him home in the back seat of an old Chevy. And while he sat there, Moms, sitting in the front seat, said, almost in a playfully devious whisper, "Sure, Limey," she said, "I will believe you. Now, what's your dad do? And your mom—what's she do? Them is both Limey people, I suppose too, is they? Or is they African people—with woolly hair?"

"I don't know—anymore. I was in Africa—but it was a long time ago. And then I ran away in Belgium, but I get headaches and can't remember and am right back where I started from."

She turned around once more to glare at him and then turned back.

"Right back where you started from, that's right. You had better watch yourself or they will take you down to the provincial hospital here and you don't want that! That's where Melon's mother is now, after she burned Melon with cigarette butts."

Bunny now turned from the cliff. Why hadn't a barrier been put up there? Why had they waited so long to decide such things?

He could see soft, mercurial lights of the neighbourhood in the half drizzle and fog, faintly hear the sounds of music from the street below, and everything seemed the same. When he had looked in the bag, it was as if he was seeing another world in a small pair of children's boots and an old shirt. Why this all seemed mysterious he did not know. He looked up once more at the sky. And then back toward the burdocks— yes, it was there he had grabbed at the bag and the coat. He walked toward the cliff once more, but there was only silence. So he turned away once more.

Bunny remembered the past few weeks with disdain. It was the first time he'd felt such feelings for his wife. She had mined a past she herself no longer recognized, in order to torment a child. "Irish this and Irish that," she would say, just to taunt him. Nor did the boy understand why she said these things to him.

"I'm Irish," she had said, "so I remember for a thousand years!"

"Yes," Bunny said. "I remember travelling to see Brendan Behan when I was a kid of eighteen, and how he whined about us. He just didn't know how many of us loved him and had travelled so far to see him. So with all due respect, the hell with the Irish." Bunny had in fact lived his life with many books, selling and buying them at one-quarter their original price.

"But you are Irish right down to your toes!"

"Yes, as much as anyone—but I don't wear it on my breast and don't use it as a weapon against a young, innocent British kid. And like any true Irishman I don't like those who do." Then he turned away.

He felt he should have said something like this ten years before. He felt he should have left Moms long ago. What he saw in the past few weeks proved who she was, and why he'd always feared her. Not because she was so cold, but because she was so empty.

And now Bunny had obeyed her until this terrible event had happened. And why did it start? It started because the boy was thought to sound a little English, and Moms liked to torment, and bring up the fact that no one catered to the Brits any longer. But why? The boy had done nothing at all to her. What added to her maliciousness was the fact that he did not remember who he was, and she smelled a rat, as she said, and spent an inordinate amount of time trying to trip him up.

"I'll pry it out of him tomorrow," she would say. "I'll pry it out of him!"

Bunny listened to all of this day and night but did nothing to prevent it.

So in a way—in more than one way—Bunny was just as responsible for what had happened as she was. He too thought the boy was a Toggle and half witted, since he knew the family and believed they were all that way. But now he had to go report the disappearance.

He started on his way down to the police station, carrying the boy's coat and bag. They would have to get the firemen to help them. But he began to think of the headlines: "Boy runs from Bunny McCrease—smashed on the rocks."

Or "Poor little kid gets chased by Bunny the bully and falls to a miserable death."

If he reported this, the police would shut their house down, and perhaps he would go to jail. Certainly Moms would lay the blame on him. "I didn't ask that no good for nothing to chase the boy, pawnmesoultagod!" is what he could hear her saying.

And the money they received for keeping foster children, what would happen to that?

Perplexed and then terrified, Bunny went instead to find his stepson, carrying the coat and the bag under his arms, treading a path through the snow. Strange that he passed a young girl named Luda Marsh—but he chose not to look at her, and moved off before she saw him clearly.

———

Vernon was sitting by himself near the back fence, near the old shed, with the night air forming ice once again over the small puddles in the yard. Vernon came out to smoke and stay out of his mother's sight. He did this at this time almost every night.

"Yes," Vernon said. "What is it, Dad?"

"Vernon," Bunny said, "I am in real trouble—your dad is in real bad trouble. It's the Limey."

Vernon, a small, thin, troubled youth, friendless, stood and walked back with his father toward the cliff, and both of them peered over into the darkness. He blinked and pondered what to do. Then he looked behind him into the inevitable darkness. The Limey was the strange boy who had so recently come to them. The boy had had two hundred dollars on him, and Vernon had secretly helped him open his own bank account just six days before. Vernon had not wanted the other boys—or his own mother—to take it from him. She might take it for safekeeping, but Vernon knew the youngster might never see it again.

Vernon had always been pressed into duty for his stepfather; Bunny was always asking him for help. Snow circled their feet as they looked down into the night.

"Can you maybe go down and look—maybe just a little?" Bunny asked.

Vernon climbed down in the dark with his father standing above, a small street light shining through his legs. Vernon smelled the wet snow, and looking far beneath him could just make out the rocky shore where he fished striped bass in the spring of the year. He was hanging on to an old root.

"What do you see, Vernon—what is it you see?"

"I can't see anything—I am halfway down—there is no body here—he must have fallen full down."

"Well, come up before you fall," said the big man finally.

"Okay," Vernon said. "We have to talk to the cops."

Vernon climbed back up, his face still terrified and his hands red raw. There was as always in his terror a look of innocent alarm, as if he had once again realized his life was tragic and that he had done nothing to make it so. He kept saying he was biding his time, and someday he would be his own man. But that someday never arrived. He lit another smoke, drew on it, tossed his head back and said again that they must now see the cops.

"Oh—no—who knows what they will do to your mom. You think they will not blame us. If we say he fell, they will blame us. And maybe they won't find him," Bunny said.

"What do we do, then?" Vernon asked.

"Take his bag and coat—no one has to know. If they come from child welfare, or that man from child protection services, we will say he simply ran away. That's the best idea under the circumstances. They will take the case back to Gagetown and search for him. The new social worker hasn't even come to the house yet. There is no way they will know if we keep quiet."

Vernon stared at his father; both their faces were white and drawn and tense. They started back together without speaking. Vernon knew this was an awful thing, but in order to protect his family, he could think of nothing else to do.

It turned much colder as they walked home together. Vernon had tried to get rid of the boy's coat, leaving it in the upstairs closet of the old, abandoned Shaw house, where he thought it wouldn't be found—or if found wouldn't be associated with them. And he hid the boy's bag and what was in it behind the back wall in their own family shed, because the ground was far too cold to bury it and it could be found if he just threw it away. He did think of throwing it away, but the girl Bunny had seen, Luda Marsh, was still standing near the back of the old school steps.

So the best he could do was take the bag to the shed. He put it behind the false wall near the sink that had been damaged two nights before, during a fight that Vernon himself had to stop; put the wallboard back and the shelf in front of it once again—a cubbyhole he had used for years—and decided that was that. Except, on two occasions he took out the bag and drove about town, deciding to get rid of it—but both times he had no better place to put it. So both times he brought it back home.

The incident on the cliff was never reported.

And in a strange circumstance, child protection sent along a cheque but did not visit for quite some time.

———

When the social worker, DeWold, did make an appearance later in the summer, he had the names of boys who had left months before, and he no longer knew who was who in the house. So he made some mistakes about who was who, and then relied upon what Bunny told him. This DeWold had taken the job to impress his wife (so the rumour went) and was hoping to show her how concerned he was.

"This is my first case," he told them proudly.

He looked at Vernon, and was quickly told by Moms that the boy was the Toggle boy.

"Goodly, goodly, how are you?"

"Well, be a polite fella and shake Mr. DeWold's hand," Moms said.

Then DeWold quickly made a few notes and talked about hockey.

Bunny and Moms received a cheque for the boy for another eighteen months, and DeWold made four or five more visits.

When DeWold came, Bunny usually talked about hockey. And DeWold would spend half the afternoon telling him stories, and laughing and joking, once taking off his shirt to show Bunny the scar from an operation he had had on his shoulder.

There was one boy in the house, Melon, who tried to find out where the Limey went. But most people told him it didn't matter—that the boy had gone back home. After a while Melon began to have nightmares. And when, after a time, Moms McCrease told him he was lying and had made up the story about the boy, he began to light fires.

So for the next eleven years Melon spent time in and out of jail. He got tattoos and he tried to act bad. And for a short time he was even sent to prison.

But in 2011 he again began to remember that boy, and this time he knew he had to write to someone about him. For in the end no one except Melon Thibodeau remembered that scrawny little thirteen-year-old boy at all.

2.

JOHN DELANO GOT THE CALL AT 7:06 IN THE MORNING. HE wasn't asleep anyway. On the radio there was an instrumental cover of "Walk Away, Renee."

It was November 3, 2011.

He lit a cigarette and looked out the window at the dry road and the ice in the windswept field and the cross of Saint Rose of Lima far beyond it, with its stained-glass windows still dark. The sound of morning, still yet, and covered in frost, came in that window and lay in that room, and said, "You no longer matter."

Since his son had died in 2002, he had woken most mornings like this; You No Longer Matter was an actual prayer softly spoken in the dark to someone who might peacefully, perhaps, without pain, as Keats said, take him away.

He poured some orange juice. On the fridge was the note he had written last night: "Melissa Sapp—arrived home safely, watched her unlock door." He flipped the notebook closed.

He was no longer an active RCMP officer—but he did get calls and still worked on cases now and again. He was better than good at them. Why this was he wouldn't have been able to tell anyone. He had in fact been around the globe doing work. He had been an officer for many years. So now the RCMP had called him about this one.

He looked across at the Rose of Lima, and the sun firing against the stained glass, and trucks moving off in the distance toward the huge mill, where the smoke and flame flashed out. Yes, he believed in saints, but that was for another time. Saints and all they went through—this idea of sainthood that was generally dismissed—yet still he thought some saints quite important. He had even prayed to a few of them. If it did any good, he wasn't certain. But he believed in them. And besides, he thought, if more people tried to be like them—no matter how clumsily they tried—there would be, or might be, less murder to investigate.

Then there was another song—Eric Burdon and the Animals, "San Francisco Night." He tried to remember when he had first heard it.

He'd flown to San Francisco one time, to transport a prisoner back to New Brunswick for trial. He'd had a day to himself while the transfer was being processed and had gone to visit Alcatraz. Two of the more famous prisoners in Alcatraz had connections to New Brunswick—Alvin Karpis, who was with the Ma Barker gang, and John Giles, the man who'd made his own sailor's uniform and almost escaped on the mail boat in 1945.

John had a dinner of fish and chips that afternoon at Fisherman's Wharf. Sunlight was bright in the window. Later, he walked to the large Catholic cathedral and lit a candle.

The prisoner said he'd had a good time in San Francisco and ultimately would have a good time back in Canada—that he would be released because he was well-known, and John was simply a useful slave of the system. He said this very subtly; it took him a while, and he had a very melodious, ironic voice. He said that the RCMP were involved in covert activity that demonstrated a lack of concern for freedom and equality, to protect the vast corporate interests of the United States. John was very used to being called names and said nothing.

Then the fellow talked to John about the lessons of Marx, the policies of right-wing governments and the death dealt the common man. John said nothing to all of this—the man had embezzled $238,000 from a wealthy elderly lady from Saint Stephen, New Brunswick, who liked cats and dogs and believed in all progressive things. But then, recently, before he fled to San Francisco, the prisoner had firebombed two logging trucks and a tree harvester on a cut in northern New Brunswick. The student papers loved him—and he gave one of them an interview. It was this that had allowed John to finally track him down.

The man was named Tim Wasson and he insisted it was his duty to protect the Maritimes, though he did not live there anymore and, among other things, had joined a health club in Toronto, one with a tennis court, of which he was particularly fond.

John had gone to San Francisco to arrest him and bring him home. That was his job. Wasson taunted him about being a member of CSIS. This was one of the five or six cases John had been working on at the time. He had worked on this case for two years—and a break had come just the week before, when the man's girlfriend in Montreal, who was setting up the interview with the compassionate student press, had made a phone call to California.

There had been other officers willing to go, and he didn't have to. Yet he insisted because he had known Wasson as a child, and he had just lost the first Bennie Cheval case. So, delaying vacation for a week, he decided to send his son to camp.

"Just go to camp, and I'll be back and we'll go on vacation next week."

It was during that trip to camp when his son disappeared.

The man spoke to him endlessly about fighting the system, wore his hair in the appropriate ponytail, spoke of unions and the working class. Still and all, he was determined to destroy what the working class worked with. Tree harvesters and pipelines, and all the rest of it.

Wasson got a six-month sentence followed by two years' probation. The elderly woman he'd embezzled from declared he had been in her will and the money was to be given to him. Wasson's cousin Melissa Sapp had organized his defence—and brought in a brilliant lawyer from Fredericton to help her.

This was nine years ago.

Wasson was now living in Scotland, married to a British actress and activist, and periodically ran for the British parliament. He had his own blog and was considered a compassionate man.

Perhaps he never even remembered John.

John put on his dark-khaki coat and went out. His marriage had ended— he forgot exactly when. Perhaps three or four years ago. Still, he and his ex-wife kept saying they would get back together, and who knew, it might happen someday in some place—and maybe in *that* place, that place where it had ended.

The sky had the peculiar scent of gas and soot, and a look of blackened ice that somehow had traces of fine-gold sunlight, which made the ice seem darker and petulant, enclosed in some brave mystery, eternal and even on the gravest sidewalks awe-inspiring.

He remembered one Christmas Day like this, and many a Remembrance Day.

On his left, small branches and withered grass clung to the sides of the lane, with dead leaves scattered throughout alders and grate. A blast of wind might be a harbinger of things to come, or things that had long ago passed by.

He stared across the street to an old hulk of a building with many of the windows gone, and those that weren't, painted green.

All is passed away.

John was at the police station for over an hour before they handed him the letter. It was addressed simply to "JOHN DELANO, police officer." It had no return address, and no stamp.

He asked if it had been delivered by hand. No, it had come in the mail the day before. Well, John asked, who paid for the postage?

The mailroom sorted it and knew where to send it, they supposed, and had just handed it in to the office.

Since his son had disappeared, John had received many envelopes and letters written to him, with people saying they had leads, and offers for help. And in this was hope—even if each new letter caused a torment. He, a seasoned policeman, had spent thousands of dollars on these fruit- less leads. He had followed his wife's almost deranged hope for years. Sometimes the letters would be celebratory, saying, "You deserve what you got; you put me away." But even those he filed.

"He was killed because of you—remember?"

These would be letters he dreamed about and he would wake up in a sweat. "Yes, yes, yes—that's why he was killed, all because of me. I allowed the idea of sin and hatred to enter into my house, to harm a little child. Someone took him when I was away and I should have been at home."

John had a heart attack in 2007, during the second Bennie Cheval case. But in many ways it was because of his son.

By then, he and his wife had been separated for a year. They had separated because they couldn't find the boy—and the boy was, in fact, the only reason for their marriage.

Now he suspected this letter was another psychic or clairvoyant writing about where to locate his son, and he hesitated in opening it. For he was only human, and there was no offer of help that he had refused; if hope sprang eternal for his son, John had such hope.

Still, he left the envelope on his desk and went out for a smoke. The wind seemed to peel back the small, dirty puddles, and the hydro wires above his head vibrated. He threw his cigarette down in the mud and went back inside. It was almost nine o'clock. He drank a coffee, black, and leaned back against his desk. Finally he tore the side off the envelope and took out the letter.

He did not know if he was disappointed or relieved: It was not about his son.

"Dear Sir," the salutation said. "I do not want to bear false witness," the letter stated, "but there was a boy here some time ago in 1999—and he left Shelf Street is all I remember. He walked up Shelf Street, and said he was going to go away. And I do not want to covet my neighbour's wife or bear false witness or anything like that there, but he was just a kid of thirteen—and I always wondered about him. For years I did wonder. I racked my brains, wondering what happened to him. I let him down, I think, for I told him he had to go meet someone one night—and I don't want to be blamed on that there. He was the kindest boy I ever met, and I don't want to think someone hurt him. He was always alone, and some called him the Limey—but I am not sure where he was from. He came here and they put him in a home, but he wanted to go away. He said once he had to go to the biggest building to find his mom and dad. So I said there was a big building downtown and was that it? And he said no, but he was sure he had to go to the biggest building.

"But I am thinking we wasn't supposed to cross the line—'cause some boys threw rocks at the boys above the field, those big guys who went to the high school, and they wanted to get even. But he didn't even know where the line was—he was only here a few weeks—so he knew nothing about the line or about the girl. He liked a girl, but I told him to stay away from her. I was just young myself—just twelve years old. So I've been trying to think of what happened to him, but I am not sure! I asked the police after the boy, and one big shot said he would look into it and never did. When I went back, he said that boy was not missing but home with his sister. So anyways, I thought you might help."

John glanced away and took a breath, and tried to think. This was and always would be his response to the madcap. That is, he was not sure if it was true. Still, something in the letter made John pause. So he turned his head quickly and then went back to the letter just as quick. And then continued reading.

The letters were small and the words very close together, as if the man or woman—though he thought it was a man—was frightened of what it was he was writing. This meant the fellow had probably thought about it a long time, and had kept it to himself—and was even now uncertain of relinquishing a secret. Or perhaps, as the letter suggested, he had told someone in authority before, and they didn't believe him. So he was wary to tell it again. The secret must have been a difficult one to bear. That meant it was perhaps a violent one. Or he thought a violent thing may have happened to the boy and he was worried that he would be implicated. The man who wrote this letter by the way the letters were formed was left-handed, and John felt his hands were probably used to doing some kind of work—perhaps he did some motor mechanics or welding.

The secret the letter imparted was of a youngster who had come to where . . . a foster family? When . . . ? Just a few weeks or a month before the incident? The person who wrote the letter did not give certain information—which meant what? He did not want to get someone at the foster home into trouble, or he did not know what foster home it was—or perhaps it was all a lie?

That was as far as John's thinking went at the moment. He looked over the timeline again.

Over time the boy, dubbed the Limey, decided to leave: "He said he was in the wrong place. That he had come here searching for his dad.

"So he left that night, and no one saw him again. But did he leave, or did something happen to him? He didn't know much about winter—so I thought I'd tell you that. He said he was born in December—what day I am not so sure—but that he would go and meet his dad at the biggest building. That's all I remember—except—well . . ."

The writing was so light as to be indecipherable at times, which meant, John decided, that even when the fellow was writing, he did not want to. Yet this was something he had to tell and he had wrestled with it for a long time. So he knew the boy better than others did. The boy did not know much about winter—which meant what? That he was from the south? Possibly, but he did have a British accent.

So—Australia, perhaps?

The person writing was religious, or at least believed in the import of more cosmic forces in our lives. And the incident had plagued him enough to write to Delano. And John knew why: He was a very well-known RCMP officer, that was true—but he had also lost a boy years ago, his own son. He had never solved his own son's case. It had driven him to despair. Perhaps the fellow was thinking that John might solve this case. To make up for it. Or—and this might be possible—was in fact teasing him.

In a strange way John had circled words and had written notes about the first paragraphs already:

"The boy was searching for his dad."

"He said he would send me a postcard—like that of the CN Tower."

So John now wrote: "Like that, or like that?" That is, was it going to be a postcard something *like* one of the CN Tower—or an *exact* postcard of the CN Tower? Therefore, if he was going away—was it to Toronto? Why did this fellow think something had happened to him? If there was even a missing kid in the first place. Maybe the boy had just left that night he was last seen and got back with his family again.

Because, John thought, reading between the lines, the fellow didn't get the postcard—the boy was important to him and he wondered about it. Someone had something against him, or maybe bullied him? In the foster home, perhaps? And perhaps that was why he did not send the postcard—because they would know where he went? So he decided against the postcard—but in fact this is what the fellow who wrote the letter remembered and is now wondering about.

John thought of this, and then jotted down a few more notes:

So then he left Shelf Street. The boy had turned and walked away. But he had crossed a line—which meant, if John remembered Shelf Street, the boy would have had to be going northwest—and the bigger boys had told the kids from Shelf Street not to. Nothing more than a neighbourhood war between some kids? Still, it might have been something else entirely. Then there was this: "He gave a girl a book—I do not know if that had something to do with it. But he bought a book and said it was for a girl."

Well, this could be, and probably was, utter foolishness. The fellow had sent the letter to John just to make him worry about someone else.

Perhaps, at its worst, it was sent to provoke him, knowing he had lost a boy. Every note he received about his son, he passed on to other RCMP officers. Sergeant Melonson kept a file on these notes out of compassion. Nothing came of them.

John set the letter down and went to the coffee machine once more. Still, the line "you might figure it out" meant the boy was relying on him.

He came back to the letter because of this line, scrawled a bit more forcefully in the second paragraph of the second page—which meant this paragraph had been written to protect the good memory of the boy: "My friend knew books but didn't like school. But he told me a poem about a nightingale, talked to me about a whale out in the ocean some-place and told to me about an operation Hitler had. He read all kinds of books because he said his mom read to him, and he wanted to find the line she read, which told him who he was. So he went to the library— can you imagine."

John Delano leaned against his desk and pondered this paragraph for quite a while. Would the fellow who had written the letter make this up? No, no one would bother making this up, really. This was written because he was proud of the boy—a boy as young as he was knowing so much—not because he was telling a falsehood.

Say the boy was here for only a matter of a few weeks. He could have come and gone, and been forgotten. Nor did this fellow who wrote the letter know what the boy was actually talking about in those books he mentioned, so in some way mentioning these historical and liter-ary anecdotes proved that the missing boy existed. So, far from being a fabrication, these two had known each other some time ago. They must have.

By this logic, the missing boy was self-taught—and had a kind of eclectic knowledge. Why? He didn't like school.

He gave a girl a book. Maybe he gave the wrong girl the book? But what book? And what girl? If there was a girl, this boy who'd written the letter might have known her situation was not very good.

Maybe this Limey was strange enough in himself—he quoted Keats and talked about Hitler's June 1941 invasion of Russia, called Operation Barbarossa. Very few thirteen- or fourteen-year-old kids would know about this. The fellow who was proud to write John about it didn't know this either—only enough to remember what the boy had told him. But someone who read whatever he could did so for one reason only: to find out who he was. So someone had read to him as a boy and perhaps had given him a love of reading and a sense of himself.

John walked outside and lit another cigarette. (Although he'd had a scare a few years ago, a heart attack, he still smoked—up to ten a day.) He was not supposed to drink, for if he did, his psychiatrist was sure he would start taking pills again. And pills made him extremely violent— not taking them, but coming off them was horrendous. It all happened after his son died, and there was nothing more he could do about it. He had apologized to everyone for it. He would not apologize again.

But he had been off booze and pills for over three years.

He was still searching for his son and had looked over every lead he had in the past nine years—was it that long now?—just two nights ago. That is why he couldn't help but think there was something made up about this boy. But then again, the letter seemed so simple and kind-hearted and truthful that John determined it wasn't a ruse. What was painful is that the letter mentioned that the boy had been looking for his dad.

The wind was bringing rain, and it hit his face, and the smoke blew out and up from his mouth. Snow then began to come down too.

If he is missing, why wasn't there a search sooner—or why didn't anyone report him gone? No, maybe there is no one missing—maybe this is just about a kid who said, "Oh, I'll send you a postcard," and never did do so—and that is that. He went off and lives somewhere in Canada and doesn't even remember people here. That is one way to look at it. But the boy might have been a loner who had decided to leave them all behind. He must have left a lot behind over the years if he was alive. Even in this age of reckoning everything thousands of people are still lost—perhaps he is lost to a factory somewhere, a small truck route along a city street?

John asked a few officers if they had heard about a missing kid a few years back, a boy who might have had the nickname Limey. They

shrugged as they walked by. He for some reason always hated it when
police officers shrugged.

He flicked the cigarette into the dirt and went inside. He climbed
the stairs to the main office—the hallways small, with old yellow walls.
Here and there was the smell of heat, and near the window the smell of
air and snow.

————

Trevor was sitting at her desk, smoking, with the window open and a
candle lit to mask the smoke. She had been the RCMP officer dealing in
domestic violence, which she hated, and child abandonment, which she
hated. She dealt on a daily basis with Melissa Sapp, who was provincial
coordinator of child abandonment. It was a new department, recently
formed. Why, Trevor said, couldn't her credentials allow her one good
crisp murder? But there were murders of children all the time. And John
knew that. She had been a friend because of his own son, but it was no
longer an open case—everything had been exhausted. She had emailed
his son's information to the new branch, to Melissa Sapp, without knowing about the years of confrontations John had had with social services,
and how Melissa had stealthily blamed him for his own boy's death. (Or
at least, this is what John thought.)

Now Trevor said, "I don't remember anyone searching for a youngster—well, that wasn't accounted for in the past ten years. There are
missing children still, and in the past number of years, two from foster
homes we have in the database—but we know who they are . . ."

She butted her smoke. Then she realized what a mistake she had
made. John's own son was not accounted for and had been lost to history,
it seemed. They had searched everywhere for him. John and his wife had
driven across Canada and back through the States, thinking in some
mad, mercurial way they would find him, walking toward them holding
out his arms. Barbecues in the summer and the smell of flowers along a
window bed brought it home to John Delano every waking instant when

July came. For the past few years he had continually read two books: *War and Peace* by Tolstoy and *Demons* by Dostoyevsky.

She knew this as well, even though she herself had read neither.

"I am not sure. I will look," she said now.

He smiled, nodded his thanks. He went back to his desk and again read what the fellow had written.

If there was something to this letter, it would most likely be hard to prove. A book, a girl, a jealous boyfriend. That was one side of it. But the boy had been only thirteen or fourteen—so a childhood crush? The girl would have been young too. But perhaps a little older than the boy. So then, what book? One that spoke of love? Or one that spoke of the life of the girl? And if that was the case—then was it a local book, or a romantic one? Then there was the war between the two neighbourhoods—yes, that was probably the reason. The boy crossed the line somewhere and got caught on a street where he shouldn't have been. Happened all the time to youth.

But John soon dismissed this, reflecting that here in Saint John among kids that age, disputes about territory most often resulted in a slap on the head, nothing much more. And the thing that bothered him about that scenario was this: Kids talked. If it was a group of kids who had done something terrible, accidentally or otherwise, it certainly would have been known and gossiped about, at school and elsewhere. On the bus and off, as John used to say about kids. So the girl and the book might be clues, but they were not the reason for the disappearance.

Everyone would have known in a day or two about something that had happened between kids. The boy would no longer have been forgotten.

But he *had* been forgotten—therefore John assumed something else must have taken place.

That is, within an hour or so John determined it was probably a crime committed by an adult, if it was a crime at all.

Trevor came back after an hour and said there was no missing-child case resembling what was written in the letter—in fact, there had been no missing-child cases at all in 1999. There had been the murder of a girl about twelve years old by her aunt—that was sensational, and the family was not poor. It happened at their cottage—a frivolous argument over a late-night bonfire and roasting marshmallows.

Still, about this case. Trevor phoned the local police in Saint John and the police in Rothesay, and John waited in the office. It took almost thirty-five minutes.

"No one the age of that child is remembered to have gone missing and unaccounted for. A report here and there about someone running away—but they turned up. The files don't show an outstanding case," Trevor said, hanging the phone up with a display of quick certainty.

The quick certainty meant what, John wondered—that she had already solved it?

That is, there was a fly in the ointment. John had brought frivolous cases to her before—about children—all since the disappearance of his own boy. There were seven of them. One about a boy in Jackson, Mississippi, who did not know who his parents were. John took a leave of absence and flew down to see the child. Of course it was not his child.

That is why when today she had got a skeptical reply from the social services department, she was not surprised. They had taken some time to look at back cases—and the middle-aged woman she'd contacted had the most up-to-date data for her. But social services actually spoke for others when they said they believed John might want to fabricate cases about missing children now. This had been hinted at many times, especially by social workers who had dealt with him before, and it certainly seemed it might be true. The idea quite prevalent—without being said—was that John was fighting an ongoing war against women who had tried to take his wife's child years before.

"I am not saying he dislikes all women, but he certainly disliked us," the woman at social services explained.

Trevor listened to this as if a sudden clarity about John and his motives might be emerging.

"We've had a history with him," the woman said. "And it's been a painful one."

She explained to Trevor what had happened with him some years back because of the fight over the Aube boy, a child John had wanted to adopt when the boy was with social services. The child was turned over to him and Jeanne Aube after they were married, and a few years later disappeared.

"Now here, suddenly, is another boy—so I guess he will blame social services for something bad. Well, I'm retiring in two months, so let others handle it," the woman said. But she said she would turn the inquiry over to the new child protection department, headed by a woman named Melissa Sapp, and leave it with her.

"But I know nothing will come of it," the woman said.

Trevor did not tell John anything about this conversation, only that the new department dealing with child protection and endangerment would look into it.

"That's good," he said. "Thank them for me."

John asked Officer Melonson, who had been a city cop at the time, if he had heard anything in his department about a boy who had gone missing in 1999. A boy who'd had the nickname Limey.

Melonson said he probably had, but not anyone who was gone for long, and not one with that nickname. He had been leaving city police work at that time and going to the RCMP. But he also said there were many kids he'd dealt with, but none who disappeared.

So John shrugged as if it was probably nothing, and then read the letter once more.

But then he went back to Trevor. He said he believed it wasn't a case that had happened outside the city; therefore they should concentrate on the police force inside the city—that is, the city police—and see if anyone on the force remembered, and they should perhaps make some phone calls.

Trevor was sorry for him. But she knew he was not immune to being censured over some of his actions. There had been those erratic years when he had demanded they comb a section of the Hammond River again for his child, and all the backwoods ponds, and they had spent eighteen thousand dollars on a futile search of two fields because he remembered a phone call he had received three years before that. Once he went almost hysterical about a young girl who had run away. He was incensed no one was doing enough. The girl was found at her boyfriend's eating pizza. And after that John was considered a dud in the department—his great talent diminished.

Melonson too had to try to forgive an episode John had had with Melonson's own wife, Judy, who had taught his child. John, reports went, had come very close to striking her. He had been placed on administrative leave for a time. And people said he had gone crazy because his wife had been sleeping around.

John suddenly realized the position he was now in.

Another missing-child case. He could easily sense how his colleagues felt.

Yes, here it was: a no-named child had gone missing. And the letter with the information had come to him.

Searching for a mythical boy after spending forty thousand dollars on clairvoyants to try to find his son seemed slightly made up. His face suddenly buckled into a kind of resignation when he thought of this. Still, he took the envelope, took the letter, put on his khaki coat and went out into the cloudy autumn day.

———

Later it began to snow and a grey came over the land—the wind was fast and hollow and the trees seemed burned by the cold. John Delano turned and walked back up Shelf Street, which was adjacent to the old west-side bowling lanes, smoking a cigarette and pondering what might have happened.

If the boy had left from here—from here, where to?

Evening was coming on and little girls in pretty coats and hats were coming home and a new new new generation of people had been born since he was their age, and all of them seemed now to listen to songs in their ears, and carry Harry Potter books about wizards, or fall in love with vampires, and in the grand distance the church of Saint Rose lay beckoning in the storm with only one faint light.

He walked up and down Shelf Street for two hours, retracing the supposed steps of a boy who had gone missing some years before.

"Maybe he turned left here," John would mumble. "Maybe not, though—however, it is probably quite likely he got to the train." Then John would look up and see a woman staring at him, and he would nod, as if he was addressing her with what he had just said. "Got onto the train," John said, nodding, as the woman scurried around him.

Still, John decided to put that idea away for now—not to think of it as a simple case of the boy leaving on a train. He looked along the ground, and then looked up toward the autumn streets beyond.

"Okay, okay," he told himself aloud, feeling now the sting of the wind, and remembering he had not taken his pills today.

A local police car had been dispatched to see who he was.

"I'm fine," John said for some reason, thinking of the pills. Then, realizing how perplexing it all was to the bright, sunny officer, he pulled out a badge from his inside pocket and showed him. The officer reminded him of his one-time protege Melonson, whom he had helped ascend in the RCMP until he himself started to descend.

So then, what did he have?

If the boy had simply left, fine.

But if so, child protective services should have been all over it. If not . . . then something happened to him, and no one had discovered what. He had seen much bitterness and anger toward children in his thirty-five years as a policeman. Much kindness too, and much of both from the same people—adults trying to cope in a world that had done them no favours either. So he wasn't blaming anyone—he was trying to find a thread. Someone had missed the ball—and this happened, and could happen in any profession, at any time.

So he continued his walk.

The church bells gonged in the shrouded distance. He blessed himself because he had promised his ex-wife he would do so when he heard church bells, and so he did.

"It will help your heart heal," she had told him.

"Ah, my heart heal." He had smiled.

He put his hood up and kept walking with his face to the ground, and the sound of traffic running close by, a kind of dull whizzing and asserting noise.

"Of course, if the boy did come to serious harm, you must understand the nature of . . . what?" John said out loud, not caring that another woman stopped and turned to catch what he said.

"The nature of something many are too abashedly sophisticated to mention," he said. She looked at him. She was about forty—a woman on her way home from work. As she turned away, he said, "Sin."

John then walked to the end of the field. There was a long fence here now to protect you from Saint's Cliff—but it wasn't here in 1999 . . . Ten more yards, and if you weren't being careful, you'd fall ninety feet.

Could the boy have gone down there eleven years ago, never to be heard or seen again? Just a stumble in the darkness. If he was not familiar with the land, it could have happened. So: perhaps it was just an accident, John thought.

Or could someone have chased him?

He turned and started back.

Evening flurries had started one more time, and the little girls shrouded in Saint John cold and mist walked past him in their yellow jackets and colourful backpacks. It reminded him of school in Newcastle when he was a child. Once, when he was in Ireland, he had been lucky enough to see Thin Lizzy—and all those young Irish girls and boys had reminded him of the Maritimes because of their shy Irish defiance.

Oh, the book bags had changed since he was a boy. They were once no more than utilitarian, but now they had spread their wings, were superb representatives of the children on whose backs they sat. Little pilgrims.

Although it looked as if John Delano was doing nothing and having no success on this small out-of-the-way street with its few houses, gates in the famished autumn afternoon, John was narrowing his focus and his ideas and his theory. And he was continually concentrating on the huge, neglected building far away, above the road beyond those cliffs—he had been looking at it most of the day, in fact. It was a singular house cut off from all the rest, on its own gated acre of land, with its four gnarled oak trees that now protected it. It had been the house of one of the city's most influential families—but a name that by now had been almost totally forgotten. It was a house where kids congregated after school in the time that missing boy might have been here. And perhaps the boy could have congregated there too out of loneliness and hope.

There in the cold fog it stood in its nakedness, its brokenness, its nineteenth-century lost splendour like some artifice rising out of the years of the lumber trade. It had been abandoned by the Shaw family— the prosperous parliamentary members and lumber barons since 1893— fallen after the son in whom they had put all of their hopes had died in battle at Ypres in 1915. It had been cut up into apartments in the late forties—a very desirable place, a convenient location for postwar secre- taries or teachers working downtown or young men come into the city to find a trade. It had been broken up further into rooms for men solitary in the mid sixties, men who longed for and dreamed of an apartment they would never have—part-time dock workers, men who laboured, night-shift taxi drivers—and then in the nineties, even those rooms became damned: the corridors became long and empty, the walls water stained and cracked; the east wind penetrated the broken-up floors and windows; small grey rats scurried over broken glass in dry cellars; old fireplaces filled up with garbage; and by 1994, boys and girls found the derelict place and partied and drank.

Then the police closed it down. Now there was a fence around it and a darkness about it, and it loomed like some relic from the age when Canada believed in some destiny it no longer had.

It stood, ready to be bulldozed away, and John Delano, walking between Shelf Street and the Cragg Road, was staring toward it as little girls walked around him, giggling and talking, and living life the only way it should be lived.

He started back toward Shelf Street, crossing Station Street toward the old strip mall to the west.

Yes, yes, he kept saying to himself whenever an answer came to the questions he had been posing himself all day.

The boy had existed, and no one had cared.

He went home and had supper, and thought of the cliff, the building and the kids. Then he took the five pills he had to take for his heart, including blood thinner and a pill for cholesterol, and sat by himself thinking of the letter. He took off his heavy leather shoes, their rims streaked in mud, and picking them up one at a time, he polished them—concentrating as much on doing so as anything else he had ever done. For he polished his shoes every night.

Then lighting a cigarette and staring out the black window, he thought: What would I do with myself if I was a child alone in the world? Would I get along so easily—or would the fact of my being on my own harm me? How would I make out in foster homes, with people paid a salary to care—would I know this in my heart? Would finding my father and mother begin to obsess me, so that I would travel the ends of the earth? Of course! And how would the social workers or police come to view me? Well, I know full well how they would—some of them would imagine I was a liar at thirteen years old. The idea of my difference would plague me. The boy had only needed one person to believe him—one person old enough to help—and he did not find this person. Sooner or later he would have been determined to leave.

John sketched it out on a pad of paper: If the boy was cornered in the field, he would have had only one of two places to run to: toward Shelf Street or toward Saint's Cliff above the Reversing Falls. If he fell, he would have been gone in a second and no one would have found him.

But then again, probably the only way he would have run there is if he was chased. But—and this was something of a hope—if the boy fell, wouldn't his body have been found by someone, washed up somewhere?

After nine that night John made his way out into the street again, and passed the old sheds that lay battered by the winter. And he was moving up along Ridge Street now toward the Shaw house.

The building was still solid, the dormers still above him on the third floor. He caught his jacket in the fence as he came off it, and had to hesitate to unhook himself, and walked through some cold, reddish, leaning brambles that snapped against him as they do in autumn.

When he reached the front door, the wind was more ferocious and his split front lip was bleeding. Yes, he remembered the poem by Milton Acorn: "I've Tasted My Blood." He had even written an essay on it for an English course. But now, because he was taking blood thinner, his lip would bleed most of the night.

He walked back toward the broken side street, and reached the set of bushes he had come through where the snow had lessened and slicks of ice had formed over last month's puddles. He rounded the building looking for a way he might enter and saw only one possibility: a fire escape. He got up on the lowest rung of the old fire escape, climbed onto a side porch twelve feet above the ground, and threw his full weight against a half-rotted back door that entered the second floor.

It opened with a jar, swollen as it was, but it was high off the ground and unlocked. Here he found himself in a corridor, the ceilings twelve feet high, with ceiling fans placed there sometime in the fifties. All along this corridor, with its bits of broken pallets and old boards, there were doors—and some were opened, and the moonlight filtered into various rooms through iced-over windows, and in some places snow crept through and lay across the floor, now and then sparkling, and the corridor led to huge stairs with a thick black banister that led down to the front of the house, and other stairs that went up to the floor above.

Rotting lace curtains lay over cracked windows and the stairways were littered with broken bottles. On the wall going down to the first floor were a number of names scratched out in defiance against a world that could not defy them here, names like Reg and Doc and Blair and Uma—and down at the back it said, *Vernon was here.*

I am your pal was scratched in the corner, along with the date March 7, 1966. He wondered where that pal was now.

He had read about the Shaw place. Seven trees at Christmas when trees were still lit by candles, and men and women in great gathering would arrive in horse-drawn carriages on those icy and frozen evenings—when back then our province was less a backwater than it is now. A band would play in the front room, a barbershop quartet would sing—smoked salmon on cedar boards, mince pies and cherry brandy, imported champagne. Guests stayed a week, danced till dawn, slept in quilts, went ice fishing, and the men played high-stakes poker in the back room at night, dressed in black tie, overseen by a doorman in a red jacket.

John Delano's flashlight illuminating the end result of the past century; those cracked or broken plaster walls that told him a particular kind of story separate from the daylight story—and besides, he was mentally at his best well after nine at night. A broken picture of King George V still sat in the corner, George looking plump and well pleased with himself at his coronation in 1911. The Shaw family were one of those moneyed yet entirely likeable families—a family of lawyers and shipping company executives, railway owners who never took life without a joke and looked upon their good fortune as a chance to give back. There were always eight of them at breakfast and fourteen of them at supper. And then slowly it eroded—their finances suffered after the *Titanic* because of their involvement in the Cunard and White Star lines; there were three deaths in two years, a scandal in the government, and Herbert Shaw resigned as finance minister in 1914 to keep the government from falling. And then the young man, Daniel, killed at Ypres.

The family came to grief over the lost empire, split up, and in the twenties and thirties after their fortune was lost one of the boys headed out west. His name was Winston. He left a trail of half-formed businesses from Red Deer, Alberta, to Victoria, British Columbia. He was in jail for a while in Moose Jaw, and was said to have known Al Capone. And then people lost sight of him too.

John came to the front of the house, to those rooms people would have first entered when they visited. A cloakroom was on his left—a room about as big as his bedsitter at the motel. Then he went to the biggest room, except for the living room, on his left, with tall windows facing down the hill toward the old motel he himself stayed in.

There wasn't much in this room. A bookshelf, a small couch and a fireplace. This is where the kids had gathered half a generation ago to drink and party a bit.

He continued on and came to a corner of the building that led down toward the back stairs, and saw on the far back wall: *Luda Bam Bam was here—2001.*

He then walked slowly up to the third floor, while faint ghostly traces of moonlight shone on the broken bits of plaster, and saw the railings torn off, and the stairwell smoke stained, overrun with graffiti.

On the third floor he went into three rooms and looked into the closets and out across the scarred landscape at the huge, glowering mill and its smoke. He checked every closet, trying to imagine who or when people had been here.

In one of the back closets, in a cubbyhole at the back of the closet itself, in the room just off the room with the skylight, and covered in a half-rotted tarp, he discovered what he thought might be an old blanket. He ignored it at first, looking under it. But then he realized it was not a blanket.

He picked it up and shook it. It was a canvas tarp, he thought—but when he went to throw it down, his fingers caught a pocket zipper.

It was a coat, with some kind of a scorch mark on the front. It was almost rotted. But strangely, the remaining fabric, especially around the sleeves, felt new.

He went into another room, the one with the skylight, and looked through the pockets. The front pockets had been rifled through before—he could tell that easily after all this time. But a top pocket on the left side of the coat wasn't pulled out. Here he found two bits of paper, and what might have been money—maybe a twenty-dollar bill.

After midnight he made his way back downstairs slowly, and then out onto the street above the Shaw house, where all the houses along the way were dark. And two street lights burned out. He carried the coat with him, of course. There were burrs across the front, and on the left arm.

John climbed the fence and then walked back along the field toward the falls one more time, just to check things out.

So, John decided, that night the boy in question was moving up the hill and he came from a house on Shelf Street. A child protective agent or a police officer in all likelihood had brought him there.

So why was there no record of him?

John pondered this for some time, and decided it could be only one thing: there was no record of him because he had been a foster boy and no one had reported him gone when he'd left the house he was taken to. So, by that reasoning, an adult in that house may have had something to do with his disappearance.

———

John himself lived in a motel, in a bachelor suite with a sofa and kitchenette, on Matters Road, and could look down over this very hill where that new boy was last seen by his friend all those years ago. He had a shelf of books, a plaque that was given to honour his achievements, and a small gold medal he had won for bravery—which was tossed on the bookshelf and forgotten, just as his career was forgotten.

He looked over his notes.

"Melissa Sapp" was written on a page and underlined. Yes, he had to deal with that, sooner or later—the sooner the better.

The next morning, which was bright but without any sense of pleasure in the cloudless sky—reminding a northern man or woman of the stringency of cold, the empty hearts of school brick and masonry,

John brought the coat and what he had found in it over to the station. Melonson, after an examination, told him it could have been any coat. John knew that. There were grease and marks on it. So he held the coat up and tried to decide if he could tell if the coat was being carried when those marks had occurred. The right sleeve had been ripped and there were spots on the inside, at the back of the collar. Then there were the burrs. It wasn't a large coat—a medium one.

So he decided that it was a boy's coat, and he told his colleagues he was working from the premise that it was that boy's coat, and for them to bear with him as much as they could.

"It is a theory—but let me elaborate on it. What do you think?" he asked Trevor. "Could it be the very coat? You see, it either is or is not—I either have something or I don't."

"I'm not sure—we have gone over most of what we know and have no missing anyone. I spoke to three people today, from social welfare, child welfare and child abandonment, and no one was missing—not in 1999."

"Well, let's just say for a moment that the letter is right. And this boy did go missing unobserved. And the letter says he did have a new coat. Well, this coat was hardly worn. I think the boy crossed a line—you know, where one neighbourhood stops and another starts—but there it is, there it is."

"There is what?" Melonson asked.

"They must have had a dispute—they ambush this boy and chase him. What do you think? Or he left and was on his way to Toronto to try to find someone."

"Who?"

"Well, who would he be searching for? He was a boy—still a child of thirteen. Let's say he was looking for his dad or mom, just as the letter says—that's why he was off to Toronto."

They looked at him.

"I am thinking he was a foster boy from Shelf Street, and Shelf Street was at war with the kids above Matters Road—what do you think? Well, here is what I think: I think maybe that is what the writer of the letter thinks happened—but perhaps something else did. Some other more terrible reason that the boy disappeared."

Trevor looked at him.

"I am thinking it happened another way!"

"What other way?"

"I have been thinking all night—and maybe someone was chasing him to stop him from going away? Is that possible? I mean, we know something terrible happened."

"How do we know anything terrible happened?" Melonson asked. Suddenly his face flushed just a tad.

"Because of the coat," John answered. "The coat tells us that. He did not know winter. He had a new coat, the letter says—and this was a new coat when it was last worn." John looked at the others with hopeful expectation. But they made no sign of believing him.

"I think someone tried to burn this coat to get rid of it. Well, it *is* possible!" he said.

"That is, if there even is anyone missing in the first place! And since I have the report from social services that no one went missing in 1999— well, I phoned Melissa Sapp. She was too busy but had someone else look into it yesterday and came to the same conclusion," Trevor said.

John nodded but remained silent.

Yet he had to do his duty, and so he continued with the evidence he had now. There were two little slips of paper he'd found in that coat pocket, along with a crumpled bill, and another piece of white paper almost empty of marks.

He put them all down on a desk and looked at them.

He decided the ragged, faded, damaged bill was most likely a twenty.

They were still viable as evidence—but of what no one could be sure.

"Anyone know what these are?" Delano asked, holding up the slips of paper.

But Trevor and the young constable beside her simply shrugged.

"Some Kleenex?" the constable asked.

"No—receipts," Trevor said.

John nodded that a receipt might be what they were. He played with them, with a pair of tweezers, and unfolded one slip of paper—or what was left of it, and then the other. He did this slowly. It took him half an hour. There were just a few marks on them, and nothing else. They were evidence of some transaction, faded with time. Maybe someone had attempted to steal the coat and then decided not to. There was a bit of blood over it, and the right arm was ripped, and those responsible may have decided it would be better to burn it. A tag in the pocket, some crumpled papers—that was about what was left, except for an old drawing of a building somewhere, almost invisible now, and a piece of chalk.

"So he went to school," Trevor said.

John shrugged.

"The chalk is pristine and was kept in an inside pocket with the drawing—so I am thinking the chalk and drawing were part of something else he was carrying."

"What something else would that be?"

"Some graver mystery! As Proust might say, 'a remembrance of things past,' " John said. "Not of here but of somewhere else. So I am inclined to think he came from somewhere else, somewhere far away maybe." Then he looked up at Sergeant Melonson.

"I was thinking you might know—but you were no longer here then. You had gone to the RCMP?" John said, partly as a question.

"Yes—I was gone. And it could be anyone at all who wrote that letter," Melonson said.

Melonson was sure John had written the letter himself—and so were others in the department, and everyone had already been told not to get involved until Melonson gave the okay. That was not a completely irrational observation—John had not even been in the office for a while. And suddenly he had shown up and received this letter—without a stamp or a return address—and had started a case. But against whom? The social services he had once battled with over his own child? And when had he done this?

Six months before he was to retire.

But the only problem was—this was a lie. Melonson had been very involved in this case. He was happy that John did not think so, but he was.

There was a child Melonson had dealt with years ago, and a boy named Melon Thibodeau, who had come to him before as well, searching for this boy.

That has nothing to do with this, Melonson now thought.

Besides, some part of him would rather lie than agree with John Delano. The boy doesn't exist, Melonson told himself. And never did.

3.

JOHN DECIDED THIS: THE BOY EXISTED AND HE'D HAD SOME
bad luck somewhere.

At ten o'clock the next morning he went over to the child welfare
department in the building near the court house. His animosity toward
social services was well-known. It had all happened during his fight with
social services over custody of his own son. The dispute had simmered
for a year, until the child was returned to Jeanne Aube. The salient point
was this: Social services had taken Aube's child away and placed him in
foster care —John married the woman to help her get the child back—
no one ever knew why. And then the child disappeared. So now John cut
a very strange figure in the waiting room, a heavy form surrounded by
an unfavourable history.

Then finally, with the help of one of the women in the office, he began
to look for the year 1999.

It was not easy, and as he searched files in back rooms the lassitude
of despair seemed to creep over him. Lights glowed on his balding head.
His skin looked parched and white; his eyes were still brilliant, however. Still, there were only file numbers and the right-of-information
forms that said naming these children without express consent was forbidden by law.

But he managed to see one thing that intrigued him.

In 1999, two foster homes had existed on Shelf Street: one at 87 and another at 66.

Crosby and Lemieux, he thought.

The family at number 66 had moved, and had only fostered girls. In fact, he remembered now—that this is where Luda Marsh once lived.

But the child was a boy—so unless there was more information forthcoming, he would assume the house was number 87.

Could the boy have been under foster care at 87 Shelf Street in 1999?

If he had been, John would have to find the caseworker who'd been in the field at that time.

He went back to his office and waited impatiently for Trevor and others to come in. They all had other cases, and were already feeling he was intruding on them. How could a man who was once so special to them now seem like a real bother? Well, he knew he was.

It was true that often when he was sitting by himself in the large front office, other officers would poke their noses in the door, see it was him and keep moving.

But Trevor came in, and sat down finally.

"The parents must have been dead or completely uninterested in him," John said right off the bat. "So he was sent to a foster home and decided to run away. And if I was in a foster home, I too would run away. But we won't get anywhere with child protection—I'm afraid if the woman in charge sees it's me, she will think the whole thing a wild goose chase."

That is, he was going to have to rely on Trevor, and she sensed this.

He then went back to the little evidence they had.

Yes, it might have been spots of blood on the coat, the medical examiner said, but the wet test did not determine this. And there was nothing on the letter he had been given—except his own fingerprints. Melonson, who had walked down the hall to see him, said this with particular gravity, and said he wanted to move away from this case until any further evidence surfaced. Melonson believed that John was fabricating evidence now, in order to get noticed. This was unforgivable; the trouble was, he could not say this outright.

"Only yours," Melonson said about the fingerprints.

"Well," John said, "that was stupid of me. I should have been more deliberate in handling it. Still, I am thinking they are spots of blood—and that they are not the boy's."

"Why?"

"I think he freed himself from the coat," John said, holding the coat up and twisting his body, "as someone chased him—that's why the sleeve was ripped. That's what all of us would do if we were being chased. This was at the cliff—and I think someone may have been trying to stop him from falling, and perhaps cut a finger doing so. The boy fell over the cliff—the fellow who grabbed at the coat had a cut on his finger and his blood fell into the inside of the coat. Then he walked to the edge of the cliff, looked over, called out his name, and headed back to the old Shaw house, or at least in that direction."

He paused once more. "Or the coat was handed over to someone else. Were they scared? Probably scared to death—and someone tried to burn the evidence. But someone else is finally willing to talk, and then the dominoes are going to fall."

"So," Trevor said. "Not that I don't believe you—but how have you come to this conclusion?"

"Well, if I am right, and say I am, the boy ran through burdocks. There are only a few places where they'd still be that time of year—at the back of the field toward the falls is the only place nearby I found. So say it was there. They hit the front of his coat. Here he turns, so his left arm gets burrs on it. The right sleeve tears as someone tries to grab him, but he gets out of the coat—and he had no idea of the falls being so close because he doesn't know the area like the people chasing him. That does not mean those people wouldn't have cared for him. The real fact is, most of us would care for anyone in trouble—the devil only likes to make us believe we wouldn't. But it is simply that fear may have taken over those who chased him, and they covered up what happened, and after a while he was forgotten. Lost—just like that child in jail a few years back, forgotten for months until she committed suicide. Except, someone who wrote the letter—and who I think is an ex-con—did not forget about him. Is always wondering about him. And wrote to me."

"An ex-con?" Melonson asked.

"Well, he didn't want to write this letter—and as you know, there are no fingerprints on it, so his whole belief system is one where being an informant is the world's son of a bitch—so he is either an ex-con—or, and this is still plausible, had something to do with it himself. But I think he was worried that maybe the wrong policeman would look at it—so that means he knows who is in this department, which indicates an ex-con even more. He may have brought it up to someone here—who scares him—but, well, probably not—I am only thinking out loud."

Melonson stiffened and looked at Trevor. Snow had started in small, mean flakes, but the day was still bright, and Melonson's face betrayed the recalcitrant skeptic he had become after twenty-two years in police work. That is, he could joke about the most sacred matters. Although they had once been good friends, he now disliked John—and felt his reputation as a great policeman unwarranted. He had heard about John growing on the Miramichi, and how unsavoury he was. But it was more than this—it was personal. John had had a disruption with Melonson's wife, who was a grade-school teacher, after John's child had disappeared. Melonson tried to be big-hearted and forget it, but he couldn't.

John looked at them and nodded, to affirm his own veracity, then looked at the slips of paper and the bill. He was sure it was a twenty. He continued speaking:

"Well, the reason he sent the letter is his own. So back to the boy. If he had a wallet, these weren't in it—these were put in the pocket—perhaps after he bought something. And this bill—what is it—" He lifted it to the light. "A twenty-dollar bill? Is this a twenty? It has the colour of a twenty."

"I don't know."

"Well, we don't make twos anymore and it's not the right colour even if we did.'

"Maybe he bought something, and that's the receipt and twenty is the change."

"Yes," John said, holding the bill to the lamplight on the desk. "You usually don't get twenty dollars back as change—it's usually less, or more if you are lucky—but never exactly twenty." Here he looked up at Melonson and then looked back at the bill. "So I am going to speculate that these slips are not receipts, and I am going upstairs to magnify them—and I am going with the hypothesis that this is a murder or criminal negligence causing death."

"Why?"

"Because someone tried to burn the coat, destroy evidence—and it was done by kids, or a kid, because it was so poorly done. So that points to a murder of a kid by a kid—simply that. Except . . ."

"Except?"

"Except, no one talked. So I doubt it was kids . . . Maybe an older person directing a kid—that might be the way it went. But this means they are probably related."

"And," Melonson said after a suitable pause, "why in hell is that?"

"Because if they weren't related, then it would have been some kind of terrible partnership—some kind of criminal bond even sexual in nature, and another crime like it would probably have happened. So I think they were related and were covering something up."

"What would be the motive?" Trevor asked.

"I'm not sure—I am thinking, well, maybe an accident. Something that gets out of hand. You know I have lived in many places and have learned that anything can be used as a motive for a crime. Hell, we don't need Alinsky to destroy the world—"

"Who is he?" Melonson asked. His face flushed and he looked upset, as he always did when John mentioned things he wouldn't know—he suspected John thought himself to be very bright and was making fun of him or his wife, who was a schoolteacher. And he thought about his wife, who tried hard with all her students, and remembered John's outburst against her.

John was very, very bright, but in fact had never made fun of anyone—though Melonson, with his feelings of inferiority, often made fun of John and what he knew. (He made fun of John's Catholic views almost continually, and equated them with sexism and bigotry because it was fashionable to do so, and his wife, Judy, was a fervent admirer of what she took to be progressive views.)

Melonson had never heard what had actually happened to that boy who had lied to him about being from Africa. He had heard that he was a Toggle who went back to Gagetown and lived with his sister, and was later unfortunately killed in a car accident. He knew John believed Melonson had been in Regina studying to be an RCMP officer at the time all this had happened—and Melonson would not tell him differently.

Melonson was about to be made superintendent of the province—about to be, that is, if things went well in the next year. He'd had an impeccable career, was bilingual and had solved his own cases. But he knew in his heart of hearts he was not as bright or as good as John; he knew in his heart that John was supposed to have been made superintendent fifteen years ago. And he worried that something in his own career would make him look bad before his promotion happened. He felt John would want this bad thing to happen.

John glanced at him for a moment and simply said, "Alinsky was a man who believed the world should be destroyed— and made fresh and new for people exactly like himself. This is what we dealt with in Rwanda, and in some respects with students in our own country today parading their virtues against our oppressions. So what does that mean?"

"I don't know."

"It means a reign of terror would exist against all those who disagree with progress that relied upon shedding blood. A reign of terror would exist like it did during both the Russian and French revolutions. In fact it does exist—it always has and always will. A reign of terror does in fact exist constantly against good men and women. I think it existed against this child for a long time. I think he came from somewhere else—maybe even another country—I think he was a little boy no one believed and it was as if he suddenly entered hell. Or maybe he came from a worse place than that."

"You believe that?" Again Melonson gave a kind of gasp and looked at the other officers present to show his disbelief, hoping the look would influence opinion.

"I believe and always have that someone who does not belong is always on the chopping block. Sometimes it is obscene, what occurs."

"Obscene?"

"Well—that is not an overstatement, considering what happened."

Neither Melonson nor Trevor spoke, but they glanced at each other.

———

John went upstairs into another room, and snapped on the light. It was now ten o'clock in the morning. He put both slips of paper under a computerized photo enhancement machine and studied their images. He couldn't tell much about them. He again took tweezers and tried his best to open them and then flatten them out. Then he left the room for quite a while. He came back into the room with a piece of plastic about twelve by twelve and put it over the computer screen, and traced what he could manage from the small, almost rotten bits of paper.

From this he was able to come to some conclusion about what was on these slips. He deciphered a "2" on one slip and what he thought was a "1" on the other slip. He decided it must be a "1."

He went back downstairs.

"Well, what do you think they are?"

"I think the slips of paper are from an ATM—and so is the twenty."

"You sure?" Trevor asked.

"I can't be sure of anything. Still, I am betting he had a wallet and the wallet was taken."

"Why wasn't the twenty taken?"

"Because he had just got the twenty out of the ATM and he shoved it into his top pocket—and he had the other money in the wallet. The wallet was zippered safely up in his new coat with the other money."

"What other money?"

"The money in his wallet. As for the money in his pocket—on these ATM slips, the date is almost indecipherable. I don't know the year— that is gone. But if we believe what was in the letter, it would put the year at 1999, wouldn't it. I believe the ATM was on the west side—"

"Why?"

"Because this is from a Kmart machine, and there was a Kmart only three blocks away across that field. And the nearest bank is eight blocks past Shelf Street near the bowling alley, and others are farther than that. So it's a guess, but I'm going with it—that his little account was near the old bowling alley, and these rotted slips were once brand new and came from a machine at Kmart. How did he get the account? Well, it wouldn't be hard if he had been given a bit of money and had an older person with him to help open the account—and that is what I believe. The letter said he had some money on him, so we will go with that—if he used an ATM, then he opened an account or had one opened for him."

He paused, looked at the others and added, "Maybe he worked at that bowling alley for a little bit and opened the account at the bank nearest the school. But I am thinking he had money on him when he came here. This older person might have been at the house—so maybe he had a few dollars on him that were with him when he got here. And I don't think he spoke much himself."

"Why?"

"There was some speech impediment or something else unusual about him."

"How in Christ do you know that?" Melonson asked. He blames my wife for treating his boy badly—so he wants to get back at me. He has heard something about this and is concocting it all, Melonson thought.

"I am just thinking," John said, "there was most likely some prob-lem, perhaps shyness or a stutter—or an inability to remember who he was exactly. I think he did not really remember who he might be. He did not explain who his parents were, just that he wanted to find them. He hated school, yet could talk of things like the stand at Marathon by the Athenians in 490 BC and events from English history. He spoke of Operation Barbarossa. The letter writer wasn't sure what that was, but I am."

"What is Operation Barbarossa?" Melonson asked.

"Hitler's invasion of the Soviet empire in June of 1941," John said. "I think if you learned that on your own by the age of thirteen, you might be wary of school. So many people don't remember him at all because he didn't go. I already checked and no one really remembers him. I am not fond of school—"

"Why aren't you fond of school?"

"Oh, I don't know—let's just say that those who know all the answers are often the ones never able to ask the right questions. But, you see, his parents were dead—or missing, weren't they?"

"No one in the world knows that—in fact, we don't know anything at the moment, John," Trevor said. "I think you are overreaching—"

"Well, I think I am right. Look at it this way—parents wanting to instill in a child the idea of the Battle of Marathon might be willing enough to run ten of them for their child, unless they were killed at the battle!" John explained, searching for a cigarette. "I think he continued reading and learning in order to impress his dad and mom when he saw them once again. That in itself is heroic—and more heroic than we are!"

"You are not allowed to smoke," Melonson said. "You are not going to have another heart attack on my watch!"

A young constable walked in, his uniform impeccable, his sideburns clipped, his hat in his hand, and handed Melonson something.

John held the cigarette in his hand. He paused, then said, "At any rate something happened. So whoever wrote this letter to me picks a cop that is—well, kind of well known."

They stared at him.

"For better or for worse I am well known. I have had trouble with the social services, I have myself lost a child, I am alone and I am willing to take this to the end. That is, I am not going to be cowed by police or social services—if I think I am right, I will continue to work from the premise that I am right until such time I am proven wrong. I should have done that with the young Smith child and I did not—or at least, not in time."

As far as Melonson was concerned, John had written the letter himself, and what he'd just said proved it. The note from the constable had one word: "Ambidextrous." John certainly could have written it with either hand; moreover, he knew every reference to the history spoken of.

John flushed because he felt this is what they now thought. Still, he continued. "The boy quoted Keats—the letter writer didn't know it was Keats—and spoke of Melville. And you know something, I hate to say it, but some of the teachers at our school wouldn't know Melville from Keats."

"Anyone could have bought the coat anywhere in town—and the coat might have been torn anywhere," Melonson said. He, like John, was a very good police officer. "One hundred kids used that place to party back then. A kid pukes on his coat, is frightened his parents will know he was out drunk—decides in panic to get rid of it? In fact I know kids who did that—and maybe I did that once myself. So these are unsustainable facts, really, aren't they?"

John took a moment to answer.

"No puke, really," he said. "I think our boy did everything at that Kmart. If we look closer at the slips, we see what looks like a separate 'o'— just below the '20,' but not quite in line with it. What does that mean?"

"I don't know."

"It's a service charge—$1.50 for using a generic machine and not an actual bank machine. So he used a generic machine like they had at Kmart. Say the 'o' was the last digit in the $1.50 charge. And that means something else, doesn't it?"

"What?"

"It means he did not close the account. And there is something else— say the account wasn't in his name, but in the name of someone who helped him get it."

"But it doesn't compute—if someone helped him, why didn't that someone report him gone?" Trevor asked.

"Ah—because that someone is the one, or one of the two, who knows what happened to the boy. And once he had the card, the boy could use it at his will. So here is what I am thinking. I am thinking that I am going to say the letter writer is being truthful: The boy came from some other country and someone gave him money for his journey—say, a few hundred dollars."

The others simply looked at him. So John continued.

"Well then, it is a possibility he went to the adult and asked to open up a bank account, for he had a few dollars on him. And the adult said okay, and helped him do so. Anyway, there was still money in the account when he left.

"But," he said, interrupting what Melonson was going to say, "never mind that now. Just say one withdrawal was for a hundred dollars, or I think it was a hundred. It can't be one dollar, and it can't be ten dollars—ATMs often dispense in twenties. Or at least, that Kmart one did, because I used it myself. Dispensed twenties but not tens. So that accounts for the '20'—there is, I think, a '1' on the other slip, which would make it one hundred or one thousand. There is no way it is one thousand. For one thing, there was probably a daily limit on the card. And in any case, the boy most likely never had a thousand dollars. The other was for twenty, an hour later? Three hours later? Sometime later. He put the twenty in his top pocket because he was going to give it to another boy—he was going away and he wanted to give something to this kid who wrote the letter. I think that is how it went. But they were watching him. Am I right? I think I am in part right."

"Who was watching him?"

John shrugged, then said, "I will find that out."

"What bank? There should be a number on the slip that would tell you."

"I don't know. And it won't be so easy—I see nothing of the account number. It is faded to a small blue dot in an ocean of nothing. But I have a feeling the bank was far enough away from Shelf Street to make this Kmart easier to go to."

"Boys, this is some fantastic stuff," Melonson said, his exasperation suddenly showing. "This is bizarre, strange and fanciful. You just keep coming up with stuff!"

"Yes—it is," John replied seriously. "And I do keep coming up with stuff."

John stayed where he was, looking out the window, and the wind scattered snow along the pavement while the day was still bright and the sky still blue. By now it was coming on to noon hour. The banks Melonson had ordered a constable to phone had no way of knowing—not really, not without the number of the account. Nor were they that helpful, but they said it could be determined within a few weeks by looking back at accounts.

Still, the ATM was a generic machine and the police did not have an account number to go with it. The account number was faded, and only printed in part, and the ATM itself no longer existed—cannibalized and eaten away by time.

John looked at Ms. Trevor, whom he considered his only friend. He still held an unlit cigarette in his hand and he was shaking just a little bit.

"Maybe he didn't have enough with the hundred," Trevor said. And she looked at Melonson, who had come back, and who was upset that she would now placate Delano.

"Maybe," John answered, "but the hundred is gone. So the hundred was taken. I think the hundred was in his wallet—if he had a wallet—or in his pants pocket. He turned in one motion to keep running, and he fell over. And was gone. Now, there is one chance in three he could still be alive. That is, if he hit the drift of snow on the ledge six or seven feet down."

"What drift of snow?" Melonson asked.

"The drift of snow that would have been on the ledge I climbed down to two nights ago. In one or two places it juts out four or five feet and is quite safe—if he landed there, he would have been fine. It is a large enough ledge to drive a car—a small car—but if he missed that . . . he would be gone forever."

"You shouldn't have been doing that—climbing down there. What if you got stuck there?" Trevor asked. "We are supposed to take you off any case that is strenuous!"

"Well, I climbed down with a rope—but then I saw that to the left, a person could come back up more easily, and there might be a chance the boy did that. Kids probably climbed down there for hellery for years. Then he came up. Say he came up—he would have had a sweater on, some money still on him, and he would have made his way down to the train station."

"The train station?"

"Well, let's just say that for now—best-case scenario."

"Why didn't he go to the cops if he survived?" Melonson said. "That's a flaw in your idea right there, isn't it?"

John simply shrugged. "No, not really. He had to know the cops would have simply taken him back to the social worker, who would take him back to the foster home, because—well, I think some officer just considered him to be someone else—not who he said he was. 'I am a boy from some other country' didn't make sense. It did not compute—and so he was called a liar. It is so easy to call kids liars."

He paused again.

"So he would have bought a ticket—yes, he would have . . . but, you see, that is not so certain. Late at night a boy buys a ticket . . . no. Maybe he gets on the train and buys it—or just perhaps . . . has it already bought."

"Then the ticket would have been zipped up in his coat," Trevor said.

"Sure, it could have been—but I have been thinking of this all morning: He was carrying the ticket in his hand—and his hand was in his pocket, and when he ran, he hauled the ticket out," Delano said.

"That's too farfetched—even for you!" Melonson laughed.

"Maybe—sure. But maybe not. The ticket is precious. He holds the ticket in his pocket as he walks across the field—he is in a hurry to give the boy who was his friend the twenty and get to the station."

"Why didn't they believe he was from somewhere else, or was someone else?"

"Because the officer in charge did not do the simplest thing when the boy first got here."

"What didn't he do?" Trevor asked.

"He did not phone the airport and find out. The boy was supposed to meet someone there, but something went wrong. I don't see any other way it could have come about."

Anyway, that was all they could do that day.

John took the chalk. He left the station, still with no answer. He went for a long walk along Manawagonish Road toward the bay, looking out over the hills and dark clouds, the little side streets running away toward the water, and the foul evening darkness that held in its dark shafts of sparkling ice the first tangible scent of snow. The snow fell into his eyes, and he thought that like any crime, it started without anyone thinking it would end like it did. Especially the girl who the boy gave the book to. She might have toyed with him, just as she toyed with other boys, he decided. That is, if the book was true. But let us say it was. Perhaps the boy had wanted her to go with him. Perhaps that is why he headed across the field. Of course, John couldn't be sure of this yet. But he felt that someday he would be sure. So the book meant something to someone, and still might be somewhere.

So by this reasoning—and John was reasoning all the time—the girl he gave the book to was poor, and did not have much in her life and perhaps was headed down the wrong road, and this boy might have wanted to help her before he left. And he was only a child himself—but, John reasoned, what if she kept the book? That is what he was thinking. If he found the book, he would find the girl, and the girl would authenticate the boy.

John remembered every name he'd seen written on the walls of the old Shaw house. But he was now thinking the boy was not dead, now thinking the boy had escaped and was alive. There was one thing in particular troubling him. The boy was certainly an honest boy, from what the letter said—so where was the postcard he was going to send?

But, John reasoned again, the boy feared detection, and decided the postcard would only give him away.

4.

It is women who will change the world, John often thought when he was talking to Corporal Trevor. He had met enough women to know this change might not be for the better. Some of them were as kind and as gentle as rain. Some smiled at you like cobras in full hoods. Trevor was a young, well-informed officer who had come through Regina with high grades but had a difficult time adjusting not only to the work she was given but to having John Delano, at the end of his career, looking upon her as someone he could rely upon. That is, he was too much a lightning rod for a young officer—and she had been warned not to become too much his protege. She now knew this and tried her best to stay away from his cases. All of this would have been acceptable if she did not like him, which she did. But she liked Melonson too—and to say she could not be flirtatious was untrue.

John was in the office by eight the next morning. Trevor was also there. He had given her things to do, simply believing that she would do them for him. And on the way to the office expected her there, because as far as he was concerned, this was the most important case, and she could do no less.

On his request she had once again been in touch with provincial social services and child welfare, and with their field officers, and had spoken to Melissa Sapp's assistant for three or four minutes, but no boy had gone missing for any real length of time in 1999. "So the foster-home theory is a dead end," she said, almost too emphatically.

"Well—are you sure?"

"I am as sure as they are—and they are sure. Melissa Sapp's assistant phoned me last night. All the boys of 1999 were accounted for that year."

"Oh," John said, and he sounded more mystified than upset.

She told him that since she did not have a name or even the social worker on the case, it made it much harder to narrow someone down. But that Melissa Sapp's assistant had said she would get Trevor the name of the social worker who had been responsible for that Shelf Street area during that time.

Eventually, Trevor returned with the name. It was a Ms. Fern Hershey, who had retired in 2004. She had been given the Shelf Street cases by a Ms. Blanchard, who had retired years before.

"Okay—when?"

"When what?"

"When did she retire?"

"I do not know, John—they just said she retired."

"Well, can I ask you a question? What do they think I am actually trying to achieve?"

"They wouldn't say—but you were in a big fight with all of them before, so . . ."

"Was I? Oh. Well, I did not think it was that big of a fight—I just wanted Jeanne to get her child back." Again he sounded mystified, and looked over his notes as if he did not take her comments to heart.

Trevor watched him and shrugged.

John said nothing for a moment, hummed and hawed, and then said, "It shouldn't be that hard for anyone to track a missing boy unless . . ."

"Unless what? I am sure it's not hard, but I have been working half the week for you on all of this. And we don't even know if a boy went missing!"

"I know, I know—and I don't mean you. But what do you think—who was the social worker, Ms. Fern Hershey? Maybe she made some little slip-up that widened—a small tear in the fabric of time that was left unattended. Some little elemental thing—as happened with my own boy—someone missing something—missing where he went or who last saw him. Now, this case is similar to that of my own boy, I feel, don't you? It is similar to that of my own child." He said this rather excitedly.

"I don't know, John," Trevor said kindly. "I hate to ask, but what does this have to do with your own child?"

"Well, nothing except—but no, you are right, nothing—nothing at all." He said this last "nothing" plaintively, almost as an apology. "Ms. Blanchard—dead. Ms. Hershey—retired? What comes in between?"

He looked at her.

"I don't have a clue what it is you are saying."

"I mean, from what I know, Blanchard retired before this boy disappeared. Who might have come in between—or after—Ms. Hershey? That is, did Hershey keep this case or did it go to someone else?" Then he added, "Oh, I'm just being suspicious. I'm sure there was no one else at all. But here it is. There is something about Ms. Hershey you might not know. She had breast cancer—much radiation treatment. But before that I think she suffered some kind of demotion, when Melissa Sapp was promoted—so she may have not even been the caseworker there. Someone else Melissa Sapp wanted may have taken it over. But, well, Ms. Hershey is dead and I do not want to bother her daughter with this case. Still and all . . ." John said.

Trevor had much more sympathy with social services than John did. In fact she was a new officer and of the popular, polarizing opinion that the social services did little wrong—and those like John who maintained they did sometimes do wrong were intolerant and in some way anti-female, since most social workers were feminist, just as she herself was. There was a war on women, she had decided, and she had seen evidence of it too. John was known to dislike feminists because, he thought, they believed he was intolerant and old-fashioned.

So then, might John be trying to pay them back? She smiled slightly but actually missed what he was saying; he was, in fact, trying to defend both Ms. Blanchard and Ms. Hershey. By now he felt that neither of them was responsible for Shelf Street at that specific time. And in fact he had been defending Hershey for four weeks now. No one knew this but him. He had been looking into what cases Hershey had had—and he did not think she had Shelf Street in 1999, though he could not be positive.

Still, this is what Melonson told Trevor to be wary of yesterday evening when they went for a drink. Melonson told her there were far more important cases to deal with—and he had ordered her not to spend time on this new Delano fiasco. Delano would be retired in six months, he said. Retired and gone from their lives.

"Maybe the boy just went somewhere else and is living a good life," Trevor said, sympathetically, as if to end it here and now. "Maybe the letter is right—he just went away and it is out of our hands. And we have three assaults to deal with here—two assaults in the last week. Then there was the prostitute beaten out on Waterloo Row. Then this boy. The story in the letter does sound made up. There is the idea that he fell but is still alive, or his ticket was bought and he is carrying it in his hand?"

"Well—yes, but I have something precious on me. I am holding on to it, thinking of it—perhaps I am holding it, my hand in my coat—holding a ticket to take me away, and suddenly I am chased. No, I would not let it go, I would hold on to it as long as I was able. They take his coat and he still manages to hold it. He trips and falls six feet—who chases him is gone, his coat is gone, his bag gone—but the ticket is still in his hand and some money is in his pants pocket."

John paused and considered, unaware, it seemed, of her intention. That is, he did not know that she was thinking he had fabricated a story and she was trying to enable him to soften it and change direction while there was still time.

Then he said he understood this too about the boy just leaving and living the good life, but did not believe it. He believed the boy came here from somewhere, after his parents divorced or died, and was left by himself. But Trevor took a gamble and said, "It is troubling about the letter—and the letter is everything. I mean, the letter is not a sham, is it?"

He stared at her a moment, not quite catching the fact that she might be accusing him. Then he shrugged and said, "Probably if someone did harm him, what we find out won't be pleasant."

"Murder never is," Trevor said, suddenly, caustically, turning to open the filing drawer. She was angered that she had asked him about the letter, and angrier that he didn't quite answer her. Still he did not quite catch it. He believed she was a fine person, but that many times she missed the point. And she did so in a psychologically complex way, to prove herself to him. This is what he was thinking at the moment—that is, that she needed to prove that she was a bright police officer too, and an independent one, and just because he had more years and many more cases, he shouldn't look upon her as naive. In fact, the suggestion was implicit—he was naive.

———

John left, his head filled with ideas, and walked back along the road to home. Here and there the front of small convenience stores, beaten down by the wind, and an ancient weather vane poised on the top of the hill. Now and again children solitary, with book bags on their backs, stumbled past him in the fresh snow, heading away to home. He suddenly got an impression of this particular boy: a look of earnest ambition, his eyes focused on the future.

He felt a twinge in his chest as he moved along.

But he now thought: I will quit for good when this is over and I will go back to the Miramichi, and I will fish the dark waters and look at the sky. Although in his home of Miramichi, he was looked upon as an outsider as well. He would notice this at the strangest times, recognized in restaurants or walking a sidewalk, and people would lower their eyes or turn away.

He had always been an outsider—fame did not change that; it only heightened it.

There was a message on his phone when he got back to Matters Road. He listened to it with great expectation: "Did you look in the well—that's where your boy ran to—I told you this before." Then a laugh in the background and a sudden click.

"You are the loneliest person I have ever met," a woman John once loved said when he'd visited her in the middle of the night four months ago, in loneliness and confusion. "But you have changed so much—you are not the boy you used to be. I could have loved you if you were, but I can't now. And you've become famous—so how can I go back to you without people thinking I am going back to you because of your fame?"

He had brought a copy of a book to give her. He was startled that she thought he was the only one who had changed—that in fact was the idea; that is, that they both had, and must.

"Ah." He smiled, looking at her, her aging face, her little dog. "None of us really are the same, are we?"

He thought of what this thinning, middle-aged woman with her shih tzu said to him, as he sat eating by himself. Lonely? Well, at times, who wasn't?

He decided he must solve this case or go mad. He was angry at himself for not doing the right things in order to solve it. He was also angry at himself for how much he relied on Trevor.

But she likes me. So she will help out, he thought. And resting on that, he lit a cigarette.

It was impractical to categorize loneliness as something gained by maturity. He believed loneliness was quite possibly this boy's defining emblem, though he was not sure yet. Loneliness is also akin to bravery. It had stood beside the brave for centuries. Had it stood beside the general at Marathon? Yes. Marshal Zhukov and Churchill too . . . it was also a state of being that in the end exuded joy.

Loneliness caught in the waning sun of October; the loneliness of Thanksgiving in mid-afternoon, or of those half-empty Paris hotels just coming onto dusk, when the streets are bare and quiet and there is the sound on the steps of someone going upstairs in solitude, a wine bottle or a paper bag in hand.

He felt it in the summer in Madrid, and singled it out too in the false fronts of small-town stores when he roamed the back highways of the Midwest. He saw it in a farmer's long, diligent fields of grain along broken highways in the sun, and under a shimmering London discotheque in October of 1979.

He thought of a thirteen-year-old buying his own coat, and being by himself. Perhaps having his own job at a bowling alley. If, as John suspected, the child was from somewhere else, he might not have been used to Canada or its weather. He might not have been adept at being with anyone. He would hear the snow swishing over the tarpaper sides of old, forlorn sheds, and hear the wild storm against some tin roof, or in the quiet of a winter afternoon feel the constant vagary of smoke-tinged darkness coming on.

And then not to be believed by anyone at all about who he really was.

His coat so new it still had the tag in the pocket. The coat so new all the zippers had not been used. And the feel of it must have been so different with its heavy lining. That is why he would have clutched his ticket.

Loneliness is all of that and more. That's why, if the boy existed, John was duty bound to find out what had happened to him.

"Limey."

Perhaps. But he doubted it. He remembered Malamud, the Pakistani man he bought a coat for in the winter of 1985. Malamud had come here as an immigrant with his wife and two children. The children burst out laughing when they saw little Malamud in his huge coat with the fur collar—and Malamud had taken the coat so seriously until the children went into paroxysms of fun and laughter. Finally his wife started to laugh as well, and then he did. All of them laughing hilariously over a brand new coat, in a country so far removed from where they had come from everything was not only new but somehow catastrophic.

John ate his soup in silence, except when he opened a packet of crackers and crumbled them into the bowl. Poor Malamud and his wife and children—where had they gone? He did not know.

The phone rang, and stopped and rang and stopped, and rang again. He did not answer it.

Malamud's wife was so tiny he did not know if she would be able to make out doing anything. He had helped her get her driver's licence, helped her as much as he could. He felt she would be lost in this country. But then one day to his surprise he saw Malamud's wife, wearing her own huge coat over her sari, barrelling down Somerset Street, driving thirty children in a school bus.

He knew that many women who saw him from their own particular vantage point believed that men like him were the enemy. Since the seventies—that is, since the age of feminism—he always had been their enemy. He knew he wasn't. Once upon a time, he had cared, had tried to tell them they were wrong. That in so much he was on their side. Now, nothing about their opinion mattered at all. And because of this he was a much better police officer. He had seen as many self-serving and wounded feminists as chauvinists. A few of them had murdered. But more of them had done something even worse, in John Delano's mind unforgivable: Like some of the writers he had got to know from Newfoundland to Saskatchewan, they had pandered.

———

Melissa Sapp had been in her new position only ten weeks. She had first met Delano in New York years ago—and to think his name had once again come up.

She went home and had a glass of red wine.

She did ask her husband, DeWold, about Shelf Street, and he simply shrugged and said it wasn't his jurisdiction at that time.

"Oh," she said, trying to remember. "So it was Fern's?"

"Yes, it must have been."

"Okay," she said. She drank her wine and took a bath. As she lay in the hot tub, a feeling of unease crept over her. She was not a stupid person—far from it; she was brilliant. Her only shortcoming might have been a certain lack of empathy. Worse, she believed it was a sign of brilliance to care less for others.

She did not worry about Shelf Street at first because what she had heard about Delano had allowed her to think his request a sham. No one knew as much as she did about how he had manipulated child protection before.

"He's trying to make up for a lost son and a life of mistakes," she told her husband.

So she shrugged and did not return his call, and thought the case would probably die.

———

John, at the same moment, ate his soup, staring at the bowl. In fact, he stared at the bowl in the same way he had when a boy had hauled a gun on him one night in a restaurant far downriver on the Miramichi Bay. He simply ate his soup, and then salted it, and stared at the bowl. The boy turned and fled, throwing down the gun as he ran.

Still John had continued on, case after case exactly like this, alone, determined and relentless. He never wore his uniform if the creases were not just so, his buttons so shiny they glittered.

One might realize that at one time, some years back, John Delano had gone to parties with the very powerful and sat in rooms at the UN listening to discussions about world affairs—and in the sun beaming across wide, red-cloth-covered tables he saw loneliness, both in their laughter and their faces. And in the end most of them at the UN carried a certain shame at doing nothing—but they held this shame at bay with salaries of more than a hundred thousand dollars a year, and pensions of just as much, as they walked the corridors and engaged in amused litigations. But in the end it was shame, shame in everything. So at the UN, much like Sartre and other ineffectual French intellectuals after the Second World War, they tried to rewrite history or redefine their role in it. They pretended there was no Vichy France; or if there was, they were not a part of it. Just as the Canadian intellectuals and politicians did after the Rwandan genocide; tried to deflect the blame to other organizations and other countries, or to religion.

And he supposed that was loneliness too. But long before his child had disappeared, before his failed dreams, before his ruined and fruitless career, he had seen loneliness.

He saw it when he rode the train one day to take in a Patriots game and came back late at night through Harlem and saw flares and fires and buildings left to decay, and a woman of fifty in filthy white underwear, her dress torn off, staggering just east of the river.

He saw it in Haiti with young children looking up in hopeful silence at adults who'd had the audacity to believe these children were not as human as they were; he'd seen it when he was trying to train police officers, and saw interspersed with desire and innocence an almost compulsive corruption and mistrust.

But now he came to the memory he had tried to erase for fifteen years—and it plagued him as he continued to eat in silence. Now and then he shrugged and put more salt on his soup.

That is, he saw the starkness of Rwanda when he went by Jeep to try to save a certain Canadian family in 1994, a family that had seemingly disappeared from the face of the earth. This was the Forrest family from Edmonton, Alberta.

His driver had been a young private first class from Camp Gagetown, a man who had by March of 1994 put his life on the line five times for people he did not know, being ordered to go to certain places by people he'd never met. His name was Jean-Paul Aube, and he was an Acadian boy from the Miramichi.

John had asked for a driver and this man had volunteered. And they got out of headquarters before anyone told them they could not go.

"Where off to?" he said with a smile.

"Well, it is at least forty miles up the road," John said.

"Oh," Aube said, "that's going to be fun."

The man they went looking for was an engineer from Canada, and his wife taught grade two. They had a little boy. A little boy named

Jack. John had seen a picture of him sitting on his mom's knee, in a bow tie and navy blue shorts. He was holding his blanket or comforter. John remembered the boy's birthday: December 15. Why he remembered that is simple—it was John's birthday as well.

John discovered they were the kind of people who tried to do right by the world; had, like so many of the university crowd, become proactive—if that was the word. John did not know if that word had changed yet. So many words did.

But this family was willing—willing to change the world. To become, as the word said, proactive, engaged, involved, progressive. All the right things.

The words he had heard Ms. Midge Nolan Overplant use in her testimony for change—just like millions of intellectual North Americans did every day. It was a different world from the tough heated world John grew up in, the world of spit and pain and blood, and maybe it was supposed to be. Only, it knew nothing of John's world, as it tried to redress it.

And so the three of them, mom, dad and child, left Edmonton, Alberta, for the great and glorious unknown.

Africa.

They left long before the Rwandan crisis, of course, when the boy was one or two. But the crisis came and they were there—the three of them—and in the end they could not escape to anywhere. John simply went that last day in Rwanda to look for them. Not finding them changed his life forever.

Back in New York, it was more civil during those days and weeks before the genocide. It was as if there was no real crisis in Rwanda, or as if— and this was even more cynical—it could be used to one's benefit if one was seen to be proactive and understanding and concerned. Now to be fair, this was not so much calculated as it was an unthinking reaction to the times. For unthinking people will always be unthinking for their own benefit.

These times, which African and French, Belgian and Canadian intellectuals used it for; that is, a benefit for themselves. They squabbled over the wording for a resolution, pretending that the correct wording was more important than the saving of a life—or as John once said, "More to the point, without the correct wording what did it matter if the life was saved?"

The intellectuals at the UN in New York were giddy with the idea of solving some world problem and becoming well-known advocates of a better world. So when he began to say that they were using their concerns for their own advantage (when he was finally dumb enough to say it), it was then he started being called a bigot by those people who had initially secured his position at the UN.

"I do not want the position at the UN," he had told his superior.

"Why not?" his superior had said, and his tone was one of astonishment and hurt that John would give up such an opportunity.

"There are two cases I am working on here in New Brunswick," he said, "and besides, for the first time in years I am content."

"No, I won't let you make this mistake because you are content—this is your career, so you have to go. The prime minister himself has asked for you."

"He has asked for me?"

"Well, he has asked for someone just like you."

But after a month or so, they began to see their mistake. Though he solved cases and was considered brilliant, tough and resolute, he was not at all like them. He considered them frivolous, vain, and in some cases, when it came to understanding their own motives, stupid.

One well-known person, passing him by in a fluster of winter coat and high-heeled boots, said, "He would drag us all back into the Dark Ages."

Ah yes—the Dark Ages, how all of us had escaped from that.

So John's place in the upper echelons of the police force in Canada, his chance at superintendent—which he wanted and believed he deserved—became less secure once that UN posting was over. It was as if he had fallen suddenly from a great height and could only now and again look up in confusion to where he had once been. He had believed the UN must take direct action in Rwanda, but was not allowed to say so. He knew there were Canadians who had believed the same thing but were not listened to.

Still, he had known his fall was only a matter of time. That is, taking action was never really a part of the theoretical. He began to see this when it came to Rwanda, for Canadian intellectuals and politicians were masters of the theoretical.

During his UN posting he would get up in the morning—usually at six o'clock—and look over the list of functions he was to attend that day. And he was tired from it within a week, but he had to carry on. Midge Nolan Overplant was one of these people. She was from one of the most prominent New Brunswick families—or so she liked to remind him in curious ways. And initially she smothered him with attention that was driven by false intimacy.

So his trip to the Canadian consulate began with the kinds of pleasantries and compliments that these things always do, and ended very badly—and his relationship with Midge Nolan Overplant and many in New Brunswick who knew her—like her favourite niece, Melissa Sapp—was forever changed. He became what was he realized the poster child of intolerance within the police.

And during all that time, the horror in Rwanda loomed.

Still he remained as he was told, polite, loyal and noncommittal, and listened much more than he spoke.

He was already feeling the strain of being there, of having to deal with people he did not respect, when two writers came within a few weeks of each other to promote Canadian works of genius. This reinforced John's strange feeling of desperate alienation from his own country. He saw both these men as being exploited and used as window dressing.

The first writer who came during this time was a former First Nations chief and political activist, a First Nations man who had the sympathy of influential Canadians as he promoted his book *Racism, White Shame and the Canadian Mosaic from the Days of British Colonialism*. He was trying to stop the exploitation of mining in the North and spoke about the Arctic region being autonomous.

John had never disputed that there was racism in the Canadian mosaic. The problem was, John had arrested this man for gross misappropriation and embezzlement of funds slated to build community houses some eighteen years before. The man had blamed this not on himself but solely on the Canadian government. "The courage to confront racism in Canada" was the quote used on the jacket of his book by one of our well-known female public intellectuals. In fact, without saying so, both John and the chief understood after a few short days that to evoke the idea of suffering and mistreatment at the hands of the Canadian government and police was the only justification for this man even being in New York. He was forced into a corner by this and could do and say nothing else. So John realized this First Nations man, too, was being used. John, during the evenings in his spare time, was studying a course from Saint Thomas University, and he would go into his room and open the books he had to read, worried about getting essays done and passing an exam.

The evening of a party given in honour of this Native activist, it seemed one could only understand suffering if one had posh rooms, hors d'oeuvres and lived on $125,000 a year. Midge Nolan Overplant succumbed to this new feeling of contriteness, without giving up her own position or her own salary. She suddenly wanted to show how adept she was at catching on to the white lie of colonialism.

This, then, was where John's fall from grace started—that is, when he saw through Midge's mask of concern. After this he was not the wonderful person Midge Nolan Overplant had heard admirable things about but someone odious and intolerant.

"I think you have had a bit of a fall from grace here—maybe you can get back on track," Midge said to him the next day.

"Oh, I doubt it," he said, completely unfazed.

They rarely spoke again.

He put in for a transfer, but was told in no uncertain terms that his orders came from the highest office and he was to remain.

He shouldered the responsibility of his fall from grace, his political alienation, his loneliness, in Haiti and Panama and at the UN.

He shouldered it wherever they needed him—like on the trip to San Francisco that day long ago, where in the slopes of the great hills, the tolling of midday bells, the sounds of trolleys like those of a carnival ride, he saw in all the grandness of the moment the frozen timeless pulse of emptiness and sorrow. So he spent that day after lunch in the City Lights bookstore reading from Bukowski and thinking of the world as a surreal journey into the dark. There he remembered Rwanda—and seeing laying in the street the heads of little boys.

His shame came because he had never fathomed that this might happen to him. He never fathomed he would be in a situation so grim, so outlandishly horrifying, that he wouldn't be able to help anyone at all; and that in a curious and hallucinogenic twist, he would be held suspect by influential intellectuals for wanting to.

And then he shouldered the death of his own son, and lived himself in self-pity, drink and constant self-blame for five years. He did not go out, he did not speak to friends, and he would disappear for whole weeks at a time. He believed the death of his child was retribution for not finding that Forrest family when there was still time. He had not disobeyed orders quickly enough and tried to find them, like he should have done. And he hated himself for it, even though it may have cost him his life.

He hated himself for being alive.

Then three years ago, his career almost over, he started to work again. He showed up at the office one day with a case that he was working on in his spare time. The case of how methamphetamine was getting from Halifax to the streets of Saint John.

So little by little he became valuable all over again.

Melissa Sapp was Midge Nolan Overplant's niece. The woman who had once wanted him dismissed from the UN. Melissa had known all about him for a long while.

And now he saw a fight looming with this Melissa Sapp over a boy everyone said did not exist.

—

"Evil?" John told his psychiatrist, Sue Van Loon. "Oh yes—evil. Sin too! Always—if you want to know—we have to combat it. You can see it often only when it is too late."

So Sue Van Loon told him he once again was showing his conservative side, which is what always got him into trouble. The world, she said, had done with all of that—given evil up—why, read the best writers today—and you will understand. "Mentioning sin to some of them is, well—sinful," she proclaimed.

He was saying there was sin in Rwanda.

His psychiatrist did not particularly believe in sin anymore. She had grown out of sin because she had grown up where everything was. She was a well-educated young woman who had studied at Dalhousie University. She could not suffer the word *Satan*, or *saints* for that matter. She would never say *devil*. Well, she would, but not mean it.

Being brought up a Cape Breton Catholic had caused a healthy skepticism to all of this. She had been at the trial of priests who had betrayed the trust of her own family. She hated them and there was good reason to. Now she had liberated herself from Mass and all it stood for.

She believed her background allowed her to understand John's convictions as a Catholic and to try to subtly undermine or subvert them. That is, you cannot put new wine into an old sack. To enter the new world, a man must be new. That is why he did not get on at the UN, she told him. There was no other reason. She believed John actually wanted to be new, and needed people to instruct him on how to be new. Once he was new, he would get on at the UN, she said.

But John had no intention of being new at anything anymore.

His psychiatrist was filled with wisdom about the church; believed, in fact, that Catholicism would end rather soon. That is, since she had given it up, the world should too. "Just because you are old and virtuous, should there now be no cakes and ale" had been replaced with "Cakes and ale prove virtue is a sham."

To her something of a psychosis had happened in and around

Rwanda—a kind of mass hysteria—but there was no evil. It was the product of two hundred years of colonialism. Now people had learned better. They had not before. She seemed to have missed the implication of the elderly aunt in *David Copperfield* saying there should be no "meandering"—as a progenitor of anti-colonialism—but this in fact is what John thought of.

So did it matter if John had seen death and horror? No, to give her credit, it did very much matter. It was the main issue. But why did he subscribe to a tenet as old-fashioned as evil? Christ almighty, people said he was a brilliant man—so, Christ almighty, be brilliant!

The word *evil*, which John insisted on, perplexed her. That is, she had come to his case with her mind made up. She could not believe a man as intelligent as John Delano would begin talking the way he did about fasting at Lent and praying—and when he very much spoke of this as a need for atonement, she was suddenly puzzled. And so she tried to redirect his obsessions into something manageable. She had read Russell Banks and believed in afflictions too. But you see it had to be managed within the context of a social platform—something studied come to grips with, quite like Russell Banks's books.

"Where did you see evil?" she asked. But she asked it not as if she was trying to understand and grapple with dark forces, but trying instead to understand the reason for his primitive reassertion. So he told her of a man he knew being burned alive.

"Certainly criminal," she said.

"And one synonym of *criminal* is *immoral*?"

She did not answer.

"And one synonym of *immoral* is *wicked*."

She did not answer.

"And one synonym of *wicked* is *evil*—so, yes, you are correct. It was certainly an evil act, perpetrated on one man by a group who found pleasure in being depraved and exulting in it for the benefit of their own hubris. And do you know why I know it was evil?"

"Why?"

"Because afterwards, after it was all over, they ran and hid under leaves in the wood—like Adam and Eve hiding from God's question, 'Where are you?' And at the trial of these men—just as God asked Adam and Eve 'Where are you?' they too were asked 'Where were you?' And none of them could answer—because like Adam and Eve, they were hiding."

The problem was, as with most patient–psychiatrist relationships, John found himself more than slightly in love with her—and her slender body and long blond hair. And he wanted to please her by getting well, by not returning to a life that others considered violent.

He also discussed the Cheval case, in some detail—it was a case where he did not address a suspect in French when he was making an arrest. The case was overturned and the man walked free. This was a major victory for the forces of liberty and equality, one paper had said. And John was the man who had subverted this liberty and equality in order to get the job done.

"What is it about that case that bothers you?" Sue Van Loon asked.

"Well, I was looked upon as a bigot."

"But I do not think you were looked upon as that. I think you made a mistake—you did not give the man the choice of language. It was unsettling for you—but all in all, the right decision was made. It was a landmark case. And say you were allowed to address him only in English—and then another man, and a man who spoke only French and did not understand you were warning him of a danger on the road ahead, drove over a cliff—you see how jurisprudence must act?"

Like others John had dealt with, Sue Van Loon knew how to modify the meaning of vicious language in order to suit a preconceived notion of what his enemies were trying to do, and to relate it to him in an affable tone.

"Oh yes—I see it very well," John said, smiling. "It was not at all personal, and to be suspected of bigotry is just part of the job. The rumour that I was intolerant to the Acadians—even though I married one—the rumour that I badgered people . . . I know very well how it all worked. But I look at it another way."

"What way is that?"

"If Cheval had been convicted—if he had been, he might be alive today—but that is not what bothered me about the case. I am averse to how it played out in my life."

"How did it play out in your life?"

He told her straight up.

"He is let off. So to get me away from the office, I am asked to go out to San Francisco, to arrest a man named Wasson. I agree to go, but because I am to be busy, we send my son to camp—and because we send my little boy to camp, he disappears. And was never found. All because I did not say *bonjour* to a man who never in his life needed to hear it to understand he was under arrest for throwing an incendiary device at a former partner in crime."

Sue tried to respond, did not, and finally said, too flippantly, "I think you are speculating a little too much."

"I think not as much as you, Ms. Van Loon."

He was hoping very much for Sue Van Loon to like him. But he knew he had hurt her with his last comments. He also had to remind himself he was old enough to be her father. Still—she asked him these questions, even though he was becoming exhausted and more and more uncertain about how to answer:

Where, then, did he see evil—where did he see what he believed was his life's great moral nemesis, the falsehood of sin? Do you actually believe in the devil? Of course that might be where your problems begin and end. If he could explain that to her, then, she decided, he would be on the road to healing. He thought of the smile of a young seventeen-year-old Rwandan showing him the shoulder, half torso and breast of a young woman that he had just killed.

Piqued that she had not solved the Cheval question, Sue Van Loon went back to it once more.

"And did you really dislike him?"

"Who, for God's sake?"

"Cheval."

"Oh yes, for more than a few reasons."

"Well there—maybe they had a point, and were trying to save you from making that blunder about language."

"Yes, yes—of course!"

"Well then, what happened to him after?"

"He killed a girl I knew, in a domestic dispute, and then killed himself. But there is something about it I never figured out—that is, I am not sure if it happened that way or not."

John told her that the day that he had not gone on to read Mr. Cheval his charges in French, Bennie Cheval and Melissa Sapp became friends who had nothing in common except their alliance against him.

"That's insane," she said.

"Yes, of course it is," he answered. "She helped free a man who later stabbed his child bride in the stomach and let her daughter watch as she bled to death on the floor over a reason that is still obscure. And . . ."

"And what?"

"And that was when I had my heart attack. I never got back to that case. Still, I am not certain he did stab her or kill himself—I do not think he would have. I have been rethinking it all—something else may have happened there, at that farmhouse. Do you understand?"

"No. I am sorry."

"So am I," John said.

The only friend John had in New York was a young man named Joel Finnegan, who he met first in a bar and then later at a hockey game, and had a few beers with. Since they both loved hockey and Mark Messier, they'd go to games together that year of 1994 more than a few times, and afterwards walked down to a small bar on Fifty-Seventh to drink. John always thought fondly of Joel Finnegan. For a long time that is all he said about him.

But other than Mr. Finnegan, he made few friends in New York or anywhere else. He had in many respects ruined every relationship he had ever had. And at this moment he was quite proud of that fact.

Still, for a while he put all his energy into studying law. But of course that never happened. In a real way it showed the immense futility of his desire to belong. Many simply considered him a racist. He felt that this was used against him to inhibit some of the cases he was on.

"The fights I had were not about race at all," he told Sue Van Loon once, when she asked him point-blank about it. He told her that, like Midge Nolan Overplant and a thousand professors, she had intentionally missed the point. "The fights were about using race for one's own benefit—that is a grand difference almost no professor understands for it diminishes them to admit it. And this small difference is universal and has a multitude of ways it tries not to be looked at in the light of day."

The only time Sue Van Loon had ever seen Bennie Cheval was when his picture was in the paper—in the photo he was leaving the court house after being released on the charges John had arrested him over. His eyes were black like a shark's, and his forehead had a scar that ran down toward his left eye. And yet in some way, for all his trouble, his smile was still gentle and endearing. He was the type of ruthless man that women sometimes fall for, write letters to the penitentiary for, and Van Loon knew this. In fact, in a strange way she knew why Melissa Sapp eagerly took his language rights case to the provincial human rights commission. In the photo, just coming from the court house, was Melissa herself, in shadow, most of her face hidden by a hat. The idea of subterfuge was embedded in that picture and in her personality. But standing to the left of her, in deeper shadow, was another person—a strikingly impressive person, it seemed to Sue Van Loon—a child who grew to womanhood in alleyways and vermin and drugs, and who was now in the company of Bennie Cheval: Luda Marsh, his child bride, six months pregnant at that time and fifteen years younger. Her eyes were looking at the camera in a moment of sudden, glorious accusation against the world—they were hardened like steel, but there was a trace of innocence in her expression. She was nineteen. This was the girl John had tried to take care of when she was little.

It was one of the many newspaper clippings about John that Sue Van Loon kept. "John Delano should be fired—he should be taught a lesson," Bennie Cheval was quoted as saying.

The idea Sue Van Loon got, and correctly so, was that John was unloved and did an unlovable job, and often protected people who would not protect him, and exacerbated this alienation by his analytical approach to those about him. For instance, he had tracked the eco-terrorist Mr. Wasson halfway round the world to bring him back, and lost his own son at the same time. Last year this man Wasson was given an honorary doctorate from the university where Melissa Sapp sat on the board of governors and Midge Nolan Overplant now headed the sociology department.

So John was unloved. He lived alone as an outcast, and was considered such.

In not being loved—especially in those years he was alone—he forgot that he should love himself. So he had put all his energy into his work and little into any relationship. In that, and in many other things, Sue Van Loon was right.

5.

JOHN HAD BEEN A LIAISON OFFICER BETWEEN CANADA AND Africa during the crisis in Rwanda. All of a sudden he was called on to be a security guard to a very important special envoy, and flew down to New York from Ottawa in late October of 1993. The government wanted an efficient and loyal RCMP officer to be part of the envoy's entourage, more than likely only as window dressing. What happened, as it often did, was John did little and then ended up doing too much.

For two or three months he did little or nothing at all. He simply listened to the ongoing discussions about the climate in Rwanda—that is, the climate of dissension. Everything was going to change, become a variation and a moderation of what once was—this was the endless hope. And Midge Nolan Overplant, new to the consulate and fresh from a course called Political Ramifications of Sub-Sahara Colonialism, was the most hopeful of all. The last thing there would be was war!

Still, John began to see how procrastination was an art form, as a folly and a pretense of progress. For instance, he told Sue Van Loon, Canada's special envoy had a huge position, was from a famous Canadian political family and went to meetings with Security Council members because Canada had sent one of their top soldiers into Rwanda under the auspices of the UN to keep the peace. This special envoy had the pallid, studied look of a world-weary intellectual and a practised, face-saving inscrutability when he spoke of delicate matters—matters when to actually be concise and forthright was critical. That is, like so many diplomats, the more vital the need the more tenuous the response.

Our special envoy once quipped that he did not know the difference between a platoon and a battalion. John mentioned that what was somewhat unfortunate about this is that this particular envoy was in New York at the UN as a broker for our Canadian commander in Rwanda, who in keeping our envoy informed at all times of the situation in and around Kigali expected our special envoy's help.

"Our special envoy was called the Lion of Justice," John told Sue Van Loon with utmost seriousness—not because he believed our envoy was a Lion of Justice but because he had been called it—whenever John looked serious he had the puzzled look of a little boy, his shirt collar pressed and clean.

John told Sue Van Loon that he flew to Africa with our Lion of Justice, and sometimes a young colonel attaché.

But John did suspect, and did not want to disrespect, that in fact these trips were quite useless.

By December of 1993, Canadian command in Rwanda wanted the authority to stop the majority Hutu from perpetrating a massacre on the minority Tutsi.

"Did you think this would happen?" Sue Van Loon asked.

"I wasn't sure what would happen," John admitted. "I was not at all familiar with the conflict between Tutsi and Hutu, and only knew the history briefly. But I believed Dallaire."

"Because he was a general?"

"Well, he wasn't a general then—but he was Dallaire! I believe it has been shown he was absolutely heroic. I think we can grant him that."

Still, he told her, the UN and our special envoy were emasculated by a modern reaction against a history of colonial infamy. And then he told Sue Van Loon this: "Both blacks and whites poached off of a reaction against this former infamy in order to make themselves look concerned—both did it in their own way, and both succeeded in doing nothing. And—"

"And what?"

"I flunked my essay." Again he said this very seriously. "And in the end I did not get into law school."

One day Midge Nolan Overplant came to him and said lightheartedly that the Canadian First Nations writer, the grand chief, had been there in New York and would become over time a member of the truth and reconciliation commission in South Africa. "So," she said, "should we not now have a young black writer who was" (as our Lion of Justice had said admiringly) "almost revolutionary?"

"Of course," John said. "Why not?"

The young man arrived in January.

It was at this moment, John Delano told Sue Van Loon, that he realized a massacre would ultimately happen.

"Why—because of a young black man trying to promote his book?"

"No—because of how they believed they needed him to assure themselves of white concern." He said this with a certain amount of exasperation, as if he believed she intentionally wanted to misunderstand. "And their concern was feckless."

And he told her something else. He smiled almost dejectedly as he said it. By some trick of fate, our special envoy was Timmy Wasson's very progressive and liberal father. That is, the father of the young man who some years later he would be sent to San Francisco to arrest, and why he would send his son to camp.

———

John remembered there were diplomats from Africa who often visited the Canadian consulate because of the Canadian military presence in Rwanda. Especially starting in January of 1994, they promoted some brilliant idea or another, and looked askance when you were introduced to them, and smiled when you were told of their tremendous accomplishments in human rights in Africa. There was always a particular region of Africa mentioned, and each man John was introduced to had some deep association with that region, just as he himself, John supposed, had some deep association with the Miramichi. So looking at it like that—as men from various regions interplaying connections and government monies—he only believed about one-quarter of what they said and sometimes did not believe them at all.

One Rwandan man was a constant presence there. His name was Harry Sabota, and John got to know him well. Or well enough, he told Sue—and he did like Harry very much in the end.

What Harry Sabota wanted from the Canadians was 2.9 million dollars for vaccinations. And for a while he was at the consulate a great deal. So John had seen loneliness too in Harry Sabota's smile—in his thousand-dollar suit and tie, and Brazilian shoes. He strutted past John—who he called Marky when he addressed him at all, as a vague thing—a person who did not understand the significance of Harry Sabota himself, the entrenched scent of perfume and aftershave and the opal ring; and now, all of that was past, gone, as delusory as disgrace in a moment of grey water. The disgrace was not Harry Sabota's, John told Sue Van Loon, but us all.

"It was all your disgrace?" she asked.

"Oh—yes, absolutely," he said. "All of humanity's—all of us—each one!"

They spent some time together because John escorted Harry up and down the elevator. Sabota travelled back to Kigali quite often—and seemed to be restive, and without sleep. Even in December there were rumblings against him. Certain strains within the Rwandan government believed he was unreliable, believed he was an informer. This came without anyone saying or doing anything. It simply happened. Harry was at the consulate; meanwhile, a Canadian was in the field in Rwanda. Harry must be an informer. No one knew how the rumour started, but once started it was believed.

Harry would disappear down to Fourteenth Street looking for bargains, and come back and tell John about them, the shoes and bold sandals and the little shoulder bag, which he loved to carry when he went on planes.

But what John saw in early January—and saw it, it seemed, before Harry himself—was how he was no longer spoken to by the Rwandan ambassador, Jean-Damascène Bizimana.

His trauma was so great, however, that John could not keep the events in their proper sequence. He would forget things for years and suddenly they would appear as bright as a new dime. And if these memories became too insistent, he would have a headache that would incapacitate him. That is why pills and booze overtook his life. He would talk about cases twenty years old, or say something about a purse with the name Amy written on it in 2001. Or he would talk about poaching and confiscated moose meat from twenty-four years before in a clear, concise way.

"And our eco-terrorist, Wasson—do you still think of him?" asked Sue Van Loon.

"No," he lied.

"And the obscene phone calls about your son," Sue asked recently, "are you still getting those?"

"Oh no—that's long over," he lied again. He was still working to solve his son's case, and monitoring what his wife was doing, though he told no one. He had also, though no one knew this, prevented a man from attacking Melissa Sapp just two weeks before this present case had started. Melissa knew nothing of this. John was still working out what he should do about it.

But John went back and forth, trying as much as he could to prevent the headaches that plagued him. And the thwarted attack on Melissa was having consequences no one seemed to know—not only in this present case but in a case from years back that he had long been struggling with. So despite his efforts, the headaches were coming.

Sometimes he would fool his head by pretending he did not care if the headache came; just as he would try to fool himself by staying in his clothes so he could go to sleep when he was working on a case. The strange thing was, when he did have his heart attack in 2007, he had been feeling better than he had in months.

He had waited seven hours before he went to the hospital. And of course, he didn't remember going.

———

It was in March of 1994 when John was sent for the second time with a delegation carrying a message to the Canadians in Rwanda: that the weapons confiscated from the Hutu had to be given back—it was not UN policy to interfere in the internal politics of a sovereign nation. And the Hutu informant, who had revealed to the Canadians that weapons were being stockpiled, had to be returned to his people so they could deal with him within the parameters of their own justice system.

It was on the long flight back to New York when our special envoy instructed John about what must be UN policy, whether they liked it or not.

"Policy—difficult times," he said.

Then, after an hour or so, our Lion of Justice pushed his felt hat down over his eyes and fell asleep.

As he was sleeping, the informant was being murdered and the Belgian peacekeepers who had been ordered to give the confiscated weapons back, because knowledge of them had come through an informant's subterfuge, were being shot by those weapons in a barn outside Kigali.

The news about the Belgians certainly came, by all reports, "like a thunderbolt."

At the Canadian consulate in New York a week later, John remembered Harry Sabota walking by him with a serious, preoccupied gaze, sometimes his handsome face looking awestruck; then, recognizing John, he would stop and nod, putting his manicured hand to his face, his long finger showing his beautiful opal ring, as he tapped his finger against his chin and said, "Marky—right. Yes, man, you are the policeman from

Canada. Yes—Canada. How I love Canada, Marky, between you and I, a very civilized country. You must come see me in Rwanda someday—things will straighten out there. If I can get ten thousand malaria nets for the children, I will pay your government back. I have an interest in two malls in and around Roanoke, so I can get the money back. What do you think? Do you think I will be able to become a Canadian? That is what I would like—what do you think? Between you and I—my ambassador is not in my corner anymore. In fact, we do not speak the same language, it seems."

John was as outclassed as poor Harry Sabota—for he did not know what to think. And those who once thought so highly of him no longer spoke to him either.

———

Of course, all of this had happened years ago. But it came over John in waves as he spoke to his psychiatrist about it. This and his young son disappearing had made his life so bitter that for days on end he did not get out of bed. Once, when people told him he would die if he did not eat, he replied, "Well, why in God's name do you think I am not eating?"

Sue Van Loon paused. "I want to go back a moment, to something you said earlier. It was about the writer from Canada. Did you dislike this young black man—this writer from Canada? He seems pretty harmless and naive, and somehow nice?" Sue Van Loon asked.

"No—not at all. In fact, I liked him. In fact, I believe I liked him much more than he liked me. I do believe there was some residual prejudice toward me, by him—for being a white police officer. I believe you are right to say he was nice, and pleasant and naive, so he had to believe I was the enemy. In order to be pleasant and nice he couldn't really be nice to me and to others at the same time. He had to pick his adversary. And he realized, and rightly so, that the others were definitely uncomfortable with me—so he became uncomfortable as well. In fact, I now understand what the mark of Cain might actually be. It may be that

I have it and I cannot get rid of it—that paying for it means I have to perform some duty. I must recognize something, and do it."

"Ah, a biblical reference!" she said in triumph. She paused, looked down at her notes, looked up with a rather more intense gaze and asked, "You don't think he liked you?"

"Well, at least what I might have represented."

"Do you dislike black people?"

"Not as a rule. But then again I wasn't born in a place that had many African Canadians in it. I may have disliked more of them if I had known more of them."

"How about academics like Midge Nolan Overplant? Their concerns."

"Well," John replied, "some of them entered grade one, went on to grade twelve, on to university doctorates, post-doctorates, tenure, fellowships, research money, and have never left a classroom—could not function without one. And you see, most of them over time become imitators of one another."

"And the social services?"

"I did not care one way or the other about them. Never much thought of what they were like, or what their ideological bent was."

"But what about Jeannie? Why did you marry her—pity? Duty? Arrogance?"

"Yes, well, there you go. When they tried to take Jeannie's child away, I went to bat for her simply because her brother asked me to do so—he was my driver in Rwanda, so I was obligated, and I got involved more than I thought I would. Rightly or wrongly I got involved—at first simply as a favour. I suppose at first it was arrogance, and then duty."

"But then you did something rather—well, impulsive?"

"You mean I married her to help her get her child back? I know what it looks like and I do not blame them for their accusations. In fact I threatened to steal the child, didn't I? That wasn't smart. But Jeannie was a test case for social services. She was paraded about—looked upon as not quite as human as they were. I suppose I could have just walked away and let it all go. But once I discovered the very way they had wanted to help her child—at first to destroy it, and, barring that, to take something precious away from her and say it was for her own good—I realized they represented the kind of world that I had fought against since I was eighteen—a battle I was bound to lose, yet a battle I was condemned to fight. For you see, they would look upon me as being the severe one, the extreme one. While their position, that of taking the life of the unborn child, was considered practical.

"But perhaps abortion at certain times is necessary?"

"Well, maybe yes. It is. I am not saying it is not. At first of course they wanted her to have an abortion, and that decision was made by people who believe they never have an ulterior motive. That is, it was her body, her child, yet they were making the decision for her own good. And yes, maybe they were. But no one thought she would say no. After she refused, they wanted to rescue her body for her—by controlling her body and saying it was to keep others from controlling her body. They were supposedly giving her control by making the decision for her. I know how she got pregnant—and I know 90 per cent of us would say they were right. But you see, Jeannie did not say that. So that in fact destroys their own argument forever—that is, a woman is entirely free to make her own decision until a woman like Jeannie actually does.

"You see, let's suppose just for a second that abortion is murder—"

"I do not believe that," Sue said.

"Well no—but let us assume for just a moment. I have come to believe that in a murder the victim is the one who is the important entity—the entity that is recognized by the murderer as important and valuable. And what a murderer does is always try to lessen the value of the victim by lessening the very imprint of their humanity and saying they are nothing or are in fact so terrible that they do not deserve life. But by saying this, the murder victim actually becomes even more important. Those who murder cannot destroy the importance of that which they desire to destroy. The very fact that such a horrendous action is taken against the victim proves that they are the most important entity in the world to the perpetrator of the crime. That is what Jeannie's child was:

the most important person, born or unborn, in that moment to Melissa Sapp and her colleagues. The idea of it being nothing was totally false to those who proposed the solution to make it nothing. For the solution counted on the destruction of something they focused on and obsessed over to prove their own ideological worth."

"You are making this quite dramatic."

"Well, I know. But we were all in that exact same position at one time—that is, in a womb somewhere—and it would have been dramatic for us if those already outside the womb were calling us nonentities."

"In the womb?" she repeated as a question.

"So," he continued, "do not think I do not know how this child came about—how they picked her up and took her to the prip-prop field, how they set her drunk and laughed when she tried to sing them a song— how she passed out over the hood of the goddamn car. I know it all.

"Oh, I know too that the idea behind the abortion was that it was for her own good—that it was not the child but she herself who was the most important entity. And you see, I believe some of them thought this. But if she was the most important person, then she was the one who should have been free to determine the worth of this supposed nonentity they wished to destroy. Ah, but there's the rub. When she refused, put up a fuss, they were furious. So they changed tack. How could she, a woman like Jeannie, with a low IQ, ever know what she herself wanted? But you see here is truth to power—for if she had said she agreed with them and wanted an abortion, they would simply have said she was determined and independent enough and wise enough to make up her own mind, and no goddamn priest was going to interfere in her life. But since she did not want this from them, how could they now assume she knew what was best for her? She was like one of the millions of women who they supposed had to be educated about her options. None of them had been tormented or beaten or raped like she had. But she was the one who had to decide.

"So, they said, she must be crazy. And yes, maybe I believed she was as well. And maybe you are right that maybe at times abortion is necessary. So they got a psychologist to test her. They decided her IQ was not all that high, so they knew better than she did. They spoke of her cognitive ability.

"You see, they felt they knew what was best for her: to make her independent and free. The child would be better off not born, although they had been born. The child would be a burden on society, although they, who couldn't live a day without others carrying them on their backs through the storms of life, were not a burden on society. The child was unwanted, although they themselves were a generation of people who for the most part were conceived without being wanted, and had been coddled in school and coddled in university, where they had learned to blame others for the problems of the world.

"No, they could not cook dinner or heat water or flush a toilet without people such as a friend of mine who climbs poles for a living to keep electric currents moving. Yet they—who endlessly had everything and complained of burdens on society—were going to see about her, about Jeannie. That was when I turned against their self-infatuated cabal forever.

"So they withdrew their horns and left her alone, and she struggled through her pregnancy working at the Dominion Bakery. Yet after her boy was born they got together and decided that the best thing to do to help Jeannie was to take her child—and they did, telling her they would take care of it. Jeannie had no idea this meant they were taking her child away from her. So her brother came to me. And the woman named Jeannie Aube, who I used to tease and torment, whose face I spit into when I was a boy of twelve, came back into my life again all of a sudden. As if it was preordained. And I took one look at her at the Dominion Bakery and I decided to help. But in helping the way I did, I destroyed any idea that I had the same ideals or vested interests as the well-established, civic-minded, goal-oriented people I had to fight."

"And who was this woman—this so-called friend who took the child away?"

"Melissa Sapp."

"Are you sure?"

"Yes."

"And who was the psychologist who saw Jeannie and tested her IQ?"

"Well, Sue Van Loon—that would have been you."

Afterwards he went back to his small rooms and sat in the dark. He saw that his wife, Jeannie, had phoned, but he didn't return the call. He had names of social workers who worked Shelf Street—a Ms. Blanchard who had retired in January of 1999, and a Mr. DeWold, who, he believed, took over from her—but he could not be sure when, for there was no real timeline about when DeWold had come into the picture. They said it was Fern Hershey who had come and gone from that house. But John felt Ms. Hershey, who had replaced Ms. Blanchard, did not go back to the house after January 20. So then Melissa Sapp's husband, DeWold, would have taken that house. However, he put the idea of DeWold aside for a moment and concentrated on the house itself.

Then he lay down in his clothes and tried to sleep. He woke with a start, thinking he had been tossed over a high cliff. As he fell in his dream, he had tried to grab the top of the World Trade Center.

John remembered how Midge Nolan Overplant had simply carried on after the UN days, after the terror in Rwanda. John could for months not look anyone in the eyes because of Rwanda, but she looked completely sincere, affable and refreshed. She became the titular head of bilateral talks between Canada and Panama over trade and embargo, and a confidante of a confidante of an aide to Hillary Clinton during the health care days, when the Americans wanted to plumb Canadian ideas. She had a position in Washington for a few years at our expansive embassy. She knew everyone, from the Clintons and the Gores to rather famous American actors—and this is what endeared her to Canadians of all walks of life.

Then in mid December of 1998 she left the civil service, and was now head of the university's sociology department and, at $167,000 a year, considered an expert in gender politics and international peace.

One of Midge's latest papers was on the redefining of Canadian geopolitical landscapes and the formulaic anti-female aggression of male language in twentieth-century Canadian literature. This pursuit had produced three papers, the last on the "diversification of primary function, and role reversal in utilizing new dynamics for preteen males." She spoke on this at symposiums across Canada. That is, the world had fallen into a linguistic horror that she herself duly celebrated as being a positive advancement in selfhood. Language in fact—like the dynamic nonviolent resolutions that she had supported at the UN—meant nothing whatsoever to the intellectual class who championed language and nonviolence. Midge was now in Budapest, giving another paper on "recidivism in chauvinistic thought processes among white heterosexual management," but would return home sometime by the end of the month.

John, two weeks into the "bogus," case, had a photo and a piece of chalk, a coat and some ATM receipts. But in fact he had no name, and no date. Still what he did not know was that external affairs in Ottawa was becoming interested in the case of this boy as well, not only as a diplomatic matter but as a police matter, and was beginning to look for this child too. This was due to evidence in Rwanda that had recently surfaced, and because of a man from Rwanda who was now well-known and had inquired about this boy.

His name was Sebastian Ebusantaini.

He was a successful writer—and not only had he published his own book but he had also edited and published a book from Rwanda by one of the men who had died there, a man named Edgar Furaki. Ebusantaini was twenty-nine or thirty years of age, sophisticated and energetic, and explained to Canadian immigration that he was inquiring about a boy he had known during the genocide. The boy had been separated from his parents, but Ebusantaini had contacted, through a variety of organizations, Belgian authorities, who said the boy had in fact been sent to Canada early in 1999.

As this was beginning to happen, John Delano was staring out at the gas fires flaring up at the distant oil refinery in Saint John, while closer to his window he could see some scattering of snow in the black night air, which reminded him of the snow that usually fell in front of the theatre doors after a movie, just beyond the marquee lights. He had toast and tea, wrote down some things about another case—a case about Luda Marsh—then stared at a late-night movie about cops and robbers, and a blond femme fatale back in the fifties on the sad, sunny streets of LA. Sometimes those sunny streets had the faint shadow of a person passing by out of camera range, who John wondered about—a shadow of a life lived, over a half century before.

———

It was snowing, and young Melon Thibodeau made his lonely way along the streets of Saint John past old houses built well over a century before, small alleyways and corroded iron fences, and was thinking of home and supper. He was considered a lost soul, this Melon—a picture of him in school in grade two reminded one of some Dickensian child left on his own. He had in fact always been on his own.

It was well after work, and after he had visited the grave of his sister, Amy, which he did once or twice a week now that he was out of jail again. He had laid flowers down, but they blew over and he spent until dark trying to get them upright and steady. He became immersed in this task and the snow fell on his winter coat and he shivered as he brushed the grave off, brushed away the snow from the top of the small gravestone. The immense graveyard was dark and long, and its rows of brown stone tottered under naked elm trees, from the Loyalist days on. And far back in one of those lonesome rows a man stood watching him.

He noticed this man, and thought nothing of it as he was going home.

Yet as he turned a corner somewhere on a street in the upper south end, he saw the man straddle the wrought iron fence and approach. He thought he might know this man by the way he walked, so Melon quickly turned and started back down the way he had come, now and again looking behind him. He took two side streets, and when he moved toward Pitt Street, the man was standing in front of him, near a sewer grate. He was just out of the light and the wind, standing near a sand-coloured building. He beckoned, but Melon pretended not to notice.

He turned again and went back the way he had come, always looking over his shoulder. Well, he could go and speak to this man, but he did not want to. That was the whole point. He knew by the way the man moved it was Constable Melonson—now Melon thought he was probably a sergeant. Melon had written the letter to John Delano without putting his own name on it, hoping Melonson wouldn't know it was him. That is, innocently—he did not want to bother Melonson with this, because Melonson had said before that it was so foolish, and that he was lying just to get the people in Shelf Street in trouble. That is what Melon had wrestled with for so long—he did not want people to think he was trying to get anyone in trouble. So for a number of months before he wrote the letter he tried to decide how he would write it, and who he would give it to. And just off the cuff one morning he thought of John Delano. That is, he could have sent it to Constable Trevor, but suddenly he thought: No, it has to go to Delano—he is the only one to trust! So he did write the letter, then folded it carefully with the tips of his fingers, wiped both letter and envelope off, all in the hope of not making Melonson angry or getting the people of 87 Shelf Street in trouble. But now that he saw Melonson, he thought both things must have happened.

Little Melon the Felon, five feet four inches tall, who had never really harmed anyone—except that he lit fires when no one believed him about the Limey, and ran away from foster home—stared back over his shoulder. He was beaten three times for saying the Limey existed: twice by Moms and once in jail by a man who had laughed at what he was saying. He had been beaten before that too—and before he was taken to a foster home, he sat in the courtroom while his deranged father screamed at him, "I'll get you—you little, thin-boned bastard."

And Melon would shrink down so only his ears were visible, or turn and give up a pathetic smile.

"I'll get you, you no good little rat bastard," his father would yell.

Once he gave a pathetic wave, and his father stopped his cursing and ranting and waved back.

Now Melon hurried along, alone, as he was most of his life.

The night air was filled with frost; the windows in the buildings were all dark.

He turned the corner, and was now safe. He was going home, and thinking that no one knew where he lived. But in fact all the police knew where he lived.

Melonson was standing sideways under the awning of a closed convenience store far down in the south end. "Hey, Melon," he said, "you have a light?"

Melon nodded, his fingers numb from the cold, looked through his pockets for a match. The thing is, Melonson did not smoke and had not even unwrapped his cigar.

"Here you go," Melon said, lighting the match with a snap of his thumb and watching it flare up in the dark.

"Oh, you see," Melonson said, almost heartbroken, taking the light for his cigar and watching as the plastic covering caught. "Look what you did!" He drew on the cigar and frowned.

"What did I do?" Melon asked, looking behind him. "You should have taken the plastic off—is what I think."

"Well, well, well," Melonson said, " I don't care about that." And here he tossed the cigar away. "But you—you broke your parole. You have matches on you."

"But you wanted a match," Melon said.

"But didn't it stipulate in your parole hearing that you are to have no incendiary devices? Well, what is a match?"

"But it is only a match. I was sure they were talking about flares and diesel and, well, maybe dynamite—but everyone has matches."

Melonson said it was a far graver disciplinary situation, and the parole could be revoked. Then he began to talk in a rambling way—about things that had happened ten years ago, and that maybe someone wanted to go back to jail.

"But that's crazy," Melon said. "I don't want to go back to jail—ever again."

"Well, you are back to the same thinking—thinking about a boy who does not exist. So then you are quite delusional—and maybe should be sent for psychiatric treatment. Did you write a letter?"

"No, I never even heard of a letter." Here Melon spit into his palm and placed it over his heart to prove that he had heard of no letter.

"But," Melonson said, "you might have been talking to someone—about a boy. And maybe a policeman wrote the letter trying to get me into trouble."

"No," Melon said. He looked behind him a moment, at someone crossing the street farther down.

The street itself was dark and hardly lit.

It smelled of burned tarpaper in the wind, and the unpleasant smell of burned plastic wrapper.

"I'll let you keep your matches—but I know about them," Melonson said. "You shouldn't mention that boy again. If the department has to investigate and find out it is all made up, you might end up in some home for the completely insane." And he turned and walked away—disappearing quite quickly in the direction of the park. The way he moved, strutted away as he did, seemed to emphasize the last word: *insane*.

Melonson was in fact enraged at having to act like this. Still, he was completely sure John had written the letter himself in order to blackmail him. He was sure John was trying to keep him from being made superintendent. He cares for nothing, he now thought, but he will never ruin my career over it!

Little Melon watched him walk away. He put his hands into his jean pockets, glumly thought of insane asylums like his mom went to, glumly thought of what Ms. Sapp had told him: that he came from a dysfunctional family.

The next day, Delano was called to a meeting and told not to take the case about the missing boy seriously, because all of his evidence was not only circumstantial but whimsical. Take it off the board, he was told.

"There is very little evidence supporting anything," Melonson told him. "All of this evidence is unlikely to point to one solid case."

"Of course you may be right—I am not sure myself," John said after a moment, staring into his black, lukewarm coffee.

The uncomfortable feeling John was beginning to have is that the more he did, the more he himself would be suspected. That is, John, in bringing the truth forward, would make this very truth be considered a lie and he a prognosticator. So in some significant way he was damned. But the very marrow of his thirty-five years of police work told him he must go ahead. That the boy did exist.

"Yes, of course," John continued, looking up from his coffee, "you're right on that—but I think a few people know I am on the right track and might be worried. For instance, the train conductor."

"What conductor?"

"Dan Furlong."

"What about Dan Furlong?"

"He took a ticket from a boy travelling on the express from Saint John to Moncton in early winter 1999—he remembers him to this day."

"Oh, come on!" one of the junior officers said. He had just driven up in his RCMP car and walked in, fresh and dedicated, and wanted to show how attuned to the issue he was.

"Well, you could ask him yourself," John said to the young man.

"What does that have to do with anything?" Melonson asked.

"Nothing—it might mean nothing at all. I know I might be grasping at straws. I felt that when I spoke to him—but no matter what, some would want me to think I was grasping at straws. For instance, the only reason Furlong remembered him was that he had a ticket—plus no winter coat, and looked as if he had been in a fight. But you see that is not why he remembered him. It was a stroke of luck that something else happened that night."

"What?"

"Some youngster did in fact start a fight in the bar car, forced everyone to show their ticket again—so Furlong remembered the young boy he remembered very well. Because when he first heard the commotion, he thought it might have been this young boy."

"So the boy was rowdy?"

"No—another kid, about twenty, was drunk and rowdy. That is why the conductor remembered the whole night—the youngster without the jacket sitting there. And he went to check on him, to make sure he wasn't the fellow who had started the commotion. Then he went back again to make sure the little guy was okay."

"Why is that important?"

"Well, some could say I planted the memory in him. Some would say that, wouldn't they? But no, this memory was seared into Furlong because of the other boy, who took a swing at people in the bar car and they had to restrain him. So Furlong remembered making sure this little fellow was in his seat. He in fact checked on him three times to see if he was all right. So the little fellow without the jacket must then exist."

"Who would say you planted a memory?" Melonson asked.

"Some police officer who made a mistake a decade ago, who simply did not know his job."

"Do you really think that is true?" Melonson asked.

"I am sure of it—or almost sure. Let us just imagine if this now was being handled by you. I mean, if you got the letter instead of me—"

Melonson said, "I am handling it, and I am trying to make people see it from my point of view."

"Of course," John said.

"Yes—and perhaps I am speaking to someone others have indicated may have written the letter. Who in fact may have planted a memory or two."

John said nothing at all to this.

"Well, I know that is unfounded and sounds unfair—but you realize what people might think of you getting involved in a case like this? They would think of it as payback or desperation or something along those lines. That is, if it does involve the social services head, who is the head of the entire province now—head of child welfare."

"Of course—Melissa. Sapp. But I have never dealt with her before. At least, not directly."

"John, you are either very naive or very clever—she has always been an adversary of yours. She dislikes you intensely because of your views on women."

"My views? I didn't know I had views on women that were so peculiar. I was thinking this case might not involve her at all—"

"Well then, why were you following her this past month?" Melonson asked. He smiled at this and looked over at the new constable, who smiled as well.

John looked at them both and said nothing.

"You were following her out to her house . . ."

"Ah. That," John said as though he had completely forgotten. But he couldn't say that he was following her for her own protection. That would be viewed now as a completely fraudulent answer. So he said nothing.

Melonson nodded, as if he had him.

"Now, for Christ sake, following her—and now a missing boy—her department, your son—"

There was a long, embarrassed pause.

Then he said more sympathetically than John had heard from him before, "John, your child is lost—trains and kids and jackets and tickets and ATMs . . . this child might never have existed."

"Of course—you are right," John said, shrugging, as if to say why are you bothering to tell me things I know.

"Don't, for God's sake, do anything else," Melonson said. "Promise me."

"Well okay—I promise," he said.

He walked home after work. I will not do anything else, he decided, and he was going to stick to this decision. He was. That is, until he was almost home.

"I will only do one more thing," he said. "I will go to the house on Shelf Street."

6.

"Principles to Live By" was faded over the door of 87 Shelf Street.

The residents of that house had kept foster children for seventeen years. Today, fog had come in across the bay to make all the houses gloomy. It swept toward the city that noon hour. Car lights shone bleakly, and all the trees reminded one of "The Fall of the House of Usher" by Poe.

The house on Shelf Street was enveloped in this fog as well. There was a small yard with an iron gate out front, the flower bed trampled and dead. The second-storey windows had bars on them. The bars looked more recent than the gate, and they looked decorative.

The house had been re-roofed as well, sometime within the last little while.

The brass knocker hung under the slogan Principles to Live By.

They no longer kept children, the woman told him. They were "good and retired," she said. But they had kept all the boys for years, she said, fed them and loved them too. She said. There was nothing much more to say than that. "Them little bastards," she said, quaintly, almost with affection.

Still, she invited him in.

The woman was heavy-set, and when she spoke, her teeth were still hidden—you could only make them out slightly. There was a look of battle readiness about her—and an acute civic mindedness, or perhaps parsimony, that John detected. She wore a red wig, and a reddish mark distinguished her double chin. She told him they had gone through all the stipulations and programs of the Family Services Act in New Brunswick—and bragging just a tad, she said she knew more about child welfare and family services than a herd or two of social workers, some of whom didn't know their arse from a hole; and she said she'd sometimes had four children—sometimes six—rarely less than four.

She had kept children for almost twenty years, when no one else would take them, not even other foster homes. Yes, she'd had a couple of young offenders as well. That was because she and her husband were trusted. They had been trusted because they were honest and scrupulous.

She gave the boys, she said, "their 'three squares a day.' They were the unwanted lot I took in. Some of them had nothing, poor things. Fetal alcohol too." They were the forgotten ones who no one wanted, for the most part. She took them in.

That was admirable and John would never say it was not. But he did not like that expression—"three squares a day." It came from army manuals and was said almost always as posture by people who wanted to show their compassion had a functionary rule others were supposed to admire as being concrete, or at least utilitarian. That is, there might be dinner, but there would be no hugs. Now, to be fair, many of the foster parents John had seen were not at all unattached to their charges. But it seemed as if this woman was.

He stared at the expensive ring on the forefinger of her right hand. He looked along the walls behind her. He glanced along the hall toward the basement door. He looked toward the upstairs, and then back toward the dining room. He saw the map of Ireland, and the photo of Saint Patrick's Cathedral in New York. These were the trappings of the expansive Irish—the kind that could be found only in Canada and the United States, as a kind of aggressive assertion of cultural identity with a country most North Americans had never, nor would ever, visit. Therefore, the cultural identification was even more compulsory for those who lived here than in the country of origin. And John knew that many in the country of origin, Ireland, or for that matter Britain or France, disliked Canadians, thinking of them only as backward colonials. He was not about to say that now.

The woman sat down in the front room, with its round throw rug in the centre and its old hardwood floor almost black, and rubbed her great left knee, which was sore. Her face was pale and she wore bluish eyeliner. There was a small leprechaun sitting on the end table.

"How many kids were here over the years?" John asked.

She yawned and rubbed her hands together. "Oh, thirty to forty, maybe fifty in all—some stayed, others were here only a few weeks. Then they got back with their families or into adoption or something like that. Some went into provisional care homes with other relatives."

"How did they turn out—those children?"

"Oh, most of them turned out okay. Some went to jail. Fine for the most part."

"And do you keep in contact with them, those foster kids, or have their names?"

"Oh, you know, some come to see us now and again. The names— I remember a lot of the names, actually—but we don't give out their names. Privacy is what we want."

"I am aware of that too," John said.

At this moment John heard someone coming down the stairs. Both the woman and he looked toward the arch in anticipation. The sound stopped, hesitated, and then continued. A man came to the bottom of the stairs and stood listening at the arch as if pondering his entrance while a conversation was ongoing.

This was the woman's husband.

And the husband was a large, overweight man with a sad, brimming face, flushed and almost comical.

John Delano nodded to him, and continued to listen to the woman's stories about these children. The man seemed to listen to them also, in the way a person does who expects to hear something complimentary about himself and will be appropriately startled. He had a huge round face, small little eyes, and wore a shirt tie and vest—the shirt was almost yellow; the tie too was old. He had large, white hands that stuck out of his torn suit jacket and seemed to hang against his legs. His eyes continually looked here and there, lighting on nothing in particular.

John kept glancing at him. He was the owner of a second-hand bookstore where John himself went in the evenings after the lights came on in the stores and the sidewalks were still bathed in twilight. There John would go over the volumes of paperbacks left to distill under the dry, dust-caked, immobile ceiling fans. John always searched for the books that would take his pain away—and found, in the end the pain remained. Comedies didn't help as well as the tragic works, unless they in a way were tragic too. Still, the books—like church—assisted him in staying alive. He was, at sixty-one, entirely on his own as a police officer, as an intellectual and as a man.

John had some twenty-four hundred books at home, in boxes and on shelves, in places he had once lived that were forgotten. He would come across them now and again. He had met many writers and some had signed their books for him:

"Thanks, John, for seeing to me when I was here."

"For John—good to share a beer with you."

"John—with admiration."

And all those books, and those authors he had met during his time in New York and Ottawa, were mostly forgotten, the oracles gone on to other places, the writers now deftly being whittled away and forgotten and replaced.

Still it was very strange for John to go into a bookstore and see the books of once-famous men and women he'd spent an hour or two with drinking, who were not so famous now. The store had a burned-out neon light at the window and an apartment above the main floor. An old heater ticked all winter long, and a bell jingled as if to announce the snow that fell without a sound on the heavy streets. At Christmas a lone Santa Claus beamed and a plastic Christmas tree sat on the counter.

The store in fact sold mainly romance novels, semi-erotic books, and more explicit works in plastic wrap. John poked about in that old store perhaps five times a year. He always ventured in with his hopes high that he would find the one book that would set the world straight. Conrad came close, and was far funnier than many would suspect. When he said this one night to a writer who had immigrated to New York, believed greatly in puns and frivolity, and who found Canadians fair game—the writer mocked him endlessly: Only a Canadian would think Conrad funny.

"I agree," John said, "but Conrad is much funnier in places than you ever could be." It was always revolutionary to tell the truth, especially when deceit was so fashionably applauded.

He liked Dostoyevsky, Tolstoy too. He read MacLeod, and others.

But one book? There was no book like that.

He thought of all of this fleetingly now. And he was a little disturbed and looked closely at the man, and then the woman. Yes, he had seen them before. The woman too seemed to suddenly recognize him, then let it go. Glanced at her husband, who did not seem to recognize John.

This was the family who had long ago kept Jeannie's child for three or four months—during the tension when social services pleaded with Jeannie to be reasonable with them. He was never at this house, had met them only once when the child had been handed over. This was the greatest dispute he had had with social services and it involved people he might have to question again. In fact there was an email and a fax circulating at the Department of Social Development and in the child welfare office, with John's picture on it as a troublemaker.

Jeannie's boy had been ready to be adopted by what was probably a very good and caring family when John stepped in and took it upon himself to get the child back for her. There was a leeway of six months, and this six months' grace is what John used. He married Jeanie for this reason—some said ruthlessly—but he did what he did, and he did love her. He did it not for Jeanie but for her brother and the memory of Jeannie herself as a child. The one he had tormented.

Nor did he disagree with adoption, not like some childless authors of popular books who made fun of it—in fact, it was one of the great arguments for allowing the child to live. But John did have a prejudice. He very much disliked the idea of couples being childless by choice. He always thought of Vera Rostova and Colonel Adolf Berg in *War and Peace*.

But there was something else he had become aware of since his last talk with Melonson: how much Melissa Sapp was involved in most of the things his investigation was centred on. And this gave him a very uneasy feeling. That is, a month after her achieving this new position for displaced children, he was known to have followed her home and now was investigating a case she said did not exist.

He now mindlessly picked up a magazine, glanced at it, set it aside, and asked them if any of the girls who had lived next door at 66 came from the same families as some of the foster boys. He was already fairly certain the book the boy gave away was to a girl from 66—to him it stood to reason.

They said, no, not that they remembered.

There is almost always a good rapport between police and individual members of the public until the police are seen as intrusive, and once that happens—as it had with John Delano—then the public believed it could be excused for being impolite and even hostile. John, of course, registered this always, and knew now that if their attitude had become more tenuous or reticent, they would have recognized who he was.

The woman, secure that her husband was there, now talked about the children a little more freely.

No, she didn't remember if any of the girls at number 66 were related, but some of the boys went as far away as Victoria to work—a few went to university, and did well, she said. One boy was in the States, a real bigwig who had helped run President Obama's campaign. Or so she had heard. He lived in Chicago and taught at the university.

He reflected their amazement at this, and looked at his notes.

He finally asked if a boy had come to this house under the auspices of social services in 1999—and perhaps left after a short time. The boy would have been brought here by someone who had found him with little money and nowhere to go. He was a runaway or perhaps a vagrant . . .

The couple said they weren't sure there had been a boy like that, apart from an x number of boys like that, who had come always that way, and this was ten or more years ago.

"But you might remember this one?" he asked. "He may have had something of an accent?" John added. "And he was probably quite bright?"

They said they weren't sure; so many kids did come in and out. And it was not unusual to have gangly kids pulled off the street who became mainstays for a month or two. In fact, half the older kids came from streets on their way to somewhere else. Once, they had to fight off a father who was coming in and trying to hurt his child with a lead pipe—and there were others too. Phone calls? That is why the boys' names were sacred and the phone had been unlisted for years.

But John said there was now a right to information, which meant he would be able to access these names if a case was warranted.

"But otherwise they are private," the woman responded.

Well, she said, maybe that was the boy he was looking for—someone whose father was like that, and had come in and tried to take him away. But they did not know of anyone who had just left.

"Did anyone disappear, Bunny?" the woman asked.

"No—disappear—no," Bunny answered. "A few tried to escape, but we got them back." He smiled at this lightheartedly.

They paused then and tried to think. They furrowed their brows. They paused for a moment of reticence and silence, which made the lassitude of the day seem more weary with the chime of the grandfather clock somewhere along the carpeted hall. John looked over at the Irish leprechaun with his little green Irish hat.

"But, you see his accent made people think of him as a Limey," John said.

"A Limey?" the woman repeated, and gave a chuckle, and looked at her husband as she scratched her arms.

"Well, in some cases," John said, "he would be called that—you know by people who observe a certain—oh—tradition."

The woman put her fingers to her chin and looked off into the hallway where her husband stood, and the clock chimed. When John glanced in the direction she was looking, her husband was silent, looking at his feet.

"And he would have been here in 1999," John said. "So would that narrow it? What I am thinking is he came in perhaps by plane—and someone was supposed to be there for him and wasn't, and maybe he did end up here? I am now thinking he came to the wrong city—there was a mix-up, and perhaps he was supposed to be in St John's, Newfoundland. But I am uncertain—and why I asked about 66 Shelf Street is that he is reported to have given a girl a book—I am thinking she may have been at 66." Here he paused for a second, selected a page of his notes, and asked, "Was Fern Hershey taking over from Ms. Blanchard?"

"I'm not too sure—" Bunny said. "That's so long ago."

"She was supposed to—and then she didn't. Isn't that right?" John said. "I mean, I do not know this—I am simply remembering what I remember. Hershey retired and sought a university position. She did not get it, and then came back to work. Her caseload did include this house, but after she returned it did not—"

They didn't answer this, and John simply shrugged.

"Maybe someone else came in to take the case—someone who was new."

Suddenly the woman spoke. "You see," she said, "many of the foster children came from distance places." She continued happily as if she wanted to show that she regarded what he had asked as not being unusual at all. "One from North Carolina, one from Manitoba. Some poor things were brought here by one parent and left alone." She tried to include John in her amazement at this, and her concern for them. She smiled at him hopefully.

"By one parent and left alone," she said, as if she was astounded.

"That happened from time to time," the man said. "Then the other parent would try to get them back. Then one baby boy came, and then the mother got married to some rich cop, so they gave the child back and he died—should have kept that one," the man said. John kept writing in his notebook. He looked up quickly and nodded, and then wrote again. The woman looked over at him and then blurted, "One was crazy as a bag of marbles, and said he was from Africa." She said this as if she wanted to put to bed any idea of being furtive.

John said nothing for a moment. Then he shrugged.

"So what did he sound like—this African boy?" he asked.

"Ordinary, I'd say," Moms said. "But he was no more from Africa than I was—we had a time with him. Some of them can't help but lie, you know. He was the one who said he come here from Africa."

His heart beat wildly, and he thought of taking out his bottle of nitro. But he did not. He said nothing for a long moment. He however loosened his tie.

"And do you have their names—I mean a list of those children?" John asked. "I'd hate to get a court order for all of this."

They saw him struggling to catch his breath, and were concerned for a moment that they had let a madman into their house. Bunny had for a long time feared a madman would arrive. (They had thought it would be a relative of this boy, and they had always had that thought deep, deep in the back of their minds—that someone would come in and demand something from them.) Not that they believed the boy had come from Africa; but they feared that someone who knew who the boy actually was would come to find out where he went.

"Well, I am not sure if I have a complete list—and I would want to know why you want it. We pay our taxes," Moms said.

"We pay our taxes," Bunny said after her—and his bald head was shiny even in the forlorn gloom of the day, making John think of waxed floors in the middle of autumn long ago.

"And there was so many here then that half the names I did forget—half of them, at any rate, are now gone on to jobs and families. They would be the ones to contact."

John had finally quieted his racing heart and was writing in his notebook. He had his legs spread and his arms across his thighs and his notebook in his hands, always uncomfortable with the written word. He looked up and Bunny was smiling, almost in conspiracy at him.

He was not in the lead in this family.

"Nine in this house then, perhaps, over that year or so?" John said. Then after a suitable pause he asked, "Africa—when would that have been? Or how did he get from Africa?"

"Well, we stopped taking in kids in 2002—so the boy who went missing would have had to belong to another foster home, for we shut her all down in 2002," the man said suddenly, in a strange and pleading tone. He did not try to sound pleading, mind you—but the inflection was similar to someone in an interview room at police headquarters whose crime had just been revealed.

"In fact the boy went missing years before then. I am thinking 1999. So, Africa . . . was he black?"

The woman chuckled in spite of herself and scratched her arms suddenly. The gold setting of her ring glittered, there was a smell of wax, the clock chimed fifteen after.

"Not that I know of," the woman said. The man chuckled too, and looked at John conspiratorially once more. "No, you have to realize the stories that people make up. He was no more from Africa than I was. He was a Toggle or something like that. He came here and had a history of running away—later on he went back and lived with his older sister and was killed in a car accident—and I got the newspaper to say it."

"Jack Toggle." John said, realizing who they were speaking about.

"Yes—"

"Yes," John Delano said, turning to the woman again. "Well, he just may be that Toggle boy—or he may have been mistaken for that boy, you see—and I have been looking for him now for the past two weeks. I think a boy might have run away or gone missing from here—well, from a foster home near here, I am not saying here exactly—a boy who was not the Jack Toggle who died in a car accident but was actually someone else."

"How could that be?" the man asked.

"I think it could have happened very easily—Jack Toggle was really never lost, only put into the file as missing. So a boy is picked up, and seems strange—and say he says his name is Jack—so he is misidentified."

John suddenly started to cough, and asked if he could go to the washroom. He made it to the stairs and then straightened himself, and holding the banister, he made it to the top and then into the bathroom, where he put water on his neck and his face. Then he sat on the edge of the tub for eight minutes. He suddenly had a powerful sensation that the boy had been here, in this very house, and that something had happened. He also felt it would have been Vernon, the son, who had helped this boy open his bank account twelve years before. He sat on the edge of the tub contemplating this for a moment or so.

"No," the man said as John came back down the stairs "Kids said a boy was from Africa—that he said he was or something. But I don't think that was true. It was just a rumour kids got going—"

"Were there any fights here—at night over something, perhaps?" John asked.

"No—oh, a squabble here and there, but never too much," Moms said.

"I would give anything to have a picture of that boy," John said.

"Well, I don't know if we have one—you could check the paper for the article when he was killed," the woman said.

"No—I know what Jackie Toggle looked like. I was in fact the police officer who found out he wasn't missing—in September of 1999 he was back living with his sister. So I knew him, and I knew—or know—his sister. I am speaking of this other boy—so that's where the confusion lay. A picture would go a long way to clearing it up."

There was five minutes where almost nothing more was said. The man and woman looked suddenly chagrined and embarrassed. The woman now and again drubbed her fingers on the cloth of the chair and glanced angrily at her husband as if she had put up with this too much.

"But it doesn't mean Jack Toggle was with his sister earlier in 1999," Bunny said, as an explanation.

"No, you are right there—it does not mean that."

The woman said she might be able to solve it and went to the old, overflowing desk in the small den, where she looked through drawers for a name or a picture and even became upset when she couldn't find one for him. Bunny then went upstairs and looked in his back bedroom closet, where he kept old folders. And he went into a bedroom—John listened carefully for what bedroom he did go into. It was the front bedroom that now had the bars over it.

He opened some dresser drawers and a closet door.

But they found nothing that went back beyond 2002, the last year they had paid taxes on the monies for the foster home.

They came back to their places. They looked at him and then at each other.

John felt he knew what had happened. The boy had disappeared and they had managed to forget about him. But the problem was, they had continued to take the money for his keep—because no one in authority had checked up on them or him.

John was not interested in holding their scam against them. He simply wanted to know more about the child he was looking for.

"Well, just tell me this much—who did he room with?"

"Oh—he didn't room with anyone, I don't think." Bunny said.

"He did not room with Melon—the little Thibodeau boy who was here in 1999?"

"Melon—oh, so you know Melon. No—Melon liked us a lot and after he left he even used to send a Christmas card to the taxi stand, to Vernon," Bunny said.

John looked at both of them, then dutifully folded the notebook and put it away.

"He sent Christmas cards to Vernon?"

"Vernon said he got a few over there, a birthday card too" Moms said. "Vernon took the time, you see, to visit him when Melon was in jail!"

"Yes, well, that was nice of him. And you might be right about this being nothing at all—do you know what I think?" John asked.

He left this silly provocative question that never in the whole wide world has an answer, and went home.

The school above Shelf Street was filled with small children. The lights had come on in the big, vacant-looking rooms. John could see their heads through the long, lit windows. For some reason he could not go in that direction. He had made a mental note, as he always did, of the plaques hanging on the walls of 87 Shelf, the old records in their cases, the map on the wall in the dining room and, more importantly, of the shed in the backyard, down by the broken cement fence. Perhaps the shed might have something left in it from all those years ago. It was locked at the side door.

He decided that the missing boy's roommate was the boy who had sent the letter. He couldn't be certain yet, but he felt it might have been Melon Thibodeau. But fear or honour was preventing Melon from signing his name or admitting to it.

When John got home, there was a message on his phone:

"I am quite aware of your intense dislike for me, but I refuse to be followed to my home. I have sent a report about it to your office—I hope you do understand."

Click.

It was the first time in fifteen years he had heard the distinct and authoritative voice of Ms. Melissa Sapp.

———

John had supper and did a wash of laundry in the motel's small laundry room. He stared at the green cement walls, the detergent dispenser, and listened to the hollow sounds from the warm pipes. Here he was closing in on sixty-two, and he was alone.

He had checked with authorities in the last day: Melon still went by the name of Melon Thibodeau and was working at the car wash, just down the hill, and John went and visited him that night.

There Melon was, five feet four inches tall, scrubbing away at a bumper and a turn signal as if the task was the most important in the world. He turned to John and smiled. Then, realizing who it was, he jumped up and tried to run, but hit the side of the door to the office and fell back on his rear.

"I am just going to talk to you awhile," John said, helping him to his feet, "and try to figure something out."

John looked over his notes as they sat down quietly and spoke—and as they did, John told the car-wash manager that Melon was not in the least bit of trouble but was in fact essential in some grave way to a case. So the manager put them in the small back office where boxes of oil cans and oil filters were piled.

What one must realize, and John of course did, was that Melon Thibodeau had grown up in a world most of us would shun, yet Melon only tried to take what he needed from those who offered. Melon, like many others brought up as he was, had made his share of mistakes, but he did his best to atone for them.

Melon, like so many, knew foster homes and hallways and the small, cramped offices of social workers and psychologists; like many had experienced dedicated, somewhat naive people trying to help. Like many, he had seen the sneers of people he had been told were there to help them but who hated the sight of him. Like others, he had a young sister who was dead, and he too was parentless. But whereas many believed that the world had been terrible to them—more so than to anyone else— where they believed the only way to act was to get back as much as they could from this world and prey upon those who were weaker than they, since they had seen the weak preyed upon and had been preyed upon themselves—Melon, who had grown up far more desperate than many, who had been burned and beaten and tormented from the time he was two, could never act like that. And though others made themselves seem very important to people on the street when they wrecked lives and harmed people, Melon's soul was large and encompassed the world with a smile though he was looked upon as nothing at all by so very many.

John understood this distinction in a second—whereas many police and psychologists would not have seen this distinction at all.

Therefore, though John had never treated others with anything less than kindness, even during an arrest, he had a genuine soft spot for Melon; liked him instantly and wanted to help him. Still, Melon did not tell him much beyond what he already knew. And he looked genuinely terrified when John asked him if he had written the letter.

"What letter? No, I wrote no letter!"

John only nodded, but he did not believe him. He surmised that the one person at the foster home who had cared for him was Vernon Beaker, who John assumed must have taken the Limey's place when he went away. Melon would not turn on Vernon, and therefore was second-guessing himself, and wondered why he had written this letter at all. He kept looking around, scratching his face, staring at his shoes and saying this was a trap.

"It is no trap," John said. "I have an interest in this case and am pursuing it."

Yet whatever was bothering Melon made him afraid. He smiled and said at the last that though he never wrote the letter, he had known a boy like the one John was searching for, and it would be good if he could someday see that boy again.

John felt at this moment that someone else had got to him, and had warned him not to say anything, and that this someone else might be a police officer.

So John Delano let him go, and went and sat in the back of the church, and stared at the Blessed Virgin and the cross on the altar.

There was the faint smell of ancient obligation, the memory of ten thousand souls. These devotions that did not matter to many anymore. But that John in madness went back to—prayed and fasted and thought about more than most, although he was a person who had been a bad candidate for any of it. Even reading Thérèse of Lisieux made him realize how bad a candidate, for didn't she make known that there exists no evil to the good of heart? And yet he saw it, dealt with it, hated it, and fought it.

He thought again of Melon and of Luda Marsh growing up in this world. Luda had been a trafficker of drugs at four and on the street at eleven. Her hope was that she would have a pretty dress to go to school in and that her mom liked her. Her hope was that she would have a birthday party once in her life. She was beaten half to death at the age of fourteen.

Then her final hope was to phone a policeman, John Delano, and ask for help; asking John to come to the end of the lane of an old farmhouse and get her, five minutes before she was knifed in the stomach at the age of twenty-three. Saying, "I have something to tell you."

John had known her all her life and could not protect her for a second. Melon and Luda had grown up in south-end apartments side by side, and may or may not have been cousins. In some ways they looked alike.

John knew that world but did not have to live there. So he had no answer.

Saint Dominic or Saint Ambrose or Saint Augustine might have no answer either—he knew that. Saint Francis might not, or even Saint Jude—but he knew, after solving cases for almost thirty-five years, he had not been able to prevent one murder. And over those years he had dealt with seventy-seven of them.

Still, he felt that sitting here, at the back of Saint Rose of Lima, was every bit as logical as sitting anywhere else in the universe. It was every bit as logical as spinning above the earth in a space station, floating without gravity in a cylinder above the Pacific Islands. He had blood on his hands from solving murders—and he felt unblessed because of the work he did. There was in the human dimension the damned truth: that a man too eager to accuse someone commits the same crime he accuses others of. Self-righteous exposés of man's inequities show the inequity of the self-righteous.

That Saint Paul had said this two thousand years ago did not make it less true, though modern established prophets might say it did.

He left the church and passed a taxi stand on his way back to Matters Road.

Once home he took his mask and breathed oxygen for thirty minutes. Then he slept late into the next day.

He decided to go to the Shaw house again when he woke. There was something more there—perhaps the bag the boy had carried—something to indicate who he was. John felt he might not find everything, but he must find something.

By now red twilight flushed the windows of the Shaw house, and a bit of light filtered through after the snow had stopped.

As he went through the rooms, that feeling of disassociated life overcame him, the kind of feeling you get when you are alone in sudden vast spaces, or when you realize the quiet, or in some building when you hear at late afternoon a door shut far away or a child's call. It was at times like a dream from Marcel Proust—a light under the hallway door.

Farther to the west the great gas fire flew up from the oil refinery stack, and the sun flashed redder, as if annoyed at darkness coming. Here and there were cries of youngsters as if formed from vapours.

He was on the third floor. Two radiators painted green stood on opposite sides of the corridor. He shoved back a door at the far end of the long hallway and it opened soundlessly. A stained mattress sat in the centre of the floor, an old blanket half covering it. He took out his flashlight and shone it into the corners and along the back.

At the very back of the room the closet door was slid open. A Tim Hortons coffee cup lay inside. He went over and shone his light on the shelf and then along the floor. He bent down and picked up a card: Roy's Taxi, 858-0909.

He put it into his pocket. He turned and walked out. It was now dark, and the sound of wind babbled against the building and a breeze came up the stairs and along the hall. He walked back downstairs to the big front room and sat on an old box, staring into the gloom.

He took a spray under his tongue and put the nitro bottle away. He waited for the reaction, and his breathing quieted.

He looked at the fireplace and walked toward it. He then ran his hand along the mantel. That is when he felt it—among some loose plaster—and picked it up.

A grey coat button wrapped in manufacturer's plastic.

It was an extra button, the kind one often finds in the pocket of a new coat.

John went back home and set the card from Roy's Taxi, and the button, on the table beside his library books. He hadn't taken the books back yet. He had three checked out: Carlyle and Lukács and Ernest Buckler. He would take them back tomorrow or the next day. Unfortunately, he had not had time to read them.

He ate his supper in silence, now and then looking up, startled, at the wall.

Then he picked up his cigarettes and put them in his pocket. He fumbled with his white birch cane. And taking a flashlight, he made his way to the Shaw house again.

It was almost seven o'clock.

He walked up the stairs slowly, to the third floor, and found two fireplaces. The first was filled with rags and water. He found a book from the second-hand bookshop lying on the floor: *Pleasure Girls of the Far East.* Two voluptuous, naked Asian girls embraced each other on the cover.

He lit a cigarette and looked out the cracked window down to the street.

He left the room.

The second fireplace was in the second-last back room, with blackened brick encasing it. The room where he had found the mattress, the Tims cup and the card from Roy's Taxi.

This fireplace was filled with wine bottles and beer cans. He bent down and removed the grate and felt through it for three or four minutes, sifting with his fingers slowly, touching the broken glass of a half generation ago, the remnants of some party. After a time, he felt something and picked it out. It had the feel and texture of a photograph. He put it in his pocket. He felt again and found a plastic card holder. He put that in his pocket as well. He kept moving his hand for another ten minutes. There was something round that he felt and it took him a while to grasp it—shining his flashlight to find it again. He put it into his pocket too.

John went back to his rooms on Matters Road. He lay down on the couch and took the small, round object from his pocket and looked at it. He lit another cigarette, and listened to the wind eerily wash over the room. The smoke burned his lungs.

The small, round object was a bright cat's eye marble. He got up and washed it in the sink. It seemed to glow in a sudden splendour—the yellow eye looking out at him from a great distance of both time and space, as if telling him something he didn't quite grasp.

He picked up the card from Roy's Taxi and the Tims coffee cup and looked at both for a long while. Like the book about the pleasure girls, these might have found their way to the Shaw house on the same evening—maybe two weeks before John? John believed the person who had visited the Shaw house was Vernon Beaker, the stepson. And he visited there because of sadness, and guilt.

Then there was the photograph—it had been tossed in the fireplace years ago.

The photo was small. John sat for a time contemplating what he had found. The cat's eye marble, the photograph, the pieces of a child's wallet that someone had tried unsuccessfully to destroy. Perhaps, John thought, the Limey boy had carried this picture in his wallet, and he'd had it on him as a memory of something either happy or tragic. It could be either. If John Delano knew anything about photographs, he knew this. Perhaps it was a picture of the boy himself or of his mother. It must have come from the boy's wallet. But it was a child's wallet—something a boy of thirteen probably wouldn't use. Yet something he would keep mementoes in? In fact John was certain of this now because of the plastic card holders that he had also found. They too came from a wallet. The wallet of a boy who had kept mementoes of some distant place and time. A wallet that he did not use for money, but kept souvenirs from his past life in? But when the wallet was turned upside down at the fireplace, things fell out of it?

So John experimented with his own wallet, took his own wallet from his pocket and turned it upside down, watching how the photo of his own son fell out. And the credit card holder and the medallion of Saint Christopher.

So say the wallet was taken from the coat. Someone opened it, took the money (but John was already sure that the money—the hundred dollars—was in the boy's pants pocket) and turned the wallet over. The boy was older now and put his money or another wallet into his pants pocket. He had held on to his childhood wallet as a keepsake.

Vernon had turned this wallet over twelve years ago. So assuming he did, John decided, the photo fell, and was lost under the brick. The marble fell just like John's own Saint Christopher medal. The trouble with the photo was that time and particles of soot had blackened it—so it had to be carefully cleaned.

When the wallet was turned over, the cat's eye marble fell, clinked and was lost. The photo somehow fell between the grate and did not burn. The cat's eye marble proved that wallet was zippered shut and was not used for currency.

John put the photo and the coat button on the table. He washed the marble again and put it alongside everything else. He took the drawing, and the chalk he had brought from the office days ago, and placed it alongside the rest.

He washed his hands, had tea and toast, something he had had before bed for fifty years, and sat and listened to the news.

"If the picture is nothing, I will give it up," he said. "For it is all just speculation—but if the picture is of someone, or something—?"

So after he butted his third cigarette into the ashtray he flipped the picture over and cleaned it off slowly. He was surprised to see how well that worked.

He stared at it and became dizzy—as if everything went out of focus.

The picture was of a young black boy—about fourteen, standing in a garden near a wall, smiling; there was one arcadia tree behind him, and eucalyptus trees in the distance. John knew both those trees from his time in Rwanda.

The boy had on a white jacket, like a bellboy or a house boy, with a name stitched on the pocket. It was probably midday. When taken? John did not know.

It was now a quarter to nine at night.

He put on his coat and went out, and walked down over the hill to Zellers. He arrived just before it closed.

The store was muted and despairing under the aisle lights, and the music sounded and drifted across avenues of blouses and pants and plastic toys, and a Christmas tree turned solemnly on a wheel in the centre of the floor, enticing both greed and guilt.

When he left, he picked up a stick to help him navigate the wind-swept, snow-swept hill because he had forgotten his cane.

He stared at the glimmer from his kitchen light as he moved. Almost all the rest of the old motel was in darkness.

He got back to his bedsitter a half-hour later, with a small magnifying glass. He took it out of the plastic bag and stared at the picture again.

He could just make out the name stitched on the boy's jacket: Sebby.

Sebby—John wondered. He tried to think of where a name like that would come from. He sat in the chair, moving the damp stick back and forth, wondering about it all. Then he stood and walked into the kitchen.

He was making himself another cup of tea, when he thought of it.

It was, in fact, a Christian name. A saint killed by arrows. Sebastian.

The picture was that of an African boy named Sebastian. And the boy had kept this in his wallet!

Even more ominous were the small flags stuck on the doors of the building behind him that you could just make out. The little Canadian sticker flags. It was a long cement building with six or more windows at the front and a door in the centre. The window shutters were painted green. There was something else. John was sure he had been there—to that very place. In 2004 he had visited the scene of a massacre. The massacre had taken place ten years before then, in 1994.

There had been writing on the back of the photo, but it had long since been washed away. But he knew now what the drawing he found in the coat pocket was—it was a drawing of that cement building. The boy had kept it as a memory. Not of the building, but perhaps of the man who had drawn it. That is, perhaps, just perhaps, of his father.

But here came the speculation that stopped John Delano in his tracks.

It is young Jack Forrest, John thought. Sebby got him out of the village—he was then whisked away to someplace he didn't belong. After a while the authorities determined him to be Canadian, but what if they sent him to the wrong city? Then something happened in that foster home, or he saw something and one night he decided to run the hell away too. Where would he go? To Toronto, believing he might find his mom and dad! Why was that? Well, he looked at the picture of the CN Tower—the tallest structure—he asked if it was—and then said, "I will send you a postcard just like that." So the tallest building meant something—which means he had been given some instruction by his dad or mom on where to go and wait.

Yes, of course, it was all nonsense. He couldn't begin to prove it.

Still, John Delano, as good as he was, could never have imagined how close to the truth he was at that moment.

———

Sue Van Loon, thirty-six years of age, as fine a person as she was, believed John's obsessions were fuelled by bigotry and rage. And perhaps therefore this search.

"Ah—not bigotry, never bigotry," John said once. "But maybe rage."

So John tried to explain these things to her. He told her he knew that if the coat button had come from the boy's coat, someone had had it in their hand when they had come back into the building, after the boy had fallen that long-ago night.

"Why was the wallet not in his jeans?" Sue Van Loon asked.

"Well," John said, "all the pockets were new, and that is why the wallet was in a coat pocket instead of the boy's jeans—because it was a new pocket and the boy felt obligated to put the wallet there and zip it up. Because he was a kid. And these were all new pockets, and he never used that wallet—it was used to keep mementoes."

Sue Van Loon paused a moment. Then she said, "But the ticket was in his hand?"

"Yes, yes, because he was excited and on his way to the station."

"And you believe it was the boy the conductor said he took a ticket from years ago, although you can't prove a thing?"

"Still, I think it proves what I have been saying," John said.

"About what?"

"About everything—the wallet, the ticket, the boy's coat!"

John told her he believed just one person was in charge.

"And who would that be?"

"The dad—Bunny McCrease," John answered.

"Are you sure?"

"Yes," he said, "I am sure."

"Who was the other person?"

"The son—not Bunny's son, but Moms's son, Vernon, who tried to keep the family together, who is decent and kind-hearted, who I believe helped this missing boy open his account at the bank. Bunny's stepson, Vernon Beaker—called Crow by his friends. That is who Melon is protecting. Because he is Melon's only friend."

"I know him. He drives taxi," Sue Van Loon said. "But why then did Melon write the letter?"

"Oh that—well, I have been wondering that too, and have decided on common decency."

7.

THE CASE HAD COME ON THE RADAR OF PEOPLE IN OTTAWA, for they had terribly mishandled it too, and this was badly mishandled well over ten years ago. Now they were not at all sure where this boy had gone to, or if he was even in Canada, dead or alive, but he was supposed to be. This was now revealed to them by a man from Belgium named Lebrun. The boy was supposed to have arrived from Belgium and gone to St. John's, Newfoundland, sometime early in 1999. But there was a problem: No one from immigration back then had followed up, and a day went by and then two and five, and then two weeks and six, and then the matter was laid away and forgotten, because everyone believed the boy was fine. No one reported that he was not fine because no one knew he had been sent to the wrong city. And time passed and he was completely forgotten about.

But the fact was, they now realized the mistake had started in Belgium. From Belgium's end, the person supposed to meet the boy in Canada was thought to have been informed by Canadian authorities at the end of 1998. In Canada, they believed Belgium authorities had informed this man at the same time. An email had come from Brussels to Ottawa on December 29, 1998, when both parties were busy thinking about New Year.

Both bureaucrats, in the two countries, thought the other was responsible for informing the boy's uncle.

Now, suddenly, in both Ottawa and Brussels, the serious mistake had been revealed.

He was supposed to have gone to St. John's, Newfoundland, to live with his uncle, but no one followed up until sometime four months ago, when an inquiry was made by Mr. Drew Pierce, his only relative, who had asked about the case of this child, for he wanted to settle the estate once and for all, and was looking for a court declaration of a death certificate that he had never received. He had asked for it in 2004, during the trials of men involved in the 1994 massacre, when the graves of those murdered had been found, but had not received one.

When they told him a few days ago that the child had been sent to him, and was living with him, and was now twenty-three years old, so was probably finishing up at Memorial University, Mr. Pierce said, "You're a damn idiot—until yesterday I assumed he was dead as a nit. So where is he now? When did he get alive again? Four times I asked for him to be declared dead. Who was I speaking about if not him? I will sue the Canadian government for negligence if he is not found."

"Yes—well, don't get upset. He went to St John's over twelve years ago and is living with you. We were sure he was safe and sound with you. So what we have to know is, are you the correct Mr. Drew Pierce we are talking to?"

"What other Drew Pierce are you talking to, you idiot? Safe and sound with me? I'm eighty-six years old. No one could be safe and sound with me. I'm not safe and sound with myself. Yer a bloody stupid mainland arsehole—he is not here!"

"Well, he went there," Mr. Paul Serone said, angrily now.

But looking into it, everyone realized there was a complete and complex silence. And no one actually knew what had happened to the child.

Finally, thinking of how this might have happened, Paul Serone was approached by a young secretary from the Miramichi region of New Brunswick, and she whispered, "Maybe they might have mixed it up and sent him to Saint John, New Brunswick."

"If that was the case, then why didn't we hear about it from immigration or child services immediately?"

"Perhaps no one knew who he was," the young secretary said.

Finally Paul Serone contacted the department in New Brunswick responsible for child welfare. The person Ottawa contacted was Melissa Sapp—a woman with a $250,000 a year job as provincial watchdog for exploited and abused and abandoned children. (A woman in fact so powerful she was appointed without anyone's approval but the premier's, and acted as a consultant on major human rights cases; being an advocate and a lawyer; considered in many respects untouchable because of the premier's hand in her career—and her own hand in championing his leadership campaign in 2003.)

In fact this special department had come about because of the agitation that had started over John Delano's child some years before. Melissa had used it to her advantage, saying she would never lose a child again. She then backed the premier in his election, knowing she herself was too much of a lightning rod to run. Now some said she had almost as much power as the premier—and of course the rumours were that she was his lover.

She was an activist. And activism is always at its best when pitched against someone else.

Melissa, after two days of searching, replied to Paul Serone by email: No, she was sure the child had not been here. It was never on her watch or she would have handled it. And at this moment, she believed she was entirely correct.

"The poor soul," Melissa said. "Whoever botched this should lose their job. How does that old saying go—heads should roll! They sent him to the wrong city? Well, they contacted no one here if they did." Saint John, New Brunswick, and St. John's, Newfoundland, were continually getting mixed up in people's minds. Especially if those people lived in some godforsaken place like Belgium. At this point Melissa did not know how close she was to one of the people who had fumbled the case entirely—her own husband, the one she berated and loved and took care of, the one she was unfaithful to with the effete premier himself.

John, who knew nothing about this but knew a child had gone missing, went to the provincial department handling social services the following Wednesday.

Mr. DeWold told him they would mail files over to him and he could go through them.

"Nineteen ninety-eight and ninety-nine especially," John stipulated.

John realized he was growing old. Mr. DeWold was younger then he was by twenty years and had the youthful appearance and the strapping gung-ho-ism of a former hockey player who had found his vocation in university. That is, he had discovered social work. It was that wholesome quality that many Canadian men have where the world tells them all their lives what to do, and they feel their way into the job thinking that whatever job they end up in is somehow their special vocation. They are always fresh faced and lively, and for the most part utterly incompetent.

DeWold had played for a major junior team and then for the Saint Mary Huskies.

Yes, he said pleasantly, he had been a fieldworker—that is, a caseworker—for 87 Shelf Street himself, and knew the area well.

"Crosby," John said.

"Hell, I never thought of it like that."

"Did you know back then of a boy with an accent—an accent that sounded English or maybe South African?"

"Hell, they all had some kind of accent," he said. Then he frowned and shook his head and said thoughtfully, "No, nothing like that."

There was one more thing, John knew: DeWold was Melissa Sapp's husband—the one everyone laughed at. The one who had never quite fit in. The one who would have made the pros had he not loved her so much.

"If you remember anything about that house—any of the boys from that time—if you could send me those files. Or give me a call . . ." John said.

—

The next day John sat down at his small kitchen table and began to figure out the money that would be earned by caring for children at 87 Shelf Street. So here is what he came up with:

Maybe six hundred dollars a week for the four children. But this amount had been collected all through 1999, and right up until 2001— and there was no mention of anyone running away. So the department was being charged for the missing boy even after the Limey was no longer there.

John felt the Limey was lost due to incompetence and Y2K. That is, all the computers had been changed over for the new millennium. And so the boy's file may have been lost to a social services overburdened to begin with, and someone, perhaps newly hired, missing this boy as their case.

But who would miss this boy entirely?

He felt sure it must have been Mr. DeWold himself.

That afternoon he went to Roy's Taxi and stood outside the door. Three taxis sat in front of the small, white building; two others were in back. He went inside when only the dispatcher was there and asked her what shift Vernon Beaker was on.

"He comes in at six in the evening," she said. "Works until six in the morning. He makes the airport run too—do you want him?"

"No," John said, "I was just wondering—between you and me—how long has he worked here?"

"Oh, five years now."

"His mom said he had cards come for him here now and again. Does he keep them?"

"Sure—he keeps them all for a while. He got one here just a few weeks ago."

"Well—can I see one? If I can, I just want to check something."

"Will it get him in trouble?"

"No. I swear. It won't even get the person who sent it in trouble," John said.

—

After this, John disappeared for a week. He went to Edmonton, Alberta. Then he flew back on the seventeenth of November, exhausted. He made a point to wait at the airport for taxi number nineteen—Vernon Beaker's. Vernon chose his taxi number after the great defenceman Larry Robinson's number—had the Montreal Canadiens logo on the back window of his cab.

Vernon was small. His face had some small beard. He said since he worked the late taxi shift he was often worried about getting robbed, and had grown the beard to look more fierce. That he never wanted to hurt anyone, but he had to protect himself.

"Do you think it works?"

"A bit," John said. "A little bit. Why can't you sleep at night?"

"How do you know that?"

"Well, you've been on night shift for a long time—so I was just wondering."

"I don't know why," Vernon said.

"And you get cards from Melon—so you must have been very good to him, visited him now and again up at Dorchester when he was there— that was kind of you. He sent one along to you to tell you he got out of jail a few weeks back."

"How did you know that—are you a cop?"

"Yes," John said. "I am—however, I know about not sleeping too."

"You do?"

"Maybe you could read 'A Clean Well-Lighted Place,' " John said.

"Who is that by?"

"Ernest Hemingway."

Before John left for out west, he had received a call from the Bank of Montreal. The account in question had been opened by Vernon Beaker. The last two withdrawals, amounting to $120, were in March of 1999. There was still forty-six dollars in it.

The night he arrived back in Saint John he had the boy's picture with him—that is, a photo of Jack Forrest—taken when he was eighteen months old, holding his comforter. The boy's picture was two feet from

Vernon Beaker as they drove in the taxi that night. A card addressed to Vernon by Melon was in the pocket of John's overcoat too, next to the letter Melon had written about the missing boy.

The writing matched.

That night, alone in his rooms after the last of the traffic died and the sound of people on the street had quieted, John pulled out the drawer on his desk and took out the money Luda Marsh had mailed him two days before she was murdered. It was taped to the bottom of the drawer.

Ninety-five hundred dollars.

Every time he looked at this money, he thought that she must have been phoning him to tell him she had mailed it, and why. But when they had talked that last time, she hadn't said anything about it. She had said, and he had it written down, "You have to come out here. I have something else to tell you." Then she said, "Just a minute—"

But once again, John could not really prove Luda sent him this money or why the money was sent. He had investigated the murder–suicide of Luda Marsh and Bennie Cheval in 2007. Both were dead when John arrived, twenty minutes before any other officer got to the house.

And now he had ninety-five hundred dollars from that farmhouse taped to the bottom of a drawer.

No one knew about this money except one person: Bennie Cheval's sister.

Two weeks after Luda's death, Velma Cheval made a complaint to the police about missing money.

John was asked about this while still at home recuperating from his heart attack. There was no way he could prove he did not steal it, so said he had not seen any money.

The sister, who was with the brand new Constable Trevor, looked at him, enraged.

"You've got it!" she yelled. "You've got my goddamn money—that's why you had your heart attack. You are guilty about stealing the money. You killed Luda and Bennie for the money! You are anti-French."

"Settle down," Constable Trevor said. But she'd looked at John warily. It did seem possible.

"He's got my goddamn money—he's a thief! It was my brother's money. Check the house—the money's missing. Bennie told me where it was!"

But since he did not know whose money it was and suspected it was not hers, he kept it.

He put the envelope back under the drawer. He lit a smoke. He of course knew that the person who had taunted him on the phone about his son was this woman.

For some reason he took out his revolver and checked it.

He woke to the sound of the air brakes of a service truck outside, at seven in the morning.

It was November 19. The air was cold and filled with the smell of gas. The trees were empty, and the ground outside flat with the windows iced in the morning.

It was his son's birthday. He carried in his pocket the picture of his boy when he was in grade one.

"Okay—if you want me to" was the last thing his son had ever said to him. And that stuck in his heart like a knife, today, yesterday and always. "Okay—if you want me to" presented itself to him a thousand ways. And no way it presented itself to him ever freed him from pain. He knew that Saint Catherine had spent the last of her life feeling the cross of Christ pierce her heart. When her heart was removed, there was a part of it shaped exactly like a cross. He knew the legend. And every day at some point his own cross would return. When Sue Van Loon mentioned wicked popes and greed-feasting priests, he never argued. His faith was in deeper things and in greater souls. The faith was much greater than the wicked and the dreadful. It needed to be, now more than ever.

After the boy disappeared, his wife began to spend time in play-grounds and daycares. She went to the schoolyard and would wait on the back steps with his lunch. She would phone the Cub leader and ask if she could enroll her boy. She enrolled him in swimming lessons as well.

Finally, when she began to wrap his Christmas gifts, John grabbed her wrists and told her to stop.

"He wasn't your boy, anyway—you didn't care!" she said perversely with a smile.

A little later he moved away.

Now his wife would phone at odd times. And he would meet her where their child was last seen. Among the foliage and branches of a desperate place. And they would begin to search again. They did this winter and summer. It was all their old friends talked about. That they had gone mad.

They called on a psychic from Nova Scotia, who turned up in a panel truck with astrological symbols hanging from the rear-view mirror and a tape of Eastern meditative chants and the picture of a brahma bull on the passenger side.

"Buddha is the superior Christ" was written on his back window.

But he had no idea where their boy was—though he charged nine hundred dollars.

John began to take pills to cope with being unable to sleep, being without the boy or his wife. And then he couldn't stop. Then he drank and took pills, but it did no good.

"I know who killed him." He would get letters in the mail, just like that. "You did!"

However, his wife was phoning him again, this time about the rim of a bowl.

"I was way up on Loman Otter Road where near the fire was a few years ago. I found this rim off a bowl. I found it in the ditch off Loman Otter Road—rusted. But this is what I know—the rim is from a Camp Fundy bowl. Remember, there was one on every table. At night Gilbert just might have crossed the Loman Otter Road—what do you think? Maybe he went in the other direction and spent until dark collecting pollywogs, and maybe that's where he got lost!"

So there was a spark of hope in that—her insanity instilled in him—hope—for what if it was a Camp Fundy bowl rim—but how did the boy get across the river up onto Loman Otter Road—well, stranger things had happened.

Man can overcome any fate by scorn, Camus said. So John would spend a day and go up there sometime soon, and look at the place where the rim was found. But even this caused his heart to ache—because it meant Gilbert was not with the group of kids but alone—he must have been left behind in the cabin. And why hadn't the children spoken up and tattled that he was not with them, as John believed the kids would have when he had interviewed them all? Because they had not even noticed he was not there.

It struck John that if Jeanie was right and Gilbert was by himself on Loman Road, then everyone thought he had got lost in the woods when in fact he had never been lost at all.

———

Melissa Sapp knew that if a child was known finally to have been lost, it would be best if it was she who discovered what had happened. Melissa Sapp had been thinking this since the call she'd received from Ottawa the week before. She couldn't conceive of anyone worse than John Delano investigating the case of a lost child. In Ms. Louise's mind he had asked his superiors for the case when he had heard about a lost child just to embarrass Melissa's new department. (And Melissa could not imagine that John had heard of this case long before she herself did, or that he did not even know that Ottawa was involved.)

Ms. Louise was Melissa's assistant, and a devoted one. She was sometimes called the Disciple by certain people, who disliked Melissa and the power she now had.

"He is a real prick," Ms. Louise said, unused to using words like that, so it sounded odd and archaic. She wore a pretty pink blouse with a half Elizabethan collar, which made her red hair seem almost historical. But what she said had the ring of some middle-school pronouncement.

Still, at this moment in Melissa Sapp's mind John had invented a bogus child to inflame a case against her new department, and was using the report from Ottawa to do so. "He has it all figured, doesn't he?" she said, looking at her friend's beauty, which was a plain, wholesome kind. Melissa Sapp knew that Ms. Louise was enamoured of her—but so were a dozen men and women. Still, there were other men and women who were false and threatening. One was John Delano. That is, in her mind he became the stickler, the provincial and the chauvinist all in one blink of the eye.

But as she sat in her large, empty office on this cold day, with the shadows playing on furniture she did not like (furniture that suggested that no matter how revolutionary she tried to be, she was what so many others were before her: an overburdened civil servant with a workload that included dealing with many petty mandates), she finally realized what was bothering her. It was her damn husband and his first goddamn case. She looked at Ms. Louise and did not say anything more, but she felt vulnerable about something, non-specific.

She did not know how John had found out about the case from Ottawa, but she was sure he was now using her husband's incompetence against her. She believed that he was doing this because of her involvement in the case that concerned his wife years before.

"All of this just to get back at me—how petty can one be?" she said now to Ms. Louise.

Up until this moment she was actually hoping the missing child had come to New Brunswick and she could solve the mystery. It would be a grand national story—maybe make *Maclean's* magazine.

Still, after Ms. Louise left the office, she phoned Constable Trevor and asked if they could meet.

—

John suspected a meeting about him would happen—almost as soon as he got the letter. He actually prayed for no one he knew to be involved in this case—

It so happened they all were.

And he had been tempted to put the letter aside and not take the case he was now on.

But he could not.

He heard there was going to be a meeting between Melissa Sapp, Melonson and Trevor about some phone call from Ottawa. So John waited at his rooms on Matters Road, putting in time by doing a crossword puzzle.

He never could complete them.

It was the evening of November 20 when the meeting took place.

"And this is the problem," Melissa said, sitting at the long table in the small committee room. "Someone is always in John Delano's crosshairs. Men like him would never get into the RCMP if they applied now. He was following me home two weeks ago, and I wondered why—now I know.

"The case is fantastic because its lie is so transparent. Delano lost a child—he is now blaming us for losing a child. He heard a child might be missing from someone in Ottawa—so he comes barrelling in and deciding what child it was. No wonder morale is low in the police department." She said this with such effortlessness that people suddenly believed morale must be low in the police department.

Then she mentioned the phone call from Ottawa, and she said John must have known of this phone call and had manufactured the entire case around it. This would be the reason he was following her these past two weeks.

In fact all of this seemed absolutely irrefutable after she spoke.

"I am aware of that," Melonson said.

At this moment he had to make it clear, to himself and to everyone, that the case was probably imaginary. Besides which the case was stalled in Ottawa, while people were busy saying they were doing everything they could.

Still the fact that all of them had now reached the same consensus showed just how implausible John's story was, and how his reputation had been sullied for years.

"He has had a heart attack, he lost his child and his wife—one must realize that he is not well," Trevor said.

Melissa told them that when she was younger, she became involved with a simple-minded woman named Jeannie Aube. She was hoping to have Jeannie's pregnancy terminated.

"Good for you," Melonson said, quickly.

"But Jeannie was insistent on giving birth to the child. So then we tried to find the child a decent home. But John had come into the picture and got the child back. Now the child is dead," Melissa said.

Melissa herself had no worries, economically or philosophically. That is, her family was the smaller branch of the Nolan Overplant tree, which meant Melissa was still worth a few million. She had an aunt who was famous, and an uncle who was a senator in Ottawa. She was a lawyer, a human rights activist, an environmentalist and a strident feminist. All the right things to be and the right time to be them.

She owned two heritage houses, one in Fredericton on Church Street and one in Saint John, and she travelled to Fredericton two times a week. John knew of her for years, kept her from being kidnapped when she was a youngster (this was a case that had also involved Midge Nolan Overplant's son). Melissa, however, knew nothing of this.

———

It was cold and dark and there was a slick of ice everywhere. Melon was sitting in his small upstairs apartment, on one of his two chairs, eating a baloney sandwich. Now and again he would speak to his dead sister, Amy, and ask for her help in a prayer. Then he would sprinkle some more pepper on his baloney and chomp down on it and shiver.

If you cast a line out to the west and one to the east, they would make a perfect triangle. Melon was at one corner.

The lines went out to other places that night as well.

In fact these three places, counting Melon's, had three different scenes.

The first was Melonson himself. Melonson knew very well a boy had arrived in the winter of 1999 and had been assigned to him. Melonson was asked to find out who he was and where he had come from by his superior and by an RCMP officer. So Melonson, a city policeman wanting to get into the RCMP and ready to leave the city police force, set about with great officiousness to do as he was asked as quickly as possible. He walked into the room where the boy was seated on a chair. Melonson sat on the desk in front of him and drank from a coffee, looking through a list of papers, which he threw on the desk after a moment. He already believed the boy was Jack Toggle, who had run away—Jack Toggle had run away before so now he had done so again. That was the paradigm Melonson insisted upon proving.

But the boy said he had arrived at the airport and no one had been there to meet him. That they had shuffled him through everywhere else, but when he got to this airport, he was entirely alone. Melonson decided the boy was lying because he had heard Jack Toggle was a liar, that he had lied his way past those looking for him for the past two weeks. So nothing could be more obvious, and he was not going to lie his way out of it this time. The boy said he had been assured everything had been taken care of, yet no one was there to meet him, and late the night before he had wandered into town.

But Melonson did not do the most basic of things. He did not check the airport—though he lied to the boy and said he had. This was the first blush of stupidity concerning the case that was, twelve years later, before them at this moment, both here and in Ottawa.

"Well, I checked the airport and you didn't come by plane," Melonson said. Just like that. And once he said it—and he had said it off the cuff—the first mistake was made, and the first lie in a case with a history of lies was given.

"But I did!" the boy responded, suddenly looking not only worried but flabbergasted. "I came to the airport!"

"What's your name?"

The boy hesitated, and said in a fearful tone that he wasn't sure what his last name was. That he had witnessed something, he was not sure what, and his memory had gone because of it. But that he was called Lebrun in Belgium.

It was what people started calling him and it just stuck. But he was not called that before.

"You were called Lebrun in Belgium—and I was called Santee Claus in the North Pole." Melonson laughed. He shook his head at this inanity. What was worse for the boy, this to Melonson more than proved that his own lie about checking the airport had worked, and the boy was now making up more lies. He loved to gloat over catching people in lies—it was part of the forte of being a bully.

So Melonson knew now he had called the boy John Delano was looking for a liar, and had thrown him headlong into a cell overnight. Suddenly that moment was as brightly revisited and clear and painful as any in his life.

So at ten at night he was looking through his old computer files at home, which he had stored in the basement of his little house on Greenwood Street, and with the light of the computer shining on hard copies of his case files, was muttering that all of this was supposed to have been taken care of by someone else. But nothing he muttered came close to the truth of what he was actually thinking.

A month after he had sent that boy to foster home, the very day he was leaving to go to the RCMP, a call came in to him about a missing boy. A boy named Jack Toggle was now reported to be back living with his sister in Upper Gagetown. Melonson, leaving one life behind for another, never gave it more than a thought.

"Sure," he decided. "That is the boy that little Melon character is talking about."

So then everything had been worked out in his mind, and nothing more had to be done. For in 1999 he would have been a complete laugh-ingstock if he'd believed that boy who had told him he had come from Africa and Belgium was actually from Gagetown.

He stared at his reddish knuckles as he grasped the papers, and his hands shook. He had never in his entire life thought he would be in this position—a position where the truth would diminish him completely. But looking at it from another perspective, and calmer, he could see how his first estimation was right: that he was becoming upset over nothing, and that he had done his duty better than anyone could imagine. So with this he would confront Delano with his own theory within the next few days.

His face was now beet red as he sat back and opened a beer—his first in two weeks.

He was at almost a complete triangulation to our Melon Thibodeau, at this moment shaking out some pepper on his little baloney sandwich.

And of course, we might follow the third line to Melissa Sapp's home five miles away.

At Melissa Sapp's house, along a row of huge three-storey wooden houses set a little back among oak trees, and with a wide veranda, only one light was visible. On the veranda was a bronze plaque stating that the house had been built by future Father of Confederation Justice High Sheriff Fuller, in 1846, and that Sir John A. Macdonald, future first prime minister of Canada, had stayed here on his visit to Mr. Fuller in 1864.

Now, almost 150 years later, in the upstairs den Melissa and her hus-band sat, saying nothing. She knew something. She knew her husband had missed the house on Shelf Street, and had probably missed the child. This was the shoe she had been waiting to drop—this was the moment she had dreaded.

One of two houses he was to go to, for God's sake. Worse, she had used her influence to get her husband that case. But she also realized this: It was her no-nonsense attitude toward others that made her vulnerable if her husband's mistake became public. She'd had people fired for less.

The stereotypical roles of men and women were reversed in this couple. DeWold had just been given proof of his wife's affair with the premier—that effete fellow who could perform like a ballroom dancer—so DeWold thought about him. And though nothing was said about the affair between them, Melissa knew he knew—or at least he knew the rumour.

"The boy he was looking for was killed in 2005—so it is not at all the missing boy from Africa," DeWold now said.

"How in Christ do you know that?" Melissa asked, sitting forward eagerly.

"Because—because I looked it up. I can have the document couriered over to the police if you want. A boy we had, named Jack Toggle, was killed in a car accident. That is probably who case number 97817 at Shelf Street was." Then he smiled. "So don't worry about it! The two cases aren't the same."

But you can say "don't worry about it" and more—that is, you can say that you will protect someone, but then inflamed by jealousy you keep doing things that ruin yourself, your wife and both your reputations. Melissa knew this. A change had come over DeWold. Not the change that happened irregularly when she said something unkind about him in front of wise people. But a different, harder change. He had been stupid enough to think he had been important enough that the premier was his friend. But the worse and more devastating crime was how Melissa had allowed him to think this as well. Now he had heard it was his wife who the premier actually liked, and the premier thought little or nothing of him at all.

He thought of this as he looked at her. He had been the premier's friend, and he had liked to tell people that he was.

"I am not very bright," he said, "and I've got you into trouble—but I am working my best to get you out of it."

She looked at him and smiled. Then she took his hand a moment.

"Guess where I was today?" he said.

"Where?"

"Saint Rose of Lima Church," he said.

"Oh." She looked a little dazed. "Well, there you go—church—what an odd place to go to."

"Well, it gave me time to reflect. And I was thinking how, a few years ago, during one of those makeup games we had for charity, the premier was coming across the blue line and had his head down—I could have stepped into him, knocked him cold. Of course I stepped out of the way—it was my duty to do so. For I was a great hockey talent and he never was—he was just my friend, who I believed was the smartest, kindest person I knew. And I often thought my kindness would be someday repaid."

———

Two days later Delano was brought into the station, into room nineteen—a small, overheated room at the back of the second floor, overlooking the graveyard, its stones today glimmering in the sunlight. He had been asked to bring in all the proof he had with him. So he sat with a small garbage bag outside the office for a number of minutes, while Trevor and Melonson spoke, and then he was asked in. In every department, in every place of work and in every meeting place, people know when they are outside the mark, outside the general concurrence of things. John Delano's career had taken this turn by 1995 and he had never managed, even with the famous cases he had managed to solve, to regain his footing.

So he went into the small conference room knowing this. And knowing, as they looked over his evidence, something was developing in the case that was out of his hands.

What was out of his hands was a couriered document from social services, saying the boy from 87 Shelf Street, one Jack Toggle, had been killed in a car accident in 2005 at the age of twenty-two. That the case was now closed, and any further attempts to insinuate dereliction would cause litigation from the Shelf Street family and child protection services.

So that was that. He knew he would find himself in an argument. He did not know this would happen. Be told his case was rubbish, and find that the very evidence he had gathered would be used against him. That is, Melonson was no fool and could see through John Delano's case. He did not want to—he respected the older man too much— but now was time to set all these things straight.

So now he laid out his response.

For to him, the marble was a non-starter—it could have come from a wallet or a coat pocket.

Perhaps—or as Melonson maintained, smiling slightly—it could have been left there by a hundred students at any time, or by a seven-year-old boy.

The coat may have been burned to hide evidence. Sure. Or it, as Melonson maintained, could have been burned as a joke one night when kids were rowdy and drunk. And that in fact was the more logical explanation, wasn't it?

The bit of wallet. Sure, it could have been thrown in the fire to cover up a crime. Or could have at some different time, as Melonson stated, been tossed in the fire by a kid who had just bought himself a new grown-up wallet.

The picture of Sebby?

Well, yes. But—well, here's the damn thing, isn't it—and this is what many would say—why didn't the picture burn? And who would not have checked to see if it did burn or not?

So then it could have been lost under a brick, which protected it from fire and brimstone, as John maintained. Or—it could have been a trick by some police officer who had travelled to Rwanda, who badly wanted to solve a case from his past and blame his past enemies because of the death of his own child. Not, Melonson said, that he himself would say this, but that other, more disreputable people might.

"Not us, but people who have long held something against you. It would all come out—your trips to Rwanda, your endless research about the genocide, your search for that family, the loss of your own child. The stalking of Melissa Sapp. And all of a sudden there's the case of this boy. I mean—where would your pension be?"

John stared at Melonson and Trevor as Melonson said this. And Melonson shrugged. "It is not what I say," Melonson said hurriedly, "it is what other people are already saying—and what they will say if you persist. Melissa Sapp is already hearing what you are saying, and is worried people might think you are saying it just to get back at her. She herself is unmoved one way or the other. She only wants the truth. The child is her concern too. Therefore I wanted to show you how your reasoning could be skewered, so much so that it would be laughed out of any court of law. All our reputations would be in for it if I did not bring this up now. A boy got on a train? A piece of wallet was found? A marble? That's all I can say about it now." Melonson said this with quick certainty, as if John was in the wrong about something grave. And that John knew he was in the wrong about something grave. There was the sense that finally being the superior officer made him look at all of this with greater clarity, that he had listened to John's theory, carefully reviewed it and now finally had a response.

He felt powerful, for his analysis of the case was indeed pretty astute. Even John knew this. It all could have happened like Melonson said. Melonson now reverted to the trick he and countless other officers always used—and the trick was this: There was a good reason for John Delano to have done this, or a less-than-good reason—and Melonson was hoping John made these mistakes because of a good reason, not a bad or calculated one. The good reason was simply that John was overzealous and had obfuscated the wrong way.

Then Melonson told him not to bother 87 Shelf Street again—for no boy was ever reported missing from that house, and no one they knew of ever resembled anyone from Rwanda. That the McCrease family certainly had a right to privacy from the police or anyone else. And, Melonson said, he knew as well as most it was tempting to try to solve a big case for Ottawa because of the prestige—but prestige never mattered to good policemen. Melonson said that yes, he too had once or twice been tempted to make more of a case then he should have—but professionalism had stayed his hand.

"Rwanda, John," Trevor said quietly, "is why you took a leave of absence before."

"Well—yes, you are both right, of course. But was there any boy here that the SS" (here he used his name for social services) "or the police could not identify?"

"No one that we know of," Trevor answered.

"No one we know of—but someone we might not know of." John smiled. "Someone who ever said—well, who said that he came from the airport. Maybe someone was supposed to pick him up on a January night long ago. He was perhaps sent to the wrong city? I mean anyone like that?"

John knew what Melonson said might be true as well—if he himself was wrong. But if he was right, then he could not stop. And he had been following Melissa Sapp only because of information that she was going to be assaulted.

He said nothing about any of this, of course. No one would believe him—even if he suddenly said that she might have been assaulted. They would simply say he was fabricating it.

Still, he should have asked a policewoman to help with Melissa. He did not. For the letter came and got in the way.

The one thing Melonson did not do is command John to leave his evidence with them. So when they left the room, he picked it all up and took it home again.

John went home, made himself supper and suddenly felt the need for oxygen. He turned on the tank, and breathed quietly.

Goddammit, he thought.

———

"How many people think you are on the right track?" his psychiatrist asked the next morning when he told her about the social worker DeWold and the caseload, and the probability that a mistake was made at the very outset.

"Pretty well no one at all," John admitted.

So Sue Van Loon told him he had returned to blaming his old enemies again. "That is," she whispered, "all your old enemies! From New York onward."

He shrugged.

"Well, maybe that is why they are my enemies," he said, almost asked. He gave a startled look and then smiled. "I don't dislike them—but Melonson's wife, Judy, did not give my son enough stars on his scribblers."

"But you have so many," she said.

"So many stars?"

"So, so many enemies."

"No—not really?" he asked, with complete innocence.

"You go to the press or anywhere else, they will accuse you of making it all up."

John shrugged. "I know."

"So you know that's what people will say—what the papers will say, what everyone will say."

John took a hit of nitro. She had never seen him resort to this before.

"Almost certainly they will, yes!" he said.

"And you might die?"

"I might—yes, I have thought of that."

"Well then!" she said, as if the thought of dying would make him stop—when in fact to stop was to die anyway.

He told her he had gone to Saint Rose of Lima and prayed for an answer to this case, when he had discovered who it was he might be looking for.

To take the cup away from his lips.

"Take the cup away from my lips," he whispered.

"That's what you prayed for?"

"Yes."

"So you do not pray for your own boy?"

"No."

"Why?"

"I don't deserve to."

"You don't deserve to."

"No," John said, "I do not deserve to. I was away when I should have been at home. I caused his death—"

"But that's not true at all. What I mean is, you never caused his death—it was an accident. No matter what people say, you have to realize it. He ran into the woods and was never found—that happens to children every year in this goddamn country. That is what I have been trying to help you with."

"That's not what my prayers tell me. My prayers hold me culpable. My ghosts won't leave me be."

"You believe the world is made up of spirits who can help you?"

"Oh yes—ghosts too. Ghosts are different than spirits—spirits have freed themselves. Ghosts, as yet, have not."

"Well, I am sorry to hear that, John —they will laugh you right out of a court of law."

"Why should you be sorry? They are my spirits, my ghosts. And in the end my court of law."

Sue Van Loon paused a moment, and then said, "But what if Detective Melonson is right? As he told you, any of these things could have come about in some innocent way. All of it is explainable just in the way he says it is. It makes perfect sense to me."

"I know that. He is right."

"He is right?"

"Well, in so far as any of these things could be explained away and they make sense to you. And they are explaining them away because—I am now sure—they need to. They need to explain away what they have been trying to hide. They did not know they had to hide it until three weeks ago."

But then he said, quite out of the blue, "I became sure I was right when I went to church."

"Why—because you prayed?"

"No—not because I prayed! But because I saw DeWold there, praying. DeWold has now remembered—he has committed no great transgression, yet he too has eaten of the tree of good and evil and is no longer free."

There was a long pause. John sat there quietly blinking.

"So who is this family," Sue finally asked, "that this imaginary boy came from?"

He told Sue Van Loon this: They were exactly the kind of people Sue Van Loon would get along with. A young man and woman with a child bringing what they believed was their modern understanding to a far-off land—and they must have believed in the idealism of the father—the father must have been an idealist in some way—or an adventurer, perhaps—bound up with the love of his job, and the idea that things could be improved. So many Canadians were so fashionably willing to improve the world.

"Don't you think that is true?" he asked.

"What is that?"

"So many Canadians are so fashionably conscientious. I saw them in New York, first-hand. They were so conscientious. And proactive—I guess that's the word." He was serious, his face puzzled a second. He'd had that serious look since he had tried to study and become part of the world. He remembered himself sitting in class with children half his age—his seriousness gave him away, almost always. He was so comical to the youngsters he had studied with. Working on things like the Trojan War.

"I would like to write about Achilles's response to Hector," he would say.

The youngsters tittered and made jokes behind his back. He heard most of them—some of them were quite funny.

She did not answer. She almost never answered those direct questions.

"Or fashion conscious," he continued. "We would wear haute couture—and the same day don masks and burn police cars, smash windows, light fires on cue, have havoc and student unrest as if we were regulated by a need for world approval—from the US. The Occupy Movement this year was like putting on the latest wardrobe—shouting the latest slogans, being in the right place, waxing enthused about nothing, having the world of the internet say we too finally mattered—saying we needed an end to capitalism, while eating a Big Mac and carrying a gas can. On the CBC they held our Occupy Movement as a force, waxed enthused about it. That is, it validated all they believed about themselves from the sixties—but of course no Occupy Movement would get past all the security on Front Street."

"So it was about nothing?"

"Oh yes—destruction and meanness and fire are always about nothing at all."

"Are you sure of that?"

"Yes—pretty sure. Well, mostly sure."

"That is a very cynical view."

"Yes, it is—but just because the word *cynical* is used does not mean the view is false."

"But about this case. This boy. What if no one believes you?"

"Oh, that's all right—I have spent half my life with few, if any, believing me. In and out of classrooms. But think of it this way: A boy comes in the night. He was sent by plane and comes to the wrong city. No one is here to meet him. Worse, no one is informed anywhere that he is coming. And it is dark and winter when he arrives. That was the initial mistake, not here but in Ottawa—some memo given to someone and simply forgotten about. No one is informed.

"Melonson is a city cop and has nowhere to put him—he is also a bully—worse, he is a bully with authority over children. So what does a cop do? He has two choices: He can check out the boy's story, plainly or truthfully; or, succumbing to his own self-infatuation, his own whimsy, he can put the boy in a cell for vagrancy. And within a millisecond, he decides on the second option. And that in so many ways condemns the boy to perdition—unless he escapes. And I am praying he escaped.

"But you see, DeWold is now also in a terrible bind—I realized this when I saw him at church. His wife does not love him, and he is trying to be a good social worker. She gave him his first case. What will this do to her career in the end? He doesn't give a damn about his career, but what will this do to his wife's career? And, you see, he does not want to appear like a complete fool."

"You are certainly passionate about all this—but are you right?"

"I do not know yet—I don't know if I will ever know."

"Are you being self-pitying here?"

"Yes—I think so. I mean, of course."

"And what are you going to do now?"

"I am going home to supper."

But then there was this other case. And he had it in his crosshairs too, and knew he would have to deal with it. It plagued him. It was, as they say, on the back burner, but it certainly felt like it was not.

In fact, anyone less honourable than he was might have used this other case—the case of Fern Hershey—to truly rehabilitate himself in the eyes of others. But those who know honour—like Sue Van Loon— would know why he could not.

———

It was a grey house set back from the road, a small house with a front porch. The curtains were off green and potted plants hung in the windows. And in the foyer was a picture of Ms. Hershey and her daughter, Jane, who was now back home at thirty years old. In the picture she was sitting on a pony and Ms. Hershey was holding the reins. Jane's father was never a part of their lives.

Jane's graduation picture was on the foyer table.

And beyond that, there was a nice, quiet living room with a glass door that opened into the dining room, and two loudly ticking clocks, and it was seven at night.

So Jane Hershey was sitting in a straight-backed chair near the fireplace. And a nice fire was burning and snapping sparks at certain intervals. Her mother was now dead. She had died of breast cancer. Oh, there was going to be an honour for her and a dinner that had been postponed many times over the past few years—Melissa Sapp was to see about it, of course.

But Ms. Hershey had died and no dinner. She had been forgotten by her former protege, Melissa Sapp.

This is what Jane mentioned.

A woman like her mother, who gave her life for social services. One hundred thirty-eight kids she had rescued over the years.

Brought out of scalding places at night—walked gauntlets of shrieking, debilitated parents, and was spit upon. Given a bloody nose, and had her hearing damaged in 1988. And now Jane, her daughter, was on her own and hoping to adopt a child. This is what she told John. She was not hired by social services, though she too had studied. She blamed Melissa Sapp for a good deal of it all. John pretended he did not know this. At least, pretended he did not know for a time.

"Melissa Sapp destroyed my family," Jane said. "She is evil. I know we are not supposed to say that—and you might not believe in evil—but I think she is quite evil."

She asked her visitor—it took her four times to get his name— DeLanO, is that it? Yes, that is right, John said, smiling slightly at this final mispronunciation, in a self-deprecating way—was it fair that her mother was cast like a stone against the sky, dropping into a pond of water to drown alone?

That was exactly how she expressed it.

John nodded, noncommittal, then asked how she liked living back in the house of her mother. Yes, it was hard on her. He asked if she had known some of the people her mother had helped. Those who were from the lower depths she spoke about, those affronted and befuddled ones, affected by drink and violence, who had set out upon the world in a different way.

"Oh yes, I knew more than a few," she answered. "Some of them are my friends. I see them at the market on Saturday. I give some of them a few dollars now and again."

So John asked her some more questions, fielding them as brightly as possible—that is, with energy and good humour—mentioning many people that he knew as well—even the old man, the Toggle uncle, who gave her mother the broken nose. Yes, he is gone now, John said, rezoned into the heavens and at rest, hopefully; he spoke of this before zeroing in on someone. That is, she felt he was after a name, and wanted her to supply it.

But John knew the name—and all the names. And it was now raining outside and the air was filled with flapping wind and the slight scent of smoke backing up in the chimney. Then, after about a quarter of an hour, he mentioned Roland Roady. Then he mentioned Velma Cheval, Roland's girlfriend.

"Yes," Jane said, "I've heard of them. They were my mother's case—Velma Cheval, that was her name. So, yes. She had a hard time—I heard she was incarcerated in Ontario for a while."

"Yes," John said. "Velma!"

Jane tossed her head and looked at the small golden statue her mom had received for her thirty years of work. Thirty years of trudging out after dark into the half-lit streets of the south end, and her daughter waiting alone in terror, only hoping for her return—and the return coming often so late the terror remained.

The statuette was like the Madonna and child, but it was a social worker and a young girl—service without prayer, as Mother Teresa called it. John thought of this fleetingly.

John then said, "I would like you to tell me if you went to the Canadian Tire store on October 14."

"I hardly ever go," she said. "On October 14?" she repeated.

But suddenly she turned as though she was reaching for something—she was reaching for her mother's picture, and realizing something dreadful about this meeting.

In fact she dropped the picture, and as John picked it up, she got up and changed her chair to one farther away from the fireplace.

"Yes," John said, turning to look at her, and carefully replacing the picture. "I think that was the day—October 14."

"I am not sure. Why?" Jane asked. She had a long face, and a red blemish on her chin, and was wearing a green turtleneck sweater and a plaid skirt. She had little jewellery on, as if her face made jewellery deceitful. She looked like a painting, called *Unmarried Woman*, from the 1960s.

She had short brown hair. Everything about the evening was somehow conditioned by the rain battering the porch windows and the small fire. And this made her realize, like the sudden, dark shadow that entered the room, that she was caught suddenly, within the paradigm of blame—and she could no more escape it than she could fly straight up in the air and disappear like a spark.

So she now finally knew what his visit was about: It was not about her mother's cases—some forlorn child swept up in the sea, as she had led herself to believe. No, it was about her.

And as with all the guilty, she tried to direct the conversation—away from the inquiry and onto other topics. She spoke of her mom's last days and how Fern Hershey's own mother, her grandmother, was now eighty-eight years of age and still going strong.

Although John listened politely and patiently, he made sure the conversation remained focused on the fact that she bought a tire iron and left it in her Mazda on Front Street across from the marketplace on October 14 on that crisp day with the sunlight on the gold window frame of a new-fashioned restaurant—and that this was what his visit was actually about. And now, in the same spirited manner—the kind of spirit that truth always has—John was talking about Mr. Roland Roady, a degenerate. It was a hard word for John to use, he admitted. But getting mixed up with him was, he said, "bad policy."

It was, in fact, the worst thing Jane could have done, the gravest error she could have made in her life.

"I believe, though no one would say this, that Velma Cheval—Bennie Cheval's sister—is quite . . . well, as you said, evil. Velma and Roland live together."

"Evil." She looked at him, and said this almost as a plea.

He answered, as always, quite straightforwardly. "You hired Velma to harm Melissa in some way," he said. "I mean, to hit Melissa. You may not even have believed you did until it was happening—but even so, you cannot do those things. Velma told Roland and asked for three hundred dollars. Velma is constantly at the tavern. Now, you might think men brag and gossip in places like that, but at the Union Street Hotel it is a woman— and that woman walks with a brace on her right leg and is named Velma Cheval, a murderer—I believe she would have blackmailed you for years. In fact she was going to demand that Mazda you left the tire iron in."

"Tavern?" Jane said, almost mortified. "Murdered who? When? I don't remember."

John said, "No. I think you were half in a daze to do what you did. Still, Roland went to the tavern to get drunk, and bragged about what he was hired to do—and worse, said that someone important had hired him. I heard about it on the seventeenth of October—so it doesn't take long to get back to the police."

Here John looked at his notes for a moment, as if the last part of the conversation was incidental and he was trying to decipher the timeline. "Velma is the sister of Bennie Cheval. Do you know who they are?"

"I think so," Jane said.

"She would never be satisfied with a mere three hundred dollars," he said, continually looking through his notes; and then looking up at her, almost startled, he concluded, "She would end up making you pay three thousand to keep it quiet. She would have taken the Mazda, and the worst of all is she would have started visiting your house. She would be friendly, even compassionate, insinuate herself into your life and take whatever she could from it."

"But she ruined my mother's life. She was Mommy's best friend. She just tossed her away."

"Who?"

"Melissa. Then she kept putting the dinner off."

"What did she do to ruin your mother's life?"

"No one would care how she did it—it's just that she did it. Mom thought Melissa was her best friend—and then when Mom got sick, she was never there. But it's her!"

"Who?"

"Melissa—it's her. Don't you see it's her!"

By now, John noticed, she was crying; tears were running down her face. She sat there looking at him as he made his notes.

"Am I going to jail?" she said.

He suddenly smiled, in spite of the seriousness.

"I don't know, Jane—I am not yet sure."

For some reason he wrote down Sue Van Loon's number and gave it to her.

Then he left the house. He walked along the little avenue down toward the docks of Saint John. And there for a long while he stared at the water. There was oil on the water and the night was bitter.

If he said he was not stalking Melissa but trying to protect her—and the woman and man he implicated, Roland and Velma, were the very people who maintained he had stolen money from them; were family of Bennie Cheval, a man they accused John of falsely arresting—no case would come to trial. Two days before, he had gone to Velma's small convenience store (the same one Melonson stood beside when he spoke to Melon) and told her what he suspected. She simply yawned and smiled, her leg with the brace thrust up on a chair. She said it was nonsense— she had never heard of Jane Hershey.

"Make sure you remember that," he said.

"Remember what, dar-o-lin'?" she asked

"That you have never heard of her," he said.

He now took the note about Roland Roady and tore it up.

———

John packed a suitcase and left town for four days.

The door to his room on Matters Road remained closed.

Then, four days later, the door was unlocked at midnight and Delano came back in.

Exhausted, he sat in the big chair beside the window and stared at the imitation pine wall, and all of the evidence he still had placed on the table.

He lit a cigarette and thought the case over.

Still as he was drifting off to sleep, he thought of other cases.

Of all the cases that plagued him, the case of the little girl who was murdered might have been the worst. He had been the lead investigator on that case. For three days the police could not find the child. When they did, she was cut up in a garbage bag behind a house near a ravine. She was one of the many little causalities of life—she was Melon's sister.

She had a red whistle that Melon had attached to her wrist, and a Mickey Mouse wristwatch, and a plastic purse with "Amy" on the front. The purse was lying beside her. In the purse was a half stick of Juicy Fruit gum and a hairpin. Melon had shared his last stick of gum with her.

Some police said even cavalierly, if she had been born just two houses away from where she was born, this might never had happened to her. Her mother had died in provincial hospital and her father was gone. The two children were living in an upstairs apartment with an aunt who locked them inside when she went out drinking. A couple lived downstairs in a small apartment at the back. That is who the suspects were. But there was no way the police could prove anything. Their names were Velma Cheval and Roland Roady. They moved away a month or so later. Velma had short black hair and walked with a brace. They went to Toronto and lived for a while on Parliament Street. Then one day in 2005, John noticed Velma in a convenience store in the south end.

Melon had saved his bottle-collecting money to get Amy the whistle and the Mickey Mouse watch. He kept walking back and forth saying, "Have you seen Amy?" He asked everyone on the street and then went to find his aunt. She was at the Union Street Tavern. He came home, and sat at the kitchen table for a long while, waiting for Amy to come in.

Later he was sent back to the foster home. And after that he started lighting fires.

John, of course, had many cases, a few of them quite a bit like this. He had tried to get a timeline on the child and on Velma—but just didn't have enough information. Still he went over it in his mind, almost every day. He hoped and prayed a DNA sample would come, sometime.

He thought about the idea that if women were more powerful, it would automatically make others safe. This was perhaps the greatest falsehood in the world.

———

There was no mirror in John's apartment on Matters Road. Sue Van Loon had bought him a mirror, but as yet it was still in her office. That is how he got to meet her. He had covered all the mirrors in his former apartment near Grand Lake. But one morning, waiting for his toast to pop and seeing his reflection in the toaster, he picked the toaster up and threw it through the window.

The toaster hit the top of Sue Van Loon's Toyota. When he went outside to apologize and offer to pay for the damage, she handed him her card, and said, "You might come and see me someday."

After he was evicted from his apartment, RCMP detachment told him he had to seek some counselling.

"Sure," he said.

And one day two months later, he was sitting in her waiting room, without an appointment.

PART TWO

PART TWO

1.

In March of 1994 Harry Sabota was sitting in a large room off one of the offices where Canada's special envoy, whom Harry had nicknamed the Lion of Justice, was almost never in. Harry was waiting to speak with the envoy about money for measles vaccinations, money for mosquito nets. And poor Harry was hoping to find a way into Canada, where he would remain anonymous. He wanted to go to New Brunswick, where John was from, though he had never heard of it before and did not know what it was like. He asked John if the winters weren't too, too bad. He asked this because things between him and the Rwandan ambassador had come apart in the past few months, and now Harry was a moderate Hutu on the outs.

"Are there many grizzly bears?" he asked.

"There are quite a few roaming around," John said. Then, seeing the fearful look on Harry Sabota's face, he said, "But not in New Brunswick."

The mosquito nets and malaria pills had all been promised weeks and weeks before. That is, the idea of foreign aid was a very grave matter to the special envoy, and he always promised it unconditionally.

"But there are problems in our country too," Midge Nolan Overplant assured Harry with a knowing look.

Harry Sabota listened to all of this with bemused and sometimes astonished tolerance. The problems of their little province and even of their big, pink-coloured country seemed somewhat removed from Rwanda with its foreboding.

Still, with his degree in business and his understanding of foreign currency, Harry had inestimable credentials. He kept trying to get permission to trade large amounts of Rwandan currency to offset the economic collapse of his country, hoping to bolster his Rwandan franc, which was approximately three hundred to the Canadian dollar. But such trading was considered unorthodox and speculative, and he could not get it started. Still he felt it would bolster a Rwandan economy and help long term, and perhaps if both Hutu and Tutsi regulators were on board create unity through joint economic stability. Of course, as always, it was an unreasonable pipe dream. So, like much else that he tried, it withered and died on the vine. And each time something died on the vine he was put further on the outs, and made more and more redundant. But the fact was, like some office drone who still hung on to his position, he had been redundant from the time he'd arrived.

Still he kept telling people his credentials, traversing through the halls of the UN and the World Health Organization. He told people these things because he didn't want them to think he was an ingrate. And of course he was not.

But what had started in great optimism now could not be done, because of the fear that the money he needed from the Belgians, Canadians and the French would somehow go to aid the Tutsi rebels, who Harry Sabota was now secretly being accused of supporting, by the Rwandan ambassador. So our Lion of Justice did not want to be duped by a man willing to funnel arms. (How astute the Canadians could be. They often said no to what was valid, and yes to what was invalid, with a shake of their heads.)

So, little pills for malaria, and mosquito nets, were not forthcoming. They would be, of course, but not at this moment. The Rwandan ambassador, fearing Sabota had actually complained about him at the Canadian consulate, worked secretly against it. So even though Rwandan children might die, there was certainly a precedent for such hesitation, and the

Rwandan ambassador chose to exercise it. The Rwandan ambassador often wore a flower in his lapel and gave parties at his luxury apartment on Thirty-Ninth Street.

Harry was despondent that day at the consulate, waiting in the outer office. He could get no answer from anyone about anything. And he clung unceremoniously to Midge Nolan Overplant, who was restive and wanted him gone, so continued to make excuses about where she herself had to be.

It was the first time Harry had a look of genuine concern in his eyes. And when Midge left, he said to John, "Marky, my good boy, there is madness in the wind—and now we will see what happens. Where are the pills I need?" And then he spoke about the devaluation of his country's currency, not only now but from the time of the Belgian occupation in the 1950s. It seemed to Harry that disease and pestilence and murder surrounded them all, but in an ethereal way as his colleagues delved into shrimp cocktails and complained about the infringement of rights because of new smoking laws.

Harry Sabota had flown into and out of Rwanda three times in the past six months, always looking more and more concerned about something indefinable; something in the nature of man he had once believed was gone—some irrevocable sin he thought we had diminished or conquered within our own natures now rearing its ungodly head. He spoke of two little ones, a six-year-old girl holding a three-year-old boy's hand, bringing him to an orphanage in the hope of getting the younger child food. She promised if they gave her brother some, she wouldn't take any for herself.

He had tears in his eyes.

"What will happen to us?" he asked.

His business degree—he was a great champion of safaris into the mountains to see gorillas—seemed to leave him spent and hopeless, without a vision for the new reality. Economic principles had been diluted and in their place had come certain horrific revelations. And yet he said, truthfully, "Most of the people are just like you and me."

The young African Canadian writer entered, wearing a new, bright-red scarf, beautiful fitting black gloves and his all-weather coat, opened recklessly. He had just missed Midge Nolan Overplant. They had the kind of relationship that relies on mutual pandering. Both accepted it.

He was lingering in New York because he wanted to find the right literary agent. All of a sudden he felt his work was too broadly focused for Canada.

Now someone important from one of the dinner parties he'd attended at Princeton had just called him a genius for "telling it like it is." Our young writer had never been outside his upper-middle-class neighbour-hood in Ontario before, and so fit exclusively into Princeton quite well.

He seemed exuberant. And Harry congratulated him on his impressive victory. For Harry knew that as a gentleman it was important to celebrate victories not your own.

Four days later John was on a plane himself—two of the people he was responsible for were flying into Rwanda to have a meeting. John was with this Canadian contingent, simply as a police officer, and people treated him with the familiarity they sometimes reserve for people who are kind and dull and would know very little. Maritime Canadians often got treated like this, and usually ignored it. Or they got treated in another way: with unbounded and superior familiarity by outsiders, like bounders might treat a peasant while flirting with his wife. Treated as the kind of people who were not as intellectually astute as you were but you could use as pleasantly brief acquaintances, and access their rustic stories to tell others when you went back to the real world.

John also knew very well who he was looking for during that desperate time.

The husband was an engineer, from the University of Edmonton; his wife, a schoolteacher. They were north of Kigali in a compound—and the husband was responsible for feeding electricity into the villages and protecting the grid, which was shut down when the genocide started.

He was the last of the Shaw family—the grandson of Winston Shaw, the great-grandson of Herbert, who had a portfolio in a New Brunswick government cabinet in 1914. His name, however, was Forrest—Hugh Forrest. This is what John had found out in the past fifteen years.

John had never given up on him, and never forgot the fact that people said the son, the little boy, had never been accounted for when they exhumed the skeletal remains.

A note came back from Rwanda in 1995 saying there was a Canadian family who were casualties, had died in the uprising in 1994. Probably in April of that year. But it also said there was no real proof this was the Forrest family. No definitive proof. Some years later external affairs said they would declare the Forrest family dead because the last living member of the family, an Uncle Pierce, wanted to see about the estate.

"But where was the boy?" John inquired at least twenty times in the next eight years.

"Well," the people at external affairs said, "he would be dead as well—all of them were killed in and around the compound—it was pretty grue-some—no one got to them for over seven weeks. The placed reeked of death. The bodies were hacked apart and burned. They were all buried in the mass grave near there—there is a marker there today."

They were all officially pronounced dead, except the boy, because no skeletal remains of a boy his age had been found. Mr. Hill, the mayor, was charged with helping incite genocide—he was convicted at his trial.

John always believed the boy was still alive and that he had a legacy to obtain—perhaps three million dollars; that the boy was alone in the world and would not know this.

The father, Hugh, with his whimsical attachment to positive energy, must have believed in the world, or his part in helping solve some of its problems; and the mother must have been devoted to the father, or at least to the idea that they could do something to better mankind.

This is what John discovered: Hugh had his master's in electrical engineering and had an errant love of mechanics. Then one day, out of the blue, he decided to help better mankind. He had begun to talk to his friend Tim Wasson, who was studying environmental politics at the university back then, and who his wife did not trust. But Hugh listened to him speak of terrible situations in the world, and the hardships of people in those places.

"Yes—well, someone should do something," Hugh had said. "Will you help me find a way to make a difference?"

"Oh, of course," Wasson said, in a lighthearted, attractive manner. "Of course. I am willing to do whatever it takes."

Hugh ran home and told his wife this, that very night.

But yet it came almost as a whim, a bright, almost obsessed look in his eyes. And it seemed as if he simply needed to give up his tenure and set out to someplace else. It came as a complete shock to everyone who had ever known him, and to his young wife most of all. She sat at the kitchen table listening to him, in mute silence, her eyes wide.

The idea of bettering mankind overcame him. It was always somewhat of a fashionable idea—so there was always a lie thought to be attached to it. The inherent naïveté of it was what galled so many people. But though it galled so many, it no longer galled John—and though he knew the naive were dangerous to both themselves and others, though he knew all this, he could only ascribe his understanding of these people, so far, as one of sweet sadness.

Hugh told his faithful wife he now championed the idea of helping mankind through electric circuits. He was determined to organize the building of transformers and a power grid in Rwanda.

They probably had the support of people much like themselves, those devoted to causes in a middle-class cleanliness, conscientious way, always willing to blame themselves for the terrible inequity of the world. The problem being they continually blamed themselves more than they should. This is what they never caught on to—this was their great flaw. It is what the Indo-Canadian activist from Osgoode Hall who interviewed John about Rwanda always counted upon whites feeling; and was furious that John Delano refused to pay homage to it. That is: white shame.

That is why he took on social services when he came home. Anyone with such preconceived notions about people's humanity shouldn't be allowed to place children anywhere. So he went and asked Jeanie to marry him. It had been a ruthless decision; he knew that now.

At any rate, Hugh did not feel this either—that is, white shame. He only felt he had the credentials and the God-given ability to help someone else. So Hugh, Lily and their child were given a send-off in some respectable way from the university where the husband worked, where he had cashed in all his chips, and John knew by 1995 that this was out west, Edmonton—in some department perhaps too. In the University of Alberta—on one of those cold afternoons when the sun shone pink on the plate-glass windows for an hour, and the rooms remained opaque and sullen. It took John some time to find out he was right. But he was right. That is, that it was the University of Alberta and Hugh Forrest was an obdurate technocrat, obstinate yet heroic—believing he could be the moment of change for a people who still dug out wells by hand.

How did Hugh's conversion happen? It happened when he watched a TV program one night on well digging and poor water quality in a remote village. He was upset over this waste of time and lack of knowledge. He kept scratching the side of his face in frustration and annoyance, and eating his bowl of ice cream in silence and consternation, with the bowl balanced on his long legs. He had tinkered with machines and electricity and circuits all of his life. He even shorted out an entire building accidentally.

"No," he would mutter. "No, no, no, no!"

"Damn," he said to his wife. "What are they up to over there? Someone should go over and see to it!!" His eyes suddenly brightened when he looked at her, his obdurate, bony knees stuck out in the half-dark room. Then he was fixated on the program again—watching in silence with only a table lamp on in the corner.

"Are you coming to bed?" she asked.

He waved her away without taking his eyes off the screen until she disappeared down the hall, and then he looked up for a second at where she had been, and then back to the TV.

Yes, the university was a disappointment to him. It was filled with idleness and with people who knew and loved idleness and used idleness with pretentious swagger, always agreeing or disputing the ideas and inventions of other people and smugly asserting themselves into the limelight because of that.

Hugh realized the security professors had, the safety they enjoyed, the coddling they experienced, the idea they fostered that malevolent forces were against them when no forces were; their intolerance was considered blessed, their liberal prejudices considered enlightened, and the monies they received seemed disproportional to anything they ever achieved. If there was an ideal idle class, a class that pretended to have great experience, even great suffering, without experiencing the pain, professors certainly came close.

It made his muscles and bones ache, and he had to do something to help the world. So there and then that's what he decided to do.

"Wasson is sure to come as well." he declared to his wife while crunching cold cereal the next morning. "He is sure to—wait and see!"

But poor Tim Wasson, the celebrated activist who had the famous ponytail and the famous blue eyes, never came.

Hugh would have been younger then, of course—strange how those pictures of oneself even ten years before give away an energy and a youthfulness that is both raw and unworldly, or show some strange incompleteness of the soul —even though at the time one thinks one is mature. And the picture of the woman—if anyone ever looked closely at it, would be one with a faint decorous smile that might have been wiser than the husband's; her looking out at the camera with an exquisite, hopeful smile—that masked her own delusions. Yet in that smile there might be the faint apprehension that the greater world did not belong to them. An apprehension, perhaps, of the desperate struggle yet to come after the final goodbye at the Edmonton airport on some soft mid-winter day. They were Canadians, of course. There was something about Canadians that did not fit into the world, it seemed. Gullible when it came to their countries of origin. Always believing that England or Wales, France or Ireland had answers they never did, and yet not enough of the answers to have kept them from journeys across the ocean to cling to this new, desperately snow-laden hinterland.

The young child would be on her lap, dressed in a suit of lapis lazuli, and like in so many pictures, she would be dressed appropriately in some post-feminist way, modest yet serving a purpose. And he would be six years away, John would be, from searching north of Kigali for her, and for them. He would search for them back in Canada too—and come to believe that he had found them—come to believe that Hugh and Lily had succumbed to the massacre at the orphanage in April 1994, but that their son had not.

He was a toddler on her knee when the picture was taken and his name was John Patrick.

JP.

Their names were Hugh and Lily Forrest.

JP was the boy who had made it all the way back to Canada when he was thirteen.

But what had happened to him?

By the time John opened the door of Matters Road and sat in the chair after four days, he believed he knew the answer. He even decided he knew where that boy, who was now twenty-three years of age, might be.

———

Afterwards—that is, after the drink at Dandy's—Midge came into the consulate and declared that she was particularly hopeful that "our troops can be kept in check until peace can be worked out. All violence—any violence—is bad, but killing is worse. Men never seem to know this."

The next day at a sitting at the UN, half the membership did not show up for a speech by the minister from Kenya, and of the half that did, one-quarter of those yawned, fidgeted and fell asleep. The speech

was about a last-ditch effort to "thrust forward" the Arusha peace agreement. This is what Midge was hopeful for.

One of the people who most approved of Midge's stance against
supplying the Canadian command with more troops or weapons, or
even a new protocol, was her Hutu friend Rwandan ambassador Jean-
Damascène Bizimana. They were constantly in each other's sight, constantly networking. He told her that the Canadian observers in Kigali
were making vastly libellous and ridiculous assertions in the hope of
military intervention, which he said would never be tolerated, because
he said it would lead to a return of colonialism. To the age of Cecil
Rhodes and the De Beers diamond trade.

This idea of being in any way accused of participating in the return
of colonialism repelled her and the Lion of Justice more than almost
anything else. And to speak of diamonds and DeBeers now—was odious.

Midge was at the Rwandan ambassador's grand apartment on Thirty-
Ninth Street many times in those days, and never took a moment to
notice the two diamonds on his fingers.

———

In his memories of all this there was a rage John could not escape, and a
hope from Sue Van Loon that he would someday let it go. From his first
unscheduled visit he had thought that she would simply speak to him
once or twice and everything would get better. He did not know how
paralyzed he in fact had become.

At first she simply believed he blamed everyone and had no real
insight into what was bothering him, but over time she became aware
that he was acutely perceptive and blamed almost no one but himself.
He felt he should have stayed in Rwanda and died there. That was his
first bad decision: to live. Then to marry Jeannie—out of some kind of
almost mean-spirited obligation. To take on the elusive and brilliant
Melissa Sapp.

How did Sue Van Loon know this? She secretly knew more than John thought she did—she had been a young physiatrist for social services back then. She knew of the furor around Jeannie Aube. She had heard the name John Delano as well, and heard that he was exceedingly intolerant. At that time in her life, she had believed it.

Sue Van Loon once tried to emulate Melissa Sapp. Until Melissa turned against her too. For Melissa's strength lay in turning against everyone she loved.

Sue Van Loon had felt that Jeanne was justified in wanting her child born, if it was her decision—and then justified in wanting her child back. A fissure formed between her and Melissa that could not be healed. They had gone over everything—the house Jeanne lived in, the terrible way she was brought up, the poverty. And still Sue Van Loon felt Jeanne should have her child.

When John told Sue Van Loon he knew she had been the physiatrist in this case, she did not mention that this was when her falling-out with Melissa had come.

"She should have the child," Sue Van Loon had argued, after investigating it all for three weeks. "I might not agree with her—but it is her decision. You can't make this decision for her—that is what is actually at stake."

"That is not at all possible," Melissa said. "She needs our encouragement to do what is right for her."

"Or," Sue Van Loon said, "is it to do what is right for you, who wishes to legislate an abortion clinic in the province?"

"What in God's name would that have to do with it?"

"Oh my soul." Sue Van Loon laughed. "Everything. But I tested her and she is certainly competent enough to make her own decision."

"But she doesn't even remember what happened that night—she has no recollection of where she was, or who these men were."

"I know."

"So I suppose it is an act of God."

"I am not saying that at all."

"Would it be your decision—"

"I don't think it would be—I have no idea—I am not sure. But I am not her, and she is as capable as well—if she remembers what happened or not. She now knows what is at stake as well as you do!"

Melissa's eyes sharpened, then she smiled slightly—almost imperceptibly—and turned and walked away. She waved her hand up in the air, as if to say goodbye to a fool.

So Van Loon was left in the corridor alone.

And Melissa would strike out at her soon after, and leave her alone for good.

Sue Van Loon knew about Ms. Fern Hershey being betrayed as well. This came shortly after the Aube case.

In fact, what had happened to Fern Hershey was at one time called a great coup by Melissa and her friends. And Van Loon always felt empathy for the young daughter, Jane, whom she admired and liked.

But this "betrayal" had happened quite simply—and perhaps wasn't calculated. It was during the search for a new vice-president at the university. The head of the sociology department was picked, and that left a vacuum that needed to be filled. All of this happened with few people noticing or caring.

But then two people applied for the position who were not qualified.

That was when, one cold autumn day, Melissa came to work and asked Fern Hershey to apply for the job as head of this sociology department at the university, almost guaranteeing her the position. In fact, she planted the idea that Ms. Hershey must apply for it, for the good of women and the good of the university itself. When Hershey, who had not thought of doing so beforehand, vacillated, Melissa said, "Listen, do you want a career or a job? I am going to give you a career with inordinate power and prestige. So let me give you some good advice too—I'm on the university board of governors—the best thing for you to do is to step down here."

"Step down?"

"Yes, from your job, " Melissa continued, with her arm on Fern's as she whispered into her ear, with her eyes directly upon her. "It's the best card in the game. That is, retire, wait a week—then submit your application to me personally at the board of governors. Who doesn't listen to me there?" Melissa smiled briefly and conspiratorially.

"But—you think I should? I will stand a chance, you'll vouch for me?"

"Stand a chance? My God, I will guarantee it. Now, what do you want for the rest of your life? I said I would. Now, make up your mind—do you want the position or not? Can you handle the responsibility or no?"

"Of course—yes," Hershey said, like a little girl.

Melissa smiled, patted her arm and walked away.

Fern thought it over for a day or two, and asked her daughter what she should do. Her daughter was like all children—thinking of how good it would be to have her mother as head of a whole department at a university.

"Of course," Jane said. "With Melissa as your friend you can't lose!"

So Fern gave up her position—gave her cases away, and applied to take over the sociology department. But something happened in the interim. Melissa, terrified of not filling the position with someone she wanted, had asked not only Fern to apply but two others also.

In the end it was a rather heavy sleight of hand.

For Melissa had asked Carey Newman, and then had emailed her own aunt Midge Nolan Overplant as well. And she did so because she wanted an ally at the university when it came to the gender battles she felt she would begin to wage across the province —so to Melissa the job easily could have gone to Hershey or to Ms. Newman, but unfortunately once her aunt applied from the States, Melissa's hands were tied.

"My hands are tied," Melissa told Fern the day of the meeting in question. "I have to recuse myself from the vote because my aunt Midge Nolan Overplant applied as well—so I cannot speak on your behalf. I am sorry. I wanted to, as I told you. But it is an uncomfortable position for me to be in. I had not foreseen this, I assure you. But if you don't get the job," she said, "come back to work for us—how's that?"

Fern looked as if she had been crushed. Never before had her daughter seen her so humiliated. And she had to go back to work. She had no other choice. With Melissa Sapp as her boss.

A few years later, Fern Hershey was struck with breast cancer and resigned.

This was when Jane Hershey began to hate. At first, of course, she did not hate. She only listened, thought that there was a mix-up, a mistake—something had happened that no one could foresee.

Was baffled at the silence from social services. Her mother died, and she was alone. But she believed that the worry and stress of it all had helped cause her mother's breast cancer.

Then one day, she began to believe that Melissa Sapp had orchestrated it all—even her mother's death—and started to hate fiercely. She planned her revenge. Or, she did not plan her revenge—no, she was never like that; it just swept her up. She became a sleepwalker, unable to turn a corner—everything she had done in the past three months was done as if she was acting in a daze. Until John Delano came and broke the spell—and now she was mortified. That is when she began herself to visit Sue Van Loon's office.

But though Van Loon knew all of this, did she believe John about this missing boy?

In her mind, if the child wasn't real, this would prove his serious flight from reality. And would also prove her own worth in helping him adjust.

Only once, at a party late the previous summer, did Sue Van Loon defend John when Melissa Sapp said that people like John Delano should be made extinct.

"Well—" Sue Van Loon smiled, her brilliance every bit the match of Melissa Sapp's, and no longer the least threatened by her "—you do have enough people trying to hunt him down."

But of course Melissa only smiled at this, and walked away.

2.

WHEN HIS CHILD WENT OFF TO SCHOOL IN GRADE ONE, JOHN was working on a case in Saint Andrews, of the murder of a resort owner by his son and girlfriend over a five-hundred-thousand dollar trust fund that the boy couldn't wait until he was twenty-five to receive. He committed the murder when he was twenty-four—or, twenty-four and two-thirds, to use a child's timeline. That is, as far as John could fathom the unfathomable, he was only four months away from obtaining this money legitimately. John remembered that his name was Harold and his girlfriend was named Wizzy.

Wizzy was a petulant woman of twenty-one. She sat in the new blue jeans the boyfriend had bought her, with the new watch too, her large eyes accusatory. Against what or whom she did not seem to know, because they never fastened on anyone too long. Hair fell against her pouting cheeks.

She had spent half the day at the Long Locks, a beauty parlour just across the border near Calais, Maine, getting a manicure and a pedicure. John only remembered all of this after the fact. That is, once the charges were laid and she was put into handcuffs, he remembered how ordinary she seemed with the cuffs on her wrists just below the sleeves of her white blouse.

They had waited until she came back to Canada to make the arrest.

The son had shot his father in the back with his new twelve-gauge shotgun that morning. His father was writing him a cheque at the time. He had placed the shotgun carefully over his father's body but managed to get his Adidas covered in blood. Besides, no one could shoot himself so squarely in the back from a standing position while he himself was sitting.

The son, John gathered, had not really thought it through.

Nor had he thought his computer would be confiscated and the emails he and his girlfriend exchanged would be looked at.

John made the arrest that afternoon at about 3:35. He took a cup of coffee and handed it to the fellow, and stirred in some sugar for him.

Then John went back outside.

John had the coroner remove the body from the back pool house— a small building separate from the main house—at seven that night. Lights—all sorts of lights—shone on the naked walkway; the dozens of rooms inside the huge main house were lit and Halloween pumpkins had already been placed on the front doorstep. John took a drive back to the Saint Andrews detachment and went over the evidence that the young woman was also involved.

But then something else happened.

Later, John overheard a call about a boy having run to a tree to climb because of children chasing him, and having almost fallen to his death. This had happened up north in John's hometown.

He looked at the young man and his girlfriend, complicit in a senseless murder, both with wide, capricious eyes and dull facial expressions, like people from some long-ago biblical story, those who would accost their merchant father for a measly pint of gold.

Strange how this case plagued him.

He thought little of the incident of the child in the tree until he discovered, by overhearing another conversation down the office hall, that it was his own child. Not that this was known by those who spoke of it—but the telltale piece of evidence was a scribbler with leaves pasted into it, which the boy was collecting, and the same large, foreboding elementary school. He began to think of something hurting his child because of what he had failed to do at the UN.

How ultimately absurd such a thought was to people like Sue Van Loon—and yet he was plagued by it nonetheless. Each thing happened for a reason—each molecule of unseen air we breathe is allowed. The misplaced monocle of a German general allows a Russian battery to perform; you turn right instead of left and miss the opportunity to save a child, whose mother and dad have gone to Africa hoping to save the world.

Those were the golden moments of the sun.

He came home and went through his child's book bag later that night, and discovered his child's life—the small yellow pencils, one sharpened and one not, the drawings of Mom and Dad, with heads too small and feet too wide and painted green and blue, the leftover one-half of a peanut butter cup, the large and small ABCs, worked on and erased and worked on again, always outside the lines, and his book of leaves, pasted every which way, and the one star he managed to corral in all this time, from Teacher Judy. And this is what got him into an argument with Melonson's wife—though he did not know she was Melonson's wife then.

John felt there should be, or could be, many more stars—and why not? And if it was not important—if not—why, then, did his boy place his with such reverence at the top of his binder? This was the indication of such a special moment, that his son wanted—a kind of success he had not seemed to have experienced—that it made the banal little star so gravely special.

It was a foolish thing to go to Teacher Judy, as the boy called her, and tell her there should be more stars! In the ruins of that huge, dilapidated elementary school, smelling of soap and crushed wax and vain autumn sunlight.

And why wasn't he more perspicacious—why did he not realize she was Melonson's young, devoted wife, who had already heard of this awful man, John Delano, who disliked both women and the Acadians? Yes, it comes to this always, the idea of whom one supposedly disliked.

It was even funny the argument he and his wife got embroiled in that evening, she waiting to see him, scared of the tragedy that had almost occurred, the boy having almost slipped and fallen, John having driven four hours in the heavy rain, and that rain now pattering above on the roof of the large house he had, in conscientious pride, built for them. Whether to go to the school and demand his son be served up more stars!

"He needs more stars," John said, his left hand trembling slightly, as it did for the last year, as he looked over the boy's work. "He's just a child—he needs more stars."

Some weeks later when John finished testifying in court for that case in Saint Andrews, he came home and the boy's school photo was on the table in the kitchen, waiting for him.

"To Daddy" was written on it, in blue crayon that slipped off both ends of the picture.

John spent a lot of energy trying to decide over the past few years what the boy's eyes presented to the world.

Hope and love.

Sometimes he went weeks without looking at the picture.

"You never got over it," a friend one time said.

"Oh—should I have?" John asked. He asked it not flippantly but almost expectantly, hoping against hope, like a man who has struggled in his life with great things might. A man who has asked the battered darkness about him, the one question that pertains to us all: "Why?"

It was what his son had asked when he'd told him he had to go to camp.

He woke with a blanket over him—half over him on the couch. Always, over the past number of years, he would wake with a start, as if he had just remembered something, and this something was essential and he must jump up and find it, or deal with it. Sometimes his waking this way would be a complement to the rain or wind or conditions in the bay water, as if something outside was beckoning him.

So he would sit up, and then stare blankly, trying to gauge his where-abouts. For at the same time, when he woke he was often confused, and often unsure of himself. As always, within a very few minutes of being conscious, the weight would come back into his heart and he would once again carry it with him throughout the day. At times when he was enthralled by his work or had a new clue or lead, it would almost disap-pear, or become so light as for him to make believe it was gone, not so much a feather but a little pin—but even at that, there was its continual presence, like the shadow of the person crossing out of camera range on a street fifty years ago. Nor, and this was the real true secret—could he stand for it to go away.

"Do you ever think of taking your life?" his psychiatrist asked him last month.

"Oh yes—at times."

"How often?"

"How often? Oh—not so often. Four, maybe five times a day."

———

Luda Marsh was waiting for this strange boy to come and meet her, and take her away. But that did not happen. Because he was stopped as he crossed the field, and was chased in the other direction. There was a gale and snow was falling. For the rest of her life Luda Marsh thought he had forgotten all about her.

Luda Marsh had poor lungs because she had been stabbed when she was a child. She sneezed often, and had colds. But her eyes were dark and vast, like the pools in some faraway forest—well, this is what the boy had told her six days earlier.

She waited until she saw two people walk toward her—this was Bunny and Vernon. She ran back to 66 Shelf Street and put the strange book with the strange imagery and strange and awful ideas on her table.

But she did not stop waiting. Each night she waited until long after supper. Sometimes she would stop Melon on his way home, and ask him.

"I don't know," Melon would say. "I want to know where he went, but I don't know."

They went downtown together to look. Then they tried to phone Ms. Hershey, but she did not work with child welfare anymore.

So Luda waited in torn pantyhose and short woollen skirt, with a jean jacket with sparkles on the pocket. She waited with a tattoo on her neck and her fingernails painted purple in the March sun.

One afternoon early in April a train shunted down along the flat and there were orange boxcars. Someone walked toward her out of this red setting sun, strutting toward her as if it was preordained. The snow was melting away and showing the desolate signs of clumped and yellowed grasses, debris from the winter up against the buildings on the street, and now and then a swallow darting across the sky.

Velma Cheval came walking toward her, with a look of complicity and glee, moving slightly sideways, with the brace on her right leg. She had short dark hair, and her eyes never left you when they fastened on you.

Luda knew who she was, and was terrified as the woman approached. But the woman came up to her and said, "Luda, how are you, dear?" and touched her face with almost immaculate seduction. "You look good," she said. "Dressin' all up tonight for something, are ya?"

"Yes, I am fine—how are you too?" Luda asked, but as usual she was never able to look into that woman's mysterious, dead eyes. Velma gave a sniff when Luda looked away and they spoke of her life. Velma too had a tattoo on the right side of her neck and spoke of being in school. How she would go to the fence far at the back of the playground to smoke, and how Mrs. Corry would always catch her. Ha, ha, ha. She spoke of summer days when she was young and how she took care of children—and took them to the beach at Rocky Point, and how one of them drowned—Velma looked whimsical and sad when she spoke of these long-ago times.

Then she asked: What was Luda doing? Who was she waiting for? Said how much she had grown—"A real little lady—and do you know," Velma said, smoothing Luda's hair, "I like women as well as men."

Luda looked frightened by this remark, but Velma only shrugged and complained of the damp air and lit another smoke and stared strangely and scornfully out at the world as if, as a child, somewhere someone had made her stare with such scorn, and nothing could change her now. Then she tossed the match into a puddle and smiled again, as if catching herself. "No one to take care of you now? I have always wanted to help you. I watched you when you were little, and I always said, 'That's someone I can help.'

"So anyways, I have something good for you, keeps the cold away." She rubbed some hash oil across a cigarette paper, smiled as she did so, a grave little smile, and looked up at Luda in conspiratorial love. "Here, here," she said.

This in fact was the moment of Luda's death sentence.

Except, neither she nor Velma herself knew.

"You see me here tomorrow," Velma said, when Saint Rose of Lima's bells sounded at nine o'clock that night. "And I'll have something good for ya."

As the days ebbed into spring, Velma would walk across the battered school ground in the afternoon, carrying her right leg a little shorter, with the brace sometimes glittering. Velma's eyes had a way of looking at you without looking at you. She always had something for Luda, a new purse, or a pair of jeans—a hat that Luda might like. And she was always there now, always at Luda's side.

Luda at that time did not know that Velma walked up to her that first afternoon in her stovepipe jeans and woollen sweater because Bennie Cheval had asked his sister to find out who this pretty young girl was; because he wanted to meet her.

But was there a moment when Luda thought she should stay away:

A thousand moments. But one day, when her guard was down in the middle of eating a peanut butter cup and laughing at a joke Velma told— the other Velma appeared—the one the kids all called Jake.

Velma simply said that Luda owed her for all those nice pills that made her feel special.

"Owe you—what do I owe you—I didn't know I would owe you!!"

"No—well, you didn't refuse anything, did you, dear—now, don't go off your pickle—you only owe some 230 or -40."

"Two hundred thirty or forty what?"

Velma shrugged. "Dollars, for god sake. Or, you can do something else."

"What can I do?"

"You can come—with us," she said, and lit a cigarette, with her hands cupped and her face turned away from the wind. Luda looked at this woman's hands, the fingers long and the nails sharp. Then after Velma got the cigarette lit, she took a pull, and said, "Do me a favour, forget the money and the foster home—that's a dead end, let me tell you—just come with me."

"Come with you—where?"

"You'll have a better life with me!" Velma answered. "Or we can take the three hundred and forget all about it."

"Three hundred?"

"That's how I add it—I don't know about you," Velma said, smiling.

Luda went into 66 Shelf that night, and sat on the bed and thought and shivered and looked in the mirror and wondered why hadn't that boy come to take her with him? All her plans had been changed now—and besides, how could she pay three hundred dollars?

So when it got quiet, she took her book bag with the book that boy had given her, and her three pairs of panties and her bra, and left by the back door, into the soaking night air. When she came out and crossed into the glazed April night, the smell of spring in the wild trees, Bennie Cheval had driven up in his car, with the motor throbbing, and he said, "Throw those damn books away—no one did me no favours with no fuckin' books."

For a moment or two she was startled and frightened—catching on that it was Bennie who had wanted to meet her, and the throbbing of the car engine seemed part of the conspiracy. Still, she laughed and threw all those books away—except one.

Other girls at 66 Shelf had warned her that Velma killed people, that she had killed a little girl—but Luda, feeling all of a sudden Velma's warmth and kindness, the way she had forgiven the three hundred dollars, realized the people who said that must have been wrong. God, Luda didn't even know she owed that, and yet it was forgiven.

"I wish more people could be nice like you," Luda said. "You are like my mom used to be."

And Velma laughed, and stroked her hair.

———

John had testified at the trial of one of the young Hutu who went from village to village killing with his machete. He put ten heads in a bag and carried them about for two days, showing them to his friends.

But the bag got heavier and heavier, and more and more corroded by blood and maggots, and even his admirers told him to throw the things away. So finally he felt compelled to do so, for the moment of bravado had run its course, and then he looked about in sudden consternation because one of the heads rolled behind him as they walked down the hill, and other boys started laughing.

John remembered him as the young man who had stopped him at the roadblock and would not let them go any farther.

"Two hundred forty-seven," John said to Sue Van Loon.

"Two hundred forty-seven what?"

"Orphans—in that compound, hiding in the same tent."

"Orphans?"

"The age of AIDS," John replied.

Harry Sabota would bring flowers to Midge Nolan Overplant's office during those last few weeks. Often she was so busy in her position of cultural affairs attaché she couldn't see him. The bright, happy smile she had worn when first introduced to him was now gone, and she did not attend his little party at his apartment on Thirty-Seventh. She was just too busy now.

So the flowers were left on a chair outside her door.

———

John had flown out to see the Forrest family's belongings some days ago, and had stood abjectly in the basement of a remote Edmonton dorm. The last remaining uncle as yet had not done anything with them but pay the warehousing fees. Uncle Pierce. That is who the boy would have had to find if he was looking for some connection to his family and his past. Uncle Pierce the Newfoundlander—deeply suspicious, always, of mainlanders, who weren't at all like him.

There John saw a drop dresser and the ornate bedroom reading lamp, three white, spotless couches, many technical papers, and books on generating stations. Other books too—Margaret Atwood, and James Herriot, the book *Pilgrim's Progress*—and a letter from McClelland & Stewart because Lily was going to publish a children's book. Along with word games for children, left to the ages passing. No one had heard a word from them in seventeen years. It was suddenly strange how nothing seemed real—it was as if he had entered a time chamber. Only silence. Lily's children book, which was to be called *JP*, was never finished. The woman from the English department, a kindly middle-aged lady, spoke softly and smiled when she remembered them—but she said she had not known them well, and no one had. They were one of those families you do not know well. John and she picked up a few objects and then in sacred duty tried placing them back in the exact same place. In fact he realized that this was Lily's life—her life before she'd packed and followed her husband away—left now to the echoes of wind and frost and drifting sun. John felt deep love for her at that moment. For Lily and her dreams.

He asked this woman if he could take a picture with him from photos taken at the university. The photo he had in his pocket when he took Vernon Beaker's taxi home from the airport.

That picture of Hugh and Lily and the little boy.

———

"You really are a pompous ass—and a very silly fellow," John whispered to the Lion of Justice one night.

He hardly remembered saying this; he simply knew he had said it. He had been drinking.

Reports about the genocide had started drifting in to them. It was the day after they had stood around a television, in horror. Mr. Sabota was on TV and the camera followed him down a walkway of a little village as he tried to first walk and then run away. He ran so funnily— somewhat like a duck.

The problem—one that he himself did not seem to realize right away—was that he had been set on fire, and the fire crept up his legs and then engulfed his entire body. And he simply slowed down, and down, and then stopped and turned around, and spoke something, and fell. He tried to stand, to climb to his feet, but was nothing but a ball of fire.

The camera, from some news source in the Netherlands, simply followed him, without comment. The Dutch, it seemed at that moment to John Delano, always reserved comment until they could make the best case for themselves.

However, two years ago, John was invited to Rideau Hall to attend the Lion of Justice's induction into the Order of Canada. John was asked to attend because of being part of the liaison. Midge was also being inducted into the Order of Canada at that time.

" 'Tireless, dedicated and sincerely committed to the improvement of women and children the world over.' "

Midge looked at him a second, frowned just slightly before smiling. John saluted—it was his job.

John had bought his son a compass and a small Swiss Army knife. The brochure said: "Fundy White Spray Camp IS the best place for your child this summer—with twelve well-trained and friendly counsellors." Jeannie promised to tape the *Dobblebuns* for their son—and John had said, "In a week we will go on vacation to Prince Edward Island—I promise—but now you just go to Camp Fundy for one week and Mom will tape the *Dobblebuns* for you so you won't miss an episode—and she and I will watch them with you when you get home."

They took a picture of him wearing his Camp Fundy T-shirt. His was blue, the girls were pink. Fundy White Spray Camp.

When John got home after flying all day in from San Francisco, he was exhausted and went to sleep. And because of his prisoner's transfer and the amount of paperwork, he would have to work another four days before he could take his vacation. That was the only reason they decided to send the boy to camp.

When John woke up late that morning, his boy had already gone. He had left a note on the counter: "Dad, you forgot to say goodbye."

That is what John kept in the kitchen on the cork board, no matter where he moved. He kept it always.

"Dad, you forgot to say goodbye."

If Saint Catherine's heart could be pierced by the cross of Christ, why shouldn't his be?

———

So then, let's remember this about Luda: The boy did not come to meet her.

Later, when Luda drove in the car with Bennie Cheval, she was terrified. He had a bottle between his legs now, and was heading back along the Loman Otter Road, and it was coming onto sunset. And there was a dry, old, straw-like heat—and Bennie drank wine and looked over at her without comment when she told him to take the turns more carefully. She was seven months pregnant and did not want any more trouble. Two weeks before, he had been released from custody. Yes, the charges against him had all been dropped. Even at this moment he did not quite understand why. He had driven around most of the afternoon pretending to look for John Delano—telling people he had had it up to here—you know, being discriminated against.

———

The Bennie Cheval case was one of four John was working on back then. And so when he went to arrest Cheval for weapon possession and tossing an incendiary device at one of his hapless friends, John did not think anything of it at all when he addressed Cheval only in English.

At first there was nothing said about this. Most people wanted rid of this man, and this man put away. He and his sister had been implicated in a murder of a shopkeeper and robbery of a blind salesman. Both cases lacked evidence, and no charges had been filed in those cases.

But now Bennie was finally arrested and people said thank God for it.

But after a time—that is, when advocates became aware that it was John Delano's arrest, and Delano was someone they could legitimately challenge to make a case about language rights—a certain perverse sponsorship of Mr. Bennie Cheval sprang into action.

The kind of perverse sponsorship that is always at the very fringe of legality and justice.

A writ of habeas corpus was filed against the nature of the arrest. That is, the question was not about the arrest itself but the nature of the arrest—how the officer actually conducted himself during the procedure. For this officer's name was John Delano—and professors teaching criminology and law had always used his cases as cases to examine.

Bennie Cheval was then granted bail. Velma came to the court house with him. The nature of the arrest was a slap in the face to his heritage, Bennie said.

Within John's own department the argument over the expulsion of the Acadians that he had had with Melonson was remembered, with a certain amount of reticence and sadness too, and many no longer spoke to him.

Could he be a bigot, and a throwback to an uncertain time? It was harped about so much even John didn't know.

The argument had started over hockey—over a game in Tracadie—and had ended in hard feelings between Melonson and him that still remained to this day.

"Well, the English have done it to us," Melonson said, off the cuff as if it couldn't be disputed. "We were all expelled by the bastards."

But John for the first time responded—knowing he should not—by saying that few Acadians were expelled from New Brunswick, the majority from Nova Scotia. He also said that many Acadians who had paid for passage to Quebec had been left to die on the beach of the Miramichi because of the indifference of the Quebec governor, who took their money but did not send any ships.

Then, with Melonson turning away, John, upset about such casual condemnation, continued. He said that if France had won the war, the English in New Brunswick might have fared far worse because of the Reign of Terror in France a few years later. They wouldn't have been deported, but they might have been slaughtered.

John was remembered within the context of this argument once the Cheval case came to light. And Bennie was not looked upon in any particular context. Or in fact he was—the fact that he was a violent man seemed to work in his favour—the idea that Christ said, "What you do to the least of these you do to me."

So the charges against Bennie Cheval were dropped and he was released. That was because information John had against him of firearms and the throwing of an incendiary device could not be used in court.

At first John did not seem to care. To get away from it he immediately went on to another case—leaving for San Francisco, determined to bring home the man who'd embezzled money from an elderly woman who was so pleased to help the ducks and the geese.

After Bennie was released he went on a four-week drunk.

And in the background, almost unseen, was the very young wife he had impregnated, Luda Marsh.

———

Perhaps, John thought, Harry did want to use the money he'd requested to vaccinate children; perhaps he was entirely innocent, with his flashy smile and his opal ring—and perhaps the person who was waiting for these vaccinations was Lily Forrest, the lost boy's mother. Though

African Harry was like a thousand Maritime men John had met: he only wanted to look the part.

They all went out to fine restaurants and dined at night. Once Sabota bought them all lobster from Maine—and once, sea bass and steak.

It was the first time Mr. Sabota ate lobster, and John showed him how to remove the lobster meat with the lobster's own claws, telling him that utensils weren't necessary if you knew what you were doing. Harry smiled and said he would soon be a master, a master of the lobster. Everyone laughed. He looked down at his lobster with a kind of child-like perplexity and anticipation, wearing a huge bib over his silk tie and having rolled up his sleeves.

A month later, Harry was caught running with that beautiful shoulder bag toward the border with Uganda—they showed it on television: moment by moment he tried his hardest to get away, already lit afire. Like a bundle of rags he fell, stood and ran again, young kids around his body shouting like gleeful trumpeters, and hacking away with machetes.

"UN official pays with his life," the caption read.

He was a moderate Hutu—he had tried to stop some militiamen from killing Tutsi children in an orphanage, those 247 who were hiding in a tent.

In the end, the UN and the Canadian government had not come through.

3.

IT WOULD BE CHRISTMAS SOON ENOUGH.

Last year John had bought himself a box of chocolates. Each day he would wake, go over the collection of things from the case that no one believed in, look over identification photos, phone old foster children and wait for some word on a boy he called Jack Forrest.

And slowly John was beginning to recognize Melissa's involvement in this. At first there had been nothing from her at all—he had written her new department for missing and exploited children, and was surprised to have no answer for two weeks.

He checked his computer every day for an email from her—but there was only silence. Then he wrote an email again, this time to her directly. Finally late one night he got an answer: "No child pertaining to case file 97817 from Ottawa letter of November 14, 2011, within social services child protection register from January 1999. Sincerely, Melissa Sapp."

A missive acutely economical.

In such a way that he almost admired her.

Sometimes, John kept informed about the aftermath of Rwanda on his own time and money—like when he flew to Paris to a conference on international justice in 2002. There he stood in the Great Hall, with its gold-leaf patterns, the grand frescoes, the imperial statues of former justices of the many regimes, and dozens of beautiful women, judges and lawyers from all walks of life, from many parts of the world. And amid this marshalled splendour, in this huge valley of marble and exquisite drapery, John was lost, forsaken and defeated.

And then suddenly he spied two out-of-place men, side by side, their thin blue suits looking so undeserving of the marble bench they sat upon. One was a tall, distinguished man of about forty; the other, a short dark man with receding hair, of fifty or so. The younger man was a Tutsi; the older man, whose skin was as weathered as oak, was a Hutu. They had come to the Great Hall to seek justice, just like John Delano had, in a world that simply passed their little suit jackets and thin-striped shirts by—they smiled at John and he spoke to them in French. They had a stack of papers with them implicating the human trafficker Odurante, who they had both witnessed murder two young women. He had taken boys and girls from displacement camps and sold them—Odurante was their main obsession. Had John heard of him?

"Yes, of course—but I have heard of so many others," he said.

"Odurante—he was the worst," the Hutu said. "He was the worst—he dealt in such young children! He cut the arms off seventeen young boys."

The Tutsi man was a legal attorney and the Hutu had been a police officer who had become overwhelmed during those terrible weeks, and had to go into hiding himself. Now, with binders of documents and certain names of some who had participated in the genocide, of others like Odurante, who had profited from it all, they had come here hoping to help their country reconcile. The Tutsi was missing a leg—it had been lopped off in order to make him shorter—but his attackers only got the one. He'd hopped into the bush and jumped over an embankment. His wife had put a tourniquet on him. He had lived.

He was now this Tutsi head of the Rwandan disability football league.

The Hall of Justice in the middle of Paris on a damp May afternoon, with the heels of the chic and well-informed echoing as in a large chamber, dwarfed them and their concerns about legal etiquette, and they held their briefs and clung together in hope, like children. A child like John, they too were five thousand miles from home.

———

On November 25, 2011, John again brought out the ninety-five hundred dollars he had hidden, and stared at it. That is, he again thought of turning it over, but knew an investigation would start against him. As absurd to him as it was, he was already suspected of involvement in the deaths of Bennie Cheval and Luda Marsh—for he was the only officer on the scene, and alone at that scene for over a half an hour.

So certain people believed Bennie Cheval's interview of May 2002 on CBC: "Why did he want to arrest me? Well, it's a delicate matter. He has a thing about my wife—always had. She is sick to death of him coming after me over it, calling her up—just check his cell phone and see! And I will say this to him: 'Just leave us be.' He's been stalking her for over three years."

Well, he did care for her. He had known Luda from the time she was three years old. Her pull-up diaper had been filled with ecstasy pills by Velma Cheval, and she was told to go from her mom's house to her uncle's. Ecstasy pills were falling out of her diaper.

Then, at thirteen, when she was carrying a screwdriver to protect herself, he picked her up on the street and took her to foster care. He had been a kind of adviser to her ever since. In fact they were right—he had tried to get her away from the Chevals for three years before she was killed.

Still, it could be looked upon as something else for those who wanted to make it seem so. For he was there. She was stabbed. Bennie was dead. That was the day, coming onto the scene where John had a heart attack.

Who would not say he did not have a hand in it all?

He stared at the money—he counted it, he tried to reason with himself about it all, at least twice a month.

The money, the ninety-five hundred dollars, plagued John because this is what he had not discovered yet. It had started with an advertisement in the *Telegraph Journal* that Jeannie placed every other month: "Reward offered to anyone with information pertaining to the disappearance of Gilbert Delano on July 11, 2002—please call 929-4914."

Bennie read this one day—strangely, he had not bought a paper in a month or more. He had picked one up to go over the ads about second-hand four-wheelers, and there blocked in black was this plea.

Yes—a reward.

"There's a reward for the young lad," he muttered to Luda.

"What young lad?"

"What young lad? That young lad!" Bennie answered.

He himself did not know he wanted any of the money at first. He put the paper on the counter and poured himself a glass of water. But twice that day he reread the offer.

He did need money for an enterprise he had. Or at least Velma had told Luda and him that she was owed money by them both. And he thought long and hard about it.

The next day, Bennie went to see Jeannie. He wasn't even intending to go and see her. But on the way into town on that rainy afternoon, he decided that he might be able to help her.

He went into the Dominion Bakery, where Jeannie worked, and said he could help her search for Gilbert. The way he walked in was quite extraordinary—there was an instant arrogance and a flush of conceit.

He handed her his phone number on a piece of paper.

He said everything off the cuff but with charm laced with a peculiar innocence and sincerity. Then he smiled over his shoulder and turned and walked out.

Jeannie looked at the phone number and began to shiver.

Bennie went home. All his actions had come to him spontaneously.

"Are you out of your mind?" Luda asked. "You can't even think of that—you can't begin to."

Bennie had never controlled any event in his life, but was always compelled to act as a mirror for other people's wishes. So Jeannie saw him as a man who could help, and therefore he would help.

For a while they didn't hear from Jeannie, and Bennie complained that his offer of help had been rejected. Yet one day, a day bright with sunshine and wind, she appeared at the door with maps and timetables and notes on previous searches. She set them all on the kitchen table, and she was shaking, and talking so quickly Luda could not make out what she said. Something about the Hammond River and the swale beyond a certain place—and the map would show you, et cetera.

"Oh," Bennie said. "We won't be needing that. That is fine, for sure— but Jeannie, dear, I have always had my own ideas about what happened to your little boy! I think he was neglected by John, and so I think he wanted to run away."

"You think he ran away?"

"Dear, I am only going by what I know—so we will see."

After that, Jeannie started to go out to Otter Road, most of the time alone, sometimes with Luda Marsh, driving in the huge, old Lincoln Continental that Luda had. Bennie was now more focused and more determined than ever.

He told Jeannie one day he had heard something about her boy over eight months before. He said he did not come forward because he was worried it would get him into trouble with John Delano, who had a vendetta against him.

"You can't tell John," Bennie said. "Luda is worried that you might!"

"No, I won't," Jeannie said. "I promise I won't tell him—you just tell me what you know."

"I am keeping my ear to the ground—nevertheless I want you to be practical. It may be nothing at all."

"But it might be," Jeanie said, "it just might be."

So that night Bennie came to Luda as she was lying on the bed with her child. His whole appearance had changed. His eyes had that bright, hateful glow and he had his black shirt on with the collar up. He told her he was sick and tired of Jeannie relying on him; just like everyone he ever got involved with. Too many people relied upon him.

"What do you mean?"

"I mean, why is she here? I only told her what I knew—yet she wants more and more from me. So I need some money if I am going to help her."

"That poor woman doesn't want a thing," Luda said. "She is half crazy with grief. And you have not told her what you know. What we both know."

"That's a lie," Bennie said, waving his hand. "And we decided it was a lie—so we keep it a lie."

Then he mashed his hands together and thought. Yes, why was it always up to him? He and Velma wanted to buy drugs from the people in Halifax and sell them here. So he thought of this and then he looked up at Luda.

"Listen—she has insurance money, seventy-eight thousand that was left her. Plus what Delano gives her."

"You told me last month you were going to tell her the truth. We were going to start a new life—and you promised . . ."

"Ah, but don't you see? I brought her up here to tell her the truth, but Jeannie is a woman who does not want to know the truth."

Twice Bennie ignored Jeannie's calls. Then a week later, Jeannie came again. And up until the moment she came Bennie Cheval had no idea of what he might say to her.

Luda told him one night that if he or his sister hurt Jeannie, she would phone the police. He pondered Luda's warning. But money was money. So it was not Luda he kept informed about this anymore; it was his sister, Velma.

"Yes," Velma said, over the phone, "you keep me informed—and I will tell you what we have to do." That is, the idea of having to do something made it imperative that they now do it. That is, like so many of these things, it now became an intellectual problem foisted upon them that they had to solve: how to get the money and give up nothing.

So Bennie spoke quickly to Jeannie now: "Jeannie, I wasn't going to say anything to you about it, but I got some news. A man is coming who says he might know where your son is." He stood up, went to the sink and poured a large glass of water. When he drank it, the water spilled over his chin and down his shirt. His hands shook too.

"Do you think that is true?"

"I have no way of knowing," Bennie said. He put the glass in the sink, and then put his glasses on and looked through the paper for a moment.

"What's wrong?"

"Oh, nothing is wrong," Bennie said. "Nothing—except that he has to get from Fort McMurray and he has no way to do it." He turned the page of the paper and kept reading, moving his lips as he did.

"Well," Jeannie said. "Could I speak to him? If I spoke to him, he could tell me where he seen my child—where he saw Gilbert?"

Her whole tiny body was shaking. She was like an elf in a chair, wearing a baseball cap that turned her ears down.

"If we can get him money for a plane ticket, he can come home for a weekend and tell us what we want to know," Bennie said, looking up from the paper. And then realizing he was being impolite, he shrugged and folded the paper in two.

"He can?" Jeanie asked.

"Well, perhaps he can. But I don't have no money for no plane—I hardly have enough for Luda and me and the baby."

Luda nodded slowly. Her heart was beating so quickly you could see her breasts rising and falling. Little Dotty was in her arms in a torn T-shirt and yellow shorts and a pair of small cowboy boots.

"Maybe we should just leave him there," Luda said, picking up some peas on a spoon to feed her daughter. The idea of Velma now involved in this so terrified her. That is, at first Velma mothered her and loved her, yet slowly this had eroded until she could not be in the same room as her sister-in-law, suspected her of something horrible, yet did not know why.

"No," Jeanie said now. "No—we can't. It is not fair. We have to bring him home and talk to him." She said this in the desperate heat of the cramped kitchen, and if each one of them had later been interviewed about this moment, each of them would have confessed to the same feeling: that this "man" was a fabrication.

"Leave him there—leave him there. Don't be silly—leave him there. No, send him the money!" And Bennie took out fifty dollars and slapped it on the table. "Now, that's what I got to send him, but I need more—"

"I can give more," Jeannie said. "I will get the money—I will come back with it tomorrow."

"Please, Bennie, she doesn't have to give the money," Luda said.

"Well, I might be able to get it somewhere else," Bennie said. But again this objection fed into the delusion, made Bennie more convincing, and over the next few days Jeannie gave him the money.

When Bennie took the money, he looked officious and bureaucratic. That is, there was always a meddlesome and bossy side to what he did. "He will be here—I promise. He is a good lad," Bennie said. A good lad in Bennie's mind was often someone who was both vicious and stupid. But he took the money because it was Velma who was really orchestrating it all, determining what would happen, while Bennie did what she said. So he knew in his heart that he could not stop.

It was his sister he was in partnership with, and he told his sister and brother-in-law to come.

Sometimes she called herself Velma Cheval, and sometimes Velma Roady, after her common-law husband, and sometimes she called herself by a half-dozen other names—names John Delano had seen inflicted on the side of the Shaw-house walls: Dora and Uma; and Jake—yes, that was hers as well, Jake Cheval. But most of the people she dealt with knew her as V. She had three social insurance numbers and four cheques a month from the welfare office under three different names. There was hardly a person who could look into her eyes. And yet at some time in some way she had done good deeds for others, for many south-end people loved her. Roland Roady, hugely overweight, with unhealthy white skin and straight black hair that fell to his shoulder, loved her too.

—

Velma and Roland arrived on a hot day, with suitcases.

Of all the people Luda feared, Velma was the one she had once loved the most—the one who had taken her away from 66 Shelf Street and had given her a new life.

But now there was an odious feeling when Velma walked up the gravel drive. It had changed between them when Luda found the picture of little Amy Thibodeau she carried in remembrance torn into five pieces and thrown into the toilet. As she had tried to retrieve those pieces and put them together, she heard Velma walk up the back stairs. Velma was the only other person in the house. Luda pasted the picture back together, but never again felt warmth toward the woman.

Now Velma walked up the gravel drive and hooked her way across the threshold and into the house.

They came and there were two more days of drinking and pills—mainly uppers—and many fights over the amount of money they would ask for.

Bennie and Velma were now planning to take all of Jeannie's money, and Velma's husband was to play the part of the man who came from Fort McMurray. So Roland Roady wore his new leather jacket as if he had just arrived from the plane, and his black cowboy boots polished to a shine and a nice white shirt, and he had his story about seeing the child seven months ago.

"Where would you have seen the boy?" Velma said. "You'd better get that straightened right now." She smoked and tried to reflect on this momentous decision—that is, where the boy would have been.

Luda took her child and went into the back bedroom by herself as Bennie and Velma instructed Roland about how to speak and what to say. This went on for hours, and Roland never was able to get Gilbert's name right, nor Jeannie's either. Velma would scold him, then laugh, and curse. Then she began to ask for Luda.

"Why don't you come out—are you ashamed of your own?" Velma said. "You silly little girlfriend (this is what she called Luda—girlfriend, and she wanted Luda to call her Jake), you're the cause of all of Bennie's problems—why he got arrested before. Dotty is not his kid. You come out here now."

"Dotty is Bennie's child—of course she is."

"No Cheval child was ever cross-eyed! Child should have been a bortion." Velma said; she herself had had four abortions. That was probably true. The idea of what was sanctified in the world had changed, and the change gave her great satisfaction—and even elation that it all had.

Two mornings after Velma and Roland arrived, Luda woke up to find Dotty in her Mickey Mouse pyjamas twitching and gyrating in the corner of the room.

"What did you do?" Luda yelled.

"Nothing," Velma said, tamping her cigarette into the ashtray. "Why blame me? I did nothing. She wants to twitch, let her fuckin' twitch! You're never around—yer always in the back bedroom."

"What are you talking about? For God almighty's sake. Why won't she wake up—what did you do?"

"I did nothing to the little twitching idiot. Just gave her some drops so she would stop her whining. Why weren't you up?"

The drops kept the little girl asleep half the day, twitching and trembling, and when she woke, she became sick to her stomach. Her eyes rolled back in her head, and it took another day before she would drink milk or eat.

"If you don't watch it, I will call the cops," Luda said, coming right up to Velma's face, glaring at her. "Do one more thing—and I will call the cops!"

"You'll do what?" Velma said, stepping up to her with a grave smile.

"Both of you—shut up! Jeannie is here," Bennie said.

Jeannie was all dressed up, as if she was meeting someone very important. The meeting happened in the kitchen. She walked in, nervous and uncertain, and the man walked out to meet her from the inside room. He clumsily hugged her and looked away.

"Here he is," Bennie said. "I tolja he'd be here—he flew all night just to tell us what he knows. That's the kind of friends we have."

"You saw my boy," Jeannie said. "You saw him," she repeated. Tears began to run down her cheeks.

"I think so." He nodded and then flushed, and suddenly tears came to his eyes too.

"You saw Gilbert—you told Luda—"

"I know where he is, I think. But you come back tomorrow and I will tell you."

Jeannie did not like the way he looked; she did not like his milk-white, unhealthy skin, or his heavy double chin, or the smell of gin on his body. And now he was actually crying as if the moment had moved and terrified him.

"Come back tomorrow? No! Why?" Jeannie asked.

"Because," Bennie answered for him. "He wants you to—so do as he says and it'll be okay."

Jeannie stared at one and then the other, and they looked at her and glanced away.

"Don't tell anyone," Bennie said. "This is at the delicate stage."

But the man, Roland, was awash in guilt after Jeannie left, and he kept crying. He said he did not want to go on.

"Goddammit," Velma said. "What am I to do with the likes of you? What a pussy you are. Well, we will just have to figure something else out."

So when Jeannie came back next noon hour, the man was gone.

"Where did he go?"

"Had to be back at work," Bennie said.

"Well, why didn't he tell me something—why did he send me away?"

"Scared of the law," Bennie said. "Scared of your husband, always was—scared of the law."

"But I am not telling no one!" Jeannie yelled. "I promise—I promise!"

Bennie shrugged. "Well, what do you want—do you want to know what he said?"

"Yes, yes—I want to know, for god sake!"

"What we think—and Luda says we might be wrong about this—but we got some information from him. Had to pry it out because he is so scared. What we think is that Gilbert would be on the Island."

"What island?"

"Oh, you know, dear—PEI." Bennie lit a cigarette and looked out the window at the haze of the afternoon.

"Prince Edward Island," Jeannie said. "All this time?"

"That's what he says. That's where Gilbert might be—on the Island. So it's up to you to take a chance on that. It's not up to us to take the chance but up to you. I am not sure if it's another wild goose chase, but it's not up to me, is it?"

Jeannie looked at Dotty and then at Luda and then at him.

"Let's go there—let's go to that place," Jeannie said, looking at Luda again, almost petrified in hope.

And as Luda looked back at her in unspoken dread she continued, "Maybe there is nothing, as Bennie says. But maybe, Luda—just maybe he is there like you think. So we should go."

Jeannie slumped down, exhausted, and began to cry. She kept banging her hands against her knees and was afraid to look up.

Bennie drank his tea, looked into the cup, put in some more sugar, and as he stirred it, he opened his eyes slowly and looked over at her. The light from the window caught the scar that ran from his eye. It terrified almost everyone who saw it, and he could only open his left eye partially.

Luda stared at the scar, realizing suddenly that there had been a moment, years ago, when she should not have got into his car, and that the boy who'd given her the book years before had been trying to tell her that. She looked toward the register. Upstairs at that precise moment, Velma was sitting on an old box, listening to what was being said.

Now Jeannie stared at Bennie as he looked up from his tea.

"It's nine thousand dollars," Bennie said, emotionless. There was a long silence. There was, in that profound moment of silence, a slight noise way upstairs. Then silence again.

"But why would I pay nine thousand dollars?" Jeannie asked.

"Well." He sniffed and looked at her open-mouthed. "That's what I thought—why would you pay anything? I figured that—I mean, it's your kid, so I asked that too. But then I said, I am not telling her about it because she won't go for it—she'll never pay the money."

"No," Jeannie said. "It's not that—I mean, I will pay, but why?" She started to cry. "I will pay—of course I will. I did not mean it—I didn't—please tell them I didn't mean it. I will pay."

"Well, I know. It's not me, but it's who has him now. That's why the lad there who came here to help us is so scared. That lad on the Island wants to be paid off—for you know, finder's fee or some goddamn thing—if it was up to me, I wouldn't do it. I am telling you, Jeannie, I wouldn't do it. I am fair—Luda lives with me, and we've had our ups and downs, but we are partners here, and she knows how I feel. I mean we are searching and trying to help—but we are innocent people and maybe in over our heads a bit."

Jeannie could no longer think—and a feeling of hope ran through her like a sudden, dull streak of lightning or the heat from the afternoon that penetrated without seeming to be present in the dry, forlorn gusts that came in from the open window. Bennie's scar seemed livid and white and shocking. The day outside was windy; the chimes tingled in the window frame of the metal door. There was the shrill, one-time call of a bird, as if in laughter, against the straw-coloured sky.

Suddenly Jeannie felt a cold sweat from her stomach down through her legs. She thought she would pass out. Her baseball cap made her seem defenceless, as did her heavy purse with its picture of Gilbert in a plastic holder at the front and a little note above it that said "Reward."

She smiled, but her lips trembled.

Bennie sniffed and rolled himself a toke, and shook his head. "Boys, I am telling youse all," he said. "I want to get yer boy back if I can. No one ever knows that more than Luda."

He licked the paper and looked at her.

There was no way to say no and be certain she wasn't throwing away her last chance at finding her child. The one she would die for in a second.

So Jeannie now had to talk Luda into allowing it. For Luda kept saying she did not want to do it. Jeannie needed to convince Luda of the perfect delusion. And she did it by asking Luda one question: Would Luda ever stop looking for Dotty if Dotty went missing?

"No," Luda said, suddenly crying, harshly sobbing in the burnt-straw sunlight.

"Well then—what should I do?" Jeannie asked.

Luda said yes, okay, yes. And she looked up toward the register, toward the upstairs room.

"But there is one thing," Luda said, speaking as if into that register. "And it is this: The man said I was the one to take the money. I was to send the money to him. So I am the one you give it to. No one else, or the man won't go for it."

And with that she picked up Dotty and left the room.

For three days Jeannie couldn't sleep while she tried to get the money. She never spoke to John when he came to the house to check on her. She was nervous and silent and was glad when he left.

She got the nine thousand dollars—in fact, she got it quite easily. She gave Luda the money. Bennie was there, and he said, "Now, are you sure, Luda, you know what you are doing?"

"Of course I am," Luda said, taking the nine thousand dollars, spread out in twenties and fifties and hundreds, and then putting it back into the big envelope.

"Let's go," Luda said. And she went inside the small bedroom and picked up a few things, including Dotty, who was wearing a dress and sun hat.

"We can't go until Friday—that's the day," Bennie said abruptly, holding Luda back by taking Dotty from her and holding her slightly away.

"Not today?" Jeannie said.

"'Fraid not—but Friday morning be here," he said. "That's what Luda understood from the last phone call." And he held Dotty harder.

"Well, maybe she should take the money back," Luda said, trying to hand the money over to Jeannie, "until then."

"No—we can't do that. There is no telling what would happen when we're this far along." He took the money from Luda. Suddenly Luda started to bawl like a child of ten.

Tears came down her face as she was saying, "I am so sorry about your child, Jeannie—I dream about that little boy all the time."

"We all do—isn't that right," Bennie said. "Pawnmesoultagod, we all do!"

When Jeannie left, Velma came down the stairs, stopping and starting as she went, walking very slowly, so that every step she made was heard as a thud.

On the Friday they were supposed to leave for the Island, Bennie told Jeannie that Luda's little girl, Dotty, had something wrong with her kidney—and Luda had to take her to emergency.

Bennie said he must go with Luda to the hospital.

They were leaving as Jeannie arrived. "You can go by yourself," Bennie said suddenly; and as if he had just thought of it, his eyes lighting up as if to include her in his delightful solution, "Just wait in Borden—once you go over the bridge, you just wait there and that fellow on the Island will find you—and he says he has Gilbert."

"Who—who says he has Gilbert? Why can't anyone come with me?"

But this is how Bennie answered: "Just think what it will be like—what it will be like with Gilbert coming back over the bridge and sitting beside you—or Jeannie, maybe you won't even want to leave the Island—because you don't have to pay nothing on the way over—you only have to pay the toll on the way back—so maybe you just would want to stay with Gilbert over there!"

He touched her shoulder as he said this, looking at her and smiling.

"No, I will pay and come back—so where is the nine thousand I gave you?"

"What do you mean, dear?"

"Well, now I can take it and give it to him directly," Jeannie said.

"Oh—Luda already sent it. He already has it. Now I owe you twenty-five dollars."

"Why?"

"Well, I took twenty-five dollars to help our friend who come from Fort McMurray, so I'm paying you back."

"No, I don't want that." She turned to look at him, her friend, not terrified suddenly, but empty, hollow and unfulfilled.

"Well, I know—but I insist!" Bennie said, taking the twenty-five dollars out of his pocket. "I insist—fair is fair."

After Jeannie drove away, Velma came downstairs.

They had just got ninety-five hundred dollars, but it immediately became a sore point with them all. Velma wanted it—now. Bennie had taken it from Luda Bam Bam and hidden it. Velma said that most of it was hers. She had thought of the scam; she knew what to do with the money, which buyer to procure the drugs from, and she wanted it.

"Where is it, then?" Velma said. "Let me see—let me look at it."

"I'll show you later," Bennie said. "Luda, make me some tea, will ya? I'd like a cup of tea!"

So then, as the poet said, they would all become like weasels fighting in a hole.

There was one place the money was hidden.

Luda searched everywhere for three months. In that time she simply played a role. Each week, when Velma came to visit, Luda would privately complain to her about Bennie hiding the money, and when Velma was gone, she'd tell Bennie she was frightened the woman would find out where he had hidden it.

So Bennie was continually checking where the money was, determined to keep it for himself, and determined to keep it from Velma. Brother and sister were not speaking now at all—but Luda had made a classic mistake. In dividing them, she had also indicated a loyalty to each she did not possess. If either found out, she would be considered the ultimate deceiver.

Still, summer passed by, and the long nights became cooler and then the days shortened. Bennie could not walk out into the junkyard without being seen from the upstairs windows at the back of the house, especially after the leaves began to shed.

In November Velma telephoned Luda to say she was coming out.

"Come Wednesday," Luda said. "And I will have the money for you."

"You will?"

"I said I would."

Both Bennie and Velma wanted the money to buy methamphetamine in Halifax and bring it to Saint John. Both of them had indicated to their source that they would have the money—and yet both of them were waiting on the other, so nothing could be done.

And every couple of days Luda told Bennie he had better check on it.

So on the morning of November 19 he left the house, and Luda ran into the attic and watched him walk out past the derelict shed, out beyond the barn—then she saw his blackened coat, his huge hunching shoulders, re-emerge from the naked trees and go beyond the spring—to the old Dodge Shadow.

"It's fine," he said when he came back in and she was sitting at the table in her bra and panties, drinking from a pint of gin.

"I hope you still love me," she said. But she was trembling.

He told her that he didn't love her, that she didn't treat him well and she had better smarten up. He told her that he was on to her. And she'd better watch it.

So she lay on her back in front of the fire.

"That's more like it," he said.

Later she got him drunk and he fell asleep.

It was dark, and the fire had gone out and she was naked. She pulled on a pair of sweatpants and left.

Luda Marsh took a flashlight and followed his frozen boot prints across the withering field the colour of piled dung. The car lay apart from the other heaps, at the back right corner of the field, tipped up on its side—and walking toward it was like moving toward a living entity. Closer and closer she came to it.

She felt under the back seat for the money. The seat had blood on it. But the envelope Jeannie had placed the money in was pushed up beyond the springs. Luda was finally able to haul it down, but in doing so, she cut her hand.

She hid the envelope in her room, behind her little bookshelf, terrified over what she had done.

She wrapped her hand in a torn pillowcase.

"What in hell happened to your hand?" Bennie asked her the next day.

"Getting drunk with you." She smiled. "You like to bite."

"Really—I didn't know I was that crazy," he said.

She walked down to the small post office off Otter Road and bought another manila envelope, and mailed it away. The ninety-five hundred dollars. To John Delano.

As soon as she heard the sound of the envelope fall and the mailbox door close, she knew her death warrant was signed.

She didn't fear Bennie—he would hit her, but he wouldn't kill her. Velma wouldn't hit her, but Velma would kill her in a second.

It was Tuesday when Bennie came out of his drunk.

He went to get the money.

He tore the back seat of the car apart with a knife looking for it—in fact, he ripped the seat out of the car.

By that time Luda had dressed Dotty, had her coat on, and was phoning John Delano. Her hand was bleeding again—the palm of her right hand, because one of the springs had gone through.

She told John she was going to find a good home for Dotty and go back to school. She had been talking to Mr. DeWold about this, and he told her she could start a course now if she wanted.

She was out the door and walking toward the road, when she stopped.

She ran back to get the strange book the strange boy had given her. She got to the kitchen, and standing there—was Jake Cheval.

Bennie had started to walk back toward the house too, slowly at first, numb with betrayal, looking in disbelief and outrage at the blank upstairs window. He turned his head to the left and spit. But once he got there, he saw Luda. She had been stabbed in the heart.

Luda was five feet two inches tall. She had been beaten over three-quarters of her life. Any X-ray would show cracked ribs and fractured bones. She had sunk between the table and the fridge.

Then Bennie suddenly heard the click of a rifle.

Jake came into the kitchen from the living room.

She had a 22:250 in her hand, and simply followed him as he ran. She had to shoot him because he would tell on her. He cried and told her to stop. He slipped going down toward the old skid road because it was icy on the hill. It was the first of his three falls, and each time he fell his sister got closer. He begged her to listen to his side of things.

John had reached the turnoff to Otter Road. His left arm was numb and his back ached, but he refused to believe he was having a heart attack even when he was standing over Luda Marsh's body. He had begun to follow Bennie Cheval toward the woods, holding his left side, when he heard the shot.

For three years the established theory had been that the deaths that occurred that day, Luda's and Bennie's, were murder–suicide.

But John had never believed that.

The real force in all of this carnage was in fact intellectual. A theme like this is always intellectual in nature—is set up to take profit by wiles and ingenuity, using intellect to create deception. And John knew, after reviewing the case so many times, that it must have involved the calculated deception of a willing victim, with the deceivers using subterfuge to suggest kindness and sympathy. So the victim must have been in some trouble or must have needed to rely upon the perpetrators. So he felt they must have enticed her or him not with force but with information. It must have been the information that was false.

This, John was now sure, was how they got the ninety-five hundred dollars.

Therefore he knew Velma must have had something to do with it—her IQ was 167, and one could see that everything she did was calculated and involved a potential windfall for herself. So he knew the money must have come from something fraudulent.

He knew since Luda phoned him Velma—or Jake, as they sometimes called her—must have felt betrayed.

So he now decided that Velma must have been at the house on the day of the murder—and when Bennie saw that Luda had been stabbed, Velma felt she could not trust him anymore. This was the biggest change in his theory over the past month: Bennie did not kill Luda Marsh.

He underlined this three times.

John did not know the exact way it happened—and he felt he himself might never know—but nonetheless he decided he would give over his notes to Trevor later on. He would send his profile of Velma and Roland Roady to her as well.

One more thing, since his wife had telephoned him about the rim of the bowl up on Otter Loman Road, he felt some dreadful connection, and realized the person they may have scammed was Jeannie herself. And he was not there to protect her.

John blamed himself for much of what had gone wrong in his marriage. Sue Van Loon was trying her best to get him to forgive who he had to be.

Once, when she'd asked him if he had any friends, he had pondered a moment and said, "Not that you'd notice."

———

When the private first class rounded the bend outside of Kigali and in his youthful kindness and bravery tried to find a secondary road, to get north to the village where they believed the Forrest family was, out of his green shirt fell his wallet, opened to pictures. John looked at him, and recognized him as a boy from his hometown. They talked for twenty minutes about who they knew in common and John asked, "Where is your sister now?"

"God, I have six sisters. Which one?"

"The one I used to torment at school, and am now ashamed of tormenting," John said. Humbly, just like that. "The little one who had a hard time learning to read and write—we used to take her scribbler and tease her!"

"Jeannie," the private said, looking over at him with modesty and grimness, "little Jeannie."

And that was how John discovered her when he came back to Canada. She was sitting behind the counter wearing a big chef's hat inside the Dominion Bakery off Hanover Street.

"Ah yes, Jeannie."

So he went back to see her after his stint at the UN—that is, some months later, and found her, in her chef's hat and cellophane mittens, selling chocolate cookies and raspberry pies to elderly men and women. When she saw him, she backed up, startled, as if she wanted to run outside and escape the horrible torment he and his friends had often thrown her way. But he only bought a chocolate eclair and left. It was July then, and the streets were shaded, and the heat burned along the sidewalks.

John went back several times to that small Dominion Bakery, always waiting for the store to be empty, entering as if he did not know she was working, while she could see him loitering on the sidewalk below the big ill-fitting front window—and finally after six weeks he asked her out.

"You want to go on a date?" she asked; her eyes widened, and she looked behind her as if a joke was being played, and then looked back at him again.

"Of course I do."

"With me? I'm Jeannie Aube."

"I know you are."

"Why?" she said.

"I don't know why, Jeannie—I just want to. I want to go on a date—I want to do something right in my life—and I want to—well, I want to make something up to you. That's if you are not married with kids." But he knew she was not married. He knew she had a child that social services had just put into foster care. The case had started some months before when she was pregnant. He had heard she did not even remember being with the men, that the night was a blur—and she was left on the side of the road.

Her brother had told John that pro-choice advocates said she should not be forced into having the child. But for some outlandish reason she said no to them. Now this child had been born and was taken from her. Her brother told him about this as well, and how she wanted her child back but did not know what to do.

So her brother was determined to get the child back for her. He went to a lawyer, but the lawyer seemed to think everything was legal. So he went to John. And John decided within a week that since there was a clause that allowed Jeannie six months' grace, he would marry her to get the child back.

This became John's great, and many would say shameful, quest. He did not, of course, tell her that he knew any of this when he asked her for a date. But somewhere in his mind he had already decided he would marry her. In fact in that bakery you could say it was a sleight of hand as he picked up his chocolate eclair.

He used to say horrible things about her, just like his classmates. But John was worst of all because he was so bright. Nothing diminishes humanity more than intelligence without compassion. But now, he decided, he would get her child back for her.

"Well then," he said, kindly, "I'll pick you up at eight, so don't be late." And he smiled.

There was a moment when everything from the past became crystal clear, as if he was looking down through ice into the deep blue water.

And he said, almost unconsciously, "I'm sorry, Jeannie. They will not take your child. We will get him back for you."

She kept her eyes down and nodded, as if she were being scolded.

The first thing he had to do, of course, was marry her.

So he asked her to marry him on their second date.

It took him almost a year to get the boy back from child services, for the hands that wrap about you to protect so often turn to claws. But beyond that, there were many days when John felt he was doing something that was dark and sinister—that is, he believed what people said about him. Yet he plowed on, hoping to do this one thing, and make her life better.

They moved into a house he spent two years designing. He spent months buying her clothes. He spent months' worth of overtime taking her and the boy to New York, Washington and Toronto, places she would never have got to.

And he became obsessed with giving something—one perfect thing for her and the boy, Gilbert.

She did not know why he did all this, because he had once seemed so ruthless.

He adopted the boy late in 1997. Still, sometime after this, about eight or nine months later, she would wake, realize he wasn't beside her and go looking for him through the shadows of the great, warm house, the smell of lilacs in the great room, the sweet potted plants on the large veranda. She would find him crouched in the living room as if he was praying. He would say nothing to her—sometimes it was as if she wasn't there. Once she asked him what he was looking at as he stared into the darkness beyond the small lamp.

"Roasting human flesh," he said.

She asked him to start going to church again, and just to please her he did. But the cluster headaches kept coming, harsher and harsher and more frequent.

And they would bundle the boy up and take him in the sled to Mass and back again, and he made a rink for the child when he was three.

It took John a very long time to tell her about the nightmares—about waiting for word from the UN and the new interim government in Rwanda, and then feeling guilty, and then trying to forget it all, and like so many other human beings feeling guilty for trying to forget.

She began to try to get him to doctors in Saint John and then in Halifax. It did no good. He had a CAT scan. It did no good.

They were told their son had been with a group of twelve children and had rushed into the woods. That they had all been going to the wish pond, and at some point, after they got there, they noticed he wasn't with them any longer.

She and John drove out to the campsite and waited with the police all that night. Then Jeannie became hysterical because she had forgotten to tape *Dobblebuns*. She taped the program for the next three years—every episode. Some kids said he was following butterflies. Some said he'd been collecting pollywogs. Some said he was in fact chased by two other boys. John interviewed all these children, in the remarkable way he knew how to do, and yet nothing was gleaned from it. The boys had not chased him, he came to believe. The youngster was trailing behind a little, but people said he had wanted to search for pollywogs. John interviewed all the camp counsellors, and waited for a lie to be discovered. But they were not lying. They just did not seem to know what had happened to him after they left the campground.

For months, John vented his anger on plate-glass windows and car hoods and ornaments in the park, until he was given a reprimand.

So one day he turned over the accounts and the house to Jeannie, and decided not to go back.

Later that week Jeannie tried to take her life. They rushed her to hospital, where she recovered. She lived in a halfway house for a while, overseen by a registered nurse named Tammy Lou. The province, under the auspices of Melissa Sapp, paid for twenty-four-hour care. People gathered about her, as if she were a celebrity, and found her a new friend. He was a professor who was in Saint John in the summer vacationing, and had learned from Midge Nolan Overplant of the strange case and of that awful man John Delano, and decided to see about it himself.

"I would like to get in touch with her," he said, with a tone of sympathy that is so common among educated Canadian men as to be valueless. "There is a definite betrayal here and I won't stand for it," he said, emphasizing the word "I."

"Oh, you must do it—you must," Midge said. Her reasons were not altruistic. As always, she was enthused; she was a celebrity in her own right, after all, having been a force at the UN.

She and the professor were out on Grand Bay in the thirty-five-foot sailing boat, and in the enclosed and somewhat cramped quarters, alone with Midge, there was a moment that seen with a clear eye on a blue day, the gentle roll to starboard, this man, this Professor Milk, seemed quite ineptly conformist.

It was the book that came later that John tried to stop. But he could not. Old friends of his disappeared, no longer returned his calls. He lived by himself and was almost always alone.

Why had Jeannie allowed this book to be written? For Jeannie it was the only way to keep Gilbert's story alive. The only way to keep hope alive—the feeling she needed that her boy might someday still come back home. And if enough people read her story, maybe just one would have seen him. Maybe that one person would know where he was.

She poured out her heart to anyone. She did not know that some people would say anything mean-spirited about her husband. That he was an unqualified father, that he had done everything out of vengeance.

For a year John did not see or speak to her. But sometime after the book was done, Jeannie became expendable. Professor Milk called her an ignoramus, went back to Toronto and no longer had her number, nor she his.

In fact, Jeannie had always been expendable, just like most of the poor always are. The professor and she had fought over the funds she had hoped to receive to continue the search. But there were no funds for that, it seemed.

Tragedy in the Campground the book was called. John had a copy. In it he was a rude, backward-thinking RCMP officer with an eye on his career—and according to anonymous reports, known as a bigot, neglecting and bullying the child, who would have been better off with people like Melissa Sapp.

"Never again," was Melissa's final statement.

But the book, which Jeannie had hoped would help, did not bring one hair of Gilbert back.

So suddenly, after it all failed, Jeannie's brother telephoned John and asked if Jeannie could phone him. "She wants to speak to you," he said. "I think she is sorry, and wants to tell you she is—I am sorry myself."

"Sure, why not," John said. But being human, and after what he had tried to do for her, he had never been so disappointed with anyone in his life.

However, Jeannie began to phone John and say, "I am here." And he would take his car and drive for forty minutes and meet her at the old campground.

They found each other on lonely, half-broken paths, season by season searching the ruins that still oppressed, and in a moment of seeing each other, still searching became triumphant—as triumphant as a flush of autumn sun on a weathered face. More triumphant in that moment of despair, their aging cheeks caught in a flash of light.

"Are you proud of me?" she asked once.

"No, I am not proud of you now," he said. "For six months you were with a man who detested me—Professor Milk. People even say you slept with him. But I am not proud of myself either, Jeannie."

"Then I will make you proud again," Jeannie said, hardly moving her lips and breathing through her nose. "I will make you so proud of me you will say, 'That's my wife' all over again."

He looked at her a moment, the wind blowing so hard against them their bodies seemed suspended.

"And," she whispered, "I did not sleep with him."

Adding almost to herself, "Even when he wanted me to."

———

John decided some time ago that he must continue on in his loneliness, in his solitude, for there was no one else. He must realize he saw it, this loneliness, against the window glass on an avenue in Brisbane, Australia, ten years before, or in the town square when he was sixteen years of age. Or when buying a pair of loafers on some autumn morning in the quiet of a small-town shoe store, with the glitter of a silver shoe horn in the salesman's hand.

"Maybe another day," he would say.

But that day never seemed to come. Sometimes—in fact, the previous night, for instance—he would take out his service revolver and place it beside him on the chair. And he would struggle against the urge to put it to his head.

Just the week before—that is, around November 15—Sue Van Loon had written this timeline about John's life after 1994. Things, she felt, were coming to a head and she had to decide if he was or was not delusional.

Also she knew much more than he suspected. This is what she wrote:

> Jeannie fed date-rape drug—gets pregnant—her family feels she was sexually assaulted by three men from her neighbourhood one night when she was working late. Jeannie thought to be retarded; psychologist Sue Van Loon is brought in to assess her mental capacity.
>
> Melissa Sapp wants Jeannie to abort child, calling it a case of women's rights. Most people agree—and this is the first time in the official record that Jeannie is ever spoken about as a human being. No one in the country disputes this idea of the abortion, except Jeannie rebukes it. She says it is her child. That no matter how it was conceived, she will have it.

Melissa calls birth of child "disgraceful." So do most others in town. Sue Van Loon leaves the department.

Melissa says she will find a home for child.

John decides to marry Jeannie after Rwanda—for in his mind he had treated this woman almost as horribly when he was young.

John gets child back for Jeannie Aube after nine months or so.

For a few years their lives are fine and quite ordinary in many respects. Then one month John investigates unauthorized weapons possession, but fails to address career criminal Bennie Cheval in French.

Melissa helps file a writ of habeas corpus with the human rights commission. John loses case. Bennie Cheval is set free, speaks of seeking revenge, wants to sue for false arrest—but remains drunk.

John is asked to resign. He refuses and decides to track fugitive Timmy Wasson to San Francisco. Therefore, not knowing how long he will be gone, decides to send his child to Camp Fundy.

Child disappears.

John and Jeannie separate.

John begins working on case of missing child from Rwanda.

John believes this will implicate Melissa Sapp's department, and her husband, DeWold. So is it bitter grapes?

So: is it true?

That is, was the vendetta against John over these many years real? And if not, how was it not real?

And if it was real, how could Sue Van Loon stare John straight in the face and pretend that what he was saying was not true? That is, it was either true or false. John was either being ostracized because of who he was, or he was not. And those who were ostracizing him were either powerful people protecting their own, or innocent people who had done nothing wrong.

———

Luda had kept asking Bennie to give her the wine bottle and keep his eye on the road. The straw-like heat of evening came in the window of the Dodge Shadow, and far off across the river was a field with six cows, and beyond that, a gentle sloping away toward a row of trees waving. And it was now twilight, and the heat in the Dodge Shadow smelled of hermit wine.

They came to the stop sign—the asphalt road led away into the distance toward the grey hill, and beyond that a highway now cut through toward Sussex or Saint John. Bennie had never seemed so exuberant. They had said in the paper—on the front page—that he was a hard-luck case whose heart nonetheless was in the right place, and he had a youthful pregnant wife he had tried to provide for. And Bennie liked the word "provide."

He turned left, up toward Loman Otter Road, in the heat of twilight in July. He drove up over the hills and around the sharp turns near Camp Fundy.

4.

JOHN SNAPPED THE LOCK AT THE SIDE DOOR OF THE LITTLE shed. Night had now come, and the lights and the doorways along the street were closed, and the squabbles seemed far away and restrained.

The McCrease shed was small, and musty too, and the windows were covered by newspapers and cardboard. In the far right corner with two bald, and two winter, tires propped against it, and a shelf of Havoline oil cans over it, was a six-foot-high white fridge—and the door of this fridge had a hinge for a lock. The lock was gone, and the door swung open easily to show three rusted grills. One of the grills was almost black.

John bent down to examine it. It was December 1. And he had just broken into the shed at the back of Bunny McCrease's house.

At one time, he felt, this fridge must have been in the kitchen of the 87 Shelf Street house, and it must have been locked at night— say, after seven at night the fridge door wouldn't be opened except by someone who kept the key upon them. That would be Moms, he thought. When he closed the fridge, the drywall behind it moved, having been only tacked in place.

So John stood up again, and pulled the drywall out, and the tacks fell.

Behind this wall many old hockey sticks and balls lay; and an old set of weights; an old, deflated child's swimming pool; a broken bathroom sink, still with a piece of soap in it.

He wanted to take the sink—he felt it meant something most important. Why was this? Because when he went to the washroom when he visited the Shelf Street house, he knew the sink had been replaced over ten years ago, but not the bath. That bath was well over twenty years old. They were parsimonious people. That meant the sink had had to be replaced for some reason. So perhaps the sink had been broken—and he felt it had been broken in a squabble. One of those squabbles that were mentioned in the letter: "at one time—I won't say who but—they bashed him up against the sink."

Sitting on top of this sink was the bag, with one of the straps broken in two. He wouldn't be able to carry a sink back to Matters Road.

However, he looked in the bag.

In this bag was a pair of black socks—and a white shirt, half yellowed, and a small black bow tie.

There were two other things as well.

John put everything he could into a pillowcase, and brought the articles home. He put these things on the table and stared at them. There were other things along the shed's back wall that he was able to carry: a plastic gas jug, with the very top of it burned and melted off.

John took the gas jug and tipped it over, as if to pour gas out—in fact a small bit of dirt-filled gas did fall on the floor.

So he jotted this down in his notebook.

Someone—he suspected Vernon—had left the coat button on the downstairs mantel, and someone had burned his hand trying to light the boy's coat. When the coat lit, the flame shot up, caught the container, and whoever it was dropped the container and in panic kicked the fire out. That's why there were smudged fire streaks on the third floor of Shaw house, six to seven feet away from that fireplace where John had found the marble and the picture.

Back on Matters Road John went over the list of what he had found in the McCrease shed:

Fridge with lock

Broken sink

Plastic gas jug with melted top

Bag with broken strap. In the bag:

>Frayed white shirt
>
>Bow tie
>
>Children's black boots
>
>Torn and dirty child's blanket (comforter)

———

On September 10, 2001, he took Jeannie to New York to one of the restaurants he'd once gone to with Midge and others. He was bragging a little, and he knew that. The waiter, dressed in a white coat and black bow tie, poured the wine and had a French accent—the menu, also in French, spoke of splendid mutton cooked in its own juices, aged beef, and brazed cauliflower tinged with just a touch of irony. For some reason, John and Jeannie were the only two there. The next day was to be the big day for them: They were going to go around Central Park in a horse-drawn carriage and take a bus tour.

And after Central Park they were supposed to go to Firehouse 61 to meet Joel Finnegan, a fireman he had got to know when he was in New York years ago. They had gone to hockey games together. They were going to meet Joel for lunch at 1:00 p.m. John wanted him to meet Jeannie, the woman who had saved his life.

———

In April 1994, Hugh could not leave his job—his job of getting power out to Kigali. He had the stubborn streak of the thin, middle-class Canadian ascetic—there was something very splendid about him. The kind of Canadian who would go to South America and work in a village in Honduras for twenty years and hardly ever tan, come home with enough money to buy a little spot on the river where he could fish in the summer.

Hugh kept wiping his glasses on the sleeves of his jacket and working into the night. He had to repair one of the transformers. But the city of Kigali kept having blackouts. People were hiding in the grand hotel there. The transportation of truckloads of natural gas to his generating station had been compromised—in fact, four drivers had already been killed, and the old road from the mountains had been mined. So he kept waiting for raw material to generate power, and the gas did not come.

Yet still, in a way unknowingly naive, Hugh was certain that the political situation did not very much concern him, and his obligation was to keep the lights glowing. There is a certain kind of Canadian—indeed, North American—who believes in a kind of reverse manifest destiny. That is, the old destiny to push forward and inhabit the places of Native Americans had been reversed, and a new manifest destiny had been shaped by our need not for a white man's burden, as Rudyard Kipling stated, but for white atonement. Yet all still sparkled through with a kind of naive arrogance. But then again, this was not Hugh—he had no dog in that fight, and up until the end he thought of the disturbance as being separate from himself. Perhaps this was a dispute best settled by the Ugandans or Congolese, he once said.

Like so many Canadians, Hugh, if he thought about it at all, was a fervent internationalist. Because that was the only way Canadians could place themselves in a primary role in the world. Of course one thought of oneself as more agreeable if one thought of oneself as an internationalist. Hugh disagreed with the policies of the United States, but knew he benefited from them. But still he did think Canadians were far more tactful. And besides, didn't people love Canadians? This was not at all a chauvinistic idea with him, but something that he had witnessed and therefore believed. He believed in Canada's obligation, in a small, unobtrusive way, to help mankind.

He was not a reader like his wife, and he did not know history—even of the Second World War—very much. He may have even been of a mind that Canada shouldn't have had a role in it, as so many naive people in Canada did. He dismissed many things—whenever ideas bothered him. That is, as far as he was concerned most things were idiotic. So he never read about these things, and continued to do what he did to the best of his ability. He had heard of Margaret Atwood. Once he'd heard that she was angry at men. He had heard that Michael Ondaatje had written a book exposing the English and Americans in the Second World War. Yes, well there you go, you see it wasn't the Germans or Japanese—it was the British and Americans. That was about it.

He was a doer, and as a doer you made electricity so elders in the villages would not have to worry after dark. He was a doer so that people wouldn't have to drink water the colour of sour milk. He was white and the people he was helping were black, and that did not matter to him at all. Sometimes people stood beside him, yelling at him, worried over something, saying to him that he would never be able to get it done, that he had ruined everything—yet he would continue to work in silence, sweating yet calm, as others tormented themselves by yelling at him, until suddenly he had fixed the problem.

"But," he would say, "I will have to do more tomorrow."

He would lay out his plans for the morning while jubilation broke out about him, and people who once again had electricity patted him on the back.

"You're a genius—genius, genius!"

So doing his duty to others, he felt he would be fine. He felt he would be as fine as he was in his office in the University of Alberta in Edmonton. He had beautiful hands with long, powerful fingers—he could pick his son up over his head with one finger, and waltz him around.

But the trucks had to come, and he had to have them. He went to the Hutu mayor, Mr. Hill, and spoke to him about this. Mr. Hill shrugged and said times were difficult, and then with a kind of momentary self-indulgence, as if forgetting that Hugh was the reason for electricity in his house and office, he dismissed him.

"You do not understand what the Hutu have had to endure," he said. "You do not understand our struggle."

"I understand a bit of it—that's why I am here."

"You understand nothing."

"Of course, but the Tutsi here have done nothing to you. Most of them are scared to death and are hoping you can help them. Most of them were your friends."

Hill nodded in a nocturnal, noncommittal way, one that indicated Hugh did not know Rwandan history, as the door closed.

Still, Hugh told the Irish doctor, "It will be fine—Mr. Hill would have told us if there was to be real trouble."

He was informed that the Belgian soldiers who protected the compound were waiting for word to leave and he simply shrugged. For some days he continued to work without sleep, trying to keep the conductors up and going. Each day he passed under the corrugated mesh fence, which he called his ER, and each day he and three young men worked to keep the generators going. One was named Chubby, a seventeen-year-old Hutu boy who came and went whenever he wanted, so Hugh had to warn him about laziness.

Each day they tried to get the word out that the gas trucks had to be allowed to get through. But the trucks had already been hijacked, the drivers killed or had fled, and the gas sold on the black market at ten dollars a litre, or simply used to set fires.

At one point Lily woke at five in the morning to see her husband atop the flagpole with a pair of binoculars, looking for the trucks to wind down the mountain roads that were already mined, while the wind blew him back and forth like a mannequin.

"What are you doing, Hugh?"

"I am testing the Arusha peace agreement," he said, smiling. "But I want you and JP to leave tonight or tomorrow—things don't look so good from this high up."

Then he went to see the captain—a Mark Lebrun—and asked him if it was true that the Belgians were leaving.

"Very true—and you and your family are to come with us."

"But what about the others?"

"We have no mandate to take Rwandan nationals—in fact we are forbidden to take them by UN ordinance. It seems that the dispute is now way out of hand."

Hugh was very silent at this news. He was very perturbed. He knew his wife would not stand for it. Nor would the young missionary nun who taught with her. He pondered something, a tall man who still had freckles and a brown beard, and as always when he pondered things, he looked like a little boy. That's why the name Hugh seemed to fit him exactly. And exactly, so too did his utilitarian profession. He walked back out into the hot April sunshine with ankle-high boots, khaki shorts and red knobby knees.

His wife waited for him just near the Belgian headquarters. She was tall, thin and blond, with curious and compassionate and searching eyes. Her face was thin and very white. They had been here in this small village for some time. She would not stand leaving the orphans, nor would her friend Sister Vanessa. In fact, all moral decree disallowed it. The difference between the two women would have been considered profound except for their agreement on that. Lily was not sure a God existed, while Sister Vanessa was sure all of us should exist for God.

Over the past three weeks children had just wandered in and sat in the middle of the courtyard with nowhere else to go—children five years old caring for three-year-old siblings. What were Lily and Sister Vanessa to do? They could not leave.

And Hugh knew as much. So it was like this: If the orphans were condemned, so were Lily and Sister, and if Lily and Sister were condemned, so was Hugh. Hugh did not believe in God either, and there was too, too much electricity to get through, but he would do his duty and not leave Sister Vanessa. That is, although Hugh would have agreed with Chekhov that steam and electricity showed as much love of humanity as chastity and vegetarianism, he could not leave Sister Vanessa now.

As fate sometimes dictates, no one was left of the Forrest family save the three in Rwanda—Hugh, Lily and the boy—except for an Uncle Pierce somewhere in Newfoundland. And this is where Lily would try to send her boy. She gave instructions to him during the last nine days—each day she told him this: Go to the biggest place he could find if he was ever lost, and they would find him—and she now instilled in him that mad and lonely wisdom. "We will find you at the biggest building," she said, and she hugged him. (She had thought she would meet him in Kigali later in the week.)

"Where?"

"If anything happens, anything at all, and we do not meet—I want you to go to Canada—you are Canadian so they will take you there. Then, if we don't find you—on your birthday you go to the CN Tower, you tell people that, and they will take you there—then we will meet you there—never forget—on your birthday, that is where you must go if we do not find you before we get there! I promise you will be found—I promise you that you will be found!"

It was then that the boy began his journey from one place to the other—and found himself in Belgium. By then he had forgotten his name because of trauma—and the people around him thought he was mentally incapable of much, because he would go to one of the great buildings and sit on the steps.

Captain Lebrun was finally called and he was taken to him in late 1997. By that time the boy had been placed in an orphanage—but had twice escaped. One time they found him at the South Tower, in the North Quarter of Brussels, sitting on the steps in the cold, his blue-grey eyes searching for people he no longer seemed to know.

Once they found him curled up asleep at the Church of Our Lady of Laeken.

Lebrun had to go through a good deal of bureaucracy within the child-care services to finally allow the boy to come to him. He did it for Lily, though he was not sure of the parents' last names. Still, finding out the boy had an uncle in St. John's, Newfoundland, he arranged it all as best he could with the embassy, so the boy left for Canada in early 1999.

But John discovered the mistake: The authorities in Brussels hadn't thought twice about the difference in the spelling of the place names. They simply believed Canada had arranged the trip in a different way. Ottawa thought the same thing about the Belgian authorities.

Which caused all the confusion later on.

"I don't give a damn about the war. I have to keep the circuits operating for people in Kigali. And my wife has a school to keep going—so then, when will this be over?" Hugh had asked Captain Lebrun. He had tried to sound polite—but also wanted Lebrun to realize he was a little impatient.

"Over?" Lebrun said. "There might be twenty-thousand dead so far. It hasn't even started yet. Don't you understand what is going to happen here? I met your special envoy from Ottawa—he, like Canada and like Belgium, is delusional—but the UN is even more so. You will have to come to your senses—it is very important that you do leave. Canadians, French and Belgians have to come with us, at least as far as Kigali! They have already killed our troops—and it is the Canadians' fault."

"How is that?"

Lebrun turned, his lips trembling, face whitened by rage. "It was your UN people who demanded we give those bastards their weapons back so they could line us up against a wall and kill men twenty years of age—who were here to help keep the peace and protect the Rwandans from themselves. But it wasn't your commander—he too was only following orders from the UN! Look what the UN has managed to do!"

Lebrun shook, and his hands trembled.

But Hugh simply turned and walked back in the direction of the great grid he was responsible for, with his wife following. Besides, they were already having power outages, and if he did not do something, who would? He sent a message to Kigali that afternoon about the transport trucks, and inquired what was happening to them.

Lily sat in the small, whitewashed building at the back of the compound with a nun from Quebec and an Irish doctor who said he would not leave either.

"Who would dare hurt an orphan?" he said, smoking one cigarette after another, and keeping up on the conversation by telling them that though he was an agnostic, he still appreciated the masses he went to in Dublin at Easter time.

At ten that night, the door opened and Lebrun entered, saluted and smiled—for he liked Lily very much. And she certainly liked him—her curious, intelligent eyes now searched up at him.

"I can't leave and neither can my husband," Lily said.

"Then convince him . . . why are you putting up a tent in the middle of a compound?"

"To have Easter Mass," the Irish doctor said.

Later that night, though, Lily tried to call the Canadian headquarters about her son, JP, but could not get through by phone. She kept trying until it was well after dark. She did not know that so many people had fled, that there was only a skeleton crew at the command post—a staff sergeant was bravely trying to do the work, to coordinate search parties when no one could be coordinated.

Then Lily, her hands now shaking, wrote a letter to some nameless person in Canada, and called someone to come see her.

A young boy appeared at the door, smiling, dressed in a white jacket with Sebby written on the pocket. For some reason Hugh liked to tease him. So Sebby was happy Hugh wasn't present now. Lily handed Sebby the letter and told him he was to go as well—he must leave if her son did. She told her son, JP, that everything would be okay.

The boy packed his bag, his blanket and a few clothes, and then Lily said, "If you're in a strange town and you do not know where we are, where do you go?"

"I go to the biggest building."

"And when?"

"On my birthday."

"And when is your birthday?"

"December 15."

"So every December 15, go to the biggest building and sit on the steps and wait—and I will be there to get you. And if we do not come, your daddy has an uncle—and he lives in Canada—Uncle Pierce—I have it all written in the letter I gave to Sebby, but we will see you soon, I promise. As soon as you get to Kigali."

That is all she knew how to say at the moment, for so much at the moment was so chaotic. People were rushing by the tent, yelling over nothing at all. She wanted to go with her son—she wanted and needed to—but she could not.

She heard through the wind that a great massacre was going to happen and by this time there was no way out. She wanted to keep JP with her, but she knew he could make it to the Belgian command and they would take him to the Canadian command. This is what she told Sebby she wanted him to do.

The next morning there was the acrid smell of burned rubber in the clear air—the day would be hot—the children were lined up and brought into class—they were learning mathematics and French grammar.

The two Tutsi teachers the school had hired wanted to leave—and had in fact come to school wearing suits and carrying suitcases in the hope of going with the Belgians. They were lighter skinned and taller than many Hutu, and now were terrified. Their suitcases sat inside the whitewashed schoolroom's front door. The two men's proximity to each other caused them to be agitated, and sometimes they stood at opposite ends of the room. The younger man would burst out laughing when he heard the radio.

The radios all day echoed the belief that there was a plot among Tutsi to retake the government and to use Hutu as slave labour—and to sell them again to the Europeans. The Hutu militia, the Interahamwe, was only fourteen miles away along the back roads into Kimisgara, waiting for the Belgian regiment to pull out. They had built fires and were singing songs and dancing. At least, this is what was reported. (This is in fact how far John Delano got to, before he was forced back.)

Yet Hugh still did not quite believe what he was hearing—even the reports that a Red Cross hut had been burned and a Canadian priest killed. "No, we will wait," Hugh said to Lebrun with a tinge of egomania. "Everything will be back to normal in a few days. Besides, it is not my concern! As I told Wasson in Edmonton when he was speaking of how corporations manipulated monies to get the most from the public for gas and new pipelines . . . I said, 'That is all well and good, but that is not my concern—my concern is to keep things up and running, for without gas and electricity your concerns would be far worse. You think you can change one thousand years of progress with a stick of dynamite—the dynamite proves the one thousand years is more important than you are.' It does not matter that Wasson was a friend of mine—common sense is far more important than cutting into a pipeline, which is what the foolish man did—in fact killing more wildlife doing it than if he had not. And now I've heard he's gone to the East Coast, where he wants to do the same things, with lobster or whatever it is they have down there. And he has a network of gullible little old ladies to give him money. I am not fond of the East Coast, though my relatives came from there. Now, you take Wasson—he buried his morals in activism, yet he has from this activism a nice life: a house in Toronto, his own TV program and his constant berating of the government, which rakes him in thousands—yet oil is needed for electricity and fisheries are needed for food and forestry is needed to build houses, and he will understand that or my name isn't Hugh Forrest."

The Belgian captain looked at Hugh in fantastic frustration and sighed. But Hugh only smiled in a kind of victory. Then he asked the Belgian if the Tutsi teachers would be able to go with them. The Belgian said no, and he looked ashamed. That too was a UN order.

Only one of these Tutsi men's names is now known to us: Edgar. Edgar taught mathematics and literature. He was a writer, and was married with a family in Malaga, Spain. But he had been foolish enough to have his papers disputed and had to return to Rwanda.

He lit one cigarette after the other and stared out the window. Now and then he would tap his fingers against his suit jacket, or pull one of his sleeves down, or rub a cufflink, just as he had done on the day of his wedding. Last night he had washed as well as he could and packed his bag with some trinkets for his own children, a little boy and girl with soft dark skin and beautiful Spanish eyes. He'd had to sit on his suitcase to get it to close, and then he'd carried it to the orphanage this morning in the bright sunlight along the dreary streets. Today the water had been cut off, and two wells poisoned.

When the other Tutsi teacher, whose name we do not know, and who had the same kind of cramped suitcase, so cramped a tie was sticking out of it, would see Edgar giggle, he would shake sporadically and go out for a walk. But only as far as the white wall of the compound adorned with nine Canadian flags. There he would stand by the crooked arcadia tree whose limbs were grey and dusty.

This was the day JP went and hid so the Belgians could not take him from his mom. That night Sebby found him under the big hut, and risked his life taking him through the forest to the rear line of the Belgian troop movement. But they then returned to the compound, only to see a horrible sight. Sebby shielded the boy's eyes, and they ran.

After that, they moved only at night.

Along the way, somewhere near a little pathway, a girl rushed out, grinning, and whisked a machete down the boy's back. Sebby yelled and the girl fled back into the trees, and Sebby grabbed JP and carried him down over the rocks to the river. But it was during this time, Sebastian related later, that the boy forgot his name and who he was. Almost completely.

———

In 2007, John had made his way back to Europe. He'd had a hand in turning Mr. Odurante over, extradited finally from Canada, from a Hamilton plaza in fact (though he had very good lawyers on his side). He saw him for the first and last time in March, in his brilliant black suit and three-thousand-dollar watch, at The Hague, being tried for human trafficking and crimes against humanity.

He was Mr. Odurante—so friendly one couldn't help but like him. His face shone like a gangster's. John asked him about the Forrest child—had he ever seen him?

"Oh yes, I have seen him and I know exactly where he is, if you can get me out of this." He smiled.

John was now halfway through Ernest Buckler's *The Mountain and the Valley.*

Midge, our cultural attaché and a Maritimer, had never heard of *The Mountain and the Valley* when John brought it up to her, saying more Maritime writers would be good witnesses of Canadian culture in New York. She was an officious lady, who, when you told her something she did not know, looked with suspicion at you—full of a kind of child-bearing accusation. She sighed and said, "It's not up to me! Besides, we always try to bring in the brightest and the best." And later she smiled beneficently when he introduced her to his friend Joel Finnegan.

They talked for a moment in the hallway—and suddenly the special envoy was standing beside them, with the Canadian flag pin on his lapel and his felt fedora pushed back, showing his broad forehead, his goatee slightly grey. He was carrying in his hand some exceptional brief.

"Sir—I would like to introduce you to a friend of mine, Mr. Joel Finnegan—he's a fireman here," John said.

"A fireman? Well, well, that really must be interesting work," our special envoy replied. He hurried on, and disappeared around the corner, where a blue orchid sat in a grand marble vase.

———

In 1994, Midge's office in New York was not very big. It was a place for gentle conversation, splendid imported teas and shortcakes. In it were posters of certain well-known Canadian writers—Laurence, Ondaatje and Atwood—the address Lester Pearson gave when he won the Nobel Prize for Peace. A picture of an African woman tilling soil with a child on her back. A map of Rwanda that she had been given by Rwandan ambassador Jean-Damascène Bizimana. She had travelled extensively and had the worldly air of the no-nonsense middle-aged feminist divorcee, wearing loose-fitting pant suits and large skirts. Always with a hat that made her look mischievous.

It was on the chair outside this office where Harry Sabota had left his last bouquet.

Later, once the massacre was over, Midge went to the Rwandan ambassador's Thirty-Ninth Street apartment, and found that when he had fled, he had taken everything with him, even the fridge, which he had locked for transport, and the seventy-two bottles of French wine that he had stored in the cellar.

————

Harry Sabota had tried to go with John to the villages—he had got out, safely away—whatever possessed him to return? It was as if he was a kid who kept turning up at a party where he wasn't welcome. When they were stopped at a roadblock, boys of twelve and thirteen trained their Kalashnikovs on them. Harry got out of the car and spoke for a few minutes in private. Then he came back and told John he had to turn around and leave.

"What about you?" John asked.

"No—I'll be fine now. I'm home," Harry said.

John told Mr. Sabota he should not leave the Jeep—and should return to the United States. "There is no place for you here," John warned.

"There is no place for me there," Mr. Sabota said.

When John told him that the Hutu militia were firing on the airport, Mr. Sabota simply took his bag and suitcase—a foreigner suddenly in his own land—and began walking northwest along the narrow, ill-defined road, with a power line to the east. The sudden clarity in the air seemed to suggest that electricity was no longer being transmitted through that line. The air was indeed fresher, but Harry's suit was already dusty and his hair suddenly seemed whiter in the sunlight, as if he had been out in wintertime. His expensive white shirt was crumpled at his waist and his belt was missing.

"I don't think it is safe anymore," John said.

"But I have only come home to help!" he said. And he turned along the road and disappeared.

John had always believed that Harry Sabota had saved his life that day.

They were forced to turn around and go back to Kigali—they met corpses along the road, in the ditch—seven women raped and murdered. Harry Sabota was himself murdered five days later.

Mr. Raul Deganda Hill—his was the face John remembered. At night he would remember it. When Raul Deganda Hill asked for political asylum in 2000, he went to the Canadian embassy in Paris. John fought for three years to have him extradited to Rwanda. During the long trips across the US, or into Haiti, or when he visited the Dominican Republic, John would see the face of Mr. Raul Hill.

Raul Hill was simply one of the three mayors from that area where Sabota finally died. He issued a statement sometime later that he personally did not know Harry Sabota would return—nor had he known the Hutu militia would rely so much upon him, Raul Deganda Hill. Still, he knew when they did rely upon him that to cross them meant his own execution. And though he told Harry to come to his house, he knew finally he would have to betray him, and to betray him meant he would have to have him killed. He turned and kissed him on the cheek at the end—why, he did not know; it was something he was compelled to do. Later, realizing it was a kiss of betrayal, he was amazed at the symbolic truth of the gesture, and tried to burn his lips.

For two or three days a Hutu boy named Chubby sat in Mr. Hill's house and drank beer, waiting for the right moment.

So Mr. Hill was one of the people who told the Hutu boys when Harry Sabota would arrive at his house, and where the Tutsi teachers were hiding. It was just a little fray within the hundreds of thousands going on around the hills and villages across Rwanda. That they happened to be middle class, and so many, many others happened to be the working poor, did not matter at all.

They lit Harry on fire with a jug of gas stolen from the compound.

"I didn't want that!" Hill stressed.

———

"I believe in God," Sister Vanessa said to the Belgian captain who had asked them to leave. "And the Vingt Deux." Sister Vanessa was pregnant with the child of the priest who had been killed two weeks before. They had been thinking of a different life for themselves—becoming lay missionaries and living together. She did not think they knew, but all of them, Lily and Hugh and the Irish doctor, did.

She kissed her crucifix, looked at Lily and smiled. Hugh stood in the corner with his red knobby knees sunburned, and looked more baffled than distressed. That perplexed look was seen on his face the next day when he was trying to keep his generating station at the "up and ready." His strong hands, with their long fingers, worked over every inch of the generators, while skyward birds flew.

Then he touched Lily's lovely face with his hand and said, "I will always try to keep you safe and sound."

It had been so silent and listless the last two days that the splash of a little water could be heard four buildings away. The machetes were at Raul Hill's house. He too was young, only twenty-seven—and he was like mayors everywhere. That is, he was pedestrian and civic and obsequious. He played the violin. Poorly. He also had hunted hyena. Once. And in the past few months he had a plan to have tourist centres where the orphanage was—and he thought of having trips into the gorilla regions for white upper-class Americans, safaris that lasted a week at ten thousand dollars a couple. He loved reading popular racy novels from India and watching sex films from Indonesia. He loved wearing a white shirt and blue tie with a glistening tie clip, and drinking a cold bottle of banana beer.

That is, up until eight months before, Mr. Hill could not have imagined killing anybody.

One morning, Mr. Hill saw his good friend the Tutsi teacher Edgar dragging his heavy suitcase along the dusty street. Edgar noticed him at the same time and waved, and Mr. Hill started to lift his hand to wave and then stopped himself. In fact he was about to go out and help him carry the suitcase, but nervously lit a cigarette and thought: How foolish I will look doing so. Still, he felt badly watching Edgar drag that heavy suitcase. They had been friends since childhood. Edgar had read some of his stories to Hill, and Hill had liked them.

Later he told the Dutch judge at the inquiry into the genocide: "No one knows what they will do until they do it—even you! When one is terrified, the only hope is to spill blood. And maybe now and again to light a fire."

And he scratched the top of his head with one finger, like a coy debutante. John was asked to testify, but he did not know exactly what Hill had done.

John would walk for miles at night, trying to figure out a way to save those who later died. Or even who to save. Even now.

He never seemed to get it done.

When Sebby, the fourteen-year-old boy, took JP, Jack, into the bush to find their way toward the Belgians, he was in such a hurry he forgot the letter Lily had given him the night before, and did not remember it at all until the boy was gone. The boy had no passport and no identification at all. So Sebby, not knowing what to do, gave the boy his picture to keep.

Then the boy refused to go toward the Belgians and they both headed back toward the compound. Jack was going back there to save his mom and dad, and hid under the farthest building. But he could not manage to get closer.

He got a great deal of dirt on his boots and mud on his hands (this dirt was now being examined by John Delano).

In the end, Sebby took him to a block of arcadia trees and they knelt in the bushes. Then when they heard the cries and saw fire, Sebby had to hold him down so he would not rush into the midst of danger. He held his hand over the boy's mouth and covered them both with bushes. Afterwards they moved out across the wall and some old barbed wire and made it into the forest—moving to the northwest with a half-million others trying to get to Uganda.

Sebby not only safeguarded Jack but kept him alive and away from the Hutu captain, a boy called Chubby, who had a small cigar and told Sebby, "Give the whitey to me and I will give you two hundred dollars American—do not, and I will kill you. Tell him his mommy wants to see him, and so too his daddy." The Hutu believed this was ingenious, the most ingenious thing. (In fact, it was Chubby's sister who swung the machete at the boy the next night.)

Sebby took the boy and ran with him back into the forest. Then six days later, running from Mr. Odurante, Sebby lost him. Over the years Sebby came to his own in South Africa, where he lived with a Mr. Butternut in Cape Town and wrote a book under the name Sebastian Donald Ebusantaini.

And now Sebby—Sebastian Ebusantaini—was in New York, where he'd had his book published. Everyone was making much of this book, especially our former special envoy, who contacted Midge Nolan Overplant.

"My soul, it's the first I heard of it," she said.

"I am thinking if he talks up here in Canada—well, he should mention you, for all you tried to do," our envoy said.

"Well, my God—you more than me!" Midge declared.

Sebastian would indeed come to Canada—he would arrive for a tour sometime in the next week. Advertisements for this event in the Maritimes were already on posters stapled to poles along Matters Road. John had seen them over the past few days and had not recognized what they were about. But this visit is why the government in Ottawa needed to find out what had happened to the boy Sebastian had written about—the Jack whoever.

———

The young boys and girls at Camp Fundy slept in cabins named for fishes and fowl. Salmon, Trout, Partridge, Duck, et cetera. They were called the Pollywogs.

Gilbert stayed in the Duck. They had a contest where they all had to waddle down to the brook and go quack.

His cot was at the back near the window, with a flower he had picked half hidden under his pillow. There was a bowl on the table at the back of the room. This was the bowl he had taken.

For the first two hours, they had not known he was missing. Then one of the girls told them he wasn't at the wish pond—that is where they had been going to. It was supposedly dangerous to go to this pond, or so all the kids were supposedly told (as a joke).

But somewhere he had gone off the path.

So they backtracked along the marked trail, calling him. There wasn't a sound in the woods at all. It had the heat of trees at twilight when the bark takes on a white appearance and now and again the bright sunlight peeps through darkened, faraway branches and a bird twitters.

When John and Jeannie arrived, one eighteen-year-old girl was shivering in the cold night, her blouse soaking and her pink shorts filthy. She had gone all the way down to the Hammond River looking for him, three miles away, calling out his name. She had scraped her legs raw on old spruce branches.

Now John was beginning to realize that the boy, his boy, Jeannie's boy, had been left behind. He had been late coming from the cabin—and went in the opposite direction. The simple fact was, no one knew.

When John went back to Teacher Judy in March 2003, he stood in the hallway of the oppressive little school with pictures of youngsters up on cork boards, slogans like "Be your own person" and "A bully has no real friends."

And he knew that neither of these was true. Not for his son—not for Gilbert. That in fact he was his own person, unconsciously and irrevocably his own, and he was bullied by those who had had many friends. Even by those like Teacher Judy herself, who sat in the lounge with other teachers and gossiped about the poor waif, son of a man who once tried to sue the Canadian government for facts about Rwanda, a man who her own husband, Melonson, had to deal with. "A bigot too," she whispered. "He hates our French."

So you see, these slogans were a lie, and Gilbert coming to this school was a lie. Someone took his star on him. Someone stole his scribbler with the leaves—because they could.

John wouldn't leave the school when the principal asked him to. She stood listening to him saying something even he could not fathom: "It has almost been a year. Where is my boy—where is my boy? I want his book bag and I want him to have his stars!"

It was drowsy late winter—still harsh with weak sunlight after three in the afternoon. He was doing this, in a way, for Jeannie, or trying to. He stood in the pale, spotless corridor waiting for his son to come out and grab his coat and boots and smile at him. That is what he was saying. That he was waiting for his son. To take the boy home to his mother. That's all he wanted his son to do—that is, run from the room after the bell rang—in fact, he would give a thousand lifetimes for it, right about now. Hell, he would die a thousand deaths. He would be crucified if they told him it would bring Gilbert home. In fact, he already was. So there and then, he understood the idea of Christ dying for us was true.

John was given new pills on December 2. He stopped taking them on December 3. That is, he did not even open the small, white pharmacy bag they came in. He knew it was perverse not to take them. But he was sure he no longer wanted to.

He picked up the bag and then placed it on his dresser.

He finally listened to his messages. Most of them were from the cardiac rehabilitation centre, inquiring why he did not show up for his appointments.

––––

The Belgians began to pull out. Hugh watched them. He smiled at Lily and patted her shoulder.

Hugh watched them packing up equipment and putting it into their trucks, taking apart and folding tents from their forward position, all with a kind of aloof and strategically professional air about them. Each clink of the tent poles signifying reticence and resignation. His tall body in khaki pants and khaki shirt with its huge pockets seemed to make him look even more vulnerable. Suddenly he sighed and turned back to doing his work, with his little boy walking beside him, trying to take as big a step as his dad.

The two Tutsi teachers pleaded with the Belgians to give them safe passage past the Hutu militia.

The Hutu militia were completely silent—in fact a few men stood by an arcadia tree smoking, as if nothing in the world was the matter. But everyone knew that if the Belgians dared take the Tutsi, there would be an assault on the Belgians.

The captain did make one more plea for the Canadians and Irishman to come. But all of them were too stubborn. They could not go. They wanted to—they desperately wanted to. But they could not.

Why were they too stubborn? Because Vanessa, the Roman Catholic nun, who was twenty-nine years old, would not leave the boys and girls; and the Irish doctor realized that Vanessa couldn't leave, even though her order had already gone back into Uganda. She would not go, so the Irish doctor would stay beside her. And Hugh looked at the great generators behind the mesh fence with the sign that said DANGER HIGH VOLTAGE and would not leave either. And Lily could not leave him. And so it came to that moment, as fruitless as it all seemed, where there were principles to live by.

Oh yes, don't worry John knew as much.

They were terrified.

The Belgian captain did not want to leave either—he did not want to leave Lily. But like the Belgian lieutenant who had been shot, he had to follow orders. And the Belgian captain, as brave as he was, he too was terrified.

Lily believed her son would be sent to Kigali. She dressed him in a school jacket and polished boots, a white shirt and bow tie. He took a bag and his small wallet. He had lost his favourite cat's eye marble the day before in a game of Eights with Sebby. Sebby handed it back to him.

"You keep this, and we will play another game again."

"If God is so cruel, why, then, is there a God?" the doctor asked Sister Vanessa later that night when the transport was leaving and the sounds had almost disappeared on the street outside. The little girls and boys were sleeping. Sister Vanessa took the doctor's hand and said, "It is not God who is cruel—something else that mocks God is. But not God."

Then she added, "Our country will not let us down. The Vingt Deux will be here tomorrow."

The Irish doctor sighed. He knew well of hopeless situations.

Suddenly, both realized there was no more sound from the last axle groaning on the last truck carrying away the last Belgian with their submachine gun.

Then the two men who had been seen a few days before by the arcadia tree, then those men started to sing.

"Imagine" by John Lennon.

That night, Midge and her friends were at a play based on George Sand's *Mauprat*. Afterwards they went up near the Dakota to have supper at Tavern on the Green. By this time Midge had said she was certain, absolutely certain, that Shakespeare did not really write his plays—no man from the untrained class could have had such a universal mind, so it had to be Elizabeth I.

"Midge is Canada," Harry Sabota had said, one night at the Consulate. That was the night they played a word game—Midge and seven other men and women—and all the words had to defeat aggression. So they had found words like *peace, love, community, nonviolence, sympathy, compassion, tolerance, devotion, need, help, completion.*

And some wag—Harry himself—had said *sex*, and everyone laughed.

5.

JOHN EXAMINED THE BOOTS HE HAD FOUND IN THE BAG. HE looked at the boots for three days.

They were a peculiar kind of boot.

He felt certain that the boots—high, black leather boots with laces—were made for a schoolboy and that they were unusual. Why were they unusual? Well, they were unusual because not many boys would wear a boot like this, here in Canada—now, they might in some other place, but here, if they wore a boot, it would most likely be a boot for winter weather.

So then, looking at the boy's boots, he realized they must have been about fifteen or so years old. They had not been worn in a long time. They were last worn in summer—or in a place that was always summer-like. And there was something else. The boots hadn't been made in Canada—initially, that is all that could be said about them. But did that matter? So many things were not made here, from toothpaste to T-shirts. So did it matter?

It did matter if you wished to find out where the boots were bought. And say a boy was going to a kind of private school and needed a boot as part of his uniform—for this is what John believed the boy must have worn. Did it matter even if it was in a poor country—John had spent time in Jamaica, and remembered those little boys and girls in uniforms, all lining up to get into Champs.

So these boots were bought for school, and the appearance of propriety.

John decided they were first seen in a shop window by Lily and bought for her young child. This was the strange connection he had with Lily, the strange feeling of following her with his mind's eye throughout those years. Lily, a woman in many ways so unlike him, was still a shadow over him, telling him that even though she was much closer in sentiment to Sue Van Loon or Melissa Sapp, she needed him to discover the truth. For she knew he was the only one who could do so.

Once he even thought she had touched his shoulder.

Ridiculous? He would be the first to say so. There was something impeccable about young Lily that had graced all that terror—he thought this remembering Sebby's white shirt. There was something impeccably good that was in the Canadian compound on that last dark night.

The boots were not bought here but in Europe, perhaps. Or, say, a trip to where the boy said his family had taken him once when he was little—Cairo?

This is what he took to Trevor. He went into her office as if she would be pleased to see he was still working on the case, and saw her displeasure at seeing him.

"Ah," he said, "it is just something I have discovered."

"What?" she said, looking up. "What have you discovered this time?"

"This time" was said with such a lightly comic, pejorative inflection that he stumbled slightly over his words and smiled. "I have discovered the boots," he said.

"What boots, John?"

"I found the boots of the child—the missing boy," he said.

"Where?"

"Well, I can't say."

"That means you did something illegal—and that is what we have all been afraid of."

He sat down in the seat across from her and said, "Well, it is my last case, so what does it matter—take a look." And he handed her a boot.

Trevor looked at the boot, and handed it back to him while looking down at some papers. That is, she wanted to pretend aloofness and seem as if the boot did not fascinate her—but in a way it did.

"Well," he said, taking the boot back.

"Well, it's a boot—could be anyone's boot, John."

"But of course, that is not true at all," John said defensively, and for the first time with her he was caustic. "Don't be swayed so easily because of Melonson's dislike—and do not think I have the least thing against women just because it is convenient to say I do by people who have less insight than myself."

She looked up, startled. She was startled because the veracity of his words stung.

He paused. "I am trying to solve a case, do you understand? I am trying to solve a case for Lily Forrest, a woman who died seventeen years ago—and she demands I solve it," John said. "So then, what does the boot say?"

So she took the boot back and looked at it once again. And feeling a little humbled said, "I don't know."

"Well," John said. "The first thing is the size on the inside is European, not Canadian—that is, it's a boot from Europe, for the size of the boot is not marked like a boot would be here but in Europe. And something else—"

"What?"

"When I took the magnifying glass and looked into the boot, I made out the name Northern."

"Well, that means it could have been made in Canada," she said. "Is there a Northern Boot Company here?"

"I don't know."

"Well, there you go—and certain children sizes are indicated exactly like you say?"

"They are—but usually for toddlers, or children not much beyond five or six—and there is a Northern Boot Company somewhere else."

"Where?"

"India," John said. "And they are sold all over the Middle East—to Egypt and in Cairo."

"Do you know they were made in India?" Trevor asked. "How can you just say that and believe it?"

"Oh, it is quite difficult, but I managed." He smiled.

"And how did you manage?"

"By looking on the bottom of the boot near the heel, where it says, 'Made in India.'"

Trevor now sat back and looked at him as she tapped her pencil. "You look like death warmed over," she said.

He didn't answer.

"Are you taking your heart medicine?"

He didn't answer.

"You know everyone here is against you, but not because we don't care about you—it's because we do care about you."

He didn't answer.

"If you broke-and-entered to get this, none of it is admissible, and you may as well be pissing into the wind," she said.

He nodded.

"And who would misidentify him when he came here?"

"Melonson," John said.

"And you are going to tell Melonson this?"

"Oh, he knows and wants to hide it—he has to."

"How do you know that?"

"Well—wouldn't you?"

———

When the Lion of Justice was freed of the enormous responsibility of doing our country's work (and what he had discovered during this time was that we did not have any carriers or transport planes, air force or navy worthy of the military men and women who actually served their country and were willing to put their lives on the line for it—and when he discovered this, he said nothing, for military situations and decrees were not a Canadian concern, but to him, steadfast in his pacifist theories, an American blight), he went on to other things. These other things showed him to be concerned about the peace process in the world, about establishing new health clinics and supporting freedom of choice and working toward parity for everyone in Canada—making sure we were seen to be fair, even if that meant being obedient to the tyrants of media-manipulated consensus, and advocating freedom for Quebec.

That is, our Lion of Justice had always been in a snare. He earned an enormous salary for being one of those people who went to conferences on international parity and economic plans, where absolutely nothing was accomplished. And in the end his morning ennui was filled with the leftover plates and dishes and the vacuous remains of hotel-room catered dining. He visited Rio, and Madrid and Singapore—always fussing over his per diem and his accommodations. Squabbling with taxi drivers, telling them to speed up or slow down, looking at maps, visiting ruins, walking on his long bony legs up the Great Wall of China, with the wind blowing and a camera round his neck.

Then making a subtle and failed pitch, with the backing of Midge Nolan Overplant and her connections in Ottawa, to become the governor general of Canada (he was, as they say, on the short list). He continued doing charity benefits for many progressive causes (but only progressive ones—ones that caught the public eye). Research into AIDS had been his biggest cause for a long time; now of course it was stopping the Northern Gateway pipeline and global warming—he did this to show his love for First Nations peoples, but in fact our Lion of Justice had never been on a reserve, or even driven through one. He had an ongoing correspondence with his son, Tim Wasson—such a good man, and often mentioned him in his lectures.

The Lion of Justice also spent many months trying to get *Huckleberry Finn* banned from schools, visiting school boards and making statements about its racism. He was trying to have certain words struck from Canadian society—words that every comedian in the United States that Canadians loved to watch used. No one could say, then, that he wasn't forthright and sincere. That is, leave it to Canadians to ban a book no Canadian had managed to produce.

The Lion of Justice was also writing his own book. And mainly he resided in New York—not as an expatriate but more as a man with dual citizenship. New York was where he felt his profile was best appreciated. But at times he looked as out of step there as the expensive peach suit he wore.

He gave some attention to the repatriation of displaced Hutu families from northern Rwanda and the damage that Tutsi revenge squads had perpetrated. Some Hutu children who had had nothing to do with the genocide were singled out and burned alive. But mostly Rwanda was behind him, like it was behind most of the world. For instance, our Lion of Justice did not suffer the enormous feelings of shame and guilt that a lowly RCMP officer named John Delano suffered, or that Jeannie's brother, Corporal Aube, did. And though he heard about John Delano from time to time, in one dispute or another, he simply said: "Touched in the noggin—hates women. All men with his background usually do."

Then he said whimsically to Midge Nolan Overplant on the night they received the Order of Canada, with the flattering and utterly false smile he always used in front of women, "As I so often tell my wife, I do believe only women should be police persons."

Our Lion of Justice seemed firm in his beliefs and he was a presence. He was doing a film. He travelled the world and was always learning—learning new words in Swahili, learning some phrases in Mandarin, sampling a certain delicacy from Turkistan. He was often called a *bon vivant*, for some reason.

So in Argentina back in 2001 he decided to learn the tango. He had a fondness for Argentina because of a friend he had met from there—a striking young woman named Mataya with dusky brown skin and beautiful black eyes. A young woman who had taught him the tango not in the large ballrooms reserved for tourists but in the small, out-of-the-way cantinas in the night. In after-hours where the tango was really celebrated, on the outskirts of Buenos Aires where the streets were dark, and the sound of squabbling could be heard in the neighbourhood.

The secret was—well, if it can be a secret today—he was married, and he had an affair with Mataya in 2001, when she was twenty years old. He had planned to bring her to New York during her vacation, which started in autumn. He often boasted to her, which he could not do with his wife, about his connections to Nobel Peace Prize winners, how he petitioned to get the Burmese dissident out of Myanmar and how he had been considered himself for a prize or two, but "I am not interested in that. I am only interested in the world." She was starry-eyed in love with him—the older, sophisticated gentleman who promised her his connections, could get her into McGill University to study.

He was going to meet her at the World Trade Center, tower one, on September 11, 2001. He of course had never faced a gun or taken a slap in the face, but he was about to meet many who had and were willing to put their lives on the line to save him that long-ago day.

———

On December 4, 2011, a man who knew a lot about our Lion of Justice, knew about facing guns and violence of every sort, was walking along Otter Road, an old, dirt-and-asphalt road that cut in through the centre of the province of New Brunswick from one half-forgotten place to another, stretching out as solitary as a crow in flight over burned trees, 280 acres of trees burned and withered two summers ago, and therefore had, after all these years, exposed what his wife, Jeannie, had found—that is, the aged, rusted rim of a bowl.

John had inspected that bent and rusted bowl rim that Jeannie had sent him, and now was walking from one turn in the road toward the other.

"You see," Jeannie had said to him. "Take a look."

And he was struck by it suddenly—that is, touching the bowl rim: for they knew there had been a bowl in the cabin and the boy had taken it, to collect pollywogs.

So John was pacing the distance between the turnoff, and looking back over his shoulder at the snow that wisped along behind him and the shadows of half-burned trees that reminded one, John thought, of some great Tom Thomson painting.

Why was he walking in one direction and then turning and walking back? He wanted to see from what side of the road the car he now believed had hit his son had been coming from. There were only two houses along this entire stretch of road, and John believed it was a person from one of those houses who had driven the car. Or more to the point, he knew exactly which house the person was from. It had taken him this long to understand that no one ever said the boy had not been with the counsellors (and he had questioned them all a dozen times) because no one knew he had not been. So they said he had been, and would have passed a lie detector test because that is what they thought.

He now believed his son had not been lost at all—that he had come here by himself, been walking along the road with the bowl in his hand, looking into the ditch for pollywogs, and was struck from behind. And that he was 180 degrees away from where everyone thought he was.

His child would be walking back toward the Camp Fundy shore at that time, so he would be walking toward the west. He would be looking at the pollywogs he had collected in his bowl, or looking for more, and he wouldn't see the car coming up behind him. So John decided if the car was coming up behind him, the sun would be directly in the driver's eyes—for it would have been well after eight at night—for that's when they began to look for him—so well after eight the sun would have been in the driver's eyes. There was one other possibility—or a multiple of possibilities. That is, John might be fabricating things himself because he was in denial about his inability to solve his own son's case. This is what had been said to him earlier this day when he took the rim to Sue Van Loon and told her he was leaving to go to Otter Road.

"Because of that flimsy rim—it could have come from anywhere. I mean, couldn't it?"

"Yes."

"So then maybe a wild goose chase?"

"Of course it could be, but there is something about it—even about the rim. The idea of him taking the bowl from the cabin—why didn't I think of it before?" He said this mysteriously. He showed Sue Van Loon the picture of the bowl. The rim caught in the sunlight of the Duck cabin at Camp Fundy, which was pictured in the brochure Jeannie had kept. So looking at the picture of the bowl, John came to Otter Road, carrying that old rim.

And now John decided that the driver wouldn't have been alone. For if he had been alone and too scared to report hitting the child, then he would have kept going. The child would have been found on the road or in the ditch, maybe even still alive. So someone made him stop and pull over to the side and take the child. And now John thought that this would be a woman in the car with him, who demanded he do the right thing.

And in the end this had kept the child from being found. Why? John felt that one reason was this: The man was someone he knew.

So John decided that a man and a woman who knew him, John Delano, were driving along on that July night, hit his child and stopped a few metres down the road, in the heat of the straw-coloured evening. They both got out—and John was now walking back toward the ditch, exactly like they would have.

The woman would have carried the boy back to the car, and she would have got blood over her.

So they both got out. The man threw the bowl into the ditch and the woman picked the child up and put him into the back seat.

John lit a cigarette and looked up and down this desolate patch of highway. This weak sun, on this day was now settling down over the burned and famished trees like the flush of crimson in the darkish-purple world of Tom Thomson.

But then what?

The man must have decided to go back and get the bowl—and hide it somewhere else. When he did, the rim had been shaken loose—or the bowl broken? And the pollywogs themselves let loose into the drain, which may have had a scum or suck of water and so survived?

The boy may have been dead then, but John suspected (although he would not tell Jeannie this) the boy was still alive. And it was all because he had been left behind in camp, and didn't know where his friends from Duck cabin had gone, and had set off on his own. So then, what did happen after that?

The woman must have wanted to take the boy to the hospital either in Sussex or Saint John—but this did not happen! She screamed that they had to take him and the man kept saying no. One reason for this entered John's mind: The man driving was drunk and in no shape to go anywhere, and did not want to be investigated, because he had been in trouble with the law before—perhaps on many occasions. John suspected he now knew who would have been on this road on that long-ago night, who had been in trouble with the law, which had the sad fatalism of the past and all the clocks stopping.

Then there was this: John Delano's picture had been in the paper that afternoon, taken as he was bringing in Mr. Wasson, the self-proclaimed environmentalist who had stolen money out of the life savings of Mrs. Clare Wilmot, eighty-seven.

John was thinking of the picture in the paper. How outlandish it all seemed for a small city. There were four officers with semi-automatics and pump actions on the roof of the justice building—not because of Mr. Wasson, but because of wild rumours that Bennie Cheval might try to take revenge. John remembered how ridiculous he had thought all of this was.

Bennie did not do anything of the sort.

He did, however, spend the next four weeks drunk, until Luda drove him to detox in August.

So John now suspected Bennie Cheval was drunk driving back roads and proclaiming to people how he would get John Delano. And Luda, the young girl who had been with him for over two years, and was in fact trapped, was in the car, seven months pregnant with a child.

John believed Gilbert was still alive yet they could not take him to the hospital because they knew he was John Delano's child. How could Bennie take the boy to the hospital after threatening the police, and then say he did not know it was John Delano's boy?

Gilbert would have walked a mile up the old road, searching for his pollywogs. Then he would have turned to go back to camp, thinking he only had two days left before he would be reunited with his mom and dad.

What was he driving that year, Bennie Cheval?

Well, John remembered every detail. Bennie was driving a white Dodge Shadow, which had a protruding front bumper that would have hit any little boy high on the legs.

So at the very moment the child was handed back to him and Jeannie, and away from foster care—at that moment the child had already picked the rose, had already written "Dad, you forgot to say goodbye."

Bennie and Luda must have taken the boy to the house. Luda would have insisted on that. Her humanity would have demanded that; all her love would have demanded it. So if that was the case (and John felt it very well could be the case), then he knew of the house.

She may have said, "I'm taking him to the hospital!"

And he may have said, "No, you can't. Sorry, but that's the way it is. They will blame me for planning what was an accident. They will say I had it in for Delano and the police—no way will they believe otherwise. I said I would take care of it at the court house the day they let me go. 'What will you take care of?' they asked. What in God's name do you think people will think!"

"But we have to—we have to."

"We will put him back on the road."

"We are not putting him back on the road!"

John seemed to see it in flashes: Bennie would have had to phone his sister. He had always told her everything.

So then twenty minutes later, Velma came in—she walked in, her stiff leg in the brace, and asked some questions and was silent—and, what is worse, perhaps even in a slight way amused.

"Well, this is something," Velma said.

"I have a face cloth for him, and he is still alive—so we have to go to the hospital." Luda ran from the house with some cubes of ice in the face cloth. Velma walked out behind her in her halter top and stovepipe jeans, her back as straight as an arrow, wearing cowboy boots as the sun teetered on the brink of going down.

And then it was night.

Those cubes of ice melted, and a swarm of wasps finally went back to nest near the back outhouse where Bennie had driven the car. And the boy gasped for air—and now and again he opened and closed his eyes.

Velma came and stood by the car, and said, "Ya got yerself in a pickle here, doncha!"

So John turned and looked far up into the solid, cold hills.

A fire had burned down Camp Fundy two summers before. That's how Jeannie found the rim in the first place. She had come here with some girlfriend to pick blueberries in the hot blueness of afternoon. The blueberry bushes that always erupt after a fire coursed over the long, burned hills, as beautiful as daisies in the sun.

You go up to the left past a heavy deep ditch and across a small, wooden walking bridge—the road itself slopes up and around a cluster of old apple trees and spruce, and beyond that, where the walking bridge ends, is a path to the grey, shingled, two-storey wooden house on a four-acre lot of land with houses and outbuildings all around, the compound that had been under siege by the police once in the seventies, once in the nineties and then again in 2007. It seemed desolate now.

But John wasn't going to the house yet—the house where he had found Luda Bam Bam in her own blood. She had the baby beside her, dressed.

John had always thought Luda was phoning him about the stolen money she had mailed to him. But he realized now her call had been about much more than that—it was about his own child.

He walked past the house—its roof almost but not quite caved in. He walked beyond the barn. His boots started to thud more as he walked, and he knew he was going down toward the gravel pit at the back end of the property, where cars lay silent like ghosts or sirens of some other time—an old Ford from the fifties, its colour undecipherable; a Skylark from '67; a Mustang; and an old green 1976 Pontiac. Beyond that was the Dodge Shadow, tilted on its side, with weeds and burdocks growing up through the shattered windows.

He had to stop for a moment and sit on a chunk of hard rock maple. His heart pained a little bit, so he waited a moment to catch his breath.

Then he moved on.

It was eerie to look into the car window. The back seat had been removed. The steering wheel had a hand knob and a fur cover. The shift was shaped like a human skull.

Luda's picture was still there, pressed into the mirror. John accidentally saw his own reflection when he picked it up.

There was white wisping snow and silence blowing over the boards of the old, dry well at the back of the bracken-cluttered barn.

He walked back to the house, the picture in his hand.

He now thought the person who had killed Luda had not come into the house like Bennie would have had to do—but was in the house—and that person was upstairs, and had come down when she heard the phone call Luda made to him. Luda Bam Bam, her friends called her, the name inscribed on the wall of Shaw house.

The sun was falling away now; and he could see it from the grimy windows inside the bedroom.

She had Dotty in her arms when she fell, and was trying to walk to the door, in a kind of desperate defiance.

John had arrived and followed Bennie. But as he ran, he had felt pain—numbness, really, on his left side, and stumbled and fell. He was lying down when he'd heard the shot and thought Bennie was firing at him. He stood and kept walking. It took him twenty-five minutes to find the man. He came along the skid road, along the haphazard buckthorn roots. Bennie was lying there in a jacket and white sweater—a big, heavy belt—and a wallet with almost nothing in it at all.

John looked around the bedroom now—there was still an empty crib. There was a woman's yellow shirt on a hanger in the open closet, and a bra on a hanger beside it. The yellow shirt had some blood on it. Some books and magazines piled on a bookshelf. A child's snowsuit was left in the corner.

He began to go through the books and magazines, now and again looking out the window toward the wooden walkway, where the evening sun was setting.

The book had been on his mind for weeks. That is, he had believed if he found this book, he would find the girl who had been important to the missing boy.

Now he remembered a book that did not fit this house when he had been here last. He remembered glancing at it, and thinking it a little odd to have seen it here—and somewhat prophetic—though he did not say anything.

So as soon as he'd read that the missing boy had given a girl a book, he thought of this book. Then he remembered bringing Luda Marsh to Shelf Street. So he began to suspect that she might have been the girl. He supposed the book could have fit—but one would have had to know the particulars of how she came to have it. A schoolteacher may have given it to her, he had initially thought. Now finding it still here, he picked it out of the shelf of small romances and cluttered magazines.

It was there in a black-and-green cover, lying against them.

It was still unread, except for twenty-three pages.

It sat behind the romance novels Luda Bam Bam loved to read, and the children books she had collected for Dotty, and a book called *How to Improve Your Vocabulary*. Beside that book was another, called *Case of the Two Fallen Sparrows*.

John took the book, *Nights below Station Street*, and flipped through it. It would be a strange book to Luda Marsh—a book she might not ever care to read. But a book someone outside the province (and this was the secret) might think she would enjoy.

He clutched his cane. Something had glittered on the shelf when the last of the sun fell, just as he was picking up the book. So he looked to see what it was. He was too good a policeman not to.

He hardly made it back to his car.

John Delano was taken to the hospital on December 5. The sky was clearer and brighter than it had been in days. And he had lost consciousness after he got back from Otter Road, and it was, as they said, "by God's grace" that anyone found him.

His wife, Jeannie, found him because he had phoned and told her he was coming to see her and did not show up.

This became known to Sue Van Loon. He was already being forgotten about—the great cases he'd worked on meant nothing to the nurses who tended him, and hardly a soul visited. His wife, Jeannie, did, and his brother-in-law—but they were the only two. And during those times he was sound asleep.

The idea that he might die this time was in fact a comforting thought to many, including himself.

But Van Loon knew Ottawa was now determined to find this boy, and now—that is, by December 5—Melissa Sapp may have realized the enormity of her husband's folly. Her husband's folly would certainly be linked to her, and perhaps because of this, the premier's folly as well; that is, to have given Melissa carte blanche within her department.

Late the night before—the night John was taken to the hospital— Melissa's husband had come to her, walking slowly in big slippers, and apologizing for the case and saying he was going to admit to what had happened and retire.

That he was going to leave her. He was going to start his own sports store, and live by himself. She knew this would be horrendous for them—but particularly for her own career.

Still, the more she tried to reason with him the more certain he became that he must admit.

"Admit—admit to what?"

"I don't know . . . I feel like I have to admit."

"Yes, yes, admit, of course admit—we will all admit, let us all admit—but to what?"

But DeWold looked feeble and sad and tired and depressed. The weight of the lie was growing every day. His big slippers made him look like a child. Then he took one slipper off and began to bat the smoke away as she held a cigarette.

"Admit," he said anxiously, his face still looking happily outward as if he could not be unhappy even at this moment. "I will tell you what I will admit to—that I lost that boy, and that it was my fault. That I shouldn't have had that case, and I did not visit that house until it was too late—that you tricked Ms. Hershey—and I botched it all. And—I—should —have been content to play—hockey."

He stopped batting the smoke. He looked at her with a serious expression, his face white and his big suit dishevelled.

Each word he spoke made her flinch, and she kept moving her head backward slightly as if to fend off the words. But then she composed herself. "Well, let me lead you through it. You don't have to admit to anything," she said, taking another pull from the cigarette. "I will figure this out. If you admit to anything, they will look at it as my interfering in someone else's caseload in order to get you a job—that is very bad for both of us. For we do not need investigations. If you admit to anything—those who should also admit to something won't, and we will be scapegoats for them. I do not intend to become that. So do not admit."

"I have to," he said. "I have been to church the last seven days—I took Communion. You said it was imperative to tell the truth—in fact, the idea I got from you during all this time was that John Delano was a big fat liar. But now I see that was wrong."

She was stunned and said nothing. Church? Communion? Well, that proved it. He was an idiot. Besides, she hated it when weak people quoted one against themselves.

"But it's all right if we are liars, for we are lying for the proper reasons," she said. "We have the best agenda." She smiled at this.

He looked at her a moment, then he said, "Hah." As if he had just caught on to something.

She wondered why she had ever married. Well, she knew why she had married. She'd married to spite people in her family. They were crazy with both worry and shame and it pleased her. Why? Well, she was a revolutionary.

Now she said that she was quite confident this would all be resolved, that she had been talking to the premier and let him know she was confident it would be.

"How?" DeWold said.

"It will be—you and I both know that the child at Shelf is not the one they are looking for—that John Delano made it all up—because—well, because he has grave psychological problems. Last month he was even stalking me. I would love to find that boy, but we do not even know by what province he entered Canada—the mix-up happened in Belgium."

She tried to get him to smile by telling him about Ms. Louise crawling about the floor in her very tight skirt, looking for a contact, and how she was totally blind, bumping first into a chair and then a desk. And how Melissa could have helped her, but it was too much fun to watch her crawling like "my slave" on hands and knees.

"Yes, I always thought she was blind," DeWold said now. "Just like me."

————

When John did regain consciousness, Sue Van Loon spoke to him. He was putting on his shoes and getting dressed when she came in to see him. In his room there was a balloon that said "Get well soon" from the department, and another one from Jeannie.

He straightened his wrinkled jacket. His face was like ash, but his eyes looked bright. He took a comb and swiped it at his hair, a few times as he spoke. He still had a heart monitor attached to his chest in a pouch about his neck. "I will know it all by next week—not only about 87 Shelf—but about my son too. I will find out by December 15. And

Melonson—what will Trevor say about him?" he said, a little childishly.

So Sue Van Loon defended Melonson now: "How could he dare believe a boy who said he only knew his first name and that he came from Africa? What if Melonson had believed him and it turned out he was a runaway from up the block—how foolish Melonson would have been, running about saying there was a child from Africa. He wouldn't have got into the RCMP then!"

"Well," John said, again with a tinge of pleasure, putting his comb away into his shirt pocket and reaching absently for his cigarettes, which had been taken from him. "The only problem is Melonson is paid not to make such a drastic mistake—but to take time enough to exhaust the possibility that the boy is telling the truth. Melonson needed it to be a lie, and set about to prove it—strange."

Here he opened a piece of gum, took half, looked at it and, shrugging, put it into his mouth. He of course thought of the little purse with "Amy" written on it.

He was not supposed to work, do anything strenuous, drive a car—and his smokes had been confiscated.

"It was not Bennie," he said to her.

"It was not Bennie—what do you mean?"

"Who killed Luda," he said with effort.

"Who then?"

"Velma."

"Are you sure?"

"Oh—well, yes. I am pretty sure."

When he left the hospital, he had to take her arm—and she walked him to her car.

"Do you know something?" she said.

"What?"

"I have been thinking about this for some time now. Yes, democracy will allow all these middle-class boy and girl protestors, and it will allow frivolity—yes, democracy will allow fascination with irony, with Angelina Jolie and Oprah and all the rest—and there is nothing

wrong with it—in fact, it is in some ways what we are all about. We
need protests and civil unrest too—but when push comes to shove—we
need—well, we need Roosevelt and Churchill. Yes, even Thatcher! We
need serious men and women willing to do a serious job. We need people
like that. Yes," she said, as if she had just discovered something, "we
need people like you—and your friend, the one you told me about. Joel
Finnegan, the fireman—whatever became of him?"

Ottawa launched a full-scale investigation on December 8. They repri-
manded Melissa Sapp for being too cautious, and asked for all pertinent
information about Shelf Street and the children who had stayed there
in 1999.

Then Ottawa got in touch with Melonson, and asked him if he knew
a boy named Melon Thibodeau. This again was done without knowledge
of John's involvement. But Melonson believed John had to have been in
touch with Ottawa and was orchestrating the hysteria.

Melonson sat in the house alone, in the chair, listening to the wind,
feeling the walls close in upon him. He telephoned Melissa Sapp but
could not get her on the phone. This bothered him immensely.

He showered at five in the morning, and was in the office by seven.
And what he said to Trevor that day, and for the two following days, was
ultimately so logical that it seemed now was the time to go to their division commander in Fredericton with the case against . . . John Delano.
That is, the lie that Melonson had to now promote was so logical it
seemed almost indecent to say it was a lie. In fact to not attack John
would be an act of diminished responsibility and Melonson knew it—
that is, he knew that if he did not promote the lie as being true, then he
would somehow be derelict in his duty as a policeman.

The lie that he had invested in over these many years had started with
"Well, I phoned the airport and you didn't come in on a plane." He remembered him saying this to that sad, likeable little boy—but why had he?

But he now promoted this lie in a way that showed he had John's best
interest at heart and wanted to save John from himself. This is what he

had in fact been pretending with Trevor for ten months now: that his only concern was to help John retire with dignity.

Trevor listened to Melonson's theory about John and Rwanda, from December 9th to the 12th:

"He said something about boots. If I went around town, I would be sure find out where he bought them—you know this as well as I do. He knew that Ottawa would be looking for this boy—he has been on this Rwanda kick for years—so he knew about it long before we did. Now is his chance to blame it on us—he waited for the Rwanda case to come up, and he jumped. He decided to take over. Shameful self-interest," he said on the 9th.

"And," he continued on the 10th, "here is it in a nutshell: He has evidence of things from Rwanda that he collected over the last fifteen years planted here and there in the city, in order to prove to Ottawa that he has solved a major case about a boy who was never here. And he did this because he was negligent with his own child. Social services was heroic—heroic in trying to get that child away from that silly woman. Melissa Sapp tried to do the right thing, but our province is so backward." (Others' backwardness was always a condition those who believed they were progressive hid behind.) "Well, they will never find this boy either—yet John will again be considered a great police officer!"

"You mean he bought the boots himself?" Trevor asked on the 11th.

"Yes—he bought the boots, or he already had them somewhere," Melonson said. "You know this or you wouldn't have mentioned them. He could have got them in Moncton or across in the US. Sure." Then, for the third time he told her the story of what had happened to his wife; that John came very close to striking the woman and had broken a bulletin board. And then he said, "I will guarantee you that the blanket John found, the one he says belonged to the boy, is Gilbert's."

"Gilbert—his son?"

Melonson sounded persuasive and practical. "He is setting the whole thing up to look like a hero—and to get his wife back. He is planting evidence. That is an indictable offence—and I might go to the Crown prosecutor because of it."

"You can't," Trevor said on the 12th.

"Well," Melonson said. "If he keeps formulating scenarios in order to indict everyone else, you know what he might say—he might say I had something to do with it myself. Buttons and slips of paper and burned jackets—he's crazy. Tell me what I should do about it."

"I don't know what you should do about it—and how do we know he fabricated it?"

"My God, he gets a call from Ottawa telling him there might be a child missing. He writes a letter about this child—and bingo, all the evidence shows up. Eureka!" Melonson laughed. "I know he is good, but is he that good?"

"Well," Trevor said, "you are right. Except . . ."

"Except what?"

"Except," Trevor said, "he is that good. He always has been that good."

6.

IT HAD SNOWED HARD ALL DAY LONG AND THE SNOW HAD drifted, but now the snowfall had stopped and the drifts of snow sparkled under the lights. All John was thinking of, beyond all the other things he had been thinking of in the past few days, was Lily. Lily, he thought, wouldn't have given a dime for all the theories about her son. For all the tormented theories of free choice, and the wisdom of one position over the other. She only wanted her boy safe, and loved, and known. She wanted him found. And now, to his embarrassment, but he could not help it, he lit a candle for her every evening after supper. He walked over to Saint Rose of Lima, holding his cane against the slippery sidewalk, to light a candle for Lily, his friend. He supposed that perhaps not only wasn't she a Catholic—conceivably she wasn't Christian. Still, he had heard "Find my child" distinctly, on more than one occasion. The voice came to him at night or in the shade of day, or in the scent of nicotine as he walked passed a storefront in the middle of the afternoon. "Find my child—and you will find yours!" he had heard distinctly. "Find Jack and you will find Gilbert, I promise!" he had heard in the dark.

"So then, Lily, my girl," John said, butting a cigarette, "that's what I will do."

The lights were on in the buildings and the streets were quiet and the shifts were changing. He parked his car on the down slope of the hill and stared at the oil tanker *Pretoria*, far out in the winter bay. (He was forbidden to drive, of course, but he shrugged and drove anyway.) Wisps of snow scuttled across his boots as he stepped carefully along the street.

He made his way into the building through the back and up the stairs to his interviewing office.

After fifteen minutes he heard the man's heavy boots squeaking along the hall. The door opened and Vernon Beaker appeared. He was a small man with an anxious, somewhat endearing puzzled face—like an old wizard.

The wind howled over the bay. His face was red raw because he had walked from the taxi stand; his scrape of beard was frozen.

John had come early to set the evidence he had on the table and said nothing about it when Vernon sat down. When Vernon saw it, and John was busy looking over his notes, he began to shake. John said nothing, just waited for the man to take off his gloves. The little man's eyes were riveted on the evidence. John handed him a coffee, and Vernon took it with his right hand trembling a little.

"I have to go to Toronto—you know why I am going there?"

Vernon shook his head, and tried to smile as if all of this was beyond him, and he did not know why he was here. That is, he had heard at the taxi stand that they wanted to see him at RCMP headquarters and he had come along, thinking that it was about the robberies of taxi drivers in the port city, which always terrified him at night—he had no idea it was about this.

"To a hockey game?" Vernon now said.

"No—I won't have time. Besides, I think the Leafs are away."

"Yes," Vernon answered. "The Leafs have been away for years."

They both smiled at this. John looked back at his notes. "No, I have to go to Toronto and try to find someone."

"Oh?"

"Here, let me put sugar in that—I drink mine black—you want sugar?"

John took the cup and went to the cupboard and got some sugar pack-
ets and emptied two in. Then he brought the cup back to the desk. He
remembered the boy from Saint Andrews—that spoiled-faced kid who
had shot his father for a largesse he would have received anyway.

"So anyway," John said, when Vernon brought the cup to his mouth,
"that scar on your hand between your thumb and forefinger—you were
holding the jug like this?" John stood, took the old plastic gas jug in his
hand and tipped it up. He stood back holding the jerry can as if it was
the most natural act in the world. Vernon set the coffee down, but some
spilled on his knee.

"You know," John said now, "I almost did that once as well—burning old siding in a barrel at my house. So I know how it can happen. So
when I saw the jug, I realized . . . well, what I realized is: Vernon simply
poured the gas on a lit fire and the fire travelled right to his hand. So, I
said, I bet Vernon has a scar on his hand—the coat did not burn as he
thought it would. But look what else happened," John said. "This stuff
got away. I mean in the fireplace. The fire did not get hot enough or go
deep enough."

Here John handed Vernon the blackened but still visible photo of
Sebby. Then he handed him the marble.

"I knew it had to be JP as soon as I saw Sebby," John admitted.

Vernon stared at the picture, and then at the marble. Then suddenly he began to cough. His face turned beet red, and he seemed to
be choking.

John handed him some Kleenex out of a box he had on the desk, and
waited until Vernon blew his nose, twice. "You see, I am now certain
the hundred dollars was in his pants pocket—the wallet was zippered
up with some old childhood mementoes he kept, so he rarely opened that
wallet, and he kept his money separate from it. He had another wallet
maybe, but I think he just put the money in his pants pocket—except
for that night when he put the extra twenty he was going to give to
Melon into his coat breast pocket. I think he had a new coat, and was a
kid and wanted to use the pockets. I think he was heading back to find

Luda—that is what is so sad—he was a young boy, just a child, yet he was brave, wasn't he? At any rate, brave enough to try to help Melon, and then to help Luda—I damn well hope a child like that is still alive."

He paused.

"He was the boy you helped open an account at the Bank of Montreal. You liked him and he liked you. And you tried to help him. I knew it had to be the Bank of Montreal—and how was that? Well, because that was the one bank that was farthest away from Shelf Street. So the boy started using the ATM instead of the bank branch. It stood to reason the boy would have a bit of money on him. He didn't work at the bowling alley—Melon thought that he did, but was simply confused. I think, as far as I can tell, he was given three hundred dollars Canadian when he came here, perhaps by Lebrun himself. Who took him to the airport in Brussels and hugged him goodbye."

John stood and stretched and looked over his notes once again. He made Vernon another cup of coffee. He asked about Bunny McCrease and how his health was. He asked about Moms, and if she had got her blood pressure under control, and said he knew what that was like, with blood pressure. Then he lit a cigarette, and he spoke in confidence:

"Much of the information I have, Vernon, is inadmissible—people could even say I planted it, but you know I did not."

"Did not what?"

"Plant any evidence."

Then he paused for a long time, looking at his notebook. Finally, he said it was not Melon's fault—Melon had wet the bed that night, and Moms beat him with a belt—but Melon was always wetting the bed. The little Limey and Melon had opened the window and tried to dry the sheets that Melon had peed on and Moms caught them. Freezing the house out at one o'clock in the morning. John said he could not prove this, but this is what he suspected.

That's when Melon was beaten—and Moms dragged Melon into the bathroom and ran the tub with scalding water and told Melon to get in—that's when the Limey hit her as hard as he could and she fell against the sink. That's when the sink broke. Then she turned and took a belt to him too. That's why Vernon went outside at night to smoke, to get away from things.

Three days later the Limey left, and a month or so after this, Moms had bars put over those windows. After a year or more, Melon started lighting fires.

Now and then as he said all this, John would reach for his coffee and drink, and look at Vernon, who had his head down.

"What do you wish for Vernon?" he asked finally.

"I wish the nightmare would just go away—so I could get some sleep."

John said he wished Vernon and Bunny had come to him with the truth, twelve years sooner.

"What would have happened?" Vernon asked.

"Everything would have been cleared up in a day," John said. And he smiled.

———

The serious fracture in Melissa Sapp's relationship with her husband caused anxiety for her during the last few weeks of the case. She was the go-to person: a brilliant lawyer, part of the human rights commission defence, part of the group of lawyers who challenged the law and brought in an appropriate women's health centre, and as usual in these cases, a child advocate who had the ear of the premier and was supposedly non-political.

Still, she knew what she had done. Years before, as both a lawyer and a social worker, she had finessed this very case away from Fern Hershey, who like so many women was intimidated by her; and she had given it to her husband, who was just coming into the job. He would be a quick riser and she would bring him along. And she had promised Fern Hershey the job her own aunt now had, in order to accomplish this. And though she had made a hundred excuses to herself as to why this was done, nonetheless it was done.

Melissa had been John's nemesis for years—always, however, in the background. She never said she was the one who had anything to do with Jeannie—but that day the child was finally handed back, Melissa Sapp was waiting in the back of the SUV, watching him. When John Delano did not read Bennie Cheval his rights in French, many people wanted to let the matter go. This was a ruthless man, implicated in so many crimes. But Melissa said no; no matter what Bennie Cheval might be implicated in, the law must be the law. It had been brought forward in New Brunswick and must stand. So she brought it before the Canadian Liberty League and the New Brunswick Human Rights Commission, but in a more stealth-like way than usual—her name was not mentioned except once in the paper. Still, why? That is, why had she done this—what motivated her and what propelled her?

One thing only that she would not admit to: revenge.

To get John Delano to seem callous and uncaring and untrustworthy. That is, she could not have cared less about Bennie Cheval's rights. And the person closest to her—DeWold—knew this, and each time she did something he was more and more distant from her. But Melissa wanted and needed revenge for being thwarted in Jeannie's case—and she would not rest until this happened. In fact, by 2007 she thought she would hear no more about John Delano, that he had been exposed.

But now she was not at all sure that this was so.

She had studied John's cases and was fascinated by this man who she took to be her enemy and a ruthless chauvinist. There was also her friend Wasson to think of—a man who, she felt, was a bright light of advocacy and revolution, who had been hounded like a criminal all the way out to San Francisco.

So in the last week she went back over the case of Gilbert and his mother, Jeannie. After reading through the files and the long court transcript, she knew in her heart that the boy should have been given back to his mother. Just as Sue Van Loon had demanded.

But still she said, "The woman was a test case. She was unable to care for a child—one should have had sympathy and she should have had an abortion." And she snapped the file closed and lit a cigarette.

DeWold listened to this, and was slightly ashamed of her. She was far too matter-of-fact when deciding these things about others. She too had had an abortion. And she'd done this to prove to those around her that she meant what she said. Though she had tried to make it up to him, DeWold had never got over it.

The case of the Limey, as he was being called, had hit the papers the past three days. Her picture was in the bottom fold, yesterday.

"I have taken the initiative," she was quoted as saying. "And from the main investigating officer there was simply a misidentification we are trying to correct."

All in all she was a political animal. So she believed everyone thought like her. She could blame others, because she felt others would blame her.

She did not have friends—she had contacts. She had tried all her life to avoid anyone who could compromise her. She was tough and brilliant and more than a little eccentric—wearing high green sneakers without socks in mid-February when she arrived at a conference. Wearing silk scarves and high hats and dyed-blue hair to luncheons— and once being noticed at a movie with nothing on but a top and leotards, accompanied by a man from the shipping industry with whom, they said, she'd had an affair. But to her it did not matter—that is, she coordinated the perception to make the best of her own invention. It was one way in which she delighted herself. She took on the church; spoke of Christ being a fallacy, when asked to address the United Church conference made a point of speaking of menopause to a group of middle-aged nuns.

You see, it was always easy to be scandalous. She would prove to women what a woman could do. She invented and reinvented herself. It was a way to be stealth-like and to keep people off guard. This surreptitiousness is what her friends overlooked and her enemies hated.

Her mistake—one of her mistakes—was thinking John Delano a chauvinistic fool. Now she knew he was startlingly bright.

But make no mistake—she was startling too. The highest marks at any university. The highest honours of anyone who'd worked as a deputy minister. The most expansive and brilliant theses and theories on the dispossessed. The most inclusive ideas about the marginalized, during her study of the law. (That is why she had taken on the Cheval case, which she described as being one of discrimination at the most basic and important level: the level of the dispossessed.) The most under-standing fact-gathering groups were formed for, and by, her to support women's rights and environmental issues. And she had been brilliant in her defence of her friend Wasson, the activist and environmentalist, during his trial, presenting information about his selfless attitude.

She popularized the idea that all women must have a minimum wage of thirty-five thousand dollars a year. "The Maritimes's answer to Atwood," one magazine had written about her.

Still, she had married a weakling. That was her mistake. And why? She could marry no equal and still have the power she wanted. She had discovered what people of power need.

So how did DeWold happen?

It happened because she was upset with her parents, and her fiancé, who saw through some of her actions—and so she decided to prove to him who she could be. She simply left a man studying microbiology, as he begged her to come back.

"No," she said. "It is over!"

She decided to find someone else. And she found him in an alley. There he was, bending over to brush off his big black boots, and she stood beside him and said, "Hello. Do you need assistance?"

She was quite tiny—five feet three inches—and quite unassuming in many respects. But she had him at "Hello."

In a way it destroyed her.

At first she was just playing, toying with her fiancé, who drove twice from Dalhousie University to try to make amends—but the more he begged, the more recalcitrant she became. DeWold was her man now.

He will come back one more time, she kept thinking of her fiancé, after she picked this hockey player, just out of the blue. And her fiancé did, and he did again. And then he did not.

God almighty, she found out he was going off to MIT on a full scholar-ship in the fall.

Finally she phoned him. But he did not answer. She phoned again, and when he finally did answer, she told him to come back. She demanded it. She sent him hate mail. Then she demanded that he come to her immediately.

But he refused.

So the game she played cost her, and she found herself alone, with DeWold, and decided to marry in a hurry with a justice of the peace presiding.

DeWold would pay for this for the next fifteen years. He was a weak-ling. As a weakling, he would be unable to resist or to leave.

DeWold was not a thing like those men her textbooks lampooned and lambasted. He was happy and joyous and not so bright, and had no ruthlessness about him. Still, quite often she made a fool of him in public and at government events. That is, he was an easy target.

But after a while—it did take a while—he began to catch on. At first he lampooned himself to please her. And then, after a time, he simply remained silent.

DeWold was considered a joke. Yet he was the man who did what she wanted, and gave up a chance at an NHL career for her. He had given up the one thing he was brilliant at doing, in order to please a woman who no longer respected him once he did. She decided she no longer loved him, and had an ongoing affair with the premier. It was the age-old ratio of sex to power. Three times she waved DeWold away, with her hand, in front of other people. "Go! We are talking."

But there was so much else to damage him with—to get him back for being too kind. And she did damage him for years. She ignored the one thing she should not have: his love.

When she told him she was pregnant (this was long before the affair), he had danced in the centre of the room like a child. "Yeahhhhh!" he had yelled.

"Well—there you go." She smiled. "But you see—you may dance, but it's not the right time for it." And she snapped off the light and left him in the dark.

And strangely, it seemed, only De Wold could help her now.

After reviewing the events of 1999 for the past two weeks, Melissa decided how they had actually happened. She spoke to Louise about it, then came home from work and told her husband what she had discovered, and what she would send as her report, and it was this: Fern Hershey had lost her chance at being head of the sociology department. She came back to work bitter and resentful and simply did not do her job. Melissa had to reprimand her twice. Finally, DeWold discovered Fern's neglected case file, and took action at 87 Shelf Street—but this was six months late.

They would say Hershey had not done her job because she was ill. This would not make her seem incompetent. Melissa said she would not mention what everyone knew: that Fern Hershey was desperately jealous of her. This would become the completely heroic possibility of the moment. Melissa knew that every moment had one. She was not a first-rank lawyer—and a woman considered one of the most powerful in the country—for nothing.

"She did not give the file to you," Melissa said to DeWold, standing over him. "She failed because she was sick at the time. Can you remember?"

She took a drink of water, holding the bottle near her chin, reflecting.

"But that is not true," DeWold said. "I had the file on my desk and didn't even go to Shelf Street for six months. You were furious with me, so upset and yelling at me that I wanted to quit!"

"Well, that can't be helped now—so forget it," she said.

DeWold was a simple man and not very bright, but he knew this: She was not the woman he married; the new ways of the world had drenched her in something. Acceptable falsehood in the name of advocacy and progress. (And although DeWold did not know this, out of fear that her old fiancé, to whom she still needed to prove herself, would hear of all of this.

Even though he lived in Boston and was married with three children.)

But Melissa Sapp did have one entirely admirable trait.

Although not in her marriage, she did have loyalty in most other things that concerned DeWold.

Though he was a failure, she would protect him to the death if need be. If need be, she would take on the world. It was a trait that John Delano would certainly admire.

Now she was beginning to feel all of this upon her, like the weight of Atlas but without the myth. So much so that on that night of December 11—though she did not tell DeWold—she said a prayer, the Our Father, as she lay down alone on the bed upstairs. For they had not slept together in months—and until he proved himself to her, she would not sleep with him again.

———

Jeannie went into the woods that morning of December 8. It was her wedding anniversary, and the anniversary of John Lennon's death as well. She knew now that Bennie and Luda had taken her money—that there was no man on PEI. How ashamed she felt, when she shouldn't have felt shame at all. She remembered seeing Luda one time afterwards, and Luda saw her and turned and ran across the parking lot in the rain. And Jeannie was left alone with a plastic bag.

It was years now since her child had disappeared. She told no one where she was going. And perhaps she was preparing herself to die.

The first major storm had come, and she worried about Gilbert being there, waiting for her, and she had no right *not* to go and find him. That was the thing about not looking. She had no right to it at all. She had many dreams that her son was sitting waiting for her. In each dream he would at some point look toward her as if waiting to be held. And she would wake in agony.

This is what sparked her continual resolve. Like any other human—a scientist, a poet, some politician who goes back into the fray; or like a man in faraway Africa working on an electrical grid—she felt she had no right *not* to search, to seek until she died.

The snow had covered up the back roads and back lanes of the province. The snow was so white it hurt one's eyes, and she had to hurry. John would be happy too, for she knew his life had been as tragic as hers. She did not remember how Gilbert came to be inside her—all her life she had been tormented and used by men—and on that long- ago day there were four men and she was alone with them, and tried to get out of the shed. This is what she did not tell anyone. She did not know who put Gilbert inside of her. It was a terrible day—terrible in all ways—but she would not give him up.

So she woke early to this snow, and she packed a lunch and went into the woods to sit with her boy. She was thinking how strange it was to have called him Gilbert—that it was bad luck. Her father had been named Gilbert and she had picked that name. But he seemed such a forlorn child, with a forlorn name. His eyes were crossed at birth, he held one arm crooked and he was shy. He was always lagging behind everyone, determined to keep up—he always lost his place in line; he always lost his mittens or his hat.

So she took to writing his name on everything he had and owned. "Gilbert." And even that seemed sad and funny and forlorn.

After he had disappeared, she had put up all of his baby pictures and pictures of him at birthday parties and at daycare —and pictures of him too on the beach the summer before he went away—on poles and in stores.

So she went into the woods with woollen mittens she had knitted for him for Christmas, and she walked and walked until nothing was at all familiar, and sat on a stump in the heavy, dreary snowfall.

It fell heavier as the day passed, the snow; and small moosebirds flitted on the limbs of birch trees in their fluffed-out grey coats, and glanced sideways at her, and hopped toward her and then flew to a branch above her. For a while she fell asleep, but not for too long. When she woke, she had no idea how to get back on the road where she had parked her car.

She had walked too far, and realized she had done it almost deliberately. That is, just as she had willed herself to get up and go into the woods with mittens, she had also in some strange way willed herself to get lost, just as little Gilbert was lost—and in this way she believed she would find him again.

She would find him and all the pain would go away. It was a pain of such horrifying precision that it couldn't stop. And a million, million pains such as this had entered the hearts of men and women, and the moosebirds flitting quietly on the limbs now covered in snow, and hidden in the spruce branches now covered in snow, told her so. Jeannie began to talk to God—she began to make promises she knew she couldn't keep—that she would be so good no one would ever be able to say she committed a sin: "Just you wait and see, if you let me find Gilbert—and I will never do or say a cruel thing as long as I live, if you let me see Gilbert—and if you just let me see his face, just once more, I will raise ten million dollars and give the money to charity—you must not be so cruel—if you are God and can do anything—then I command you—I really do, right now I command you to give me my Gilbert BACK! If you have taken him, show me where he is."

But of course no matter how she talked and how much she promised, there was nothing more than silence. A moosebird did not move any closer but simply eyed her from the side of his head, his beak now and again poking at the branch of a spruce tree. Far away, she could hear the sound of a freight train—which when they were kids they always called a fright train.

She stood and began to walk through the woods in the storm. The moosebird flitted after her, and she came to a ravine, and looked down. She decided she would find Gilbert no matter how long it took. And if she froze, she would find him. She took off her foggy glasses and cleaned them on her mitten, and put them back on again, as foggy as before— wet with snow too.

She knew John got upset with her at times because she wasn't as bright as he was, and often couldn't figure the simplest things out. But if this was simple or not, she had to know where her child was, and she would not stop until she finally discovered where he was. And once, only once, when she had asked John if he was proud of her, he had said that he wasn't proud, for she had said such silly things against him. And it had come out in a book, about how social services was nice to her and how John wasn't. That was why she had asked if he was proud of her—because she knew she had said foolish things about him. She had drunk too much wine and got very upset and said things she shouldn't have, when that man asked her about John and if Gilbert was frightened of him so maybe he ran away.

"Yes. Yes. He ran away—yes, yes, yes, John made him so scared that he ran," she said.

And the man put that in the book.

So she said what the man wanted to hear, thinking it would all turn out, and they would find the boy.

And later she had said to John, "Don't worry—someday you will be so proud of me, John. I promise you will."

Though he never spoke of that again and told her he didn't care, and to forget it, she herself had never forgotten it.

I will find Gilbert, she decided now. And then he will be proud.

And she set off down the ravine. The shadow in the trees to the left of her was of a coyote following at just a safe distance. The snow swept across the rock ridges and the stream far down below looked like glass.

She remembered her house in those terrible years—how one day her brother Jean-Paul stole some flares from the caboose and was chased to the house by a railway worker. She was crying, thinking they were going to take him to jail. The railway worker's name was Maufat—and in the end he did nothing but look kindly at them, and full of sorrow.

She remembered the smell of the flares that Jean-Paul had wanted to burn to celebrate her birthday because he had promised her a surprise.

"The flares will go off, they will cast a glow in the air and you will realize how much you are loved," he told her. He didn't say it like that, but in fact that is what he'd meant, and she knew that now. Half her brothers and sisters died of cancer in their thirties. They were considered by many to be the poorest of the poor. That was why men took advantage of her from the time she was thirteen. Once, a boy on the way home from school spit on the new second-hand dress Mrs. Dulse had given her. She knew that the boy was John Delano, and he was trying to ask for forgiveness now.

So she had lived her life as an outcast. But people were always saying they were going to help her. So much so that she relied upon them—she in fact, for a long time, thought of her life always as being in the hands of others.

When she got pregnant by one of those men (and she often wondered which man), Melissa Sapp said, "I will take care of everything for you." At first Jeannie loved Melissa like no one else. For Melissa could will herself to be loved. And Jeannie couldn't wait for her visits. Why—because the woman was so powerful, had her own car and smelled so sweet. But Jeannie liked the way so many, many men were frightened of her. And why not, so many men had made Jeannie frightened—why couldn't someone be frightened of her? That is, Jeannie, who had had so little love in her life, couldn't wait to be hugged by this powerful person. And she smiled when men nodded and said, "Yes, Ms. Sapp—of course."

But the thing Melissa wanted to take care of was the unwanted pregnancy. This was during her fight for the women's health centre.

Jeannie, you see, was the test case. That is what Melissa called her.

Jeannie did not understand any of this until they were in the car together on the way to the centre. But when Melissa began to explain it to her—that there were nice people who would solve her problem, and she would no longer be pregnant—she began to get a glimmer into this other world. It was a powerful world—and Melissa was powerful—but it had something else—and Jeannie did not know what it was. She did not understand that for all of Melissa Sapp's great power, there bloomed a hint of corruption—just as with all power.

"Oh no," Jeannie said. Then she said, as if she had made a blunder, "But well, you see, I have already knitted mittens."

Melissa said that they could sell the mittens.

"No, they will only fit my child," Jeannie said.

"Don't be absurd," Melissa said, quite calmly. "I am doing the right thing here. Don't you understand people want to help you? We all want to help out."

"No! No! NO!" is all she was able to say.

Finally, Melissa pulled over on the side of the road. "What kind of society do you want?" she said, trying to refrain from being cross.

Jeannie put her thumbs together and looked at the dashboard and said nothing.

"Tell me—what kind of society do you want, young woman?" (Melissa said this even though Jeannie was much older than Melissa.)

"One with some little children wearing mittens," Jeannie whispered.

Melissa drove her home. To her credit, she did not press the issue anymore. She let Jeannie out at the ramshackle house on the side lane beyond the tracks.

Still, as Jeannie's pregnancy wore on, Melissa made plans to have the child put with a foster family.

So this was the second option. And not only did it seem reasonable, it seemed the only way to reason. And Jeannie felt that if she did not do this, she would be ungrateful. For she could not take care of a child—it was absurd to think she could. And Melissa was upset because the first option, the primary option—and what was considered by the very brightest people the only option—had failed. That is, the test case had failed.

But then, just as she was in the process of having the child taken away, John Delano walked into the Dominion Bakery and asked for an eclair, and everything in her destiny changed. She could not believe that this had happened—and when she told John about the child, he said, "Well then, we'll just get Gilbert back. What a funny name—but we will get him back!"

She was shaking so badly when she telephoned Melissa that she couldn't keep the phone to her ear.

"Hello, Melissa. Yeah, well, I think I am going to keep Gilbert."

"You absolutely are not," Melissa said. "Everything is decided."

"But I haven't decided—you didn't even let me get decided."

"I'll tell you what—you get married to a man who makes—oh, let's say fifty thousand dollars a year—for that's what the prospective parents make—so you meet a man like that to marry you within the next three weeks—and I'll give you Gilbert—other than that—things will remain the way they are."

Jeannie hung up.

A week later she telephoned again. "Hello, Melissa."

"Well—what is it this time?"

"I think someone is going to marry me—and I even think he makes more than fifty thousand a year. He gave me a diamond ring—and I can't even believe it."

"And who in hell is that Jeannie—who?"

"John Delano."

"Who?"

"John Delano."

The line went dead.

"Hello, Melissa—Hello, Melissa—hello."

That great fight between John and Melissa lasted almost seven months. She had a private detective follow him, report to her about his off-duty hours—and little by little she began a file on him as well. And as always, John never saw her, never came in contact with her—except one night when he was entering the court house and she came out a side door, and turned and walked into the night.

But Gilbert came home.

And Jeannie was in a world she could never have dreamed of. John built her a five-bedroom house, overlooking the great river, where their master bedroom was bigger than the house she had grown up in. He treated her with such respect, such glorious and uncalculated kindness, she could not have imagined it. The mahogany library was filled with leather sofas and books. He read to her—books like Dickens and Victor Hugo, and Guy de Maupassant. And he would do the accents and act the characters and she would laugh hilariously.

But why did he do that? Why? What was he trying to atone for? For bullying a young girl when he was a boy? Yes—that, of course. But he was trying to save her life, because of what had happened in Africa.

So she got Gilbert back. And Melissa was gone from her life. But Melissa went on to other things—and the most pressing of these was championing language rights in the province. Again, really she was never in the forefront, but always present. Still very few knew her to see her, and fewer still knew her well. Now and again, however, she would ask after that woman, Jeannie Aube, because she had a genuine affection for her.

For two years Jeannie sat in her great house, mostly in one spot, frightened—frightened that if she moved, the house would disappear. She would open a closet or a door, and peek in and close it quickly. She would not go into some rooms for she felt she didn't quite deserve to.

Once, John found her in the back closet, sewing.

"You have your own sewing room," he said

"This room is about as big as I need," she said.

She was frightened that the house would disappear. Or that John would not come home. That he would phone her and laugh at her, and say it was all a joke. And he and Melissa had made it all up as a big joke.

But it was not a joke—at all.

Then John went to San Francisco. He just left to find a man who had taken money off an old woman.

"How stupid can things get?" Jeannie asked John as he packed to leave.

But then their lives changed forever. Melissa re-entered her life. She was told that John had frightened the child, and that Gilbert ran away.

How unloved he is, she now thought of John. But he must know that I love him.

The day had darkened, and she could hear strange sounds—a wisping here and there. She did not know it was the coyotes moving in between small spruce cover behind her. Cowardly as they were, they were gathering each other up to attack.

She was now truly lost. The snow was blinding, but fell so silently as silent as snow on a Christmas card. And the tracks behind her were obliterated. Then, as sometimes happens in the woods, there was no sound at all.

She turned and there was a black spot behind her. Strange she had not seen it before. It stood in the dark, not moving. Then she realized it was a coyote. And there was another one standing sideways to it, farther away.

"Where is Gilbert?" she said.

And she moved off up the hill, toward the old field beyond the village that went down to Hammond River, and she then sat down in the dark and realized she would never find her way out.

"Where is Gilbert?" she said, in defiance to the dark, to God. "If you want me to believe in you—you tell me where Gilbert is! I command you—and I have never commanded anyone before. I have never asked and you will receive before—but now I do—I do NOW!"

She would never tell this to anyone—she would always keep this to herself. But at that moment there were two great flares in the air— which seemed to glow and sputter—there was a noise too, and the two coyotes that had come up to her dashed away, bellies on the ground and tails between their legs. The flares reminded her of her brother and how he had stolen flares for her one summer day long ago.

She watched these fiery things in the sky, and then stood and walked toward them.

They were flares that had started the procession for the second week of Advent toward the church of Saint Francis, but she did not know this.

There was an old woodlot with a wooden fence on both sides of a path. And she walked down it. The snow still fell, and she saw the flares on the ground, glowing orange and beginning to disappear. Then another one appeared up in the sky.

She heard voices in the distance, and singing.

"Please, I have to know where Gilbert is!" she yelled, tears streaming down her face.

Suddenly everything became like a fairy tale—the air was soft and pure, and snow still fell—her little white hat was covered in snow and made her look like an elf. She came out along a stand of white birch trees. There was a marker and then another and then an iron gate fence. She opened it and stepped inside the churchyard.

One of the torches burned near her feet, and the lights from inside the church of Saint Francis of Assisi were turned on.

The Christmas light poured out through the great stained-glass window, and she heard Beethoven's "Ode to Joy." And what towered in front of her was a stained-glass image of our Madonna holding a child. Madonna, of course, said nothing. There are no miracles, of course.

But someone was telling Jeannie, not by words but by devotion to the human heart, that Gilbert was not only loved, but he had been taken home.

———

The next day, December 9, at about nine in the morning John went back to the Cheval house. He had left home before sunrise and had come here to meet the men who would search for his child. Trevor drove him north to this place. And on the way up the road he spoke of these things that confronted sensibility—order and purpose—but that in the scheme of things today seemed regressive and intolerant. That is, he asked Trevor what she thought might have happened if Bennie Cheval had not got out of jail on a technicality; what if John had addressed him in French, which he said was the language of his choice.

"Then he would not have got out on a technicality, attempting to right the wrong of a bigotry that in this case did not exist."

"Do you believe this was unjust?"

"That he walked free? Of course. He was not only a felon but a danger to everyone, including himself. He knew it—and couldn't believe his luck. In fact—it was more than disbelief on his face; it was a look that said, 'This is preposterous.' Yet he hugged his lawyer for adhering to a law he did not know and would never adhere to himself—and Melissa had a victory over the world. And Melonson was happy because of our own history."

"Is that fair?"

"Who knows if I am being fair," he said to Trevor. "Who knows if I can be—but he got out and came back here, with a pregnant child he had charmed, Luda Marsh. He got as drunk as he could for as long as he could. Then I left for the States."

"And you had to go to the States to get Wasson?"

"Yes."

"But you wanted to get Wasson—why?"

"Because Wasson was a friend of Hugh Forrest—Hugh Forrest, who left one night for Africa. And Wasson simply borrowed five thousand dollars from him and went to his health club."

"So it was personal?"

"Yes—I think it was personal—but Cheval is out of jail. And my child is walking along the road with his bowl—and Bennie is not in jail on an incendiary device charge but is drunk and driving a car, and how did all this start?"

"How?"

"It started by me as a cop not saying *bonjour* at the right moment—and it would have been better for all of us, for Cheval himself, if he had been sent up on those charges. He would probably still be alive—and so would Luda Marsh."

"And so too would your son." Trevor said, and added, sadly, "your boy collecting pollywogs."

John walked the dry, cold yard, with the cane in his hand. Trevor stayed beside him.

People had come from both detachments of RCMP and emergency services. One was Reese, an old friend of his, who volunteered to go down into the well. The air smelled of gunpowder and a little dog watched from the side of the barn, wagging its tail every time John looked over at it. He told Trevor that when he had been here a few days before, the cold afternoon light from the sun, cast on the window, had cast its dying light on something forgotten for years and covered in dust.

He had been uncertain what it might be.

He had walked out of Luda's room, with the book in his hand. "Good Luck, Luda" was written on the inside cover. There was no name under the inscription, but a date: March 17, 1999. And the seven was crossed, like they cross it in Europe.

"That was the present mentioned in the letter," he said. But John told her he had felt he was in a bind since he would have been one of the few to know of the book—*Nights below Station Street*—(Trevor herself had not heard of it) or why it would have been given to Luda.

"And why was it given to her?"

"Because she came from Station Street—the boy would not have known this was a different Station Street from the one in the book; he would only have thought of the importance of Station Street in Luda's life."

"And why were you in a bind?"

"Melonson will say that I wrote the inscription to sell it."

"No!"

"Yes—oh yes."

He told her that as good as it was, all his insight was coming back useless and there was no way to prove a thing—and even if he did prove it, they would not accept it.

He told Trevor he was thinking when he walked out of the bedroom with the book under his arm that Melonson would once again say he had planted evidence. It was the most effective thing to say against him since the Bennie Cheval case.

Yet he told her the afternoon sun was glinting off of something else. Something that had been hidden there by Luda years before. So he left the book on the table and turned and walked back into the bedroom.

It sat on Luda's bottom shelf in the far corner, hidden at the back. (If he had not picked the book up, he would never have seen it.)

He put it into his pocket, but he almost never made it back to his car.

Strange as it was, the Muslim woman whom he had taught how to drive, and who now drove a school bus, slammed on her brakes when she saw a man falling out into the deserted road. She called her husband and they managed to get him back home, the man driving his car.

When he got home, he called Jeannie and told her he must see her immediately.

But he ended up in the hospital.

"But what was it you found?" Trevor asked. "What was there beside the book?"

John nubbed his cane into the harsh embankment near the house. Ice crystals had formed on the stones lying there. The wind was bitter.

The small dog wagged its tail at him.

"What was it?" Trevor asked again.

"The little Swiss Army knife," John said, not looking at her. "With the spoon and scissors, which I bought for Gilbert to take to camp."

7.

Like a Maritimer, John had put his ticket to Toronto in his shirt pocket and he stayed at one of the smaller modest and run-down hotels on Wellington, and he smoked in the hallway, near the fire extinguisher. And how lonely are places like this, with their faded red carpet and the sound of the vacuum down the ill-lit hall. But he had known loneliness all of his life, or at least most of it, and he had been visited by it at celebrations, at places in the soul that were tarnished even by festivity. Or in fact, he almost always felt the loneliness in festivity itself. But this hotel had little festivity—a complimentary breakfast of toast and donuts, and a room with a small pool table, the door locked and the lights turned off.

The RCMP had looked for his son. The search had gone on for a number of days, and into the next week, and beyond that. But not a trace was found.

Velma was questioned about her knowledge of the boy, and she maintained stoic silence. "Yes, wouldn't it be like John Delano to say these things?" she said.

"I will sue now," she went on. "I will sue John Delano for all he is worth! He killed them both—stole the money. He might have even killed his son." And then, using the word improperly, she said, "That's how eccentric he is!"

Later Melonson had come to him, saying he had heard that some had wanted to charge him with fabrication of evidence, planting evidence and jeopardizing and impeding the investigation into a national case in order to bring attention to himself. That they were pressing for this if he did not retire.

That if he retired within the month, he would still get full pension, and the benefits of being looked upon as a good policeman. That Melonson would see to it.

Then the next day, under a court order filed by Moms and Bunny's lawyer, authorities confiscated almost everything he had taken, except the marble and the photo, which came independently of the Shelf Street residence. They took the jug, which Bunny said had been blackened in a lawn mower fire, the bag, which Moms said belonged to Vernon as a child—and gave them back.

This was a severe reprimand. The objects could not be used as evidence, and any evidence that followed—i.e., the examination of the dirt on the boots—would be likewise inadmissible. Doubtless they had waited the right amount of time to "spring it" on him. But he was not sure. Perhaps they did it at the exact moment he was again grieving over not finding his boy to cause calamity in his spirit.

It happened like this: Melonson had called him into the office. There were two other people there. One was the division head for the province; the other was Melissa Sapp. And when he caught her eye, she looked away. She certainly was a beautiful woman.

She looked down into her briefcase, and took out a letter and passed it to the division commander without a word. It was a letter from John that he had sent to social services about "wreaking havoc" on whoever had impeded his wife. So, the implication was, this current situation must be part of the havoc he wanted to render.

She looked at him as soon as she had passed this letter over, in victory, and then turned to Melonson and spoke quietly with him.

Then Melonson turned to John. He first and foremost went into the details of Luda's and Bennie's deaths. It was very strange to hear

Luda referred to as Ms. Cheval. Melonson also spoke about the missing money—the affidavit filled out by Velma Cheval in that regard. Which was still pending.

That is, none of this was as yet solved. Much was still under investigation. The inquiry into the deaths of the Chevals was still ongoing.

Then Melonson came tactfully to the crux of the matter. "We don't want to go against you—but by all accounts *Nights below Station Street* is a book you could easily have obtained at Bunny's second-hand bookstore. As a matter of fact, it is more logical that you did than you did not. I've never even heard of that book, or that writer, for that matter. Are we to buy this—finding the book on a bookshelf after a book was mentioned in a letter that you had in your possession?"

"Why, then, would I pick it—wouldn't that give me away?"

"But I think it shows your fancifulness. People at Bunny's who have seen you there said you could have picked that book up there as well. I was ordered to check into this last week."

"Not only could I have picked it up, but I did," John said.

"Well, there you go," Melonson said, his face brightening suddenly at this admission. He turned to Melissa and smiled.

"Yes, I did," John said, "buy a copy of *Nights* at that bookstore and a copy of *No Great Mischief* as well. But of course not *this* copy of *Nights*— this copy was bought by JP, for a young girl on Shelf Street, who was there from the same time he was until shortly after New Year's 2000."

"And can we speak to her?" Melissa asked the question as if it was a heartfelt request.

"No, we can't," John said. "Or at least, you cannot."

"And why is that?"

"Because she is deceased," John answered. "She was stabbed in a domestic dispute." He paused, and did not bring up the name Bennie Cheval. She looked away again, and over at Hurley, division head for the province.

"But can't you see how difficult this makes it for anyone to believe you?" Hurley said, with the kind of tone a newcomer has.

"Oh yes, completely—but then, that has always been so—not only with this case but with other cases."

"What other cases?" Hurley asked.

"Many," he said.

"But that is not true at all," Melonson said.

"Well, my evidence has disappeared."

"It does not belong to you."

"And the boots . . ." John said. "But—well, may I sit down?"

"Of course yes. Please sit down," Hurley said.

"How do you know this boy—this JP—gave the book to that girl?" Melissa asked.

"Because he signed the date—and crossed the seven."

"Crossed the seven?" Hurley asked.

"Yes, like a European boy would do, or someone who was used to making the number seven that way."

"And you know this?"

"Yes."

"And you know the book?"

"Yes. I know the book."

"So you could have crossed the seven." Melonson frowned. "That is what will be questioned."

"Oh, I often do cross my sevens," John said. "Since I have lived in many places I often do—but . . ."

"But?"

"But I did not do so in this case. The book was given to Luda Marsh because Luda Marsh lived on Station Street when she was a little girl— the boy liked her very much—saw the book and bought it for her. I am sure the boy did not read the book and Luda only got to page twenty-three. But she kept it. In fact, when she was stabbed, I believe she was going back to get it."

"And what kind of book is it?"

"A book that couldn't have been written anywhere else but here. In a real way it belongs to our world."

Hurley paused, and then told him that everyone involved that he knew wanted to get to the bottom of the case too. But at the moment, they couldn't take his evidence at face value—even the dirt samples from Africa.

"Maybe you are the wrong officer for this case," Hurley said.

"Then you should have found another one earlier," John answered.

Melissa left the building, and walked down along the street to the bus stop. It was growing dark; there was a smell of slush and wind. The bus was crowded with all sorts of people, and she usually did not take it, but today her car had gone in for inspection. She sat down by a small boy wearing a torn yellow jacket and woollen toque. His nose was running and now and again he put his fist up to his mouth as he coughed in embarrassment.

"You do have a bad cold," Melissa said, and she looked through her purse and found some cough drops and handed him one. "Here."

She began to talk to him about Christmas, how it was near, and what did he think he would like. Then she straightened his toque, as well, and saw how golden his blond curls were, and smiled when he told her about going with his school to see a play but that he couldn't stop coughing.

She told him, as the bus manoeuvred along the crowded streets toward the centre of town, how she had been in plays, and at one time when she was a little girl had wanted to be an actress—but had decided to do something else.

"What do you do? I bet it is important."

She smiled.

There was a smell of night and the windows were washed with slush, and she took ten dollars from her pocket and pressed it into his grubby hand.

"You are pretty," he said. "And so nice."

When he looked at her, his nose was running again and she noticed his deep-blue eyes, tender in the lights of the bus.

"Oh," she said, and kindly gave him a hug. "Yes—I think at times I can be."

———

John left the next evening for Toronto, after phoning Jeannie.

"I have your money," he said.

"What money, John?"

"It's in an old envelope in my desk—I want it to go toward Melon's education."

"Are you going to come and see me soon?"

"When I get back. Right now I have to go somewhere."

"I will say ten Hail Marys and five Our Fathers."

How quaint that sounded—how old and odd and out of date.

"Thank you, Jeannie—say them for me, please."

Now the streets were greying in Toronto, and he saw out the window the side of a parking garage and the number of a towing company on the side. And below, Beck taxis and Co-op cabs making their way in the snow. So he had left all the information that he could with Sue Van Loon. He told her each part of the puzzle, and how he had solved it.

"It is solved?"

"Oh yes."

"And you will find this boy?"

"I do not know—he was asked to go to the tallest building on his birthday and wait. Tomorrow is his birthday—he will be twenty-four, I think. I will be sixty-two."

The snow was like ash coming off the top of the grey buildings; and the sky was red and angry; and small, dirty mounds of slush and ice lay like law-abiding ghosts at the corner of the street.

He sat in his hotel room with the TV on and the sound off, and stared out the window. One o'clock came, and then two in the morning. He drank coffee and smoked.

Sue Van Loon was with him. She in fact monitored his pulse that whole night.

It was seven in the morning, and not yet light, when John Delano put on his suit jacket and coat and made his way out under the flat grey sky, the great skyscrapers shuddering in cold, where steam floated up through the foul vents of the streets toward the CN Tower.

He knew why he was doing this, even though he might be the only person in the world to know.

"Go," he imagined Lily must have said, "to the largest building on your birthday, and we will be there to find you. Don't worry how long it might take. Please, please remember."

"And do you think he would still go after all this time?" Sue Van Loon asked, taking John's hand to help him along.

"Well . . . wouldn't you?"

———

Peace and Security at the Summit: A Diplomat's View on Courage and Tolerance was to be published in New York in the fall of 2001. Its author, our Lion of Justice, did meet Mataya at tower one. They were going to go to the Top of the World restaurant. For breakfast on September 11.

He wore a light-blue suit, with a polka-dot ascot. She wore a simple black-and-white print dress that showed off her gorgeous legs. And he loved the effect it produced when she walked ahead of him. Somehow there was a swish and a sway to her whole remarkable body.

It was, he told her, a simply beautiful dress for a beautiful late-summer morning, and as always, he walked quickly beside her, trying to explain his latest book, *Peace and Security at the Summit*, while she nodded and looked steadily ahead of her. She was moneyed—probably richer than he was. He was aware that she was more than ten years younger than his son, Tim Wasson. He put his hand on her back to guide her like the gentleman he was, and quoted a line—a line from a poem by Maya Angelou.

They took the wrong elevator and had to come back down to the lobby. He made the mistake of standing on the left side of her—a mistake because it showed his hearing aid—and he was conscious of this.

Then, on the way up again, on a whim, she decided to see if a friend of her father's was at work that morning—and perhaps entice him to have breakfast with them. So after changing on the seventy-eighth floor, they got off at the eighty-seventh. He was not at all happy about having a friend of her father's with them and didn't hide his displeasure, which she noticed.

"Don't be too angry," she whispered, and took his arm.

They turned left off the elevator, and started toward the offices of Conner, Halpern and Linn. Suddenly she looked at him strangely, went sideways, and hit a printing machine at the side of the office door. She simply fell, and a hunk of marble wall fell over her. It happened in a rush.

He turned and looked at her, his own head filled with dusty particles of wallboard, the lapels on his jacket flapping as if in a wind.

Suddenly water started to drip on his head, someone said, "Watch it," and a large red ball flashed in the sky above them. These things could have happened simultaneously—he wasn't sure.

He went to young Mataya and tried to get her to stand, but the impact had broken a number of her ribs. A beam or a slab of marble had been cut from the ceiling and had fallen on her left leg. (He was dazed and unsure of what it was.)

She lay there looking at him and he realized she was in terrible trouble. He would stay with her until help came, he decided.

But after a while, fires were starting to show in the ceiling. Smoke was everywhere. After twenty minutes or so, people were making their way from one end of the building to the other—a great many people were moving away from one end, trying to find another stairwell. They had handkerchiefs over their faces. Some were actually screaming they were trapped.

From behind a wall of a conference room where the metal of the door frame had jammed, no one could get out. He saw their shadows, as smoke began to engulf them, and a woman said, "Get on the floor."

"Break a window," another woman pleaded.

Smoke was beginning to engulf sections of this floor as well.

He sat beside her more and more anxiously. He had taken his ascot off (he had spent ninety-two dollars on it just yesterday) and put it over his face.

"Please don't leave me," she said as he started to leave.

"No, of course not," he said. He came back for a moment.

He waited until she closed her eyes, and let go of her hand.

He needed to find a pathway for himself over shattered glass and wallboards and running water. When Mataya opened her eyes, she could see him crawling like a child. Then she closed her eyes again.

He is going to get help, she thought.

Our Lion of Justice stood and made his way toward an open stairwell.

A young man walked past him at the same time, coming in the opposite direction—a man named Harold Morelia. At first he had been trying to help by opening the conference room door and then trying to get the sprinklers to work. Then he took a piece of metal pipe he had found and banged open the wall beside the conference room, allowing the people there to escape through that hole and make it to the stairwell.

He turned to go with them, but saw this young woman lying alone in the corner. There was another woman, a young secretary of twenty-two, sitting beside her.

"You go—now!" he demanded, and the woman hesitated.

"Someone should stay with her."

"I will. Go on now—go."

So the young secretary did move, and found the stairwell.

"Well, we will have to get you out now," he said to Mataya. But the piece of pipe he had with him did not work at all.

Harold Morelia was a courier and had a wife and three children. He lived in Brooklyn. He was working another man's route today as a favour. He refused to stop trying to lift the slab off of Mataya. He tried for the next quarter of an hour. She groaned and told him to stop, it hurt too much, that her leg was shattered, to wait for the people to come and rescue them.

"Oh —I am sorry, sweetheart, but I have to keep trying—where are you from?"

"Argentina."

"Ah," he said. "That's a fine place. 'Don't cry for me, Argentina'—that's what we will say."

"I cannot breathe—where are the sprinklers?"

"I don't know, love. They don't seem to work—but wait and I'll get something." He ran and found a small flowerpot in that conference room and took out one of the rags he had in his pocket and wetted it from the pot. He made it back through the hole in the plaster wall he had managed to cut twenty-five minutes before.

He noticed when he went to find the flowerpot that some others were in the corridor. They had lain down below the smoke and had simply gone to sleep or were unconscious now. From the large back window of the conference room he saw men falling, and jumping. If he left at this moment, he might make it down those stairs.

He came back in and looked at the door to the stairwell—now was the time to go if he was going to go!

He took the rag back to Mataya and placed it over her face. They sat for another ten minutes, and breathing became extremely difficult.

He phoned his wife on the cell and said, "Don't worry—I am sitting beside a pretty young woman named Mataya. Kiss all the children for me one at a time." Then he turned to this child again.

"Here, love," he said, "here, hold my hand. I always like holding hands with pretty girls."

She squeezed his hand.

There was a big *SWISH*—and they fell toward earth, enveloped in a thousand degrees Fahrenheit, and disintegrating in each other's arms.

An hour or so earlier, when he had met her in the lobby, our Lion of Justice had thought: It's a pity she is wearing such a nice dress this morning—she should have saved it for tomorrow when we go out to visit.

She was supposed to go to the clinic just north of tower one to see a cosmetic surgeon that afternoon about breast enhancement, and hadn't told anyone but him.

But that all seemed a lifetime ago. And he had forgotten all about her.

Our Lion had actually fallen and cut his head open, and lay almost unconscious at the eightieth floor. He was picked up and put over the shoulder of someone who had been coming up when so many were going down.

He was then carried by a man down to the seventy-eighth floor—actually sliding over board and debris.

The man set him down and gave him oxygen from his own tank.

"You can't leave me," our Lion said. "I don't know how to make it!"

"I have to go back up—there are people trapped above—I have to go and see to them. You'll be okay—move along with these people—hold on to them as tight as you can. Hurry down now—it's clear all the way down if you hurry—but you have to hurry."

And he pried Our Lion's hand from his arm and left him.

Our Lion of Justice did just as he was told, standing and stumbling forward, holding on to others, until he got to the lobby and then outside. The lapels of his coat crinkled and his hair and clothing filled with soot and blood and water at the spot where the cosmetic surgeon Mataya had been supposed to meet was trying desperately to save a young girl's legs.

On the seventy-eighth floor Joel Finnegan watched after our Lion a moment to make sure he was on his way. The seventy-eighth floor, once so spacious, was a living hell of soot and fire, of broken electrical wire scattering fire in the wind.

Then he turned and made it back up almost to the completely blocked ninety-second floor, over bodies and debris. He felt a groan in the structure. So he called his wife.

"Hello," he managed to say, "I won't be able to make it to lunch with John—tell him I will see him in—"

————

Van Loon was with John at the end. She felt in a way it was a horrible thing to say, now that he was more famous than he was when alive, and now that people were saying they were his friend and boon companion. Still, not one of them had been—not the man who was now doing his biography. Not the woman with the little shih tzu dog he had gone in the night to visit.

But Sue Van Loon had been his friend and companion. Yes, she'd been. She had travelled with him to Toronto, and they'd stayed at a hotel downtown, on Wellington. They took an airport bus into town, and he had an overnight bag. There he booked two rooms, but she stayed in his, for she was afraid he might not make it that night. He was breathing laboriously and his arm pained, and he refused to put out his cigarette. He now and again took nitro, and spoke in a harsh whisper about the twenty-seven cases he had solved on his own.

"You are a legend now," she said.

He told her (and she did not know if he was fabricating this) that the silt off the blanket and boots had come back as "notably African in origin, probably Burundi or Rwanda"—that was how it was said on the white sample envelope returned to the department.

When John had left the police department after his meeting with Melonson and Melissa Sapp, the December night had fallen and footfalls sounded far away, and the smell of gas lingered in the air. He called Sue Van Loon and begged her to meet him.

They went back to his place on Matters Road; John insisted he make Sue a drink.

His was non-alcoholic; her drink was a gin.

"I want you to remain with me now," he said.

"In what way remain with you?"

"In a way no one else has, I suppose—to the end."

"To the end?"

"It won't take that long."

"Then you can't go—to Toronto."

"No—you come with me tomorrow—it will be like a vacation."

She sat in his bedsitter in Saint John, looking at the little place he had ended up after all his life, the sad man at the edge of the world. "I am unloved," he said finally. Then he took out the picture of Lily Forrest and asked her to look at it.

"What do you see—or, who do you see?" John asked

"I don't know—a kind young woman with a child," she said.

"Yes—but Lily looks just like you. I want you with me, just in case he remembers," John said.

"To Toronto?"

"Yes—and no matter what, you wait for him that day."

"So you have proven it?"

"I must have."

"Why?"

"Because I am surrounded by ghosts—but you must not tell anyone."

"That you are surrounded by ghosts?"

"Yes, please—you must not tell a soul that I am. That I speak to Lily at night and Luda as well."

"Do you believe that?"

"Oh yes—very much so."

"What do you tell Lily?"

"I tell her I have found her boy—that I am going to Toronto to get him, as soon as I take care of my own child."

———

DeWold's part in the scandal—the fact that he had not visited the home on Shelf Street during the six months before the boy had disappeared—wasn't mentioned in the meeting between Melissa Sapp and Justice Minister Lorne Brait. The minister had requested the meeting on December 18, 2011.

Melissa did not give one thing away about her husband. She did not shake or look intimidated, even though the press was now aghast with rumours and had called for a complete investigation, et cetera. She did not flinch when someone said this had to be explained to Ottawa's satisfaction, or when the morning talk shows on CBC Radio mentioned her,

her large salary, and even made a joke about the devotion of Ms. Louise. Worse they mentioned her "chumminess," as they called it, with the premier himself.

Still, her husband was not yet mentioned.

Besides, Brait was not even informed she had a husband. Melissa wore no ring. It had been a civil ceremony—and one that she had often derided. But Brait did not care about that. But he did have the deputy minister with him, sitting at the far end of the room. The deputy minister in any portfolio is far more astute and knowledgeable about any given affair on any given day than the minister. This deputy minister was Kelly Backwash, a former civil litigator and champion of immigration status, and a no-nonsense, hard-nosed woman of forty-three who had no time for Melissa, whom she disliked intently—even viscerally, who disapproved of Melissa's trendy collaborations with people.

So she was very knowledgeable, very astute—had hoped some years back to have charges laid against Melissa for her part in an eco-terrorism case that had happened when Melissa was linked with radical environmentalists back in university, specifically a man named Wasson who had embezzled money from Ms. Backwash's aunt. They could not prove anything against Melissa—that she knew beforehand that tractor trailers and woodlots were to be firebombed in protest over logging.

For her part, Melissa knew in a second where Kelly Backwash was sitting. She knew all of this in one glance. That is, she knew Backwash was the real threat here but was still in the dark about much of what was going on in this case—and therefore did not know enough to make any judgment.

Melissa told the minister, "It was a mix-up not in social services or child protection but within the city police at that time. The boy is probably alive and we are hoping to have him brought to New Brunswick."

Then she handed him a copy of a letter written in 1998. "Please, Minister, this should remain confidential," she said. It was a letter written by her, requesting Ms. Blanchard, who had lied about her age, retire at the end of June of that year.

It was in fact an act of betrayal at that time against her former boss by a group who were loyal to Melissa and wanted her to take over the position in Saint John. It was a power shift within the entire department that enabled Melissa to hire her husband. It was this coup that had allowed Melissa to take the caseload from Fern Hershey to give to Melissa's own husband—after she encouraged Ms. Hershey to apply to the university.

That is, Ms. Blanchard would never have been party to such a thing.

But Melissa did not say anything about this now. That is, that this letter was in fact a complete record of her uncanny ability to betray. That she had betrayed in her lifetime scores of people who relied upon her, and considered it good politics. Now she sat forward, and spoke softer.

"Ms. Blanchard did not retire at that time," Melissa said, "though I pressed for it. I was, however, allowed to make some fundamental changes within the department. But they did not come at a fast enough pace to help the young boy who'd arrived from Belgium."

"But weren't you still an advocate and an attorney then?"

"Yes—and I still am. I work, however, within the parameters of social services."

"Is that where the trouble lay?" Ms. Backwash asked.

"Never—my conscience is clear on that. I do not interfere with anything in the justice department."

"So Ms. Blanchard was at fault?" the minister asked. "Too old and crabby, right?"

"In part yes—but so was Ms. Hershey. My husband found out that this house on Shelf Street was neglected, and took over the case, some months later."

"Your husband?" Backwash asked.

"Yes," Melissa said quickly, not looking at her for more than a second. She knew her husband's name would come out, so she had to mention him, and chose this moment to do so.

Melissa stated that she was waiting on a report before she could inform Ottawa. This was John Delano's final report. She had known he was going to Toronto, and had been waiting for him to inform her of what he had discovered.

"Delano—that is the man who died in Toronto a few days ago?"

"Yes."

"And he is the one who found the boy—in Toronto?"

"Not exactly," Melissa said quickly. "Sue Van Loon did—she was the real advocate, I think. I mean Delano was there as well, we know that. In fact I was one of the people who said he should go—even though we were not positive he could find anything out. But it is as we have suspected now for over three weeks: The boy is now a man of twenty-four. From what I have been able to gather—and I was just called to this case three weeks ago—the boy was left alone in that house because Fern Hershey was ill—she had resigned her position to apply for head of our sociology department," Melissa said. "I asked her not to. But she wanted a change. So there was a vacuum at the top until I filled it, that's what happened in this case, and the boy went missing. With my help Sue Van Loon, who once worked for me, found him. That is, as soon as Ottawa came to me I put everything in motion."

"You mean your department?" Kelly Backwash asked.

"That is why my department was formed," Melissa said with a slight smile. "It was formed to help abandoned children."

"When did Ms. Hershey apply for the university position?"

"In 1999."

"And you knew she was going to?"

"At that time—I advised her not to."

"You did?" the minister asked.

"I thought she was fine and sweet and not qualified," Melissa answered crisply. "But unbeknownst to us, her departure left Shelf Street vulnerable. Something I would have known if Ms. Blanchard had retired earlier, I assure you."

She hoped the minister would understand this and she looked at him with just a slightly pensive look—and then a glance at her enemy Kelly.

She said she believed there might have been a dispute at the house on

Shelf Street that was never reported by those foster parents, who were supposed to care for the children—but this could not be determined now. But according to her investigation, the house was not visited regularly because of the caseworker.

"Let me get this straight—who was this caseworker?" the minister asked.

"Fern Hershey—as I said," Melissa answered, as if she was talking to a child.

"Oh I see," the minister said.

"But she was a brilliant social worker," Backwash said.

"A good social worker, yes," Melissa answered. "But she wanted to be somewhere else—head of sociology. I told her she was biting off more than she could chew. Then she took ill with breast cancer. We raised money for her and in fact I insisted we have a social worker's award in her name." She mentioned that she had copies of everything she had managed to glean in the past three weeks.

Backwash asked why she didn't believe John Delano in the first place; that is, when he first brought this case forward. This struck Melissa as being a very odd and intrusive question.

That was simply never true, she said.

She was willing to go to the ends of the earth to find the boy, but she had to measure a lot of conflicting information. In fact she went to a meeting with John in order to assess the information he had, and found it very much paralleled her own findings.

"There were those who were against Delano," the minister said, with great deference.

"Yes," Melissa said, "during the meeting I came to that conclusion— he was not trusted. I had to weigh that—but I realized it was best if he go to Toronto."

"Is that so?" Kelly Backwash said.

"That is so," Melissa answered. "That is because I realized the strengths in his argument outweighed the suspicions other police officers may have had about him."

She said she had never disputed his intelligence or wisdom in being a good police officer. But that she really trusted Sue Van Loon. That is why she was very glad Sue Van Loon was on board.

"Did you oversee Sue Van Loon?"

"I was well aware of her," Melissa said. "We understood Delano, and we also knew we needed a woman on this case. Delano had a history of being angry with accomplished women. Sue Van Loon knew this too. So—it was better she was with him—"

"I don't follow," Backwash said.

Melissa only shrugged. She had got her complaint against John in, and was satisfied. She opened her soft leather briefcase and took out a report—this had all been given to her by Melonson in order to show the minister of justice that John was fabricating evidence. That was because Melissa had said to Melonson two weeks before, "Send me the proof you have of him fabricating evidence and I will see that our minister of justice is informed."

But now that the boy was found, this information pointed only to Melonson's deception and Delano's heroics. Melonson wanted the information back, but Melissa said she in all conscience couldn't return it. Melonson had even called in little Melon two nights before to ask about the case, imploring him to remember how much he, Melonson, had tried to do.

Melissa until five days ago had thought Delano's evidence was fabricated as well. Now she and the province knew much better, and she had John's collected evidence—the evidence that had been confiscated—and it supported her statement that she was "out in front of this case from the beginning."

Melissa said the one thing she was sorry about is that it had taken so long to find the boy.

In fact the minister, who knew little of the case yet, was completely spellbound by this beautiful and aggressive and brilliant woman—as so many were over the years. Also, there was a joke about her and the premier—meeting behind closed doors, and once Melissa coming from his office tucking her blouse into her skirt. Well, he could well understand why Jim would be banging her, he thought.

She seemed to catch what the minister was thinking and stared at him.

He flushed.

Then, after a pause, where he continued to look ashamed, she said that she now felt a city policeman must have botched the case by believing the boy was someone else. And that she now knew who this police officer was.

"My God," the justice minister said.

Kelly Backwash did not succumb to her charm and did not think it charm. For one reason she had been a fiancée of the premier four years ago, but was no longer so.

"This police officer informed social services that the boy he had was a boy named Jack Toggle simply to clear up another case," Melissa was saying. "It's unfortunate—but it does happen."

"I see," the minister said gravely.

"But it was his error," Melissa said. "Not ours. And it took my husband to figure it out—that is, back on Shelf Street—years ago."

"Do you know what officer?" Kelly Backwash asked.

Melissa gave a quick, dramatic smile, handed the minister a document marked confidential, gathered her briefcase and left the office.

She went home to talk to her husband.

"All you have to do," she told her husband, "is keep your fucking mouth shut—and mark my words, this is the last fucking time in my career I am bailing you out."

Then she did something inevitable—irritated, and feeling an almost sexual high, she went out shopping.

There could be no question from anyone that she was at the height of her powers.

———

The little group got together in New York that evening. Of all wonderful evenings, this was to be a wonderful evening too.

Midge Nolan Overplant and her small entourage went to La Mama in the East Village to take in an opera, *The Strange Life of Ivan Osokin*, and Midge spoke humorously about it and what it said and what it did not say about modern problems, which were so different than the problems of ten years ago. This was her fashion statement more than anything else, and she like many Canadians was good at such statements. They then came back in taxi and toasted one another with a brandy at a bar called Dandys' somewhere on West Fifty-Seventh.

It was April 6, 1994.

Midge said she did not want to speak about Rwanda that evening. She had a meeting in the morning about Rwanda. And tonight she wanted to forget. "Forget, forget, forget," she said.

And people understood how it had been for her—all these junkets back and forth to Ottawa, speaking to external affairs—she and the special envoy, who had been a friend of hers from their days at the University of Toronto, both of them tirelessly working.

There was another young woman there that evening. She was Midge's niece. Her name was Melissa Sapp. She had startling blue eyes that could stare through you. This, in fact, was the first thing Delano noticed. Melissa was already considered one of the best lawyers in the province—she worked in litigation and high-profile women's rights cases for social services.

John thought, at that moment, of little Jeannie Aube, who he had grown up with years ago. Why he thought of that waif at this moment, for the life of him he could not say . . . except that he felt she had been abused as much as anyone he ever knew.

At twenty-five, Melissa was deeply political, and wanted to relay this to everyone. She described how she and one of her university friends had published two papers in "Common Futures"—a lyrical and a satirical on the Catholic Church.

She had once argued the position of the local human rights commission to offer free abortions, without parental consent, to any woman over the age of twelve who lived in a rural community.

"I have discovered certain women must be taught to think," she said.

The person sitting next to John that night was the African Canadian writer who had just published his book on slavery in the Maritimes in the 1700s. He was to give a reading up the street—on Amsterdam Avenue—the next night. He spoke long and hard about appropriation of voice—and how he, as a black man, wanted *Huckleberry Finn* banned. The Lion of Justice said, "Hear, hear."

Our Lion of Justice was always the first to say "Hear, hear."

All of this had a gloss over it, of course—that of being intellectual Canadians, and not having much say in the world, but always a say about the world.

The person out of place in this little group was John Delano. Midge spoke for a while about Tim Wasson, the Lion of Justice's son, the radical advocate, who wanted to protest the "exploitation of Canada by American billionaires."

However, John had no opinion. Midge had once thought they would be great friends, she and John. Now he was realizing it had not turned out that way at all, and Midge too was realizing her mistake. Melissa was spoiled and brilliant; Wasson was less brilliant and far more spoiled. Wasson called himself a professional political agitator. That was how he was to become famous.

John knew, in 1994, he had already attacked the pipeline out west and had advocated that all Native land claims be settled immediately. John, once again, had no opinion. Only he knew why Midge and our Lion of Justice were so pleased to have the First Nations writer there a few months before.

"My boyfriend plays hockey," Melissa said during a lull in the conversation, seeing a hockey game on the corner TV. "But he will not be playing it much longer—the last thing I need hanging about my neck is a hockey player jerk from Canada." She did not speak to them when she said this, but spoke to her drink as she looked at the television. John was not listening to the game—because, like most Canadians, he knew too much about hockey to be able to listen to American commentators.

Our special envoy laughed in that artificial way so many intellectuals have when hockey is mentioned. "Hear, hear," he said again.

John decided not to answer Melissa's comment about hockey, and picked up his beer and drank. He smiled slightly at something the African Canadian writer said, and then listened as the Lion of Justice spoke. As he talked about the size of his office and his incompetent staff, the Lion said, "Americans are daft and obnoxious"—quite suddenly exercising an unthinking anti-Americanism that John had so often heard him use.

"Why?" John said, suddenly and out of character, as if coming out of a daze, and holding his flat beer. "I like them."

"For one thing most of them are racists," our Lion said, nodding to the black writer half in affirmation and half for support.

John politely said he did not think this was true and asked him to be quiet. Our Lion was taken aback. He studied John and suddenly became flustered. Our Lion's nose was pointed and his sandy hair was curly, and his eyes often looked startled. He moved his mouth, as if about to speak, but did not.

For the first time he saw John as a human being—and one who in many respects had a reserve of calm and integrity—this man who our Lion had never thought of as much more than a country bumpkin.

"Why, for heaven's sake?" he said finally.

"Because you are being uncivil and rude, and have been that way for most of the evening, and it is unbecoming for you to be so. Both of us, I am afraid, are in a position where we represent Canada and not ourselves, so we must show decorum and reserve our own opinions. It is not hard to do—it only takes personal honour."

"Well," Midge said, in a childish voice, "we in Canada know that America is the most oppressive regime—worse," she said, "far worse than China."

"That of course is a blatant lie," John said, looking at no one in particular, "and only a dishonest Canadian could concoct it. Only a dishonest

Canadian could so misinterpret tyranny in order to show her progressiveness in front of a niece she wants to be admired by."

"That's a terrible thing to say," our Lion responded, "and so unfair—so deeply unfair. You should apologize immediately."

"I apologize," John said.

"There now," our Lion continued with a smile, "I have been to the Great Wall of China—and America I will say is racist, and worse, anti-female. Yes, there, I have finally said it." The last statement was a bogus assertion, as if he himself had finally broken free of a diplomatic restraint. However, John did not answer.

It was then that a man sitting across from them in the bar got up and came to their table. The group became silent as the man stood over them, a broad-shouldered man of six feet, and asked them what they meant by what they said.

"Who are you? You aren't invited here," Midge said. "This is a private discussion."

"Then keep it to yourself," the man said matter-of-factly. He had a large, rough face, yet his expression was ultimately kind and passive. His hair was dark and curly and his eyes had mischief in them. "Besides, you have said enough about my country to make me invite myself."

"Oh, the home of the brave," our Lion said, "the home of the brave."

"Well, I am not sure I have to prove that to you." He smiled at our envoy, looking at his thin, red hands.

John spoke up, telling the man he was sorry they had been loud and that the group was now leaving. What John could not bear to see was how this man, who was in his own country and his own city, celebrating with his wife, looked more baffled than angered.

John turned to the others and told them again that they were leaving. "Now," he said.

"I am not leaving," Midge said.

John simply picked her up by the arm and brought her to her feet. "Come, let's go."

Once on the street Midge said she would never apologize for calling men sexist or America racist, and John should understand that free speech was still allowed.

"Yes, much more so here than in China," John answered.

The young African Canadian writer and Midge Nolan Overplant walked down the cold streets, singing "Imagine" out of tune, and breaking into laughter over something witty Midge said about "police escorts."

There was only one person in the bar that night who John Delano had paid attention to: Melissa, the young woman lawyer who was there visiting.

She had simply stood and left during the altercation. She was too bright to stay, and too tough to be worried about what others thought. She would do many things. And these brave and wonderful things would all be done, it seemed, at the expense of others. And John shuddered slightly, looking at her walking down the street.

He knew that his whole troubled life—his violence, his failed marriages, his anger—was an anathema to her. He felt at this moment he was meeting one of the most dangerous people he would ever meet. For Midge had often said Melissa Sapp was out to change the world.

Once the group was safely in a cab, John went back to the bar and asked the man his name.

"Joel Finnegan," the man said. He introduced his wife. "It's our anniversary."

"Well, congratulations—I'm sorry they are a bit drunk."

"Forget it," Joel said.

"Where are you from?" his wife asked. She was a black woman, and Joel was white.

"Canada."

"Well, I thought Canadians liked us." She looked at her husband, seeking confirmation in the childlike way Americans often do when they are somewhat disconcerted by the world beyond their borders.

"We do." John laughed. "In fact, we emulate you in many things."

And he bought Joel Finnegan and his wife a drink.

—

The argument in that bar, the discussion and everything else about that uneventful night would be forgotten by almost everyone. Yet in a number of ways this entire group of people would someday—by fate, or chance, or whatever people chose to call it—be joined again.

In many ways they would be joined because of a young boy named JP, who was sleeping that moment under a net in a small compound in Rwanda. His world, which had once been so safe and ordinary, would become in a matter of weeks one of terror and self-reliance, and he would start on his lonely trek to find his mom and dad. He would never give up that trek at all.

When Sue Van Loon met him at the end of a December day in 2011, with silt in the air and the withering sound of wind over the grey buildings in blunted downtown Toronto, he would be twenty-four. He would be wearing a knitted cap with earflaps, and a string tied around his throat. He would have lost two toes during his wanderings from the Port of Saint John. He would have been beaten half to death—and left for dead in an alley in Drummondville when he was thirteen. The only name he remembered having was Jack. He now worked as a baker's assistant at the St. Lawrence Market. He lived in a rooming house on Jarvis Street. He read books about Spain and Africa, and engineering, he read history and poetry—and he had just started dating a young girl of nineteen, a journalism student from Ryerson who thought he was loving and brilliant and hopeless, but in his hopelessness she hoped for him, and sat with him waiting for an imaginary person to show up.

And that day she said, though she did not believe it in the least, "I am sure today is your lucky day."

They sat close to each other shivering, and when she said this, he took her hand.

This was five minutes before Sue Van Loon turned to look their way.

His girl was the one who pointed Sue Van Loon out to him.

He looked up and saw a woman staring back at him with hope and curiosity from across the flat, empty spaces near the CN Tower. He stood and approached her, hobbling in the dark, his face as expectant as an eight-year-old child's, while his girlfriend walked behind him, almost on tiptoes.

"Are you my mom?" he said, carefully. "I'm afraid I do not know her very well anymore."

———

In late December 2011, Sebastian Ebusantaini was to speak at Blake House on campus. It would be a personal atmosphere, with green shaded lamps and spotless varnished bookshelves and an intimate stage.

He was brought to Saint John through the auspices of Canada's Department of Foreign Affairs, the Canadian Mission for Peace and the New Brunswick Human Rights Commission. Melissa Sapp and Midge Nolan Overplant would also speak—Melissa on the threat to the environment by the oil pipeline, Midge on her view of Darfur.

There would be a special appearance by the special envoy, our Lion of Justice, who had finished another book; what one national newspaper said "was a Chomsky-like indictment of Prime Minister Stephen Harper."

And yes, the public was invited.

Sebastian Ebusantaini's account of what had happened in Rwanda did not vary too much from what John had told Sue Van Loon—she went with a young man that night to listen. No one paid much attention to her, since she sat three-quarters back in the full house and she was sitting with a man who looked like he was a—well, some type of bricklayer or mason, or baker perhaps. Still, if it was hard to understand Sebastian's accent, it was not that hard to imagine the night he and the white boy had hidden behind the compound. As Sebastian talked, the boy who sat there quietly by Sue Van Loon became more and more the focal point of the evening. Soon there was a stir, customary in situations such as this—and then the turning of the audience toward this young man.

What brought it all out—of course—was the marble.

The cat's-eye marble that John had left for the boy.

As soon as Sebastian saw it, he said, he knew who this boy was.

The boy stood up, and before the crowd left their seats, he began to walk toward the stage. But he was beaten to it by Melissa Sapp.

"This is our surprise!" Melissa said, getting to the stage before him, and holding out her hand for him. "This is what we longed for, for the past five weeks! This is who we have been searching for—our entire resources were put to this effort—this is our surprise for Sebastian. This is the reason we commandeered him away from the bright lights of New York."

She read a brief telegram from Tim Wasson, who was again running for a seat in a by-election in England, who said he had searched to find this child of his friend Hugh Forrest himself—and that someday he would invite the boy to England.

Then Melissa stood between Sebastian and Jack, holding their hands as a picture was taken—you know, the same one that appeared in the *New York Times* and the *Globe and Mail*.

Melon too was surprised by the appearance of the lost boy. He heard of it while walking home from work, and he went and sat in the park, dumbfounded, and so worried that the boy, Jack, would be angry with him for not writing the letter to John Delano sooner. Then he became so shy he didn't want to meet him. He remembered how they had tried to get in touch with Fern Hershey to ask her to help the Limey, because Moms had never believed he was from Africa.

"You wait and I'll help you," little Melon had said.

And they went to a phone booth up on Matters Road and phoned— but Fern Hershey was no longer there. She had quit and had applied to university.

Melon didn't know what to do after that.

So he had let the Limey down—and soon after, he was going to go and visit his mom at the hospital, and the Limey said, "Just a minute—I will get you some money—wait here—then you won't have to go back to the foster home."

Melon felt that if Jack didn't have to come back with the twenty dollars, nothing bad would have happened to him. So he was terrified to meet Jack, especially when certain things had happened. For instance, Jack came to Saint John and the first thing he did was meet with a man called Sebastian Ebusantaini and go to the university.

So maybe it wasn't the right Jack at all. Melon stayed in the park all that night, shivering and wondering if this Jack would even want to say hello. There was no one left from that far-off time of his childhood who Melon still knew. His sister used to wait for him on the school steps, and they would walk back down the street together, and he would tell her stories and sing to her. Once in a while he had to tuck her mittens in. And he bought her a whistle when she was scared, but then she went away. Then he was taken to the foster home.

Still, immediately after all the gravity and weight attached to it and newspaper men and women coming and going, people began to suspect them both. That is, Jack and Sebastian.

That is always the way.

"How did they get away through the jungle—when no one else did?" people said, smiling. "In fact there is always quicksand, if you ever seen a Tarzan movie—lots of it!"

"How can we believe him—who knows what lies he would tell about it—what's his name—Ebusantaini? I can't even say it."

"Nor wouldja want to."

"Well, there you go."

Sebastian's story was simple and sordid enough and was told in simple language, about everyone in the compound that night.

Edgar, the teacher and the writer of books, had tried to run away. He had tried to desert everyone, but he was terrified, and he had dropped his suitcase and run.

But they caught up with him and grabbed him by the white shirt collar and dragged him to the ground.

"Please, please—" he kept saying in French, pleading for his life.

But they brought him forward with his hands tied. They did not know how they would kill him. Until Chubby saw a little hand sticking out from under the tent. And began to giggle when the hand disappeared. They heard some whispering in the tent and the boys with machetes came out of the dark and all gathered around it. Chubby then decided on the spur of the moment to light Edgar on fire. He would be their torch. Edgar started to scream when they began to pour the gas on him.

"You will be our torch so we can look into the tent."

That is, Chubby had said at first that since Edgar had taught him how to read, he would let him go. Then he'd decided to kill him, but with a pistol he had got from Mr. Hill. Then, when he could not find the pistol, he poured gas over him.

"You were once my teacher and now I am yours—so don't drink it," he whispered kindly as the man was gulping and crying out for help, "it will make you sick."

The whispering went on in the tent—and Chubby lit a cigar. He walked about proclaiming himself king of the compound.

"I do not think I will have to get my pronouns right ever more," Chubby said, his little belly button busting out from his shirt and hanging over his belt. He threw the match, but it went out and he had to light another one. Edgar could do nothing but try to blow the matches out, screaming for help as he did. His shrieks never seemed to match the horror in his eyes.

When Chubby lit the man on fire with the third match, the man tried to run—to get rid of the flame—and they opened the tent flap and he ran right into the tent. That had been their plan all along. Chubby's hand lit on fire and burned the skin between his thumb and forefinger, and he yelled and threw away the canister of gas.

At first there was no sound except for Edgar screaming. Then as Edgar stood in the tent being engulfed in flame, his eyes looking at them in terror, there were many more screams—like everyone had been caught playing hide-and-seek, but more and more horrifying. The children tried to run. The tent started to burn from the inside out.

There was a sound. *WHOOSH!*

Sister Vanessa, holding a three-year-old child, tried to run out the tent door.

Those who did run out were cut apart by Chubby's friends; those who did not succumbed to the smoke and fire.

At about the same time, what Chubby called his second battalion went into the long school compound. Lily was seen being dragged across the compound ground, from the school to the dorms, where all the beds were. She tried to hang on to the hands that hauled her by the hair, to relieve the pain. She was being stripped naked as they dragged her.

"Lie her down—lie her down to fuck her," boys kept yelling in French.

A sixteen-year-old (the boy who later carried all the heads in the burlap sack) bypassed the first three beds and threw her down on the fourth one. When they cut Hugh's hands off, he was trying to stop them from tearing away the last of his wife's clothes.

Sister Vanessa and the doctor who tried to protect children from the machetes were sliced apart and thrown into the ravine by the arcadia trees. The doctor's head was put into a burlap sack. It was the head that later rolled down the hill.

Lily tried not to scream, not only for her husband's sake but for her own—the darkness against her. She died within a half-hour. This disappointed them all.

Chubby came in later to find her body lying like a rag—the space between her legs covered in clots of blood, not even like a human being, dying beside her castrated husband.

"Jeepers," he said.

The only two Chubby could not find were Sebby and JP, though he sent his sister looking for the "rascals" and smoked another cigar and waited. Mr. Hill said he was sorry Chubby had burned his hand.

When they arrested Chubby and charged him, along with Mr. Hill, with crimes against humanity, he was not yet eighteen.

This was Sebastian's story.

John didn't find the boy, of course. No, the boy found Sue Van Loon.

John died at nine o'clock on December 15, while walking toward the CN Tower. He staggered on a street that was lonesome by a building he had never been beside before with strangers walking by him. Steam came from the grate. And two people stepped over him on their way to work.

Sue Van Loon was with him. She knelt beside him, trying to give him CPR. But she wasn't good at it. He grabbed at her hands to stop. His last words were "My dear, dear friend."

His cell phone had three numbers in it: Jeannie's, Constable Trevor's and Sue Van Loon's. For a man who supposedly disliked women, he certainly believed in and relied on them.

The day of John's funeral, Trevor told Velma that she was being investigated not only for the murders of Luda Marsh and Bennie Cheval but for the death of a little girl named Amy Thibodeau. And that nothing would stop Trevor this time. That is, she got the murder cases she had long wanted, and of course she was not happy about them at all.

There were two versions of how John died. Some said he died that morning on the street. But others said he died in the bed at about four o'clock—and that Van Loon was sleeping with him. This rumour persisted even when people confirmed he had tried to make it to the CN Tower and had died on the street. He had not taken his heart medicine in over a week.

There were also two versions of how the boy was found. The first was that he and his girl approached Sue Van Loon at the CN Tower in Toronto, just as Sue Van Loon reported.

The second came later, and was more sinister. This is an account of the second story, started in one of the taverns and then flowing to many taverns in our city and beyond: When the story of the missing boy, which was only a footnote in the *Globe*, was reported with some detail in the *Toronto Sun*, a young man came forward. He called himself Jack Brown. Not everyone believed who he was. He was a bricklayer who lived out toward Jarvis—or a baker, or some such.

Some said he was an imposter from the start and wanted his hands on the money. That he was in a gang.

When he spoke of the marble and the picture, Melonson was adamant it was a ruse. "Just like Canada to fall for that," he said. He even said, and more than one person thought this, that John Delano himself was involved, to perpetrate a perfect scam. Some said Sebastian Ebusantaini was a fraud, and only people like Midge Nolan Overplant would fall for his story.

Even when Melon did come forward, on the insistence of Sue Van Loon, to say he had known the boy and written the letter, and was willing to tell everything he knew as long as they didn't revoke his parole . . . well, people still said that in this day and age anyone could say anything, and the internet had proven it.

Moms said she did not remember him. Bunny said he did not chase anyone over any cliff—he also intimated that John Delano bought the book *Nights below Station Street* at his bookstore in November.

But the young man insisted he had been searching to find his parents for fifteen years, and now he knew they were dead. And that he did indeed go to the CN Tower on his birthday every year. He would wait there in the cold all day, for his dad and mom to find him.

Sue Van Loon believed him, and knew John had done his job. That it was a thankless job very well done. In fact like great men and women John had done his job heroically, without benefit of help or hope of applause. And she would never forget him. That she would remember him as a brother. And she told Melissa Sapp the last time they met, "You accused him of everything but his genius. That, my dear, you tried to claim for yourself."

The boy was sandy haired, five feet nine inches tall, had a large amount of eclectic knowledge about the world. He still spoke with an accent, and he did meet with Melon for an hour.

Yes, he remembered Melon very well. But he did not remember the name of the girl he gave the book to, or the name of the book. He remembered something about it, but he had given her the book on a whim—for the name of the book struck him, whatever that title was. He asked if he could see that girl again.

"She was a crush I had," he said. After all this time.

When the investigators spoke to him about some of the things in the letter—Keats and Hitler's Operation Barbarossa—he did not hesitate to say what he knew.

The death of his parents and how he heard it took some time to sink in. It did when he went to Edmonton later in the month.

But a few people, especially at the tavern, still said he could have read about the marble, and have seen the picture of Sebby in the paper—and though they met and said certain similar things about what had happened to them, who could ever be sure anymore? Sebby and he spoke like old friends—but there was a distance of seventeen years, and certain people were not so gullible as to think that money wasn't involved. Sebby was earning a good deal of money too—and a couple of people said he was just after the notoriety, couldn't anyone tell? And they insinuated that others were involved.

"The boy is being paid by someone—maybe Sebby—is that the prick's name who dreamed it all up—or matter of fact, who was in 'Wanda himself if it wasn't John? So John sends a few letters then over comes Sebby. John is dead, but Sebby and the boy can still manage it. The boy wants old Pierce's money—in fact he never even heard of Pierce, did he? And if he was the real nephew he would have. It's all just for the money."

"No way he knows anything. I'd love to get the likes of him in a corner and ask him some questions—Melonson is right on that—and they get Melon—what's he called, Melon the Felon, in to talk about it. Sure, Melon the Felon. Melonson said he would have been better off a bortion. Then they said the boy cried when he saw the blanket. I only know if they was going to give me three million, I'd blubber too."

"I'd go on my knees and blow you."

"Well, there you go—and he don't remember Luda's name, or anything about her at all, except he give someone a book."

"Yeah, a dirty ignorant book too."

"No, it's what I say—he's being paid by someone—how could he even think of that book to give her if he was from Africa and just come here—no, that proves it. It was John who made it all up. He goes to the bookstore and grabs the book and signs it hisself. And the lad goes along with what John Delano said: 'Did you fall? Yes, I fell. Did you land six feet down? Yes, I landed six feet down. Did you go to the ATM—yes, I went there that evening.' "

"And he's supposed to have froze his toes off?"

"Gang related!"

"What I think it is about is John and he was in this together, and John is up to Toronto to meet him and finally dies of a heart attack. And so his plans—this Jack Brown's plans—are all upset—so he gets the idea to come forward as if he just heard of it."

"That's it."

"The only one gullible enough to believe him is some psychologist or someone like that there. Some white-arsed bitch who needs a tunin'."

This was the talk by some at the tavern that Melon would overhear and become upset by, and walk home in the dark. And even when he told everyone that he had written the letter, some no longer really believed him.

And he would sit in the dark in his small apartment and wonder why so many people had turned against this boy, who had done nothing wrong except get lost. And Melon would think about this, and wonder how lives are so affected by things. For at first everyone was on his side, and CBC did a national news story. But then the media and others became increasingly wary—John Delano was not the most savoury person; well, not in Canadian terms, anyway; and the idea of the book, and the picture, and the soil on the child's boots—could all this not have been manufactured? The boy's own sad story seemed to get lost in this—and when he resurfaced in Edmonton, in that quiet room filled with the echoes of the past, with books and tapes and old furniture from years ago, he was stunned and uncommunicative, and his girlfriend had to tell the press to leave him alone. He sat in the corner of the room for two days and did not speak. He just stared at the things his mother, Lily, had left behind.

"Yes," Melon would say. "Lives are certainly affected by things."

DeWold was affected too. His work suffered and he got very ill. His face swelled up. Then his nose swelled up.

He stayed at home. He read sports magazines and fell into a mid-afternoon slumber. His wife came and went and he heard the key in the door, or the bath tumbling upstairs before she went out alone at night to some function, wearing short or long dresses, sometimes not returning until three in the morning.

By the next fall Melissa was looked upon as not only a visionary but a no-nonsense legislator. A person who had solved the entire case of the missing boy almost single-handed. There is today on the wall of her office that picture of her standing between Sebastian Ebusantaini and Jack Forrest.

Once in a while she will show up at a party with the premier, but usually she is concealed, almost clandestine. Once in a while someone will feel her penetrating eyes upon them from far across the room. Sometimes that's the only thing about her they remember.

Tim Wasson was involved in a hit and run in northern England, and tried to flee the bobbies. It was rumoured he was drunk and under his car seat were ten small, plastic bags of cocaine.

Melon went to work, and bought his own clothes and tried to live his own life.

He thought often of John Delano coming to see him at the car wash. They'd had a long talk—it lasted over three hours. This was the second occasion they had talked, and it happened just before John left for Toronto. That is, John had wanted to talk to Melon one final time.

Delano said he would help Melon take a welding course. And Melon thought this was the kindest thing anyone had ever helped him with. But when John Delano died, Melon forgot about it altogether. When John had come to see him the second time, Melon had said he thought it was Bennie Cheval who was angry about the Limey giving Luda a book, and that Bennie must have chased the boy or beaten him. Bennie was crazy, Melon said. "He was like my dad—possessed."

"He was possessed, weren't he?"

"I don't know any more than you do about who was or is possessed," John said. "I am sorry your father and mother harmed you, I am sorry, but you have to let it go—I am sure little Amy would want you to now."

"So Bennie killed the Limey—maybe?"

"No," John said quietly. "Bennie did not do that. Bennie did not know Luda then. So it wasn't him—it was Bunny McCrease and his stepson, Vernon Beaker, who chased him. But I'm afraid Bennie did harm my son—he did that. I don't think he meant to—maybe he was possessed, I don't know. I suppose this is a world of fancifiers and falsifiers and such, and most of us live in a world distorted. If we had just put Bennie in jail for a few months after I read him his rights—my son, and he and Luda too, would still be here now.

"My boy would be going to university soon. My wife would have been so proud. Who knows such things anymore."

Then John stared at Melon's knuckles, and seeing *love* tattooed on the right hand and *hate* tattooed on his left said, "Melon, you're left-handed?"

"Yes, how did you know?"

"Oh, I just thought of it—but if you do get into welding, if I can get you into welding, will you do me a favour? Will you remove what's on the knuckles of your left hand? Forever?"

"Why?" Melon said.

"And try not to hate again, try not to hate your mom and dad and how they burned you with cigarettes. And how little Amy died because no one was there during the day to take care of her, and you bought her a whistle when you were at school so she would be safe. Yes, you see, I do know about all this, Melon. I do know how your dad broke your arm, how your mom went to provincial hospital. And how Amy only had you to take care of her and that's why you bought her the whistle when you were eleven years old. I've known that since 1998 . . .

"So I know these terrible things. Really, really, I have known them since I was seventeen. It is in my heart not to want to know them, but I do—and my heart will fail me soon. Soon enough it will say to me: 'I must stop now forever.'

"But you do not have to be scared of ghosts anymore. If I find that boy, that Limey who was kind to you, you will not wet the bed again and you will not worry that Moms McCrease used to beat you with a belt, and feel guilty that's why the Limey took up for you and they broke his nose. And I know that Vernon couldn't stand it—and used to go outside to the back and smoke. And now he has to live with it all."

"How do you know all that?"

"But you will take hate away from your knuckles and you won't cut yourself like you did in jail. And you will not try suicide again, okay? You will be able to sleep again. You can keep *love* on your right hand, though—Lily is at this moment asking you to."

"Who is Lily?"

"Someone who loves you so much because you loved her son enough to write. You were the one who started the journey back, for her son to come home. Lily is someone I love very much now. She is right near us. Just like Amy—I am sure.

"So do not be frightened of ghosts anymore." Here John took out his nitro and put it under his tongue and smiled a little.

Melon might have laughed and forgotten about what anyone else said. But not those words from John Delano.

Still, he never thought the welding course would happen. But after Christmas he got a call from the community college and was asked to attend.

"But I cannot pay," Melon said.

"Oh, it's all been paid for—or will be through the estate of John Delano. There will be ninety-five hundred dollars put into your account."

"I am on probation—I steal things."

"But John said you would not steal here."

"No, I will try better never to do that anymore."

When Melon did start his welding course, there were still a lot of rude jokes going around about the Limey and how he had scammed the money. The young man's picture was in the paper alongside an article by our Lion of Justice and an interview too with Midge Nolan Overplant.

And even after Vernon came out and testified that everything the young man had said was true, some people—a few, and there would always be a few—still said the boy was a fake. And worse than that, Jack Toggle was still alive and was going to sue everyone in the province for impersonating him. He started selling T-shirts that said "I am the real Jack Toggle." And it caused quite a sensation and he sold six thousand of them.

Trevor told Velma on July 28 that she was being investigated for the murder of Luda Marsh and Bennie Cheval. And Roland Roady had turned against her. She asked Velma questions about a child, Amy Thibodeau, who had been scared of her and lived above her a long time ago, and had tried to lock the door and sit on the cushion where Melon had left her cup of milk.

Though Trevor got Roland and Velma to turn against each other and tell her where each one of them had been on the day Luda and Bennie were killed, and who was hiding in the woods and who was upstairs in the house, many others said Delano himself had been involved. That he and Luda were lovers. That the child Dotty was his, and that's why Luda was phoning him—you know, the paternity test.

That was why he wanted to arrest Bennie in the first place, and why he had given her that novel as a present—for who in their right mind would read a novel like that?

After that Velma wrote such a long, confused, rambling letter. In it she asked Melon to visit her so she could explain things to him about the little girl Amy, and things she knew about the case. She told him to come to the women's prison where she was housed as a dangerous felon, and she would tell him about Amy and how she saw her that day—but only if Trevor would drop the charges.

But Melon decided not to see her. He just wanted to remember Amy like she had been. That is, staring up at him with an eager smile when he poured her a glass of milk.

And once a month or so he would phone Jeannie Aube. He told her that at night—really late—he sometimes felt people were very close to him, people like Gilbert and John, and that they loved her very much.

He would sing to Amy. He said he sang to her every chance he could after he got home from welding school.

Her favourite songs, from the *Dobblebuns*.

And he felt like she listened to him.

For he was learning to play the guitar.

It became true, and it was sad to hear, that Velma had breast cancer, and it was advanced. Her hair was short and iron grey now, and she was so thin now some mightn't even think it was the same person.

Roland wrote her from his jail cell to tell her he still loved her. And he always would.

After Vernon's long interview and confession in the *Telegraph* was published many people began to see the enormity of JP's struggle and look upon it with compassion. That not only was he great in his soul, but John Delano also. Letters were written to the paper, expressing dismay that this could have happened to an innocent child here. And thank God for the life of John Delano, many said.

When spring came, Luda Marsh's little girl, Dotty, left the foster home for good and was adopted by Sue Van Loon and her partner, Jane Hershey, who moved into an old, quaint house together. So the world finally gave hope to the little girl, and to the two women who found love in spite of the odds. But of course that is the only thing one can ever use against those odds—love. It is what Lily knew.

Melon and Jeannie did not give up the search for Gilbert—and someday, they felt, he would be found, for people from the army base in Camp Gagetown were now involved, in honour of John Delano. And yes, even Melonson began to say he would do all he could before he retired.

They would go out to Loman Otter Road and begin to search again and again for the boy who John so loved.*

And Trevor said, "We should honour John, you know." And she brought this forward for committee debate at city council sometime that June.

So, like a man who has given his life for something precious, John Delano, for some reason scorned in life, was now, by many people, finally loved.

Some even talked of a statue.

Melonson did not make superintendent and took early leave and then retired in late August.

Jack Forrest did finally send Melon a postcard. This was in September of 2012.

He and his girl were living in Toronto. Both were attending university there, and they had received a payout from his parents' estate of close to $850,000.

He was studying electrical engineering and hoped for kindness some future day.

The postcard of the CN Tower had but one word.

It said: FREE.

Melon would go lay flowers on the grave of his sister, 1993–1998, who died because Melon wasn't there to hear her whistle, and when she tried to run away, she stumbled and fell; and he put flowers on his mother's grave too—she whose name was Florence, 1961–1999, and who was Jeannie Aube's sister.

Now when people asked, "Are you Melon the Felon, who hid in the ductwork at the jail and tried to burn down the bus depot?" he would answer, "That was someone else—gone far away."

---

* The body of Gilbert Delano was found in a hidden closed well on the Cheval property on June 6, 2013. The information about its whereabouts came from the deathbed statement of Ms. Velma Jean Cheval, October 1, 1957–June 4, 2013.

For many days when Melon first attended his course it was very hard for him to get a good weld because his left hand was wrapped. But a friend of John Delano's named Evan Young offered him a very good job whenever the course was done.

When they asked him what had happened to his hand, little Melon Thibodeau said he'd had something removed for good. Something he was now glad others did not have to see.

ACKNOWLEDGEMENTS

I thank my editor, Lynn Henry; my agent, Anne McDermid; and my wife, Peggy.